Mary Stuart White Meier-Smith

Matson Meier-Smith

Memories of his Life and Work

Mary Stuart White Meier-Smith

Matson Meier-Smith
Memories of his Life and Work

ISBN/EAN: 9783337059026

Printed in Europe, USA, Canada, Australia, Japan

Cover: Foto ©Raphael Reischuk / pixelio.de

More available books at **www.hansebooks.com**

MATSON MEIER-SMITH.

MEMORIES OF HIS LIFE AND WORK.

*"To-day the warfare of the Cross!
To-morrow the Crown! Righteousness, peace, and glory for evermore!"*

PRINTED FOR PRIVATE DISTRIBUTION.

NEW YORK:
ANSON D. F. RANDOLPH & CO.
1891.

University Press:
John Wilson and Son, Cambridge.

To my Beloved Children,

SHARERS WITH ME IN THE INHERITANCE OF PRECIOUS
MEMORIES,

THIS VOLUME IS TENDERLY INSCRIBED.

M. S. M-S.

" But still I wait with ear and eye
For something gone which should be nigh,
A loss in all familiar things,
In flower that blooms, and bird that sings.
And yet, dear heart! remembering thee,
Am I not richer than of old?
Safe in thy immortality,
What change can reach the wealth I hold?
What chance can mar the pearl and gold
Thy love hath left in trust with me?
And while in life's late afternoon,
Where cool and long the shadows grow,
I walk to meet the night that soon
Shall shape and shadow overflow,
I cannot feel that thou art far,
Since near at need the angels are;
And when the sunset gates unbar,
Shall I not see thee waiting stand,
And, white against the evening star,
The welcome of thy beckoning hand?"

PREFACE.

THIS Memorial of MATSON MEIER-SMITH is mainly a transcript of the sacred recollections of those who stood toward him in relations of intimacy. Were it proposed to prepare a more extensive and complete memoir, with a view to publication, it would be forbidden by the knowledge of Dr. Meier-Smith's strong conviction, often expressed, that unless a life had been distinctively public and prominent, any written record of its events should be reserved for those whose personal affection would give it a peculiar and tender interest.

Penned therefore as are these memories only for loving friends, among whom, it is believed, may be numbered many of his brethren of the clergy, of his former parishioners, and of his late pupils in the Philadelphia Divinity School, a freedom of expression is permitted upon the following pages that would be otherwise forbidden.

It would have been gratifying could there have been included in them more from Dr. Meier-Smith's own pen, but a large proportion of such of his letters as are accessible are of a personal and private character which forbids extensive use of their contents.

It is a compensation for such necessary omission that this volume has been prepared by the one who stood toward its subject in the nearest and most sacred earthly relationship, and who beyond all others knew his spirit, his aims, and his manner of life. Thus its recitals are peculiarly dear and grateful to those who stood within the wide family circle so long blessed by his presence, and who, in his departure, felt that they had lost the most generous of friends, the wisest of counsellors, and the most tender and loving of brothers.

They, in common with all who came within his influence, recognized the fascination of his manner, the dignity of his bearing, the breadth and liberality of his thinking, his unselfish devotion to the service of his fellow-men and his loyalty to his divine Master; but they also knew, as others could not, the joy and the strength which his presence imparted to those upon whom, as standing nearest to him, was freely lavished the wealth of his rich affection.

Too well they know that from their lives a radiance has vanished never to be rekindled until the day break and the shadows flee away.

E. N. W.

MARCH, 1891.

CONTENTS.

PAGE

SERMONS.

Memories of Life and Work.

I.

ANCESTRAL NOTES.

MATSON MEIER–SMITH came of an honored lineage. The blood of Puritan forefathers, from typical New England families, mingled equally in his veins with that of German ancestors of names revered in the Fatherland, and in their adopted country.

To this heritage he was loyal, believing in the blessings received from an intelligent and godly ancestry. The ties of blood and kindred were very strong in him, and his response to their claims always kindly and hearty. Physically and intellectually the influence of heredity was distinctly marked in him, and no portraiture of him could be life-like which did not recognize this fact.

Some notice of those from whom he was descended seems therefore especially fitting; and happily, several sketches can be given from his own pen, as he had prepared extended genealogical notes for his children. He writes respecting those from whom he received his time-honored and homely patronymic, "So far as can be ascertained, the Smiths were always a most respectable family, with no aristocratic pretensions, or quasi patents of nobility. They were thrifty and much respected freeholders and landowners of New England. The first ancestor of whom we have record was Richard Smith, who settled in Lyme, Connecticut, in 1652. His descendants in direct line remained on the old homestead, prominent men in the community, and re-spected citizens. Joseph, the fifth in succession, mar-ried Mary Matson, of Lyme."

From this well-known Connecticut family came Dr. Meier-Smith's Christian name. Among men of note, of kin in the Matson line, were the late Hon. William A. Buckingham, Connecticut's "War-Governor," and the Hon. Morison R. Waite, late Chief-Justice of the United States.

Through the Mather family are collateral connections with many New England families of this historic name. They are descended from Rev. Richard Mather, born in Lowton, England, in 1596. Educated at the University of Oxford, he became a clergyman of the Church of England; but was suspended for non-conformity, and came to this country in 1635, settling in Boston. He was the first of the family of Congregational ministers known as the "Mather dynasty," and was the father of Increase and the grandfather of Cotton Mather. He was selected to answer the thirty-two questions in regard to Church government, propounded to the New England ministers by the Magistrates, in 1639, and was the chief designer of the "Cambridge Platform," adopted by the New England Synod of 1648. He had six sons, all but one of whom were clergymen. Timothy, his second son, was the ancestor of Dr. Samuel Mather, of Lyme, who was the last of seven in succession, all of whom were clergymen or physicians. Dr. Mather was a man of much distinction in his profession.

Matson Smith, the son of Joseph Smith and Mary Matson, was born in Lyme, Connecticut, Feb. 9, 1767. He studied medicine with Dr. Mather, whose daughter Sarah he married. They were Dr. Meier-Smith's pa-

ternal grandparents. Of this grandfather he writes:
"Dr. Matson Smith settled in New Rochelle, New York,
about the year 1788. He was a man of strong personality, of tall and powerful frame, with marked features
and commanding presence, and of grave and diguified
manner. He possessed the physician's instinct and the
surgeon's instinct, in equal balance. He was the leading man in his neighborhood, and prominent among the
physicians of Westchester County. His home was a
most hospitable one, a favorite resort of friends and
clergymen from New England and New York. He was
thoroughly well read, and always abreast of the time
in the literature of his profession. He was a student
of the Bible and theology, and quite eminent among
laymen for his knowledge in this direction, as well as
for his religious character. In 1830 he received an
honorary M. D. from the Regents of the University of
the State of New York. His chosen home, New
Rochelle, one of the early Huguenot settlements, became very dear to him in all its interests. He was
one of the founders of the Presbyterian Church there,
a ruling elder, and frequently a delegate to the General
Assembly. In all matters of public interest he was very
influential, and contributed liberally to everything for
the prosperity of the place. He died March 17, 1845.

"Dr. Matson Smith had a large family; seven children survived him. His eldest son, Joseph Mather
Smith, M. D., was a distinguished physician, practis-
ing in New York for many years, and Professor of
the Theory and Practice of Medicine in the College
of Physicians and Surgeons. Afterward, under the
University organization of Columbia College, he became Professor of Materia Medica. He died in the
year 1866, in the seventy-eighth year of his age."

Dr. Meier-Smith's maternal ancestry was purely German. His grandfather's family, from whom came his second Christian name, used in all his later years as a prefix to his surname, is traced in unbroken line from about the year 1490. It has been to the present generation honorable in the annals of the free city of Bremen. Dr. Meier-Smith's grandfather was Caspar Meier, son of Diederich Meier, "Doctor and Burgomaster" in Bremen. He was born in Bremen, Sept. 20, 1774, and came to New York about the year 1800. He was Consul of the Bremen Republic, and founded the business house of Caspar Meier & Co. His place of business for many years was in Broad Street, New York. The successors of this house are the well-known firm of Oelrichs & Co., in which, to-day, some of the leading partners are his grandson and great-grandsons.

Mr. Meier's family mansion was beautifully situated on the high bank of the Hudson at Bloomingdale, commanding a noble view of the river. He was a man of gentle and unobtrusive manner, and much sweetness of character. His grandson remembered him with peculiar affection, his home life being singularly attractive. He entertained extensively, though unostentatiously; and as a Christian man, and upright citizen, he was held in high regard in the community. In many traits of character his grandson strongly resembled him. Brought up in the German Reformed Communion, he became an elder in the Dutch Reformed Church at Manhattanville. He married, in 1801, Eliza Katharine, daughter of the Rev. Dr. Kunze. They had eight children, of whom only four reached maturity. Mr. Meier died Feb. 2, 1839.

Through his grandmother, Dr. Meier-Smith was descended from the Patriarch of the Lutheran Church in America, Henry Melchior Muhlenberg, who was born in Einbeck, Germany, Sept. 6, 1711, came to this country in 1742, and died at New Providence, Pennsylvania, in 1787. The one hundredth anniversary of his death was celebrated in Philadelphia in commemoration of his great services to the Lutheran Church. "Dr. Muhlenberg's great energy and executive ability were combined with extensive learning. He was a finished scholar in Hebrew and Greek, almost as familiar with Latin as with German, and fluent in the English, Dutch, French, Bohemian, and Swedish tongues. He was a fine musician, and performed upon the organ, harp, guitar, and violin. He travelled extensively in the advancement and oversight of his Church, founding and strengthening the Lutheran congregations. He resided in the city of Philadelphia. He married, in 1745, Anna Maria, daughter of Conrad Weiser, mentioned frequently in our Colonial annals as an Indian interpreter, agent, magistrate," etc. Dr. Muhlenberg was the father of eleven children. The three sons who survived him were all men of distinction in Church and State, — honorable among the many honored names connected with the days of the Revolution, and the founding of the Republic. John Peter Gabriel, the eldest, took orders in both the Lutheran and the English churches, and was pastor of several mission congregations in the valley of the Blue Ridge in Virginia. The story is told of him, that after having received a colonel's commission in the Revolutionary army, he conducted services in his church; and during the sermon, at the close of a patriotic appeal, threw off his gown and bands and appeared in full uniform, ordering the drum to beat for recruits at the church door. Three hundred hardy frontiersmen enlisted under his banner that day. He was a distinguished officer throughout the war, rising to the rank of Major-General, and afterward served in both houses of the Federal Congress.

The second son, Frederick Augustus, also a clergyman, was a member of the first Continental Congress, and Speaker of the House in the first, second, and third Federal Congresses.

Dr. Muhlenberg's daughter, Margaretta Henrietta, was born in 1751, and in 1771 was married to Rev. Dr. John Christopher Kunze, who was born in Mansfeld, Saxony, Aug. 5, 1744, and died in New York, July 24, 1807. He came to Philadelphia in 1770, and became pastor of St. Michael's and Zion Churches, Philadelphia. He was also a Professor in the University of Pennsylvania, but in 1784 removed to New York. He was a Regent of the University of the State of New York, and one of its founders, and also Professor of Oriental Languages in King's (afterward Columbia) College. Dr. Meier-Smith writes of his great-grandfather: " Dr. Kunze was regarded as one of the most learned men of his age. He was the leading Oriental scholar in America, a man of much mathematical proficiency, and an astronomer. In theology he was pietistic and supra-naturalistic. Dr. Kunze was quite a numismatologist, and his valuable collection of coins was presented, after his death, to the New York Historical Society. Among my own papers are some manuscript letters and parts of lectures to students, in Hebrew. An old diary, kept in Latin, has some amusing and pathetic entries illustrative of his simple piety and domestic sweetness." He had seven children. Mrs. Kunze, conspicuous among the many women in whom the stirring times developed

vigorous and superior traits of character, was a leader
in social and religious circles in New York. Her great-
grandson writes: "Mrs. Kunze I remember distinctly
as a very remarkable woman, even in old age, and one
particularly attractive to my childish fancy."

"Eliza Katharine, the eldest daughter of Dr. Kunze,
was born Oct. 9, 1776, and became the wife of Caspar
Meier. She was an intellectual woman of elegant presence, — a gentlewoman of the old school. For the last
thirty years of her life, she bore with great sweetness
and courage the affliction of total blindness. She survived her husband many years, and died Jan. 29, 1863,
at the residence of her son-in-law, Dr. Albert Smith."

From the biographical notes left by Dr. Meier-Smith
are given the following sketches of his parents. "My
father, Albert Smith, M. D., was born at New Rochelle,
Westchester County, New York, March 28, 1798. He
was born on the place where he died in advanced years,
and probably within a few feet of the spot where his bed
of death stood. He was educated at the well known
Academy of Colchester, Connecticut. He studied medicine with his brother, Dr. Joseph Mather Smith, and
at the College of Physicians and Surgeons in New York,
where he graduated Doctor of Medicine in 1820. He
began at once to practise medicine in Manhattanville,
in the upper part of the city limits, on the North River
side of Manhattan Island. He was resident physician
of the Bloomingdale Insane Asylum for about two years.
Here he instituted reforms and amelioration in the treatment of the insane, novel then, though generally accepted
now.

"The residence of Caspar Meier, Esq., was nearly
opposite, and on one occasion a party of ladies from his
house visited the asylum, and under the guidance of the

young doctor ascended to the cupola to enjoy the view. Here my father was first introduced to my mother. Thereafter he was a frequent guest at Mr. Meier's hospitable home, and married his daughter, Emily Maria, May 3, 1825.

" After his marriage he removed to the ' Bradish Mansion,' on the east side of Manhattan Island, and commenced general practice in Harlem. In 1830 he went to New York, living in Bleecker Street for ten years, and then in Green Street, near Clinton Place. In 1846, after the death of his father, he purchased the family homestead and farm at New Rochelle, and removed thither, building a new house on the site of the old one, which was moved a few rods, and is still standing. He relinquished a large and successful family practice by this change, the reasons for making it being a somewhat precarious state of health, and the cares and responsibilities thrown upon him as surviving executor for the estates of his father-in-law, Mr. Meier, and his brother-in-law, Mr. von Post. He continued to aid his professional brethren in consultation, and gave his services to those who were unable to pay for medical attendance. Some old families and personal friends insisted more or less upon his supervision until his extreme old age. He was a man of great activity, and interested himself extensively in public affairs, especially as a member of the Board of Education at New Rochelle. He gave a large piece of fine woodland for a rural cemetery, and expended upon it much time, thought, and money. He took great interest in the erection of a stone edifice for the Presbyterian Church, bought and removed the old frame building which his father had helped to build, and altered it into a comfortable parsonage, which he presented to the church. He erected a transept to the church at his own expense, and by his gifts and much secular superinten-dence attested his liberal spirit and enlightened percep-tion of religious duty. For several years he passed the winter months at the home of his daughter, the wife of Robert Jaffray, Esq., in the city of New York; but for the last two years of his life he remained entirely at his home at New Rochelle. He suffered much from malarial dyspepsia and weakness of the heart for several years before his death, and during his last days was greatly dependent upon the devoted care of his friend, the over-seer of his farm, Mr. John G. Ross, who watched and nursed him with almost filial care. He died Feb. 19, 1884, in the eighty-seventh year of his age.

"My father was an example of great liberality, as well as of great economy and thrift. He began his pro-fessional life in entire dependence upon his own indus-try for bread and butter. His practice in New York was modestly remunerative, though a very extended work. It was the day when from one to three dollars were the ordinary and extreme charges for medical visits. His generous delicacy forbade any pressure upon those who found it difficult to pay him, or even upon such as were simply careless. Though entirely unused to finan-cial responsibility, the executorship of the estates before referred to threw upon him a heavy burden of study and work. He rose to the business finely, and managed with such discretion and fidelity, that, at the expiration of his trust, the estates were largely increased in value, in spite of losses by fire and general commercial disas-ters. He lived simply and without ostentation. He gave freely to his children, and to friends in needy cir-cumstances. His gifts in these directions and to various benevolent purposes, as well as to the church, amounted to a very large sum in the later years of his life. He

was a man of great modesty and reticence in regard to
his religious life, but of humble and devout piety, and
his diaries and letters for many years before his death
evince deep religious feeling and consecration. Upon
the monument erected by his descendants in Beechwood
Cemetery are the words which his son thought peculiarly expressive of his experience during the last years
of his weakness and seclusion from old age, 'Looking
for that blessed hope.'

"My mother, Emily Maria, the third child of Caspar
Meier and Eliza Katharine Kunze, was born in New
York, April 20, 1806. She received an excellent education in the French school of Madame Chegary, dear
to the memories of many of the daughters of old New
York. She was married at the age of nineteen. My
mother was a woman of superior education for the day,
possessed of keen mind, well read in history and choice
literature, and thoroughly at home in the French language, in which she read and spoke fluently throughout
her life. It was an unheard-of thing that she could
make a grammatical mistake in either English or French.
She was in youth and health very attractive in personal
appearance. Her resemblance to some of the best-
known Madonnas of the German School of painting was
often remarked. She was a woman of great religiosity.
Under mediæval environment she would have been a
saint. A saintly beauty became her well. Trained by
her Lutheran mother, in her childhood she attended
either the Episcopal or Dutch Church; but after her
marriage she became a Presbyterian, as my father was.
In the winter of 1831–32, a great religious interest pervaded the Presbyterian Communion in New York. The
preaching was of a character to alarm the careless, and,
what was less desirable, to excite the most conscien-

tious and delicately balanced minds beyond proper bounds. From this cause it was, I presume, that my mother became almost morbid in her religious experience, and suffered much disturbance for two or three years. A few years later, while I was in college, she suffered for some months from a most painful depression, which my father traced to physical causes. After her recovery from this experience, she had no further recurrence of the trouble. Her Christian life was thereafter bright and happy. She was a devout worshipper in church, a devout woman in private prayer, and a great student of the Bible. 'A perfect concordance,' was the family saying, significant of her constant study and extensive memory of the Scriptures. She was devoted to every good word and work, her only limitations being her health and strength. She suffered greatly from malarial headaches for many years of her life. A few years before her death she fell in her bedroom and broke her hip, remaining a cripple for the rest of her life. Though entirely secluded from this cause, she in some manner contracted varioloid at a time when small-pox was prevalent in New York, and fell a victim to the disease after only two days' illness. She died March 21, 1872." Dr. Meier-Smith believed that he owed a great deal to the influence of his mother's strong and beautiful character, and he gave her in return the most filial and affectionate devotion.

II.

EARLY YEARS.

1826–1839.

OUR converging lines have now brought us to the subject of this memoir. The city of New York was his birthplace. There are some now living who can recall the New York of sixty years ago, and who dwell with some fondness upon the picture. We may linger over it a moment as he loved to do. Those were days when it was but an easy walk to reach the rural suburbs from the heart of the city; when Union Square was almost "out of town"; when the broad houses of the wealthier citizens surrounded the Bowling Green and St. John's Park; when the Battery was a favorite promenade and the safe resort of nurses and children; and when one might meet, of a summer afternoon on the hills of Hoboken, the well-to-do house-father and his family. "Rapid transit" was secured to the satisfaction of the younger business men who had ventured to make their homes as far "up town" as Bond Street, by an hourly omnibus from Wall Street to Bleecker Street! Though the metropolitan policeman was unknown, peace and security were ensured to the belated wayfarer when he met the sturdy watchman in triple-caped overcoat going his rounds with the hourly "All 's well." The last of those good primitive days passed with the early boyhood of Matson Meier-Smith. Before he was ten years old, his native city began to take to herself metropolitan airs; but Dr. Meier-Smith loved to tell his children that he could remember when New York was scarcely more than a "big village."

The banks of the Hudson, and of the East River above Thirtieth Street, were lined with the country seats of those who were able to remove from their city residences in the summer, or who preferred to make the beautiful suburbs their homes for the entire year. In Harlem, then a fast growing and attractive village, very near the river stood the Bradish Mansion, a fine old villa, rented in the absence of its owners; and here, on the 4th of April, 1826, Matson Meier, the first child and only son of Dr. Albert Smith and Emily Maria Meier, was born.

The introduction to Dr. Meier-Smith's book of genealogical records, from which we have made extracts, contains these words: "This book is for my children. Two God has given me. With a father's love I shall give or bequeath these pages to them, containing in various forms records of family affairs, observations, thoughts, and hints. It is not a journal, and yet may subserve the purpose of one in some respects. It is not an autobiography, yet I shall give a little sketch of my life so far, and not fail to chronicle any grave changes which may hereafter occur. It is intended to be a book of familiar conversation with you, my darlings, undertaken in the hope that the Covenant God, whose you are, may spare you to mature life in this world, and in the persuasion that the jottings down of experiences and incidents may prove not valueless, even when the hand that penned them is mouldering in the grave. I do not approve of the style of journalism so often exhibited, in which the inmost heart is laid open, and most sacred experiences paraded before the public eye. But my children may be admitted at times within a circle whither the world may not tread; and should they in these pages find themselves occasionally introduced within such a precinct, they will appreciate the spirit in which they are welcomed thither.

" This book is undertaken in the days of your infancy, my darlings, while you are my little lambs, and I am scarcely more than a stripling. It might be wiser for me to wait until mature age brought me greater wisdom before indulging in an experiment like this. But length of days may not be mine; and lest I be removed early, I will not tarry, but one tribute at least of your father's love you shall have. Some things, too, perhaps I can better say while in the vigor of my youth, and with a strong and lively sympathy with you in your childhood and your incipient youth."

From this loving introduction it is seen that the writer intended to record reminiscences of his early life, after the ancestral sketches which immediately follow. The fulfilment of this good purpose was constantly postponed, and of his own story nothing is recorded. That it remained a purpose, and would have been fulfilled but for the pressure of work and the failing strength of the last few years, is certain, for he often referred to it, and with the promise that in a year or two more, if he did not feel more vigorous, he would lay aside other writing and study, and record the story of his own life for his descendants.

The childhood of Dr. Meier-Smith was uneventful. Life was more monotonous then, even for the children, than in our own fast moving day, when the little folk share in the excitements of their elders, and find it equally hard to live without them. " My boyhood seems to me a jog-trot," he said, "compared to the gallop of the boy of the period." He was a vigorous child, with bright, quick perceptions, gifted with a keen sense of humor, affectionate and generous, and very sensitive to praise or blame. Though baptized in the Dutch Church, he was early familiar with the Book of Common Prayer, always dear to his mother; and at her knee he learned the Church Catechism and to read well in the Bible before he was four years old. The fear of stimulating the brain by early pressure seems hardly, to have occurred to parents or teachers then, and in the little Matson's case, as in many others of his generation, we are startled to know that at five years of age he was studying English and French grammar, and that before he was eight he commenced Latin. When expressing his strong disapproval of giving such tasks to children so young, he would add: "So far as I can see, however, one little boy was none the worse for it."

When Matson was four years old his parents removed to the city, and lived for five years on Bleecker Street, east of, and within two blocks of Broadway. A little later his school life commenced at the Washington Institute, under the care of Rev. J. D. Wickham.[1] The school held two sessions, but he, with many little boys, remained through the recess, the distance being so great from their homes. A luncheon table crowned with a pudding was spread for the "good boys," and a bread-and-water table for those in disgrace. At the latter, the mischief-loving propensities of the little boy caused him not unfrequently to be found — never, he averred, for faulty lessons, for he was quick to learn, and had such a retentive memory that he was easily first in his classes.

[1] The Rev. J. D. Wickham is living at this date, and is the oldest living graduate of Yale College.

Among the older boys then at this school was one to whom by marriage Dr. Meier-Smith became kinsman, and who, as the beloved Bishop of Western New York, was ever a dear and honored friend. A few years ago Bishop Coxe was a guest at Dr. Meier-Smith's table, and as recollections of school-days were revived, the incident was recalled of an ambitious attempt of the older boys to produce the play of " Hamlet." The more important part in which the brilliant young senior appeared had been forgotten by his admiring junior, but the awe-inspiring appearance he presented as the "ghost" was vividly depicted to the amusement of host and guest.

When a little older, Matson attended another private school, conducted by Mr. Nash and Mr. Mann, where he received from an Irishman (who was a genius in his way) an admirable drilling in the rudiments of Latin, for which he was always grateful. He also commenced Greek here at the age of ten. Later, he went to the University Grammar School, and there was fitted for college.

The chief enjoyments of his childhood were found in his visits to his grandparents. The beautiful home of his grandfather Meier was very dear to him. Probably the happiest days of his boyhood were passed there, where his frequent companion was his cousin, Hermann von Post, who was a little younger than himself. His grandfather was very fond of him, and proud of his bright and ready intelligence. He often made him his companion in his daily journeys to and from Bloomingdale to his office, with the fast horse he loved to drive; and we can readily believe that these drives with the genial German grandfather were a great delight to the boy.

The river was an endless source of amusement, and here Matson learned to row, swim, and skate. His grandfather gave him a donkey-cart; and among his reminiscences was the pride he felt when he persuaded a venerable lady, the widow of General Alexander Hamilton, to seat herself in his cart, and allow him to drive her up the hill which led to her mansion.

A great treat, now and then, was a visit to one of the vessels consigned to his grandfather's firm, when the boy was made much of by the kindly German officers, and treated to the best the steward could offer, with sometimes a glass of beer or a sip of wine in which to toast the Fatherland.

Christmas was a time of great joy and of happiness such as boys and girls hardly know now, when a wealth of books, and toys, and luxuries are scattered throughout the year, and Christmas is only a little "merrier" than other holidays. But it was the one day in the year for the children in the families where it was observed, though they were a minority in New York; for between those of New England descent, who knew no Christmas, but to whom Thanksgiving Day was sacred, and the old Knickerbocker families who kept high festival on New Year's Day, Christmas had small chance of honor. To households of French and German descent, and to those brought up in the Roman Catholic and Episcopal communions it was very dear, and cherished with the more devotion because of its non-observance generally. The prizes dreamed of for a year, and the longings of the little hearts for a twelvemonth, came into the little hands under the tree on Christmas Eve, and every one, young and old, joined in the festivity which commenced then. All went to church on Christmas morning, and all the family gathered around the table for the Christmas dinner. Many quaint old customs were kept up in Mr. Meier's household, and

the memory of those early Holy Days was always fresh
and green to the grandchildren.

Very different, yet very attractive in its way, was the
other ancestral home at New Rochelle. Here, under
the care of his grandfather, Dr. Matson Smith, and the
good maiden aunts who mingled admiring petting with
some wholesome New England discipline, parts of many
happy summers were passed. It was a taste of genuine
farm life, after the good old Connecticut pattern. Matson was very much at home there, and had many a story
to tell of fun and mischief, often to the dismay of the
"good aunts." The dignified grandfather, in long black
coat and high white neckcloth, the embodiment of the
old-school doctor, often took him in his "sulky," with
the little hair-covered trunk of medicines and surgical
instruments at their feet, on his visits to his patients.

With the farm-hands he was a favorite; for, utterly
devoid of all pretence, he had from earliest years the
warm, frank manner and sunny smile which won him
a welcome in every home, and among parishioners of
all social grades in later years. So the city-bred boy
learned something of genuine farm-life.

A fine tract of woods on the farm gave a chance for
lessons in shooting; but this sport soon lost its charm,
as the boy was too tender-hearted, and always felt a
qualm when he brought down a bird or a squirrel. It
ended on this wise. Having taken aim at a "chip-
munk," the little creature jumped upon a stone and
looked at him, as he declared, with such pleading eyes
that he put down his gun and never cared to use it
again.

The earliest letter of the little Matson which has
been preserved dates from New Rochelle, and was written when he was six years old, during the first of those

gloomy seasons known as the "Cholera Summers," of 1832 and 1834. The writing is very firm and distinct, and the spelling — always a strong point with the boy — faultless. Happy as he was in this kind household, a little homesickness peeps out toward the end of the letter.

New Rochelle, Aug. 31, 1832.

My dear Father, — I received your letter by my grandfather, who brought it from the postoffice to me. It gave me a great deal of pleasure. I broke the seal myself, and read it myself, but a few words my grandfather told me. I sat on my grandfather's knee when I read it. I have had company; their names were Lydia and Deborah C. After tea they went home, and I went to Mr. P——'s, where I heard some ladies play on the piano.

My dear father, you wished me to write a full sheet, and I have not enough news to fill a sheet, and hope you will excuse me. I have been a little feverish lately, but grandpapa gave me some medicine, and now I am better. I hope you will not think I am imprudent, for I do not eat any fruit.

I am your affectionate son, Matson.

September 1.

I left off writing yesterday because I was tired. This part is to my mother, and the first to my father.

My dear Mother, — Aunt Eliza had an owl fly at her window one night, and she hallooed, "Oh, oh, it is monstrous!" And I would like you, father, to come up here to bring me home. The whole family send their love to you, and I send my love to you and my father and my sister and Katy. September 1, 1832.

I am your affectionate son,

Matson Meier-Smith, New Rochelle.

An only surviving aunt, the sister of his mother, writes thus of his early boyhood: "Matson was so remarkably bright that he read fluently at three years of age; and when he began to attend school, he had been so well taught by his mother, that he was in advance of all children of his age. He had a bright, happy disposition, brimming over with mirth and fun. He and his cousin Hermann delighted to imitate their fathers. Matson would ask to feel the pulse, if he heard any one complaining; while Hermann would look to see if the wind were in the right quarter for the incoming ships.

"Their grandfather Meier had a room in the attic made expressly for these boys, where he loved to watch them at play. Matson was a great mimic, imitating the sounds of all animals, somewhat to the injury of his throat. He was so bright and full of humor that he was always excellent company, — a happy child, and a blessing to all about him."

Two anecdotes illustrate the instinct of tender helpfulness, conspicuous throughout his life. The first of these his aunt recalls: "When seven years old, seeing his mother's grief over the death of a young sister, he told her that he would read something to comfort her; and opening his Bible, he read the story of the raising of Lazarus, in the 11th chapter of St. John's Gospel." About a year later, during one of the seasons of depression from which his mother suffered, he inferred from observation the cause of her sadness, and overheard a friend advising her to read a book by a Scotch writer. His heart was filled with the desire to do something for her relief, but he shrunk from going alone, having suffered from the usual experience of the small boy who essays to make purchases by himself; and he expected to encounter especial contempt in his quest for a "grown-up" religious book. But his busy father had no time to accompany him, so, summoning up his courage, and taking the little purse with its slender stock of silver, he entered one of the principal book-shops, and boldly asked for "Colloquion [Colquhoun] on Spiritual Consolation." No doubt it was with surprised amusement that the ponderous title was heard from the lips of the eight-year-old boy, but Matson gratefully remembered the kindly young man who, instead of laughing at him, assured him that though that book was not to be had, his slender means would purchase another, and sent him home happy in the hope that "Johnson's Rasselas" might be equally helpful! Surely the mother received some uplifting from the loving effort of the boy.

A child born and nurtured in such homes, and amid such associations, could hardly have been otherwise than thoughtful, and susceptible to religious impressions, from very early years.

The social circle in which Matson's parents moved, after their removal to the city, was a religious one. They were members of the Bleecker-Street Presbyterian Church, of which Dr. Erskine Mason was pastor. He was the son of the distinguished clergyman, Dr. John M. Mason, and inherited much of his father's intellectual ability and his power as a preacher. His congregation numbered many of the leading professional men of the city, and his sermons were among the finest of the type which thoughtful Christians of the day expected from their religious teachers. The children were trained to listen to sermons, and "tell what they could remember" at home. The little Matson, listening so often with poor success for something which he could report, decided that "Dr. Mason did not know how to preach," and brought his mother to confusion on one occasion during a pastoral call of the clergyman. "I saw you in church, my little boy, last Sunday, and you seemed to be paying great attention. What did you think about the sermon?" The unexpected reply came quickly, "I thought that when I was a minister I would preach so that little boys could understand, and have something to tell about afterward." The good minister took no offence, but was charmed with the frankness of the reply. When, however, he was of an age to appreciate the strength and beauty of Dr. Mason's sermons, he enjoyed them extremely, and always felt that he owed much of his own power as a preacher to the admirable models under which he was trained during these forming years. Dr. Mason became a dear and honored friend, and Matson was on terms of intimacy with his family, who were near neighbors.

While his parents resided in Bleecker Street, there lived, nearly opposite, the family of Mr. Norman White, which became as his own a few years later. Matson first met when he was five years old a baby girl who has no memory of a time when she did not know him. The parents were dear friends, and Dr. Smith was the beloved physician of Mr. White's household. The mothers told each other proudly of the achievements of their eldest born. Matson's sister was a playmate of the little girl whom God was keeping for him, and thus constant knowledge of each other grew with the years of these children, though she was so much his junior that he seemed to her a "big boy," of whom she stood in some awe.

During his school and college days they met often, and she recalls compositions — prose and rhyme — and caricature drawings which Matson's sister proudly exhibited to her, each confident that the writer and artist was a genius, destined to dazzle the world in the near future.

As related in his biographical sketch of his mother, he was a very little boy when the religious circles of New York were deeply stirred by an awakening under the preaching of the evangelist, Charles C. Finney. Matson was too young to attend the meetings, but his mother and many of her friends were greatly engrossed by them, and he, a very observant child, heard much conversation which deeply impressed him. He was required to commit hymns to memory, and they were often of a type of theology calculated to alarm and excite a sensitive child; so that he recalled much real suffering from the conviction that he was under condemnation for his sins, — and this before he was five years old. In the religious training of the day, under Calvinistic influences, fear overbalanced love, and the timid child hardly knew what it was to look up to a Father. The Righteous Judge filled the imagination, and the tender Saviour was almost shut out. The little ones of Christ's Kingdom felt themselves outcasts, and in distress and perplexity, looked in a vague way for the " conversion " to come to them of which their elders talked, while the bright side of the religious life was almost obscured by clouds of mystery and fear. Thus, certainly, this little boy suffered, and debated the question from year to year, conscientious child that he was, " whether he was a Christian." He belonged to a " Little Boys' Prayer-Meeting," and was often a leader ; because, as one of the other boys said, " Matson could talk and pray *easier* than the rest." So he could, for expression was easy and natural to him, but his conscience troubled him lest he did not "*feel* his prayers." It is not to be understood that he was other than a natural and light-hearted child, or that there was any more of a morbid element in his serious thought than was inevitable under his surroundings, and was more or less the condition of all children similarly taught.

While his mirth-loving propensities could not be restrained, there was an under-current of struggling unrest. He wondered if he loved God, wished that he did, and longed to be sure that he was one of the chosen. So he struggled upward; always a pure, obedient, truthful child, he was steadily moving toward the outward Christian stand. There remain no memoranda to verify the impression, but it is believed that he was thirteen years old when he resolved to assume his baptismal vows; which he did, in accordance with the usage of the Presbyterian Church, by public confession of his faith, when he received the Holy Communion for the first time. But he was not yet free from doubt and trouble, though clearer light was coming to him.

Matson's most intimate friends among boys and youth have, with but few exceptions, gone before him. His cousin before referred to, Mr. Hermann C. von Post, his brother-in-law, Mr. Robert Jaffray, the Rev. Dr. Thomas S. Hastings, Isaac Lewis Peet, LL. D., and his cousin, Dr. Gouverneur M. Smith, are among the number of early friends who remain. Some of them he knew well from early boyhood, others a few years later; but with all he had memories of happy association which it was always a pleasure to revive.

The features of character which were conspicuous in later years marked his boyhood and youth. He was mirthful, sunny-tempered, unselfish, and affectionate, of quick sympathies, and gifted with ready tact. Somewhat ease-loving, though when roused, working quickly, — he was not one of the untiring workers of incessant activity. He was retiring in general society, not self-asserting, and inclined then, as afterward, to await recognition rather than to assume it. He was not easily daunted, and would never be patronized. When once he held a position he was bold, and on occasions defiant, and by no means disposed to submit to any but constitutional authority. He was very sensitive to ridicule, but could face it bravely if occasion demanded. At college he bore not a little, for, young as he was, he took a decided stand with the few whose views of life were serious and religious, while the prevailing tone was quite the reverse.

As a scholar Matson was both quick and thoughtful; and though he was wont to call himself lazy, and declared that he only did such work as was necessary, it would seem that he hardly did himself justice, for he was throughout his school years in advance of boys of his age. It is remembered that his father was heard to say of him to a friend, "What shall I do with my boy? He is not thirteen years old, but he has gone through the course of the preparatory schools; he is too young for college, and they don't want him any longer at the grammar school."

The standard of scholarship was then much lower than at present; and a boy could pass the necessary examinations to enter most of the colleges, with perhaps two years less preparation than is now required.

III.

COLLEGE AND THEOLOGICAL SEMINARY.

1839–1846.

IN 1839, when less than fourteen years of age, Matson Meier-Smith entered Columbia College, New York, and was the youngest member of his class.

In his own retrospect, college days had but little fascination for him. Living at home, he lost the experience of good fellowship, and failed to form the close friendships which are often so pleasant a feature of college life. He had but little liking for the fashionable society he might have entered, through the acquaintance formed at Columbia, and his growing religious character led him out of such associations into those which more directly met his higher aspirations.

There is but a brief record of his college life. He was a good Latin and Greek scholar; and to Dr. Charles Anthon, Professor of Greek and Latin, he felt under much obligation for thorough discipline, and the awakening of real interest in classical study. Henry James Andrews, LL. D., Professor of Mathematics, he always remembered with gratitude. He thought himself deficient in mathematical ability, and this impression discouraged him, and caused him to lose much that he might have gained from Professor Andrews's valuable instruction. Matson maintained a good, though not a brilliant standard of scholarship throughout his course, graduating third or fourth in his class. The theme of his graduating oration was "Consecrated Talent." He received his degree of Bachelor of Arts in 1843, when he was a little more than seventeen years of age. One who was in college at the same time, but a year in advance of him, writes: "He impressed me by the same traits of light-heartedness and unselfishness which he exhibited in all his after life."

During his college course, another season of great religious interest occurred in the Presbyterian Church, in connection with the evangelistic work of the Rev. Dr. Kirk, which enlisted all his heart. Dr. Kirk's preaching and work were radiant with the light of a full and free gospel. He was a man of persuasive eloquence, of a fine and winning presence, gifted with the richest and most melodious of voices, and a magnetic power which compelled the attention and moved the heart. Few who remember Edward Norris Kirk in his prime, will admit that any later evangelist has equalled him in his power over an intelligent audience. He encouraged the most timid with his tender, pastoral counsel; and there must be many now living who owe to him their emancipation from the doubts which overshadowed their youth, through mistaken early instruction.

Among the number who received such help was the subject of these pages. He called Dr. Kirk his spiritual father, and never mentioned him but with loving gratitude. It was through his instruction that he came to the light, and consecrated himself heartily to the service of a Saviour whose love he had hitherto but imperfectly understood.

Apparently no diminution of religious purpose and consecration was caused by college associations, and Matson began to consider the claims upon him of the sacred ministry, as he approached his graduation. His mother's heart longed to see her boy in that high calling, but she conscientiously refrained from pressing her wishes upon him. A flattering position in the business-house of his grandfather was offered to him. To decline it, as he did, involved worldly sacrifice. At this time he had strong leanings toward the hereditary profession of medicine. Indeed, throughout his life he felt an interest, only second to that in his own calling, in this honored profession, and numbered many physicians among his most valued friends.

While debating a final decision, Matson decided to spend a year in medical study, and entering the office of his uncle, Dr. Joseph Mather Smith, he attended several courses of lectures at the College of Physicians and Surgeons. He pursued these studies with much enthusiasm, and always felt the benefit of them. There was that in his temperament, and in his intellectual traits, which doubtless would have made him successful as a physician, had he not been impelled irresistibly to the ministry. During these years he was actively engaged in Sunday-school and Mission work in the Bleecker-Street Church. He had also many social connections with the Mercer-Street Church, and greatly admired the preaching of its distinguished pastor, the Rev. Dr. Thomas H. Skinner. There are seldom found in one congregation so many cultivated and influential laymen as were there associated. Intellectually and religiously he found much stimulus in the meetings of such men for conference and worship. Dr. Meier-Smith recalled them as the " palmy days of the prayer-meeting," and said that he " belonged to Bleecker-Street Church and to Mercer-Street Prayer-Meeting." After such a model he tried to mould the social services in the congregations

to which he ministered. But the material was often
wanting. His high ideal made him impatient of the
formalism and dull mediocrity which so often kill the
prayer-meeting, and in his maturer years he was far
less confident of its benefits than were many of his
brethren.

When asked, after he became rector of an Episcopal
parish, " Do you not miss the prayer-meeting?" his
answer was, " I should if it meant such a service as we
had in old 'Mercer-Street' days, but alas! it *don't*."

As many of his relatives were members of the Episcopal Church, he often attended the services of that
Church, and was much attracted by them. The Prayer-
Book, as a study of devotion, he prized, and its phrase-
ology strongly impressed itself on his mind. Probably it
was to this cause that he owed what was sometimes
spoken of as his "gift of prayer." Reverent and Scriptural language, and orderly arrangement of thought, with
maturity of expression, were characteristic of his efforts
to lead his congregation in worship from his earliest
ministry. Matson was strongly influenced to take Orders in the Episcopal Church; and his father, a man
of unsectarian tendencies, would not have objected, but
at this time he was an ardent young Presbyterian, and
felt himself able to combat successfully the claims of
historic Episcopacy. Certainly he did it to his own
satisfaction, for in the autumn of 1844 he entered the
Union Theological Seminary of the Presbyterian Church.
The course of three years' study he found very interesting, awakening in him the first genuine enthusiasm for
study.

Dr. Henry White, Professor of Theology, and Dr.
Edward Robinson, Professor of Sacred Literature, were
admirable teachers, and inspired enthusiasm in their

students. Dr. Robinson's eminent scholarship made his instructions especially valuable. Dr. Meier-Smith remembered them gratefully, as well as the personal interest the distinguished scholar took in his young student, who was permitted to enjoy a warm friendship with him, and his cultivated and literary family.

These years were happy ones. Much religious fervor pervaded the seminary, and there was especially an awakening of the missionary spirit. The claims of foreign missions were strougly presented, and a number of Matson's classmates consecrated themselves to this work. His own heart was greatly stirred, and at one time his decision was almost made to give himself to the work of Christ in heathen lands. It kindled his imagination and appealed to the spirit of self-sacrifice, which appeared to him as the foundation of all successful work in his sacred calling. Throughout his ministry he was a thorough believer in " Foreign Missions." The Lord's command, " Go ye into all the world," he considered an all-sufficient justification for all sacrifice of labor or wealth, apart from any results. " Had I not honestly decided, and at much pain to myself, guided by the counsels of trusted advisers, that my duty lay in my own land, I would have gone to India," he wrote, adding, " Yes, it was a sacrifice to give it up." Some of the most eloquent platform addresses Dr. Meier-Smith ever made were in behalf of this work. In later years, during his professorship in the Divinity School, he prepared a thorough course of lectures on Foreign Missions, giving historical sketches of the work, as carried on by various Christian bodies.

During his seminary course he gave much attention to extemporaneous speaking and the cultivation of oratorical power. He had a rich and musical voice,

and was recognized as one of the best speakers of his
class. The students were not then allowed to preach
until regularly licensed, but he gave informal lectures
now and then in New York and at New Rochelle.

Toward the close of his theological course a friendship began which was of much benefit to him, and was
affectionately cherished until death interrupted it a few
years since. The Rev. Charles Hawley, D. D., for many
years pastor of a church in Auburn, New York, was
then a young man, a few years Matson's senior, and
minister of the Presbyterian Church at New Rochelle.
Dr. Smith's family had removed thither, and Matson
was often with them. Mr. Hawley was a remarkably attractive man, possessing a charm of unaffected
sweetness much like Matson's own, and very unusual
gifts as a preacher. He won his young brother's love
and admiration, and returned it cordially. In every
regard this friendship was helpful and stimulating.
Together they spent hours in walks over the beautiful
country, planning the full lives they believed were before them, and together they prayed for the blessing of
the great Head of the Church, to whose service they
had consecrated themselves. A deeper and more fervent religious life was kindled by this brotherly communion. A promise was then made, that when their
work should separate them, correspondence should be
frequent; but in the pressure of busy lives, this purpose was not carried out. Only now and then did
letters pass between them, but the old love remained
to the last.

While in the Theological Seminary he had two regular correspondents; but the letters of his friends, which
gave much detail of these years, were lost in the transition from one parish to another, and his own cannot

be found, as those to whom they were written are not living.

Some warm friendships were formed in the Seminary. The two friends with whom he was most intimate were the Rev. Edwin A. Bulkley and the Rev. James Kimball. Mr. Kimball died a few months after entering upon his ministry. Dr. Bulkley, a lifelong friend and his kinsman by marriage, has contributed to these pages the following affectionate reminiscences of those early days : —

"... In quick and pleasant recollection, my mind runs back to the September days of '44, when my ever-constant friend, Matson Meier-Smith, started, side by side with myself, upon the curriculum in the Union Theological Seminary of New York City. We came together by mutual attraction, without previous acquaintance. We were the juniors in a large class, — ourselves still lacking more than two years of our majority; and the considerable interval between us and our older and more mature classmates was one link in our association. This was strengthened into habitual companionship and close intimacy, and still further into a relationship through a marriage. In all the variations of our lives and divergence of our paths which lessened communication, this friendship was never broken till the one went on in advance of the other across the river. He was as strong as a man and tender as a woman in his attachments; and in his last days he sought to revive the early experiences of Christian fellowship in an expressed purpose and plan for more frequent intercourse.

" His temperament was very buoyant ; cheerfulness seldom forsook him. With a keen sense of humor and a sharp wit, his merriment found constant play, and animated others, while he was not without seriousness and dignity. To this spirit he owed much in times of trial, and the heartiness of his greeting and laugh was a medicine to many a depressed friend.

With a very confiding nature, he sought a close Christian intimacy with some of his fellows, evidently aiming to help them, but more to advance his own spiritual life. So always, with his proven friends and brethren in the ministry, he loved to give and receive confidence.

" After our seminary days we passed to active work in the same part of the country ; and so in all our pastorates, though not very near neighbors, we were never very far apart. The time is pleasantly recalled, when, in a suburb of Boston, he was just coming into that distinction in the pulpit which he more and more acquired as he continued to preach. His friends rejoiced in his usefulness and honor, and he in turn never failed to express his gratification when they had similar recognition in the Church.

" In his change of denominational relations, his catholicity of spirit was not at all abated. Those whom he could not persuade to accompany him into another church fellowship were still held by him in warm-hearted fraternity. Clear and firm in his new-found convictions, he always rejoiced in the greater communion of saints, and loved no less his former and cherished associates.

" It was a startling surprise when the news of his death was flashed to us ; but we knew that all was well with him. We looked with gratitude on the calmness of his face in death ; and we sang with thanksgiving his funeral hymn."

The Rev. Professor Dwinell thus wrote after the death of Dr. Meier-Smith : —

PACIFIC THEOLOGICAL SEMINARY,
OAKLAND, CAL., Nov. 10, 1887.

. . . . I was in Union Seminary, N. Y., at the same time that he was, and knew him very well. A perfectly distinct image of him comes up to my mind at this time. I can believe every word of the testimonials to his memory, and believe them faint by the side of his excellencies and the reality.

Excuse me for obtruding on your attention, but the pleasantness of early associations and memories impels me to give this tribute to his worth as I knew him when a young man. . . .

Dr. I. L. Peet, President of the New York Institution for the Deaf and Dumb, wrote under date of August 9, 1887 : —

". . . Your late husband was one of the most beloved companions of my boyhood, as he was one of the brightest. He was, in every respect, far in advance of other boys of his age; and when he graduated from college at a period of life when most young men enter, and after the usual course of preparation, entered upon the duties of the Christian ministry, I found that the promise of his youth was fulfilled in his manhood. Ever since then I have watched his career with interest, and when I learned that in the midst of his useful and honorable labors in Philadelphia, he was so suddenly called to go up higher to be forever with the Lord, I mourned his departure, — not on his own account, but on my own account and that of others. . . ."

IV.

PROFESSIONAL WORK BEFORE ORDINATION.

1847–1849.

HERE on the threshold of his future life-work, the familiar name of boyhood may be dropped.

A word of explanation may perhaps be needed for some who knew him only in the early years of his life and ministry. The adoption of his middle name as a prefix to his surname did not become general until the last twenty years of his life, though always more or less in use. As there was no descendant of his maternal grandfather to bear his honored name, he sympathized with his mother's wish to make it prominent, and the double name was always his signature. So completely is it now identified with him, that to speak of him as he was generally addressed in earlier years, would be unfamiliar to nearly all who may read these pages; and therefore the name by which they knew him will be used throughout the volume.

After passing the necessary examinations, Mr. Meier-Smith was licensed to preach by the Fourth Presbytery of New York, April 9, 1847. In accordance with the regulation of the Presbyterian Church, ordination was deferred until a pastorate or other settled work should be assumed. He preached his first sermons on the following Sunday, in the old church at New Rochelle, his parents and sister being among his hearers. The texts of these sermons he has recorded: the first, from the second Epistle to the Corinthians (ii. 15, 16), "For we are unto God a sweet savour of Christ, in them that are saved, and in them that perish. To the one we are the savour of death unto death, and to the other the savour of life unto life. And who is sufficient for these things?"

The second sermon was from the eighth chapter of the Epistle to the Romans. The text was the eloquent passage commencing "He that spared not his own Son," and ending, "In all these things we are more than conquerors through him that loved us." Looking back over the forty years of his ministry, it would seem that in these his introductory sermons he struck the key-note of all his future preaching. The first one glowed with his lofty ideal of his calling, while with touching humility he expressed his own sense of his unworthiness. The second one was inspired by the one great theme ever dearest to his heart, — the love of God as manifested in the life and work of our blessed Lord. The serious earnestness of his style and manner in the pulpit, free from all trifling and levity, and the straightforward march of vigorous thought were the natural outgrowth of the truths underlying the first sermon; while the fervor and unction which gave his preaching its power could hardly have been wanting where the ever prominent theme was Christ crucified, risen, glorified.

Mr. Meier-Smith had but just completed his twenty-first year as he commenced his work, and he was much oppressed by a sense of youth and immaturity. He resolved not to seek a parochial charge at once, but to spend a year or two in further preparation, and in acquiring greater facility in writing and speaking, giving himself the while to the occasional assistance of other clergymen, or to temporary work in vacant parishes. He had at this time an offer to spend a year in Europe. This he declined from a conscientious apprehension that there might be, from foreign study and travel, a loss of interest in his work, and a lowering of the tone of religious life which would outweigh the advantages that might be gained. Such a view of European travel and study was more common forty years ago than at the present day. He felt afterwards that he was probably mistaken in this, and that the broader views and more thorough preparation he might have acquired would have been of great benefit to him in his life-work.

He had a modest appreciation of his own ability, and was genuinely surprised when he found himself in demand and his services acceptable. The encouragement was good for him. His sensitive temperament needed it. From the record kept of his public ministrations it appears that he was at work almost every Sunday from the time of his licensure. His home at this time was with his parents at New Rochelle, and he officiated there frequently, — his friend, Mr. Hawley, suffering from a long illness. Often, also, his former pastor, Dr. Mason, called for his help, and he was welcomed in the church of his nurture with a cordiality which proved that a young prophet was not always "without honor in his own country" and among his kinsfolk. His first experience at a distance from New York City was at Mount Morris in Western New York, where he supplied the place of a friend for a few weeks, and made some warm friendships, among others that of a noble Christian woman who henceforth watched his course with loving interest, and predicted for him a faithful and successful ministry. A letter received from her since his earthly work has ended speaks tenderly of the impression he made in that community, in spite of youth and untried powers.

The next winter Mr. Meier-Smith was at home, and at work quite steadily; and in the spring of 1848 he was invited to visit Western New York. Friends who were settled in parishes in that part of the State wished to have him near them, and he filled vacancies for some months, — first in Perry Centre and afterward in Le Roy. The former place was in the midst of a farming community, and the people were a little afraid of the young minister from the great city. He wrote home, "I am the biggest man in the place, judging from the respect with which I am treated." He gave them simple sermons and familiar talks, and so won their interest and favor that they proposed to give him a call. But he now received an invitation from a more important and prominent church, and one which he felt he could serve more successfully. Le Roy was an attractive and enterprising town, with many intelligent people, and the work there looked inviting to a young and enthusiastic man. At the close of a three months' engagement, he was earnestly desired to remain permanently; but he found an obstacle in the shape of a minority who from some unlucky past experiences, though anxious to retain him, were opposed to having any permanent pastor, and desired to engage him from year to year. This he thought bad policy and poor Presbyterianism, and declined to stay unless regularly called, and with entire unanimity. It is certain that it was with great regret that the most of the large congregation parted with him, and for some months he was in correspondence with them, many efforts being made to shake his decision. He was firm, however, and felt assured that he was withheld for some good reason from the pleasant settlement in prospect.

Toward the close of the year 1848 he became engaged to Mary Stuart, daughter of Norman White of New York. The acquaintance from childhood blossomed suddenly into the close union which was to be so blessed for almost forty years.

This new tie strengthened the now earnest desire for a settled field of labor. Yet it appeared to be duty to remain at New Rochelle for a few months, as his friend, Mr. Hawley, pastor of the church, had just resigned his charge, and the congregation depended upon Mr. Meier-Smith's services. During the winter he was invited to take an old and much enfeebled church in New York; but his friends advised against it, thinking it beyond hope of resuscitation. That he now felt more deeply than ever a spirit of consecration and willingness to go wherever God should send him, the following extracts from letters to Miss White will show: —

New Rochelle, December, 1848.

. . . For myself, I live anew. The kindness of God to me, in bestowing such a gift upon me, has led me to a renewed, unreserved self-consecration. May He direct us to a place where we may together labor for the salvation of precious spirits and the triumph of our risen Lord. If he spare us to advanced life, may we be always fruitful in His vineyard. If our days be few, let our labors be abundant, that we may sleep sweetly till the Resurrection morning. . . .

After preaching twice: —

December, 1848.

. . . Let me give you some of my own experience to-day. I have found to-day, for the thousandth time, that " God worketh in us after His own pleasure." I wanted to mount to a high position, — to get far above the dust and din of earth, and into the focus of eternal realities. I wanted so to feel their power and influence as to become a different man; to get such a view of things unutterable, that I might tell upon my fellow-men; to get so high and receive impressions of such tremendous strength, that Satan could no more wound me with the arrows of infidelity. But God has suffered me to feel the clog, the weight, the drag of a depressed nature; and to realize my absolute dependence upon His Spirit's aid for strength to mount, — aye, for any life at all. . . .

In answer to questions as to reasons for conflict with doubt : —

January, 1849.

. . . Suffer me to obtrude a leaf from my own experience. Last spring I was in a strange state of mind. It seemed as if a whole regiment from hell was let loose upon my spirit, to assail me in every part with all the shafts and shots of infidelity. My creed was shaken to the very foundation, and the most vigorous use of syllogism upon syllogism, and prayer upon prayer, did no more than just keep me from complete destruction beneath their violence. It was just as much as I could do to hold fast and say, " I believe." Why this contention with " principalities " and " spiritual wickedness," I knew not, but have since seen in a measure. It just enabled me to meet the case of a Christian brother at Perry, and again to stop the mouths and gain assent to the truth of Christian doctrine from some young men at Le Roy. The experience taught me more of the nature of infidelity, and the way to meet it, than I could have learned in a year from books or lectures. . . .

. . . Looking forward to some of the trials which you seem to dread, this thought may be given. Afflictions will come, in whatever position of life we are placed. They are as certainly the portion of the children of ease as of those of a less brilliant fortune. And since they *must* come, and *will* come, how delightful to have them all in the way of Christ's service. We shall find them in the ministry, but they will perhaps be of a different kind from what we should have experienced in some other calling. Let us go forward with stout hearts, ready to encounter anything. Storms will make us cling closer to each other and to the Lord. Still, don't dwell on melancholy forebodings, nor " die a thousand deaths in dreading one." . . .

January, 1849.

. . . Let me say a word to animate you in the prospect of a life in the great work. Does it seem a life of toil and sorrow to you, my Mary? See its certain success predicted by the " Voice which rolls the stars along." " Glorious things are spoken of thee, O city of God!" Is it an employ unhonored and unsung by worldly-wise men? Lo, God's estimate of those engaged therein. " How beautiful upon the mountains are the feet of those who bring good tidings!" Let us go hand in hand rejoicing. We have a blessed business before us. The Forerunner has accomplished *His* portion, — delightful assurance that He will aid us in *our* part. Encircled in the arms of covenant love, — sustained, made effective by power from on high, — we may go forth bearing precious seed, presently to return with sheaves ripe and golden for Immanuel's garner. . . .

February, 1849.

. . . I am now ready to begin the work of the ministry in earnest. My eighteen months of licensure have been taken up with preparation more extended than I had in the Seminary. I have learned many lessons, some of them bitter. The path of duty is beginning to be more clear, away from home, but in what direction I know not. I wish to resolve *myself* away from self and pleasure, and claims of flesh and blood, and say to the great Bishop of the Church, "Lord, send me where Thou wilt. At the first beck of Thy finger will I go; no longer fastidious about the place, I will labor there until Thou send me elsewhere, if it be until the coming of the great day." And by anywhere and where Thou wilt, I mean it *all*. To China or Cape Horn, to Illinois or Rome, to Tahiti or London, to the Western Wilderness or New York City, or *even* to New Rochelle, of which I don't see the slightest probability.

I speak of being "fastidious." I do not mean that I regret my past decisions, for I have not felt ready for settlement, either intellectually or socially. Now, having a small stock of sermons in hand, and having discovered a capacity for extemporizing, of which I before was ignorant, and being *socially* provided for better than I ever thought possible before, — I am ready and feel it a solemn duty to get to work permanently, as soon as possible. In this consecration may I not ask my dearest Mary to unite? Aye, let us join —

> ". . . The Solemn Vow,
> The Vow we dare not break,
> That long as life itself shall last
> Ourselves to Christ we yield ;
> Nor from His cause will we depart,
> Nor ever quit the field."

April, 1849.

. . . You remember I came home with the intention of devoting the week to hard intellectual exertion. But not a bit of headwork have I done, save what was subsidiary to something more important. I have found plenty of heart work to do, and I think you have been praying especially for me. The past of my Christian course fills me with shame and repentance, and I long with unwonted desire to perceive more of the glory of Christ, to have Him ever before me, and to be present in spirit with Him, the ineffably glorious Son of God Incarnate. I want to realize His personality — His real present existence — to have it more of a fact to my soul. My desire is to get such views of His transcendent excellence as shall set me above all danger of preaching myself or anything but Christ. . . .

In May, 1849, he was asked to go to Geneva, where his friend and kinsman, Rev. Mr. Bulkley, was now pastor, with a view to settlement in one or other of the vacant parishes in the vicinity. He visited two or three, and accepted an invitation to take charge for three months of the church in Ovid, Seneca County. The result of his work there was an unanimous call which he decided to accept. The church was in the county town, the centre of a large and wealthy farming community. He writes to Miss White with reference to his future field of labor : —

OVID, June, 1849.

. . . My situation here appears more and more pleasant to me, — certainly as far as externals are concerned ; yet I can hardly see the evidence of permanence. There is a large and attentive congregation, many young people, and an average amount of intelligence; but all over this region there is a mischievous growth of dislike to settled pastorates. The querulousness of some when talking of the work of the late "Dominie," as the parson is called here, leads me to believe that they demand of one man more than a cohort of angels could do. I have induced the people to change the hour of afternoon service. This followed the morning services, with barely half an hour's intermission. Some are dissatisfied, and wish to return to the old plan. Should this be done, I doubt if I can remain; for, to say nothing of the slow slaughter of the parson, the cramming and packing of a spiritual dinner close upon a spiritual breakfast is enough to make a congregation of spiritual dyspeptics. And I desire no such bad work for my hands. . . .

During this temporary sojourn in Ovid, an acquaintance was formed which resulted in one of the closest friendships of his life. The Rev. Heman Dyer, D. D., was then staying in Ovid at the home of his wife's father. He took a kindly interest in the young minister, — an interest none the less cordial, that one was an honored presbyter of the Episcopal Church, and the other a mere novice in another branch of the Church Catholic. This friendship, ever inspiring and invigorating, ripened as years went on into perfect trust and harmony, and was counted by Dr. Meier-Smith as one of the blessings of his life. There was never a break or jar in it, until he, so much the younger, was called to the rest of Paradise; while in strength of soul, though in bodily weakness, his revered friend and counsellor awaits his summons in the holy calm of the "land of Beulah."

After accepting the call to Ovid, Mr. Meier-Smith was in New York for a few weeks, and in the first letter to Miss White, after his return he writes:

Ovid, October 16th.

. . . I reached *our* destination on Saturday, safe and sound and happy. Upon landing, I felt blue and dreary; but reaching the village and getting in sight of the church, the clouds were blown away, and the consciousness that I was in the right place, and that our prayers were answered, gave me great peace and satisfaction. I was warmly and affectionately received, and have reason every hour to be grateful for friendly words and looks. My kind friend, Mr. Joy, took me to his own house, where everything is done to make it pleasant for me. Mr. Joy could not do more for me if I were his own son. On Sunday I preached with great pleasure and comfort in my *own* church, to my *own* people. The congregations were good and attentive.

To Miss White.

Ovid, October 18th.

. . . My ordination will probably take place on the 23d inst. Oh how much I shall need your prayers and sympathies, my dearest one, on that day! To think that I, a sinner, so weak, so prone to err, so inexperienced, should be invested with such high office in the church of Christ! What am I, or what is my father's house? Oh that on that day I may experience a hitherto unknown baptism of the Holy Ghost, and go forth in new strength and grace to make full proof of my ministry!

V.

ORDINATION AND MARRIAGE.

The First Parish. 1849–1850.

ON the 23d of October, 1849, Matson Meier-Smith was ordained to the work of the Ministry by the Presbytery of Geneva, and installed pastor of the congregation in Ovid. The sermon was preached by his friend, the Rev. E. A. Bulkley.

He wrote of this service to Miss White, —

Ovid, October 25, 1849.

The service was in my own church, the congregation was large, and a deep solemnity pervaded the assembly. May God send his perpetual blessing upon the delightful, yet fearful relation now consummated! Your last received gave me great cause for thankfulness. I bless God the Spirit for whatever love to Christ and consecration He has implanted in your soul! . . . I know that it will be a trial to my dear one to leave that precious home, and go to the land of the stranger. I have found it a severe one for myself, and can sympathize deeply with you. Often will tears fill your eyes at the thought that you are absent from the circle of your affections and early attachments; often will the musical voice of mother or father wake you from blissful dreams to the consciousness that they are far away, — but you will find yourself amply repaid for every sacrifice in the consciousness of being in the place of Christ's appointment, in the moral elevation attained by those who sunder tender ties for Christ's work, and in the more rapid development of character and usefulness as Christian woman and wife. And you may be sure of this, that if the attentions and affection of a devoted husband, *to the utmost* consistent with his duties to his Master, can palliate any pain of soul, you will never know unmitigated sorrow.

How this loving promise was fulfilled, let the long years that followed bear witness, with their lights and shadows, their abundance of labors, and their full weight of care, anxiety, and sorrow.

To Miss White.

OVID, November 1.

I contemplate the future with much satisfaction. There will undoubtedly be many things — among others, homesickness — often annoying; but many other things, new and strange to you, will be sources of amusement to our very philosophical minds. There will be inconveniences, but I shall trust you to shorten up some very natural long-facedness, and take them as good jokes as I have learned to do; and the wants in view of which they arise, as merely *citified*, artificial, imaginary wants. The life of a minister's wife you will possibly find, when common-sense analyzes and compares it with other stations, not the worst life in the world. I feel happy as a pastor. I know not what circumstances may arise, or what kind of consideration there may be among my people, but independently of this, " I magnify my office." Oh, dearest Mary, may we have grace to be faithful and efficient! May we ever be to each other what we *may* be!   May the God of our fathers establish His covenant with us and with ours forever!   And if it be His will, may we, oh may we be spared long to each other on the earth!

On the 14th of November, 1849, Matson Meier-Smith and Mary Stuart White were married, the grand-uncle of the bride, Rev. Samuel Hanson Cox, D. D, who, twenty-one years before, had married her parents, being the officiating clergyman.

Early in December they went to their new home. To these young people, accustomed to the refinements of city life, and leaving delightful family and social ties, this remote field of labor — four times as far from New York forty years ago as it is now — seemed almost like a foreign mission.

The town of Ovid is situated on a high ridge overlooking the beautiful lakes Seneca and Cayuga.   The first impressions of the arrival at the future home are vividly recalled.   The young minister and his wife came by steamboat through Seneca Lake, landing on a cold and dreary day.   Three miles in the distance, the village crowned the hill.   A long pier ran out into the lake; and when the travellers landed, they found great difficulty in keeping a foothold on the ice-covered dock. A solitary vehicle with its driver was the only sign of life.   As they seated themselves for the long drive up the hill, was it strange if some heart-sinking, in view of the happy past and the untried future, was felt,— while yet strong purpose and united hands nerved them to the work before them?

The people gave a cordial welcome to their young "Dominie" (the local name for the pastor) and his wife. A semi-housekeeping was set up in three small rooms which were made attractive by the display of the wedding gifts. The winter months, though the weather was dreary and severe, were not without their simple pleasures. Mr. Meier-Smith's work here comprised the oversight of a large and somewhat scattered parish, with two and sometimes three services on Sundays, and lectures upon two evenings in the week. The congregations increased rapidly, and much attention and seriousness appeared. There were many young people in the place, and they gathered around their young pastor with enthusiasm. The home letters were full of interest in the work, though it was not without its discouragements. The sober, elderly, farming folk were somewhat distrustful of a young city-bred clergyman, and any new methods; and from them not much co-operation could be hoped for.

The village was embodied quietness during much of the winter. The Lecture Lyceum had then hardly established itself in the more remote country towns, and Ovid was not enlivened by anything of the kind. The social entertainments were of no more exhilarating a nature than now and then a sleighing party, or a gathering of a dozen to tea to meet the minister and his wife, when it seemed to be expected that the social entertainment of the evening would be furnished almost entirely by the honored guests.

Many things afforded much amusement to those to whom such an experience was so novel; and loving, prayerful work to raise the tone of religious life in the church and community kept the hearts warm and the heads busy. But physical discomfort was very considerable. The extremely cold weather, and the entire unfitness of the domestic arrangements to insure even a moderate degree of comfort, told seriously upon the health of the young wife, and it was soon apparent that this first parish could hardly become a settlement.

During the winter much religious interest followed sermons and services of peculiar solemnity, and a number, especially among the young people, were added to the communion of the church. The pastor was encouraged, and found his time and sympathies fully taxed with his pulpit preparation and pastoral visitation. One written and one extemporaneous sermon was usually preached on each Sunday; and the verdict was, as given by one of his hearers, "When our minister writes his sermons, we say we wish he would always write them ; and then when he preaches without any notes, we say we hope he will never use them again," — which paradoxical approbation was not at all unsatisfactory to its subject.

The buoyancy and mirthfulness which belonged to Mr. Meier-Smith's nature were a great help to him and to his wife during the somewhat rough experiences of this year. When the insufficient fare provided had to be supplemented by a supper in their own rooms, — and very privately, for fear of giving offence, — a merry picnic was improvised, with oysters cooked in the little stove, and French coffee which had to be covered tightly as it steamed, lest its fragrant aroma should tell the tale. If the flavor of oysters almost a week old was not improved by the smoke of the wood "airtight," the coffee was irreproachable, and no schoolboy and girl ever made a merrier feast in secret.

When summer came there was much enjoyment from the beautiful scenery and surroundings of the town, which afforded charming drives, commanding views of the two lakes, between which rose the high ridge upon which the village was built, or through forests with trees of such age and height that the small wagon could be easily driven under their branches.

The church was filled by attentive congregations, and continued religious interest prevailed. It was with reluctance that the decision was reached to resign this first pastorate, already endeared by promise of success and usefulness, and accept work in New York. The severity of the winter climate was a principal reason, the slowness of the parish to provide a suitable home for the minister was another. There was no parsonage, and the parish, though wealthy, was indisposed to secure one, and no house was available for renting. During the summer Mr. Meier-Smith declined proposals from a church in Syracuse, New York, from the conviction that, could he venture another winter in that part of the State, he ought not to leave Ovid. The positive advice of physicians with regard to the danger to his throat, which threatened loss of voice, and the manifest inability of his wife to bear the harsh winds of the winter, brought about the dissolution of his pastorate in September, 1850. The protests and letters received from all classes of his parishioners, treasured affectionately by him throughout his life, express strongly the general regret at the parting. A letter received more than thirty years afterward commences, " My dear and honored pastor of the olden time." From it an extract is taken testifying to the unusual impression this young pastor made upon his people during the year he ministered to them : —

" Time has not effaced from our memories your labors of love while here, and you still hold a warm place in the hearts you left. Among those was my departed brother. He remembered every sermon you preached, the chapters in the Bible you read ; and in looking through the hymn-book in his last illness, he would often say, ' Here is one of Mr. Meier-Smith's hymns.' Have you forgotten the class that met in your study on Monday afternoons? Only two are left, and but few of the choir that so loved you, — but to them the memory is very precious of those days. Our place and people have greatly changed. We have had nine clergymen since you left, but you would find hearts yet warm and true, if you would come and see us. Come and spend a Sunday with us, and bring a sermon."

Fifteen months' work in this first field was enough to make the parting hard, especially with those who had been brought into the Church through his ministry.

The stage-coach which bore away the young pastor and his wife passed through a long line of vehicles from all parts of the town, containing parishioners young and old who had gathered to say a word of loving farewell. It was nearly twenty years before he revisited Ovid. In spite of the great changes, there were not a few to grasp his hand in affectionate recognition, and refer to some word or act of his which had been an influence for good through all these years.

The winter of 1850 and 1851 were passed in New York. In the month of October came the joy of receiving the first-born child, a son, born in the house of his grandfather whose name he received. Mr. Meier-Smith was invited to take temporary charge of the Sixth-Street Presbyterian Church, pending an engagement to consolidate it with another church. The grandfather of his wife, Mr. David L. Dodge, and her uncle, Mr. William E. Dodge, were elders of this church, and their friendship and help were greatly prized by their young minister. Mr. Dodge, senior, was a remarkable man, of much intellectual vigor, and well versed in Bible study. He was an active and devout worker in the church, and prominent during a long life among Christian laymen. He was a ready writer upon theological and ethical subjects, a man of original and inflexible opinions, and in all respects a marked character. A warm attachment sprang up between the venerable elder and his young kinsman pastor, which continued until the death of Mr. Dodge a few years later. At the request of his family, Mr. Meier-Smith edited his autobiography and some of his theological and prophetical studies.

The memory of William E. Dodge is yet so fresh and precious to all who knew him, that to name him is a sufficient suggestion of what his friendship and help must have been to any one associated with him in religious or church work. Then in the prime of middle age, he realized the ideal of lay support to a clergyman. His untiring activity and zeal were tempered with such beautiful warmth and simplicity of manner, that he gave no offence to those who differed with him, and his leadership was willingly followed. He had already won the position he held so long among influential citizens and Christians. His friendship was prominent among the circumstances which made this winter in New York a restful and refreshing season.

The work in this church proved helpful and stimulating just at this time, as the intellectual character of the congregation encouraged thoughtful study and sermon making; and in the spring the young minister found himself better equipped for a permanent field of labor than he could have hoped a year before.

Two little incidents of this winter he often related. Once, when an appeal was to be made for some good cause, as the pulpit of the little church did not afford room for two, Mr. Meier-Smith took his seat in Mr. William E. Dodge's pew, leaving the field for his visiting brother.   Before the speaker commenced, Mr. Dodge took a small piece of paper and wrote his contribution upon it.   In the course of the address, as the urgent needs were forcibly stated, Mr. Dodge, evidently moved with emotion, took the paper which lay folded before him and added one stroke of the pencil.   Afterward, assisting to count the collection, the minister saw that the original sum in the tens had been raised to hundreds by the addition of a cipher.

The other incident was the presence one Sunday morning among his hearers of the celebrated singer, Jenny Lind.   She was then in the height of her first triumphs in America ; and her fine character, as well as her wonderful voice, called out more enthusiasm from all classes than has been exhibited for any of her successors ; while her refusal then to sing in opera made her the especial favorite of the religious part of the community.   She sought this little church on this occasion, having heard that her friend, the Rev. Dr. Baird, was to preach.   He, however, was unable to fulfil his engagement, and she listened instead to a simple exposition from the young and unknown minister in charge, thanking him afterward for the sermon with a winning grace very gratifying to the preacher, who may be forgiven for confessing that he did not altogether forget, while delivering it, the bright and changing face of his famous hearer.

Several prospective openings came before him in the spring of 1851, and in May he accepted a call to the Harvard Congregational Church, in Brookline, a suburb of Boston.   It was not without hesitation that this change of ecclesiastical position was made ; but he was assured that he could assume charge of the church to which he was called, without professing a preference for the Congregational form of government over that of the Presbyterian in which he had been educated. As the invitation was cordial and unanimous, and the work prospectively just what he desired, he accepted the call, inspired with hope, and grateful for the promise of enlarged usefulness.

VI.

BROOKLINE DAYS.

1851–1854.

ON the 5th of June, 1851, Mr. Meier-Smith was installed pastor of the Harvard Congregational Church in Brookline, Massachusetts.

The Rev. R. S. Storrs, of Brooklyn, a former pastor of the church, preached the sermon, and the young minister's "spiritual father," the beloved Dr. Kirk, of Boston, gave the personal charge.

The fact that the candidate was an ordained minister in a church closely affiliated in doctrine to the Orthodox Congregational Communion of New England, did not exempt him from a searching examination in theology and church polity by the Council called for the installation.

He discerned at this early stage of his new experience the influence of Unitarianism upon those professing to hold the Orthodox standards in regard to church government and the sacraments; and planting himself on those standards, he sustained the examination with a firmness and decision which elicited strong expressions of approval from many present, among whom were the leading members of his new charge. Ingenious efforts were made, especially by some lay members of the Council, to call out an expression of preference for, or at least entire satisfaction with, Congregational Church

Government. This effort was met by appeals to Scripture and church history, so aptly and sometimes so humorously presented as to silence his questioners without offending them. A prominent Congregationalist present, when asked what was the young minister's position on this point, replied, "It was summed up in his telling us that he did not think either the New Testament or church history was written to propagate Congregationalism." Nevertheless, as he then understood the system, he believed he could conscientiously work under it. Thus, with flying colors and with zeal and hopefulness, he entered upon his work, — the first he had essayed which promised permanence.

Socially, the field was very inviting. As a place of residence, Brookline was one of the most attractive of the suburbs of Boston. A pretty parsonage awaited the young family; and kind attentions, flowing in upon them without stint, testified to the heartiness with which the new pastor was welcomed. Culture and refinement were on every side; and the community was a thoughtful and religious one, free from the excitements of fashionable city life.

The mistress of the parsonage, with youthful enthusiasm, wrote to the home circle within the first month: "You know enough of my mind and my taste to imagine how things look when I tell you that place, church, parsonage, and people, each in their way, are the realization of my *beau ideal*. We feel happy in the prospect of remaining here a lifetime, if Providence so orders our way, and this is what we hardly had grace enough to feel at Ovid. We could be *willing*, but not with *heart-pleasure*." She remembers the fervor of the prayer so often uplifted by her husband, that the delightful outward circumstances might not so fill the vision that the great and serious purpose of the life before them should be obscured.

Some of the most active intellectual work of Mr. Meier-Smith's life now commenced. The necessity for meeting the needs of a thoughtful and educated congregation, three or four times every week, stimulated earnest and conscientious study; and the parish was not large enough to need too great an expenditure of time and strength in parochial care. Clerical society was congenial and helpful, vigorous young men being in charge of parishes contiguous; and in Boston there were older brethren to call upon for advice and assistance. It was not his nature to rush precipitately into changes, or improvements upon the past. He rather surveyed the ground quietly, and planned new lines of work slowly; and by causing the need of them to be felt, carried his points. His bright and cheerful disposition, warm hand-clasp, and ready smile, were almost irresistible; and when his mind was made up to any course, it was not often that he met with serious opposition.

Among the first things which engaged his attention, was the " Confession of Faith," peculiar to the Harvard Church, and to which assent was required of those seeking admission to its communion and fellowship. It seemed to him most ill-judged and unfitting, that when receiving persons for the first time to the Holy Communion, they must stand before him in the presence of the congregation, while, to use his own language, he " read *at* them a long statement expressing profound belief in Adam, and very little in Christ." Certain Calvinistic doctrines, expressed in language now almost obsolete, were quite beyond the comprehension of many candidates. Members of the church admitted that "no one believed them," and that it was a mere form adhered to for old association's sake. An element of absurdity was not wanting, sometimes, as when on one occasion, the candidates were two lads of fourteen years of age, who were not only required to signify assent to theological statements, but to promise to "order their households religiously, and bring up their children in the same faith!" The pastor was much gratified when, after some months of study and discussion, the church consented to lay aside the old and clumsy "Confession," and to substitute a simple statement of evangelical faith drawn up by himself. His preference would have been to limit the confession to the Apostles' and Nicene Creeds, but this was too radical a change.

His thorough and exhaustive investigation of this subject he regarded as the laying of one of the foundation stones for the change in his church position made so many years afterward. From this time he took strong ground against demanding any extra-Scriptural conditions for admission to the Lord's Table, or other privileges of his church.

During the first three years of his pastorate, Brookline was rapidly growing; and he had the satisfaction of watching increasing congregations, and seeing the vigor of new life in his little church as it gradually gathered to itself many of the best of the new residents. He was personally attractive to strangers, as his ever cordial manner and ready welcome made them feel themselves at home at once. This was before the days of numerous parish organizations, guilds, clubs, and the like; but he drew to himself the younger part of his people, and urged upon them united effort in various directions, guiding them personally, both religiously and socially. A class of ladies met at the parsonage for the study of the evidences of Christianity; and a course of lectures on early church history, illustrated by charts of his own drawing, was kept up vigorously for two years.

Once a month a catechetical instruction for children was given, and a short sermon preached. This was an innovation, such services for children being then unusual. The Sunday-school which he found connected with his church was of a character quite new to him, peculiar as it was to New England, and especially to Massachusetts. More than half of the classes consisted of adult members of the congregation, gathered around one of their number whom they elected as leader; and they pursued Bible study in any direction they fancied, sometimes, the pastor thought, on lines more unique than instructive. The "pillars of the church," including the deacons, were gathered in these classes; and it seemed as if the little ones were almost forgotten. In fact, not much effort was made for the class for whom the Sunday-school was originally intended.

The lambs of the flock were always near to the loving heart of him whom we are trying to portray in these pages. He could not rest until through earnest effort, seconded by some devoted young helpers, he filled all the empty spaces of the Sunday-school room with children, many of whom came from families not connected with any church, and inclined to avoid Harvard Church, from an impression that its congregation was select and aristocratic. The first Christmas festival the Sunday-school had ever celebrated, took place in the parsonage in the first year of his residence. This festival was yet something of an exotic, having scarcely taken root in New England.

Another effort was in the direction of enlivening the social services for conference and prayer. Before many months his lecture-room was crowded on Sunday evenings, in consequence of a plan he adopted for answering questions and discussing topics of interest. A box was placed in the vestibule, and inquiries on religious subjects of personal or general interest were dropped therein. On the following Sunday evening the questions were read, short answers given to such as could be quickly disposed of, and one or two were taken as a theme for a more careful discussion or familiar lecture. The ready grasp he had of a subject, — the power of getting at the kernel, so to speak, — came out forcibly in these popular services for instruction. Among those who attended, were members of the Episcopal and Unitarian congregations of Brookline, and not a few from Boston churches.

At this time Mr. Meier-Smith was of slight figure, active in movement, and sanguine in temperament. He had a laughing blue eye and a merry smile which was contagious as it lighted up his entire face. No one knew it if he was ever ruffled in spirit, for his bright amiability never deserted him, even when he met opposition. So much of the " charity which thinketh no evil " filled his heart that though sensitive and sympathetic in an unusual degree, he was slow to take offence, and invariably saw the best in a man. If so much perverseness prevailed that he failed to find the good points, he still declared that they were there, and he turned the edge of many a sharp or ill-tempered remark with a ready and humorous retort, born of a capacity for seeing the ludicrous side of almost everything disagreeable.

Without an element of sensationalism in manner

or style, he was popular as a preacher, and was welcomed in neighboring pulpits when exchanging with his brethren. His sermons were thoroughly prepared; his well-informed congregation would not have relished any others, and he was always a conscientious workman. Looking over his record of sermons written and preached during the first three years in Brookline, there appears a marked absence of any "tricks" to catch attention, such as unusual texts, or *ad captandum* themes. *Evangelical*, in the true sense of the much-abused word, applies to nearly all his sermons. Repentance, faith, Christian fidelity, the great facts of the incarnation and life of our Lord, — these were presented in varying forms, but never with uncertain ring.

Nothing could be more cordial than the relations of pastor and people. To his wife he once said, "*Such smooth sailing* cannot last. Let us take it as a time of preparation for some other discipline that must surely come to us. We must grow strong in the sunshine, that we may not succumb to the storm."

Mr. Meier-Smith took a leading position in Brookline in matters affecting the public interest. The old New England custom of placing clergymen in the front, especially in educational interests, still prevailed in Massachusetts. He was an active member of the school board, and zealous in promoting reforms and raising the standard of education. During his term of service he urged the erection of new school buildings with modern improvements, and had the satisfaction of seeing the substantial results of enlarged financial appropriations, and of much devotion of time and thought to the work.

Among letters to his parents written during this period is one to his mother dated Jan. 29, 1852: —

. . . A letter was received from you this morning, and was most welcome, as are all your letters. I had no idea that my dear father had been so seriously ill. I trust that he is now better, as the indications were.

The frail tenure we have upon life in this world is a subject often before my mind, and when it is most realized, then how full of meaning those words of the great Resurrection and the Life, "He that believeth in Me shall never die." I interpret this passage not with reference to eternal death solely, but with reference to temporal; at least there is a thought suggested which is most precious to the spirit. So far as death is an idea containing elements of horror, so far the man whose faith is full in Jesus shall not experience it. So far as it is an act of passing from one sphere of activity to another, so far it shall be realized.

But the cross and the risen Saviour, and the life and immortality brought to light, have displaced the gloomy elements, and filling the soul with assurance and triumph, they make what to Nature is the awful passage, only a stepping-stone from one place to another, — from ship to shore, from earth to where God can be served with perfect service and elevated powers; and as such not to be dreaded in itself more than the transit from any one spot to any other on the earth. To present the thought in another light, religion or the service of Christ is to the Christian an end in itself, not simply a means to an end. We delight in it, and make it the main business of life, loving it for its own sake and because it is right, not chiefly because we think it is necessary for future happiness.

When one embarks in this service it is for eternity, and the idea is, serve God now and ever, here or elsewhere, and make this service the whole business forever. Death is not even an interruption to this service, it is only the door which opens to a higher station. So I try to view the subject. As a Christian I chose the service of Christ, not caring much whether He called me to the service of the merchant, the lawyer, or doctor. When invested with the ministry, the question of *place* was the most unimportant one, and the one I tried to leave in His hands.

He sent me to Ovid, and then removed me to Brookline. I stay here until he summons me elsewhere. In my right senses and frame, I care not *when* or *whither*. If to New York, or to Philadelphia, or to heaven, whether a mission to China, or a mission of a thousand years to distant Saturn to tell of redemption in this world, — it matters not to me. The railway would be the means of getting to New York, the ship to China, the putting off this mortal is the passageway to a superior sphere. " He that believeth in Me shall never die." Saint Paul says, " Mortality is *swallowed up of life.*"

Precious to me is the blessing of such views, and if not unfamiliar to my parents, they will be ever new and refreshing, as often as contemplated.

With very much love to all, I am

Your MATSON.

In the parsonage, the family at the close of the year 1852 numbered four, as a little daughter came bringing new brightness into the home. To a friend he said, when this event occurred, " A man is proud when he is the father of a son, but he is happy when he is the father of a daughter." When this little one was but a few days old, there occurred great cause for thankfulness in a narrow escape from the terrors of fire. Mr. Meier-

Smith sat late in his study one night, and was about retiring, when a slight sound attracted his attention to the kitchen. On opening the door he found a vigorous fire in progress, commencing with some garments hanging to dry, but already reaching to the ceiling and woodwork of the room. A few pails of water, always standing ready for such an emergency, extinguished the flames without the sleeping family's knowledge of their danger. But had he not gone to the room at the time, the small frame building must certainly have been destroyed, for it was a cold and blowing winter night, and the village had no efficient fire department.

There are few letters accessible written during these years. His friend, Dr. Dyer, with whom his intimacy increased, was often called to Boston, and was then a frequent guest at Harvard Parsonage. Letters full of life and humor passed between them, and of these the following is an example. It was written in the spring of 1852, on the occasion of a proposed visit of Dr. Dyer to Europe, with the offer of a letter of introduction to the Hon. William B. Kinney, United States Minister at the Court of Sardinia, whose accomplished wife, the mother of Edmund Clarence Stedman, was the aunt of Mrs. Meier-Smith. War clouds were already darkening the horizon, and the mutterings of the storm which two years later descended, involving Russia, England, France, and Italy, were heard in the distance. This explains allusions in the letter: —

. . . We both hope you will get to Turin and see our distinguished relatives. I am sure you will enjoy the interview with Mr. and Mrs. Kinney very much. He is the Coleridge of America for conversational powers and fascination; she, one of the most classic of our female poets, with the usual woman's heart in all seasons, whether under the " Inspiration " or not. . . . And you are really going to see the menagerie, are you ? Take care that the old Bull (which his name is John) don't get into fits while you are there, because the frog-eater tries to mount his back and gallop to the universal domi-nation. And do keep out of the way in case there should be a hugging match between the old " Bear," the " Duke," and the rest of the beasts. I might give you a letter to Dr. ——, as you are going to Switzerland, — only he don't know me, and I doubt the utility of any such missive. Rev. R. B—— and his family are in London now. They might introduce you to Her Majesty. They know all about her and her ancestors, having taught school so long. . . .

Well, God preserve and bless you both, — " Mizpah ! " — and may His wing shadow your children while you are absent, through our Lord and Saviour.

Affectionately yours,
Matson Meier-Smith,
" Episcopus."

A cordial friendship existed between the pastor of Harvard Church and the Rev. Dr. John S. Stone, at that time rector of St. Paul's Church, Brookline. Dr. Stone was a distinguished writer and preacher, and a man of a lovely catholic spirit that knew no bounds of ecclesiasticism. He was lively and playful in social intercourse, and was wont to address his young brother as " My Bishop," in humorous allusion to Presbyterian claims.

Dr. Dyer and Dr. Stone were intimate friends, and on one occasion Mr. Meier-Smith, entering the rectory library, found these two eminent churchmen engaged in a literal wrestling match with all the vigor of a pair of school-boys. Recovering from his surprise he entered the fray himself, and declared that though but a *militia man*, in their view, he had brought these officers of the *regular army* to speedy discomfiture.

A letter to his wife, during her absence from home, gives an intimation of a method of answering questions upon ethical subjects always characteristic of him.

BROOKLINE, April 26, 1852.

. . . I had yesterday a delightful Lord's Day; it was one of the days " the Lord hath made." Congregations good. My morning sermon upon the " New Creature in Christ," appeared to be liked. In the afternoon I preached from Proverbs v. 11, 12. It was a little in "Dream Life" style. I 've half a mind to write a religious " Dream Life." Do you think my genius adequate? In the evening I talked about the Sabbath and keeping it. In answer to the very common question, " Is this breaking the Sabbath, the holy day? Can I do this or that, and not sin ?" I advanced the doctrine that to holy beings duty and privilege are intimately related, indeed are synonymous terms. God's law tells the Christian his privilege and honor, — that is, what he *may* do, — and is not to be construed as *must* do, though it implies the latter. We should be so delighted with the privilege of being holy and serving God, and so grateful that we are not left to hopeless spiritual death, or sin's bondage, that we should esteem God's commands as our charter of liberties, and not as a set of restrictions.

After service until midnight, I had a grand chat with our friends in Linden Place upon heavenly things, and some of the mysteries of redemption. We talked also upon the inspiration of the Bible. I declare I think that however wonderful may seem the idea of the Bible being from above, if we view it otherwise and deny its divine origin, it is a greater wonder yet.

To his Wife.

BROOKLINE, April 11, 1852.

. . . I wish my little wife would not reproach herself for any fancied or real shortcomings. Love is in spite of failings, if not strengthened by them. Certainly it is strengthened by commiseration and sympathy when the failings occur in the midst of a sincere conflict against them and all sin. And if you have faith in God's assured forgiveness through the blood of Jesus, for any unwilling sin, you should, dearest, honor God by acquiescing in his forgiveness, and gratefully press on with smiles shining above the tears which memory brings, unto more and more perfect service. You ask me to bear patiently with your failings. Do you think I fancy myself in no need of your patience and forgiveness?

Good-by, dearest,

Your MATSON.

Throughout the years of the Brookline ministry there was a growing excitement upon great national questions. The Anti-slavery agitation increased rapidly, and there were many, who, anticipating a desperate struggle, yet hoped it might be averted through the wisdom of conservative leaders, while themselves in sympathy with the progressive element. It was characteristic of Mr. Meier-Smith to move slowly toward a new position. The next letters show this cautious treading; but, three years later, he was prepared to be among the first and the firmest in a steady march toward the high stand on the great moral questions involved, which was reached by a large proportion of Christian men of the North before the commencement of the Civil War.

To his Father.

BROOKLINE, April, 1852.

. . . Last evening Mr. E. D—— was at Mr. T——'s, and we had a regular tilt upon the "higher law" question. I believe his principles are sound in the abstract, and that he would act righteously in a real case, but his conclusions logical seem to me to be *il*logical from his strong attachment to the Webster-Whig school. Mr. T——'s views were developed too, and I find he is no more an Abolitionist than I am, holding almost the identical position I do, with the exception that he votes the Free Soil ticket *certainly*, while, just at present, I feel inclined to vote for Mr. Webster. It was the briskest fight I 've had for three years!

To his Parents.

BROOKLINE, June, 1852.

. . . The first subject of conversation here has been as everywhere else the nominations at Baltimore. Mr. Webster seems to have been entirely distanced. As a matter of national vanity I had some desire for his nomination and election, but it is doubtless best that he is so thoroughly rejected. Magnificent as are his mental powers, his principles are so defective that he ought never to be President; and if ever a man righteously deserved defeat for truckling to Southern principles as to slavery, with New England blood coursing through his veins, and New England's stern lessons of justice ringing in his ears, *he* has deserved it. The grand political game started about three years ago — of which the Fugitive Slave Law and the other Compromise Measures, and the many speeches and sermons in favor thereof, and the wolf-cry of "danger to the Union," "no higher law," etc., were parts — has been a deep game and a desperate one, but the chief players have all burned their own fingers. It is righteous retribution. What is in the future we know not, but if such events will produce more manliness in our statesmen, they will do good. And if, as I trust, the agitation of the last two years will only swell the grand shout in favor of Freedom and Free-soil and Anti-slavery to the detriment of the leading parties, I shall think that our prayers are beginning to be answered on behalf of our country, in earnest. I am not an Abolitionist in the ordinary use of the word, but I am every day growing stronger in my Anti-slavery sentiment, and this not merely as disapproving of slavery as I disapprove of Hindooism, but in the conviction of the increasingly pressing duty of Christian men to begin to act, and give no countenance to the system, nor be longer wheedled into a dead conservatism by unpriucipled politicians and worse stock-jobbers!

Allusion has been made to the pleasant ministerial associations of this period of Mr. Meier-Smith's life. He was one of a select number who organized the Winthrop Club, vigorous yet in the maturity of more than thirty years of life. Now and then during the many years that have passed since he met with his brethren, messages of fraternal friendship and good cheer have gone from his pen in answer to invitations to their meetings. No clerical social gatherings were ever more prized and enjoyed by him. From the Rev. Dr. Dexter, of Boston, editor of the "Congregationalist," who was at that time pastor of the Pine-Street Church, Boston, a letter was received after Dr. Meier-Smith's death, giving the impression he made upon his associates during those years : —

Boston, April 8, 1887.

. . . The sad news of your dear husband's death was a great shock to me, as I had hardly thought of him as growing old. Indeed, he struck me as being perennially young. I can remember exactly how he looked when I knew him so pleasantly and well, and how like a sunbeam he went everywhere. I find it very difficult to realize that he is withdrawn from all the service of earth, and that we shall see his face no more.

It cannot but please you to know that at the meeting of the Winthrop Club on Monday last, he was the subject of affectionate remembrance, and such passages from the early records as recalled him were read by the Secretary.

I can assure you that there was not one drop of bitterness generated by his changing his position from our denomination; his own genial and charitable soul gave all too good a guarantee of his sincerity and of his catholicity for that. . . . His bright face is distinctly before me as I write, with that rich and genial smile, just ready to break forth into some glad or merry word, making his presence always cheering and delightful.

From the Rev. Dr. Furber, of Newton Centre, Massachusetts, one of the first members of the Winthrop Club and the present Secretary : —

November 2, 1887.

. . . Mention was made in our Club of the death of your dear husband, our very highly esteemed former associate. It is nearly thirty years since I saw him, but I remember him with the greatest distinctness. I exchanged with him five times. He told me that once while preaching in my pulpit, it suddenly occurred to him that he had preached that very sermon to my people before; "but," said he, "I determined to *brass* it out and make the best of it," which he wisely did, and probably no one in the house thought the sermon an old one. In proposing an exchange to me he said, "Please bring plain spoken sermons, for we have some religious interest." I remember once hearing him preach in his own church. In the pulpit he was stately and dignified. In social intercourse, though he was never undignified, he was genial, sympathetic, and vivacious, and his conversation was enlivened with pleasantry. One of his brethren came to him on Saturday morning in distress for an exchange. Your husband could not accommodate him. "What am I going to do?" said Mr. ——. "Go home and write a sermon," was the answer; "that 's what I 'm trying to do!"

These reminiscences of early friends illustrate a side of his personality which was as marked thirty years later, as in the days of his youth. In this aspect he never grew old.

Beginning with the year 1854, some of the shadows which he had predicted as likely to fall over his smooth pathway began to be discerned.

First among them was the loss of two faithful men, John Dane and Nathaniel Dana. Harvard Church and its pastor were rich in the possession of such office-bearers. Mr. Dane died in the prime of life, in July, 1854, after a very short illness. Mr. Dana, venerable in years, slowly passed to his rest, in January, 1856. Both of these men were such as a pastor may lean upon in confidence. A warm love was mutually felt, and each in his way was a valued counsellor. Mr. Dane's bright and sunny nature was much like his young pastor's, and they were always in sympathy. He was an untiring friend and helper, and one with whom Mr. Meier-Smith could freely unbend. He was a faithful, loving Christian, and his death was a loss never made up to the church or its pastor.   Mr. Dana's lovely piety and large Christian experience were an example and stimulus to the clergyman whom he took to his heart in his youth and inexperience, and who mourned for him with almost a filial affection.   These losses were also felt by him as withdrawing strong influences for the spiritual prosperity of his congregation.

VII.

BROOKLINE DAYS.

1855–1859.

LIKE golden threads running through all the web of Mr. Meier-Smith's early ministry, and here and there shining out as light fell upon them, were the influences which were leading him to a stronger churchly position. The position of children in the Church, as indicated in the usages growing more and more prevalent in New England, was a perplexity to him. Infant baptism appeared to have become only a pleasant custom, justified by use but not otherwise to be strongly maintained.

The Eucharist was regarded only as a Memorial Feast. Not such was his view of the sacraments, or of the place of the children in the Kingdom. Old Congregational standards he found taking ground with Presbyterian formulas, but modern practice and instruction were widely different. Investigating the subject of what the fathers of the New England churches called "Infant Church Membership," he had a discussion of some length in the Boston "Congregationalist," with its editor, at the close of which it was courteously admitted that he had the weight of testimony on his side of the argument. He ended the discussion by the following inferences: —

"1. That baptized children of believing parents are members of the Church, unequivocally. They stand as young trees in the orchard, rather than as young trees in the nursery, which are hereafter to be transplanted. There is no more indefiniteness in this statement than in the statement that a minor or infant in law is a citizen. The fact of being under age does not render the term improper. The law of one State says, 'Every free white able-bodied citizen who has attained the age of eighteen years is liable to military duty.' Yet these *infant citizens* cannot vote, and in some cases cannot hold property. Is it then absurd to speak of infant citizenship in Christ's kingdom?

"2. Infant members are entitled to such privileges and subject to such responsibilities as their capacities will admit, and these only. Those six months old have fewer than those sixteen years old. They are not entitled, for example, to the Lord's Supper, until they can discern the Lord's body and will come forward with right hearts. On the other hand their position creates an obligation to receive the Lord's Supper with right hearts, as soon as they are old enough and wise enough to discern the Lord's body.

"3. This doctrine does not conflict with the right of a church to prescribe its own terms of communion and fellowship for infant members who seek for privileges, and it may require profession of faith.

"This profession is not 'joining the Church,' but *simply* a profession. They were joined to the Church, according to this theory, in infancy."

It will of course be understood that these conclusions express the shape the subject took in his own mind in that forming period, and do not, except as they foreshadow them, present the full views of his maturity.

As a source of disquietude there appeared a weakness of throat and voice which at times threatened entire disability. The east winds of the winters and springs were always severe, and a harassing cough became chronic during the cold weather.

He was compelled to take several short rests and to keep under constant local treatment for his throat. On one occasion, while preaching an especially solemn sermon to a crowded congregation at a union service, while in the midst of an earnest appeal, his voice grew thinner and weaker until it was almost a whisper. The audience grew proportionally still, watching the speaker with strained attention. He did not stop to explain, and closed his sermon with a benediction, pronounced in a whisper, which deeply moved his hearers with the fear that the faithful servant might be delivering his last message. It was some time before he spoke aloud again.

This throat weakness improved during the next year, and he regained and held for many years nearly his former strength and ease in speaking. In 1856, and in the following year, financial disasters spread over the country to such an extent that a general gloom prevailed. Among his own people there were some who suffered greatly. This was followed by a remarkable season of religious reviving, or *awakening* as he called it, giving the old name he preferred to *revival.*

Such serious interests now engrossed the attention of thoughtful Christians, that his preaching changed in a marked degree. He felt that the times called the " watchmen on the walls " to exhort the people to deep self-communing and repentance.

He endeavored to arouse his own flock and to enlist their interest in the work of the Holy Spirit as he saw it manifested in the communities about him. He carried many of his people with him, but some of his most respected friends, upon whom he relied for sympathy and support, differed from him, and freely criticised the "advanced" views and methods, as they regarded them, of their pastor. This wounded him, and an entering wedge of separation appeared. Among his advisers at this time was his friend the Rev. Dr. Kirk. He was in full sympathy with the spirit which stirred the soul of his "dear son in the Gospel," and that his course won Dr. Kirk's approval was the compensation for some heart-aches.

While the unusual services of this time of religious interest were in progress, Dr. Kirk sent an invitation to him, inspired by tender thoughtfulness. Being universally revered and beloved he knew that such an open indorsement would strengthen his young brother's hands, and wrote to him in these words: —

My Dear Son in the Gospel, — Will you stand by your father in his advancing age? I have to preach on Tuesday morning and evening, on Wednesday morning, and Thursday morning and evening. My nervous energy is almost exhausted, but God can supply my wants and he may employ you in doing it, — a service from which I know you will not shrink. Can you be with me to pray for the people on Tuesday morning, and to preach on Tuesday evening? Come and stay with me.

Mr. Meier-Smith's preaching at this time was more doctrinal in subject and more personal in style than hitherto. Upon certain subjects he had not felt constrained to preach before. Death, judgment, retribution, sin, conscience, and responsibility for great moral decisions are among the topics of sermons written at this period. In his review of this time, some years afterward, he believed that some who stood aloof were conscientious in differing with him, and he recognized also that this was a time of expansion in his own religious life, and of a more entire consecration to Christ, resulting from the discovery that he must not rely too much on the most trusted human help and sympathy.

In January, 1857, the death of Mrs. Meier-Smith's mother brought great sorrow into Harvard parsonage.

From his early boyhood the loveliness of Mrs. White's person and character had inspired an admiration in her future son-in-law, which grew into filial love when he came into close relationship with her. Years of great suffering preceded her release, and throughout them her beautiful character ripened until in the eyes of her family she seemed a saint. " I love her scarcely less than my own mother," Mr. Meier-Smith often said, and when she was removed from the husband and children whose lives she had blessed so richly, he who had been adopted into their circle was one of the most sincere mourners.

In the year 1857, he received an honorary degree of Master of Arts from Williams College, Massachusetts. Within two years he declined overtures from several churches, among them one in the city of New York. It was not until he felt that a change was imperative from a sense of overwork, that he consented to consider a call elsewhere. The disturbed feeling of which we have spoken had then disappeared completely, and entire harmony prevailed. The church had doubled in size and strength during his pastorate, and the outlook was promising; but the intellectual strain had been steady, and he desired an opportunity to reach other classes of people for the sake of development in certain lines of work. A change of climate, also, was advised for the tendency to throat trouble.

In the autumn of 1858, he received, simultaneously, calls to the Presbyterian Church in Bloomfield, New Jersey, and the First Congregational Church of Bridgeport, Connecticut. While absent from home, visiting these parishes, and while yet undecided in regard to leaving Brookline, he wrote to his wife: —

I am on my way to Bloomfield, of which I cannot say more than that I am entirely ready to go thither, unless I can be more useful in either of the other *Bees!* The Bridgeport people are very pressing. Is this of the Lord or no? I am only solicitous to be directed by the great Head of the Church. . . .

What is the Lord ordering for us? I do not see a boat's length ahead. The Great Pilot does see however! He ruleth! Be of good courage, my love. Whether there lies before us an ample and congenial work, or a faith-trying disappointment, we shall find out. If I know my own heart I only want to be guided by His Will. . . . Their father's warmest love to his boy and girl. Ever, dearest, your

MATSON.

The call to Bridgeport was accepted, several reasons contributing to the decision. Probably stronger than Mr. Meier-Smith knew at the time, was the drift of his thought in certain directions, which made him doubtful of returning to the Presbyterian Church, lest he should feel himself more trammelled in following out his inclinations than he would be under the independent system of Congregationalism. He was being led by a way which he knew not. Had he returned to the Presbyterian Communion, he might have remained there, for he would have missed an experience which had its influence in strengthening latent convictions as yet not fully recognized by himself.

On Sunday, Nov. 14, 1858, Mr. Meier-Smith read his resignation to his people, from which this extract is made: "My decision has not been reached without prayerful deliberation, and unfeigned sorrow at the thought of parting with those whom I greatly love, with this church to which I came in its feeble youth and in mine, and which under divine favor has attained maturity and masculine vigor. I am under the painful necessity, in order to enter upon the field which opens before me, of tendering the resignation of my office as pastor and teacher, and I ask you to unite with me in calling a Council to dissolve the relationship existing between us."

The resolutions passed by the church in reply were as follows: —

"*Resolved*, That this church views with profound sorrow and regret the event which has thus in divine Providence been brought upon them. That, understanding that it will be acceptable to our pastor as a proof of our confidence in him and our love for him, and that it will be received, not as evidence of our willingness to part with him, but of our readiness in a spirit of self-sacrifice to defer to his desires, it is therefore —

"*Resolved*, That this church accepts the resignation as tendered by their pastor.

"*Resolved*, That in accepting the request of their beloved pastor this church desires to present to him their Christian love, their warmest thanks in remembrance of his past faithful labors, and their prayers to our common Lord and Master for his future happiness and usefulness."

From the Minutes of the Council called to sever the relation : —

"The Council cannot part with one whom they have known so long and well, and in whose pleasant and fraternal fellowship, and hearty co-operation in all departments of Christian and ministerial activity, they have had so much comfort and strengthening, without bearing witness to the tenderness of the relationship that has existed between them, and their deep regret that this beloved brother is to be removed from their immediate neighborhood.

"Their prayers and their sincerest wishes for his prosperity and success in his work will follow him hence to the new field of labor understood to lie before him. And to those with whom he may hereafter be associated in any function of his calling, we heartily commend him as a faithful, earnest, and wise minister of the Lord Jesus Christ."

With universal expressions of sorrow at the parting, and very many substantial tokens of love and appreciation, the farewells were said, and the Brookline life ended with the closing year.

A letter from Mrs. Edward A. Strong, of Boston, finds an appropriate place here, bearing its loving tribute to this early ministry. The writer and her husband having been for more than thirty years among the dearest friends of Dr. and Mrs. Meier-Smith, there was ample opportunity in this long and close intimacy to verify the impressions formed in Brookline, of the character and influence of her young pastor.

". . . Ever since you wrote to me, asking that I would try to recall some of my impressions of your dear husband's life and pastorate in Brookline, I have been searching the depths of my memory to find something which might aid you in your labor of love. But you will realize that thirty years ago is a long way back, and in this lapse of time many things which might throw a valuable light on the story of those days have quite dropped out of memory's grasp.

"I have always felt that my long and close friendship for Matson was colored by the peculiar circumstances of its beginning. It was under the very shadow of death that I first knew and loved him.

"He came to Brookline, as pastor of the Harvard Church, when I, a girl of seventeen, lay low with typhoid fever in the very next house to the parsonage.

"My first impression of him is dim and shadowy. I knew that he came daily and sat by my bed, speaking words of sympathy and comfort to my mother, repeating Scripture promises to me, and praying for me, until soon there came a night when he bade me good-by, as he thought, forever, never thinking to see me in life again.

"How often in after years he spoke of that solemn farewell! But, when I was raised up to life again, all through my convalescence, how faithful and tender he was to me. How gently he encouraged my feeble faith, and strengthened my new resolve to come out on the Lord's side and join myself to his people.

"When the time came for me to meet the examining committee of the church, and I naturally shrank from the ordeal of their questions, I remember how his wise and kindly words gave me courage.

"I wonder if you have any remembrance of that November Sunday of dreary storm, when I, the only one to 'join the church,' sat by your side in the front pew of Harvard Church and took the solemn vows upon me. You, as the pastor's wife, young as you were then, were never behind him in your sweet helpful devotion to his sacred work. You held up his hands and encouraged his heart. You lightened not only his burdens but those of his people, by your cordial tact and always ready sympathy. What Matson was to me as pastor, I know he must have been to others. His whole heart was in his chosen work of preaching faithfully the gospel, and ministering in all ways to his people, and I know they dearly loved him.

"His sermons seem to me to have been strong, sound, and fearless. I wish my memory would serve me to recall any of them in subject or treatment; these have vanished, and only the impression remains of the influence they had upon me and on others. I recollect how earnestly, at one time, he persisted, even at the risk of unpopularity, in preaching some truths which he felt sure that this particular flock needed to hear. But I believe he always spoke the truth in love, — who that ever knew him could doubt it? Who can ever forget the warmth of the cordial greeting he always gave one, the hearty grasp of his hand, the welcome iu his eye? 'Great-heart' indeed he was. You could never do him a greater favor than to allow him to do one for you. One rested on his absolutely true, strong friendship as on a rock, and knew it would never fail one.

"How vividly comes back to me your life in that Brookline parsonage, dear home that it was for you both, in spite of its deficiencies. But how cheerily you and your husband made light of them all! My mother was never tired of praising you for the patience and cheerfulness with which you bore the discomforts of small and few rooms, poor servants, and a hundred petty inconveniences.

"I recall so many pleasant things about that early Brookline life, and my associations with you and Matson. They have been for all these thirty years bright pictures hung up on memory's walls.

"I love to think that he was with me in two of the supreme moments of my life. One I have already spoken of, where I seemed to be just stepping out of life into eternity; the other, seven years later, when he performed my marriage service.

"As fully and heartily as he had always given me his friendship, so now he gave it to my husband, taking him into his heart once for all; and to us both this world will always seem a sadder and a lonelier place, now that this noble soul has gone out of it. Such unselfish, great-hearted ones are rare, and when our Father calls them upward, we who remain behind must forever mourn over their unfilled places.

"I know that Matson was greatly valued and beloved by the circle of clergymen in and around Boston, with whom he came much in contact during his life in Brookline. After all these years, one of them, with whom he must have differed widely in theological views, remembered him so tenderly as to write for the Boston 'Congregationalist,' at the time of his death, an appreciative and affectionate tribute. Many of that circle have passed on before him, some are in distant parishes, others linger on in the old places, but are weakened by disease and burdened with infirmities; but I am sure that all would bear glad testimony to the nobility and sweetness of nature, and the manly sincerity and courage of this dear friend."

VIII.

LIFE IN BRIDGEPORT.

1859–1863.

IN the first week of January, 1859, Mr. Meier-Smith was installed pastor of the First Congregational Church in Bridgeport, Connecticut. A very heavy snow-storm was in progress, and many who were invited as members of the Council for installation were prevented thereby from attending. The sermon was preached by his friend the late Rev. Dr. Roswell D. Hitchcock, of New York.

The new home and work contrasted strongly with the life in Brookline. Bridgeport was a busy and thriving city, its population largely engaged in manufactures, and it presented elements of variety in social and religious aspects, as heterogeneous as those of Brookline were homogeneous.

An extract from a letter written by the pastor's wife, after the first Sunday, gives the early impressions: " Matson had crowded houses on Sunday, and in the evening the Sunday-school concert met in the church. The school seemed large and animated. We feel that we have indeed commenced a new life. Such engrossing labor as Matson sees before him is just what he has longed and prayed for, and I shall try not to give a sigh now and then to the life which lies behind us, and with it a great deal of our domestic quiet and home enjoyment. But if my dear husband can only have strength of body and mind, and warmth of soul, for all his labors, we shall both rejoice that he has been counted worthy of a more arduous and extensive field."

Mr. Meier-Smith was at this time three and thirty years of age, youthful and vigorous in appearance, and full of ardor at the prospect of work which would call out all his energies. He was gifted with a charm of manner which few could resist, and his frank greetings naturally met a cordial response. It was often said of him that he went a great deal more than half way to meet every one. The geniality which made him so approachable was perhaps the more felt in his pastoral work, as in his public ministrations he was unusually dignified, never, even under the excitement of a popular address, forgetting for a moment the sacredness of his high office. All who recall him as friend and pastor will appreciate what has been said. But only those who were admitted into the nearest circle of friendship, or the intimacy of his home, can understand the place he held there. He was a born care-taker, — a burden-bearer by nature as well as from a sense of duty. The little thoughtful attentions, the patient fulfilment of small domestic duties, so irksome to many men, and so impossible to some from their temperament or education, seemed entirely natural to him. He was singularly frank and open with those whom he loved and trusted, and there were no secrets at his own fireside. He talked freely of his cares and responsibilities to his wife, and to his children as they matured, and recognized their right to share his burdens, while he entered with readiest sympathy into theirs, no matter how trivial. Prompt response to any appeal for his sympathy or help was a marked characteristic. He never had to apologize for forgetfulness when his help was sought, for he allowed no time to pass before giving the request his attention. If assistance could be given, it was always in a manner that seemed to lessen the obligation ; if it must be refused, it was shown that it was real pain to him so to answer.

The attempt has been made to give such an impression of him as his new parishioners must have received, but the sketch is very imperfect.

In contrast to Brookline, Bridgeport offered a more hopeful field to the pastor who desired to be the intimate friend and guide of all his people. In this busy working community, living in comfort but without pretension, the good New England traditions of social equality were generally observed.

The congregations were usually large. In addition to the regular people of his charge, a fair share of the floating population were drawn by the attractive church, the excellent music, and the style and manner of the new pastor. All this was very stimulating to one who could say, as he so often said, " I do *love* to preach."

After his removal to Bridgeport, Mr. Meier-Smith cultivated more freedom as a speaker, being resolved to gain in force and animation at the risk of loss in rhetorical finish. He was more distinctively a popular preacher during his Bridgeport pastorate than in any other period of his ministry, for his sympathetic temperament responded to the stirring events which marked these years. Although he never became a careless or slovenly writer, he now wrote *currente calamo*, and usually finished a sermon in two sittings. But his preparation was thorough, his notes very full, and the language more or less chosen before he put pen to paper. His manuscripts are found almost without correction.

During the first two years, parochial work occupied much of his time, as the parish limits extended over all parts of the city and its suburbs. He spent less time in his study, and was much among his people, learning their needs, and how to adapt his sermons to them.

Among points which first interested him as he surveyed his new field, was the aspect of matters ecclesiastical. Connecticut Congregationalism was not altogether unlike Presbyterianism, a centralization being obtained by a standing council known as Consociation. Perhaps this feature gave to the officers of the Church, — the deacons, — some coloring to their assumption of a position not altogether different from that of the ruling elders of the Presbyterian Church, while limits to oversight being undefined, more abuse of it was possible.

This glance at the situation before him seems necessary, in view of the possible difficulties he foresaw, and the influence they were destined to have on his future.

An incident occurred within the first month of his residence, foreshadowing coming events. An old man of large frame and striking appearance introduced himself as formerly acquainted with Bridgeport and its churches, but for a long time resident in the West. " Accidentally," he said, he had been present at the *examination* of the newly-called minister, and being much interested in some of his replies, he would be glad to get his views still more clearly upon certain doctrinal points, and upon church government. Accepting the statement of his visitor in good faith, Mr. Meier-Smith answered his questions, which showed much shrewdness and considerable information, without reserve, and afterward found out that he had been catechised by one of the oldest members of the church. Some natural indignation was felt when it appeared that an undue advantage had been gained by stratagem, the long absence from Bridgeport which his words implied having been but for a few months. He had purposely refrained from an earlier introduction to his new pastor that he might " sound him," as he expressed it, when he was entirely " off guard."

Only brief notes remain of the first years of his pastorate. The " Record of Services " indicates that in his study and thought, prophetical Scriptures took some prominence, and particularly such as refer to the Second Coming of the Lord.

He became a believer in the Pre-Millennial Advent, and testified to the gain in his own spiritual life from the study of this subject. Two or three sermons advanced these views, and they were often brought out in his familiar talks and lectures.

The younger members of the congregation were strongly drawn to their pastor, and his personal influence appeared in a steady increase of the number admitted, on profession of their faith, to the full communion of the church. Not a sacramental celebration occurred without accessions to the communion. There were a few among the candidates who had been educated as Unitarians, and the pastor received some criticism for admitting them to the church. As early as the second year of Mr. Meier-Smith's work in Bridgeport, his broad and catholic views with reference to the privileges of the Lord's Table attracted attention and aroused some opposition.

From a few whispered doubts as to the course pursued, the seed was sown of a persistent conflict, which, unable to make much headway during the exciting years of the Civil War, appeared in the latter part of his ministry in Bridgeport.

By earnest personal effort, and a relinquishment of a part of his salary for one year, he secured the erection of a handsome building for the Sunday-school and for general parochial purposes, toward the close of the year 1860. This chapel was first used at the Christmas celebration of the Sunday-school. It is hard to believe now that there could have been at that time serious opposition from some members of the congregation to such an observance of Christmas.

But so it was, and the pastor, always ready to sacrifice his own wishes where no principle was involved, offered to postpone the festival for a few days, if the objectors would decide upon another day in the Holiday week. They selected the 28th of December.

On the appointed evening he remarked that it was a happy coincidence that his friends who disapproved of Christmas celebrations for the children, had selected the day observed for centuries by a large part of the Church in memory of the *Holy Innocents!* The dismay of a few, and the amusement of many, may be imagined when this view of the situation was presented.

In the spring of 1860, he with his wife and a party of friends visited Washington, and Richmond, Va. It was a period of much repressed excitement. The crisis was rapidly approaching which the ensuing presidential election precipitated.

The party were favored with an interview with President Buchanan in his private study. It was the morning after a stormy session of Congress, when the President's policy had been rebuked by a strong vote. Mr. Buchanan, dressed in morning *négligé*, and standing on the hearth before the smouldering embers of a wood fire, looked careworn and dispirited. Mr. Meier-

Smith afterward remarked that "We had seen the President literally in 'sackcloth and ashes.'" In Richmond, they tried to see something of the Southern "Institution" where it appeared under the most favorable light. They were much touched by the conversation and songs of the slaves in a large tobacco factory, and afterward by the prayers and speeches at a negro Baptist church having the largest communion of any in the Southern States. Everywhere it was plain that the deepest unrest prevailed, and that the slaves were looking forward with terrible anxiety to the result of a struggle which all felt sure was impending.

With his brother-in-law he visited a slave auction, and they must have been among the last from the Northern States who were allowed to witness this feature of slavery, as the estrangement between the North and the South became so bitter from this time that any visitor from the North was looked upon as a spy, and shut out from all confidence. It was indeed with much difficulty, and only through the efforts of the pastor of the colored church above referred to, that they were witnesses of the painful scene.

A New England clergyman at this time was expected to be a guide of public opinion and action, and not simply to be carried along by the current. Mr. Meier-Smith was not behind others in boldly expressing himself on the exciting topics of public interest. The nomination and election of Mr. Lincoln, the threatening attitude of the Southern States, and the deep disapprobation of the loyal North at the timid and vacillating course of President Buchanan and his Cabinet, overshadowed most other subjects during the remainder of this year. The pastor of the North Church did not feel that it was "preaching politics" to set forth the principles of civil government, considered as a trust from the Almighty Ruler; or to rouse the public conscience on the important questions involved in the unhappy conflict.

Two or three sermons were preached in the autumn of 1860 which attracted much attention, and provoked violent criticism from local journals which took the other side. Some of these attacks were extremely bitter and personal.

During the winter and spring of 1861, in spite of the engrossing public questions, a steady religious interest quietly made its way, and the pastor had the happiness of welcoming a number of his young people to the communion of the church. Good Friday of this year being appointed by the Governor of Connecticut as a State Fast Day, union services were held by the Congregational churches. The burden of the prayers and addresses was the distracted state of the country. In the address made by Mr. Meier-Smith, especial mention was made of Good Friday as observed by a large majority of the Christian Church. Much exception was taken to this by a few of his parishioners. On Easter Sunday an appropriate sermon was preached; and in the Sunday-school, instruction was given regarding the great festival, and the hope expressed that at no distant day all Christians would keep the Feast of the Resurrection. Open disapproval of this teaching was expressed by one individual, who complained tearfully in the evening prayer-meeting of the training of the children in such " heathenish customs!"

This is not the place to speak at length of the events which followed so rapidly the inauguration of Mr. Lincoln. The fall of Fort Sumter, the first call for troops, the upspringing loyalty of the nation, the attack in Baltimore, the defeat at Bull Run, — all that these things meant to the loyal people of the Northern States, is yet fresh in the memories of those who were on the stage at the time, though it can be but slightly appreciated by a later generation.

Mr. Meier-Smith's " Record of Services " during these years shows a choice of practical subjects. The great questions of the day were plainly and solemnly presented with increasing vigor of style and rhetoric. Sermons on the personal religious life were characterized by much illustration and fervent appeal. The influence of the times was seen in the directness of the presentation of any truth. The excitement of the period influenced expression on every subject, and quiet argument would have attracted few listeners. In July, 1861, Mr. Meier-Smith was appointed to preach the *Concio ad Clerum* at New Haven. His subject was the Personality and Work of the Holy Spirit. The sermon was received with very gratifying commendation by the large body of clergymen before whom it was preached. In the autumn of this year, he preached two sermons on Civil Government; and on the Fast Day appointed by the President, and on Thanksgiving Day, his topics were appropriate to the crisis through which the nation was passing.

Some of the members of the North Church, by reason of birth or associations, were sympathizers with the South, but their pastor's hold upon them was retained through all the trying period of the war, as he never suffered them to feel that his interest in them was lessened, or forgot, in private intercourse, the respect due to their opinions, fearlessly as he expressed his own on all proper occasions.

In 1863, Columbia College conferred upon him the

degree of Doctor of Sacred Theology. He was especially gratified by the kind remembrance of his Alma
Mater, as it was out of its usual course to confer this
degree upon non-Episcopal clergymen. A characteristic remark appears in his diary: " Columbia College has
given me D.D., which I consent to wear because my
unfortunately common surname demands all the dis-
tinctiveness I can get!"

IX.

LIFE IN BRIDGEPORT.

1863–1865.

ALLUSION has been made to a small number of persons who had constituted themselves critics of their pastor during the first year of his ministry in Bridgeport. They were represented by the old man, whose surreptitious introduction of himself to the new clergyman has been already mentioned, and by two or three others who, jealous of ministerial influence, were ambitious to control the spiritual as well as the temporal affairs of the parish.

During the latter part of Dr. Meier-Smith's pastorate many efforts were made by these men to create extended dissatisfaction, but with small success beyond the annoyance of constant friction. The parish generally was thoroughly loyal, and, whenever a question of policy was fairly presented, always sustained its pastor. The grounds of fault finding were that he was "no true Congregationalist;" that he was "at heart a Presbyterian;" that he was "half an Episcopalian," — witness his regard for solemn, reverent worship and his wish to observe "certain days;" that he made "too much of baptism;" and, as a crowning offence, that he was loose and unguarded in his invitations to the Holy Communion, admitting youth whom they considered unprepared, as well as persons of "Unitarian tendencies."

Little sympathy was aroused on most of these points, but on the last mentioned some anxiety was manifested by a few of Dr. Meier-Smith's warmest friends. He assured them that his practice was strictly in accordance with that of the leading churches and ministers of the Congregational denomination. Animated and sometimes heated discussions upon this point became the rule in the evening meetings. Some of these discussions were amusing as well as annoying, and Dr. Meier-Smith's old friends tell various stories of his wise, and often humorous methods of confuting his opponents. The vexed question was settled on the pastor's side, by the answers received from distinguished authorities in reply to questions as to general New England usage.

Before this finale, however, an incident occurred illustrating Dr. Meier-Smith's prompt action where a question of principle was involved. By representing that the pastor cared little about the matter, and would willingly concede the point if he were assured of the wishes of a majority, the leading spirits of the opposition secured a large number of names to a petition requesting him to alter his invitation to the Communion, so that only members of Congregational churches could be admitted even to occasional participation in the Lord's Supper.

This paper was handed to Dr. Meier-Smith on a Friday evening. After reading it, and asking a few questions, he saw at once how the names had been procured. Handing it back he said, "The Table is the Lord's, not mine. All baptized persons who love our Lord and wish to obey His command, and who have professed their faith in Him, are welcome. I will never give a more restricted invitation, and I know that many who have signed this without conference with me, would never ask me to do anything I cannot do without treachery to my principles. If every name on this paper is not withdrawn by to-morrow night, I shall offer my resignation on Sunday morning." No entreaty from even his most valued friends, who represented to him the difficulty of meeting his ultimatum on such short notice, moved him. The result was that the parish was diligently canvassed on Saturday, and late in the evening the paper was returned to him with the pen drawn through every name upon it but those of the leaders in the movement. At the close of the Sunday morning service, Dr. Meier-Smith made a brief allusion to the matter, expressing his gratification that his friends whose names had been affixed to the paper under a misapprehension had withdrawn them, thereby testifying to their confidence in their pastor's fidelity to his convictions. His peremptory action at this crisis he considered justifiable in view of the long contest which had preceded it.

From the "Record of Services" at the close of the year 1863: "The year has been in some respects a favored one. There has been much religious interest among the young, and I trust twenty-five or thirty have given themselves truly to our blessed Lord. In other respects it has been a year of trial. Some troublesome parishioners, few in number indeed, have been very fractious, but they have been entirely unsuccessful, excepting as drags upon my ministry, in what they have undertaken."

In the early part of the year 1864, much religious interest was general in the congregations of the town. A well-known evangelist was invited to conduct union services. Some of his methods were of doubtful expediency, and though Dr. Meier-Smith consented to allow services in his church, he reserved to himself the right to guide them. These services resulted in the addition of many to the communion of the church, whose consistent lives bore witness to the reality of their experience.

The topics chosen for sermons and addresses for this year appear from the " Record " to have been of an unusually solemn and impressive character, and directly addressed to the heart and conscience.

He speaks of the apparent result of the special evangelistic work, in a letter to his mother, dated March 23, 1864:—

As I write this date, I remember that it is my father's birthday. Let me begin by offering through you my congratulations to the "old gentleman" of sixty-six. I could show him some very much older men of fifty-six.

And, by the way, I saw a woman of fifty-four to-day who looks beside you more like sixty-four than you do like fifty-eight. Ah, dear parents, how more and more I pray each year and every time I see you that God may give you both a delightful evening of life, a good long summer evening, whose twilight shall not be dim until the glorious morning absorb it and make the new day, the day fadeless and eternal. I do not call you "old people" yet, but I hope you will one of these years be "old people" always young. . . .

The results of our time of religious interest, now that the extension of the work has ceased, are looking well. Twenty-five have been examined and approved for full membership, and more are to be.

I have been working very hard since February 1st, every day.   Next Sunday, Easter, I mean, if possible, to be with you.

Your loving son,   MATSON.

Many anecdotes are told by old friends in Bridgeport of Dr. Meier-Smith's ready tact in meeting and conquering small obstacles.   He seemed to know by intuition the methods best suited to those among whom he served, as one incident may illustrate.

During one cold winter he suffered much from the many broken panes of glass in the large windows inclosing the pulpit recess.   The winds whistled about his ears, and he called attention in vain to the subject, the repairs being constantly neglected.   In the middle of a sermon one morning, he paused, glancing from window to window.   Then leaving the desk, he put on his heavy overcoat, deliberately fastening each button, and drawing up the collar about his neck.   Apologizing for the interruption, he remarked that he had previously counted the broken panes, and found that there were over one hundred through which the wind found its way.   The next morning the glazier was promptly on hand.   It should be added to the credit of the good brethren of the committee in charge of the building, that they took in the best of humor the public notice of their carelessness, telling the story themselves with satisfaction at the bold rebuke of their pastor.   "He knows men and how to meet them," was the comment of a shrewd observer who watched him in Bridgeport with not too friendly interest.

The place has now been reached in the life of the subject of this Memoir, when it is necessary to speak of the long period of thought and mental conflict which led to his decision to seek Orders in the Protestant Episcopal Church. The seeds of this change were sown in early youth. His acquaintance with liturgical services from childhood has been already noticed. Churchly ideas were always familiar to him. From the beginning of his ministry he held high views of the Sacraments and of Orders, though not higher than those expressed in Presbyterian standards, as he understood them; and it is not unlikely that he would have remained in the Church of his nurture, had he not been called into New England.

While the excitements of the war-days engrossed much of his time, in 1863 and 1864, in the quiet of his study, and in the inner life, questions and difficulties regarding his own future ministry began to make themselves heard and felt.

Reviewing his twelve years' service under the Congregational system, Dr. Meier-Smith recognized that he had not been in full sympathy with the prevailing tone of ministers and congregations.

Many things which seemed to him of first importance were lightly regarded both in theory and practice among those with whom he was associated. Lay participation in the spiritual oversight of the Church he considered unauthorized by either Scriptural rule or catholic usage.

The practice of holding the children of the Church at arm's length, requiring assent from them to a doctrinal confession and a profession of a personal experience, often impossible for their years, was opposed to all his convictions.

Subscription to the catholic creeds was not enough to admit to the communion of the church; and in the *Articles of Faith*, which were prepared by each congregation for its own use, he found unbalanced and distorted presentations of doctrine, which he could not subscribe to himself, or require of others.

Yet to all this he must conform if he remained a Congregationalist. To oppose was to suffer from constant friction. The atmosphere of conflict was uncongenial to him, and he knew that in such an atmosphere he could never do the work he aspired to accomplish.

The entire subordination of worship to preaching, and the absence of reverence in conducting worship, were distasteful to him; yet he always repelled the charge that matters of taste, or any superficial considerations, bore any appreciable weight in his final decision.

Studying the doctrine and worship of various Christian bodies, he found himself much in sympathy with the Anglican Communion. At times, again, he felt strongly drawn toward the grand old Presbyterian Church where his ministry commenced. Within two or three years, however, he was prepared to say that in worship and in doctrine, especially regarding sacraments, and in general administrative methods, he could more heartily affiliate with the Protestant Episcopal Church than with any other. But here he paused.

Were these convictions strong enough to warrant so great a break and change, a step which must involve so much sacrifice and must provoke so much criticism? He was now brought face to face with the claims of historic Episcopacy.

Although the important questions pressing upon him were not fully answered until his release from his Bridgeport pastorate, he now began to realize whither he was being led.

In the autumn of 1864, Dr. Meier-Smith was called to a Presbyterian church in New York City. Many of his friends among the clergy pressed his acceptance of this call, and from his growing unrest in Congregationalism he was almost ready to accept a position which promised relief.

The possibility however of deepening convictions on the side of a still more radical change finally influenced him to decline it. The congregation which he visited were greatly disappointed. From the letter acknowledging the receipt of his decision an extract is made.

"The unanimity of feeling that shadowed our choice, the deep and growing interest awakened by your visit to our church, and the results that followed it, all seemed to be indications of Providence that God would give you to us as a spiritual guide. . . . I shall never forget Dr. Meier-Smith, of Bridgeport, and my heart's desire for you is that your life and health may be spared to accomplish the great work for which God has fitted and prepared you."

The year 1865 opened with national events of the gravest importance. Everything pointed to the collapse of the Great Rebellion. The absorbing interest all felt in public affairs did not interfere with faithful pastoral work. It is remembered by Dr. Meier-Smith's old friends that the last year of his ministry in Bridgeport was marked by more than usual fervor and directness in preaching. The deep thinking and heart-searching concerning his own future doubtless made him especially solemn and tender in all his approaches to his people.

He was superintendent of his Sunday-school at this time, and saw many happy results from his work among the young members of his charge.

The annoying opposition on the part of the mal-contents continued, and in the spring of 1865 they were evidently preparing for a more open attack.

On the anniversary of the fall of Fort Sumter the stars and stripes again waved over the fortress, and in quick succession followed the fall of Richmond and the surrender of Lee. The enthusiasm was at its highest pitch, and the roar of the guns celebrating the consummation had scarcely died on the air, when there came the terrible shock of the assassination of President Lincoln. While the country, and indeed all civilization, stood aghast, while the churches as well as all the dwellings were draped in mourning, it occurred to the small company who hoped to coerce their pastor, that the time had come for a bold stroke.

On Easter Sunday, the 16th of April, the North Church was crowded. The solemn signs of bereavement were everywhere, and almost every face was that of a mourner. After the prayers, the appropriate Scriptures, and the requiem music, as Dr. Meier-Smith was about to commence an address prepared for the occasion, an interruption was caused by the appearance of one of the men who had been conspicuous as an opponent. He went into the pulpit and presented the pastor with a paper. Dr. Meier-Smith glanced at its contents, and found that it was a call for a meeting of the church on the next evening, ostensibly for some unimportant business. The names appended, no less than the time chosen to present the paper, were sufficient to assure the pastor upon a moment's consideration that another purpose was veiled under the innocent request. He knew that only those in the secret would attend a meeting called for so trivial an object, at a time of such great public excitement. The real purpose was to assail the pastor, and secure a formal censure upon his course with reference to the terms for church communion.   He read the paper aloud, with its signatures, then pausing a moment said, "Another subject will also be brought before the meeting which I have called at the request of some members of this church.   The church will be called upon to act upon my resignation, which is hereby offered to this church and congregation.   The reasons which call for this unexpected announcement are probably plain to all, and will be given in full at a more appropriate season.   For the apparent want of decorous respect to the august occasion which calls a mourning congregation here to-day, by the intrusion of personal affairs upon the public attention, I offer no apology.   The responsibility must rest on those who have forced the issue upon me." Then throwing aside all appearance of further interest in the matter, he delivered an eloquent address upon the great calamity that had befallen the nation.   The congregation were deeply moved.   Already strung to a high pitch of emotion, the sudden prospect of losing the beloved pastor was too much for many to bear with calmness.   The signers of the paper, realizing the situation, retired rapidly at the close of the services, while a large number gathered about their pastor, and affectionately urged him to recede from his position.   This he firmly declined to do, though he afterward consented to remain in charge of the parish until the first of July. At the church meetings which followed, Dr. Meier-Smith was almost unanimously sustained, although his resignation was accepted finally at his peremptory request.   The resolutions passed by the church were all that could be desired, in expressions of regard and affection, and of sorrow at the severance of the relation.

When this was finally settled, Dr. Meier-Smith gave himself entirely to the consideration of the important change so long before his mind. Many and anxious were the conferences held in his study: sometimes alone with his wife, who dared not advise, but stood ever close to her husband's side, and ready to go with him wherever he was led; sometimes with dear family friends, nearly all of whom were affectionately urging him to take no step so radical, and so fraught with peril; occasionally with clergymen of the Episcopal Church, from whom he did not receive much encouragement. Beyond kind sympathy in his perplexity, and the hope expressed that he would be cordially received if he asked admission to the Church, no one contributed materially to the result. His friend, Dr. Dyer, gave him the information needed for intelligent action, and promised him such kind introduction as was possible; but he plainly set the difficulties before him, and told him that it might be long before he could find a work and a position equal to that which he was leaving. Dr. Dyer wrote: "I wish some post could be offered to you in advance, but this seems highly improbable. I think you will have to shut your eyes tight and *jump;* but don't jump while providential difficulties deter you." The Canon requiring a six months' candidature without employment was a great deterrent. It required a strong sense of duty and no little faith to "jump" into such uncertainties. Dr. Meier-Smith spoke freely after this time to his most trusted friends in Bridgeport of his probable decision. Many expressed their grief, and one dear old man of really catholic spirit retained so strongly early Puritan prejudices against the Episcopal Church, that he said with tears in his eyes, " Much as I love you, I would rather stand by your grave than see you go into the Episcopal Church ! "

In the review of this pastorate, Dr. Meier-Smith writes, " I have, during the six years of my ministry here, admitted one hundred and seventy-six persons to the communion of the church, and have preached seven hundred and fifty-six times." In speaking of these years he said that they seemed to him years of peculiarly vigorous life and work. Occurrences incidental to the war contributed largely to this, in the pulpit and out of it. Pastoral visitation often included scenes of touching interest, as partings in families were constantly occurring, and every great battle brought anxiety, and often mourning and desolation into the homes of some of his people. Naturally, very tender ties were formed between pastor and people, for his ready sympathy brought him at once to every one in trouble, with the counsel and help needed for the emergency. To all such, his decision to leave Bridgeport brought sincere sorrow; the more that he seemed to be going very far away from them, in leaving the Congregational denomination. The last two months were burdened by the parting in prospect, and the service in which he delivered his farewell address on the last Sunday in June, was an ordeal he said he would never like to pass through again. On the first Sunday of July, Dr. Meier-Smith and his family received the Holy Communion in Christ Church, Bridgeport, and this was the first open intimation of what was now practically settled. Yet even then he listened to the remonstrances of friends, and prayerfully weighed anything which might be an indication of the will of God.

A delegation from one of the largest cities in Massachusetts visited him with the plan for an enterprise of which they wished him to take the lead. Dissatisfied with Congregational doctrine and worship, they proposed organizing an independent church on the basis of the Ancient Creeds, and with a Liturgy largely drawn from the Book of Common Prayer. They offered to contribute liberally, and to give him the entire direction. This was a tempting prospect, but he knew the dangers of independency, and had no disposition to lead off in another sect, even if it were limited to one congregation. He was constrained to decline the offer, though with grateful appreciation of the confidence shown him by the gentlemen interested.

By this time his convictions had become settled that there was a Church and an Order that could rightly claim to be Catholic and Apostolic.

The long period of anxious thought ended with the summer, when the full decision was reached to apply for Holy Orders and become a candidate in the Diocese of Massachusetts. Some clerical friends desired that he should be appointed to a vacant chair in the Divinity School of Gambier, Ohio, which position he could take before ordination. Bishop McIlvaine at first responded favorably to the wishes of Dr. Meier-Smith's friends, but finally decided that it was not wise to pass over the claims of others proposed, in favor of one not yet in the ministry of the Church. Dr. Meier-Smith was not disappointed at this result, as his own preference was decidedly for a rectorship. He wrote to his father-in-law after his decision, " You may be sure that it is not without much pain and solicitude that I make the transition. Yet my convictions on the score of usefulness, however greatly I may have erred, have been too strong for resistance. The positive Congregationalism demanded among Congregationalists, — the aggressive Congregationalism, — I cannot conscientiously maintain. The Presbyterian Church is abundantly supplied.

Evangelical Episcopalians need help. I can enter their Church on their Catholic ground, and work with them. So I have taken the step. I need the prayers and sympathies of my loving friends that I may be a better and more useful minister in my new relations than ever before."

In the "Record of Services," the notes of the ministry in Bridgeport close with these words: "Here endeth the First Lesson."

Twenty-one years later, letters were received from former parishioners, from some of which passages are copied. They give evidence of what Dr. Meier-Smith was as friend and pastor while in Bridgeport, and of the abiding nature of his influence, surviving the separations and changes of the long years that had passed since he was the beloved guide and helper of the writers.

From Mrs. Eliza Webster Jones.

BRIDGEPORT, April 5, 1887.

. . . I cannot forget the kindness of your husband, — his swift and dearly prized sympathy in our deep troubles. That precious letter is written in my heart ! How it comforted me ! Now he is where the mysteries of divine Providence are being unfolded before him. What precious memories he has left for you, dear Mary, and for your beloved ones. You will miss his kindly greetings more and more as years roll on ; but more and more you will be able to rejoice in the review of his beautiful life, and of his early escape from the troubles which are darkly shadowing the people of God, in these days when He is trying the faith of those who love Him, as never before. I have often said that while here, and so closely associated with our family and church, he was always the Christian gentleman in feeling, soul, and action, whatever provocation sorely tried him. To me he was a model man ! . . .

I now use your husband's gift, — the New Testament in large type, — in my daily reading, for my old Bible has fallen to pieces. When I first took it up after his death was known, I involuntarily pressed it to my heart. His words, " In memory of Golden Hours," are inscribed within it.

From Mrs. Eliza B. Wordin.

BRIDGEPORT, April 9, 1887.

. . . I was very glad to hear and to know something of Dr. Meier-Smith's last days. I cannot express to you the thoughts that come to me as I write these words. I could take him up, where I last left him. He had not gone away from me, or I rather had not gone out of his life. . . .

I think it was characteristic of him to throw his interest and sympathy so much into the lives of his friends, that they must all feel as I do. No words that may be said in his praise are enough to express what he was to those who were so fortunate as to be his friends.

. . . .

My heart is divided between pity and tenderness for you, and joy and triumph for him. I am so glad that he has heard the " Well done, good and faithful servant." I know that that was the plaudit which welcomed him, as I think of the many who have been cheered and comforted by him, of the many who have been led to the Saviour by him, and of those whose Christian life has been rekindled by his strong encouraging words. How many there are who loved him for his earnest help in their time of need ! You are rich in having had such an one for your constant companion, your loving helper, your tender sympathizing husband; you are rich now in having him at the Court of the King.

To me, Dr. Meier-Smith was always a true, helpful friend, as I know he was to others. I never had such a love for any one as I had for him. I never had such a pastor. I never expect to have another, but I thank God that I had him.

His going has made a sad spot in my life, for though I saw little of him, I was sure I had one friend to whom I could turn in any time of need.

From Miss Mary Clarke.

BRIDGEPORT, October, 1887.

. . . About dear Dr. Meier-Smith, my recollection of him is this, that while very instructive and interesting as a preacher, always feeding us spiritually, he was pre-eminently beloved as pastor and friend among his people, and a most welcome visitor at the bedside of the sick and dying. His loving, winning manner, his cheerful presence, the soothing Christ-like words from his lips carried comfort and. help, and left its impress when he had departed. Often have I contrasted him with others I have known, only to think and say what a blessed gift he had for helping sick and weary ones in this troublous life, and how willingly and freely he used it. As a family we always enjoyed his incoming. Personally as to myself, his voice always had wondrous cheer for me; I can hear it now even though he is with the angels, and with many whom he has led and helped into our Father's House.

From Mrs. Frances Lord MacLellan.

BRIDGEPORT, April 2, 1887.

. . . Next to being held close in the everlasting arms of the loving Saviour, it seems to me your comfort will be the memory of him "who is not, for God took him." The remembrance of that great, true, noble life which you have shared, the companionship of those blessed years together, all the memories that cluster round those years, the loving, protecting care that has always been yours, the wifely devotion which you gave to him, — thinking of all these, how rich you are, how few who sorrow have such a past! . . .

When I think of you without him in the beautiful home endeared by his love and life, my heart breaks for you, and I feel that words are feeble and cannot express my thought. Perhaps I ought hardly to touch upon my own sense of loss and affliction, so light must it seem in comparison with yours ; but, dear friend, you do not know how dear to me you both, are. A thrill goes through me as I think perhaps he knows now.

Why you have been such faithful friends to me I never could and cannot now discover ; but your loving-kindness to me, when I was but a girl, so bound my heart to you both, that my love for both has been deeper and truer than for any friends in the world beside, save those of my own fireside.

Oh, how I longed to stand by that casket, and look again upon that tender and true face ere it was shut out from my sight ! To let my tears mingle with the tears of others who loved him ! . . . I shall always be " sorrowing that I shall see his face no more." Could I have stood there and laid one little flower as a tribute of affection upon his casket, it would have been a " forget-me-not," as a token that I could never forget what he was to me, he who was pre-eminently my pastor and friend. He was to me always the " Great-heart " of Bunyan's allegory. His loving, faithful preaching, his earnest, personal appeals — always so tender and loving — led me to my Saviour. My mother's prayers and his words are linked together in my heart. I told him once in those days that I did not want to be talked to. He ceased talking, but kept on praying until my stony heart broke ; then he was my guide, leading me by still waters and into green pastures.

Memory has been very busy this past week bringing out of her storehouse treasured store of many years. I have recalled my pastor of the North Church, our meetings there of prayer and praise, of which he was the head and life ; so many incidents of those days showing his great, kind heart. He is linked in thought with that only brother who filled a soldier's grave. Said that brother once to my mother, " Dr. Meier-Smith is the only man who seems to care for my soul." Once, upon a railway train, meeting that brother, he engaged him a moment in conversation, then with a hearty hand-shake said, "Good-by ; there are folks at home praying for you."

Later, when H—— was a soldier, he wrote to him urging him to be a Christian.   It was no wonder, when the soldier of the Union became a soldier of the Lord Jesus, that in the letter bearing the good news to parents and sister was added the message, "Tell Dr. Meier-Smith ; he will be glad."   I did tell him, and the next morning's mail carried a letter to that brother from that faithful friend.   Later, when my brother was called from the battlefield to heaven, the same beloved pastor and friend brought tenderest comfort to our hearts.   Oh, he is linked with all my life !   I have never had a great joy or a great sorrow since I knew him, but his friendship has given token of his sympathy.   My engagement, marriage, the coming of little ones into my home, have all brought me kindly words from a great heart of love and sympathy for every event in life.

My visits to you are crowded with pleasant thoughts of his kind deeds to make me happy. . . .

When the letter came breaking to me the sad tidings, as I was crying alone, my baby came in, and said, "What makes you cry, Mamma?"   I told her a dear friend had gone to heaven, and I felt very badly that I was not to see him again here.   Slipping her little hand in mine, with a surprised look and a ring of triumph in her tone, she said, "Why, Mamma, he has gone up to our heaven that Jesus made !   Jesus sent for him, and it's nicer than the other home he had here. Don't cry ; we are all going ; we 'll see him soon."   Is my letter long?   My heart is just as full as when I began.   I think of you, lonely in your home, although surrounded by those who love you, and then of the great, noble life ended here, and I do indeed " weep with those who weep."   If I, only a humble friend, loved and prized him so much, when only a little corner of his life touched mine, and his loss brings to me such deep grief, what must it be to you all, who filled and dwelt in that heart ? Still with this thought comes another. If my little leaf brings so much comfort of memories, how the great life-book, all your own, must bring numberless pages of comfort, a store never to be exhausted. How you must look forward to the blessed reunion by and by !

8

X.

ORDAINED DEACON AND PRIEST IN THE EPISCOPAL CHURCH.

1866.

FROM Dr. Meier-Smith's "Record of Services": "On the fourth day of September, 1865, I was admitted a candidate for Holy Orders in the Protestant Episcopal Church, in the Diocese of Massachusetts, under the Rt. Rev. Manton Eastburn, D.D. It is unnecessary to state that this change has been long in contemplation, and is the result of much thought. With not the smallest disposition to cast aspersion upon either my past ministry or my associates therein, I accept Episcopal ordination in full persuasion of its Scripturalness, its order, and its expediency; and the Episcopal Church as the most Scriptural in its structure of all the Churches in this land. I enter it from conviction, and with all my heart, not knowing what is before me, but confident that the Lord has work for me to do in it."

For advice and assistance in reference to entrance upon his new work, and for favorable introductions, Dr. Meier-Smith was under great obligations to friends among the clergy of the Church, some of whom he had known for years. First ever in thoughtful kindness and wise suggestion was his friend Dr. Dyer, and he was also much indebted to his revered kinsman by marriage, the late Bishop of Delaware. Rev. Drs.

Stone, Wharton, and Bancroft were ready to assist him in any way, and the present Bishop of Central New York, then Rector of Emmanuel Church, Boston, requested that his ordination take place in that church. Rev. Dr. Tyng, of New York, invited him to preach the first time after his ordination in St. George's Church. The Bishop of Massachusetts was most friendly, and the trying time of candidature was relieved by every expression of kind hope and encouragement.

Yet no one dared promise work, and nothing was definitely in prospect. Friends who could not sympathize in the " experiment," mourned over the possible loss of position and failure of work. One exception must be made. His brother-in-law, Rev. Erskine N. White, although himself a Presbyterian clergyman, gave him intelligent and hearty sympathy, and encouraged him to follow out his conscientious convictions. One dark cloud of doubt and trouble came over him as he was about to send a letter to Bishop Eastburn, announcing his desire to become a candidate for Holy Orders. For the moment the fear that the important decision might prove a mistake, overpowered him. Had not this dear brother, believing that his mind was morbidly excited, taken the responsibility of urging him to post his letter immediately, a trying delay would have followed. That hour was the last of doubt. Thenceforward he never wavered, but rested in a calm confidence that the Almighty Guide had been surely and graciously leading him.

The decision had been reached intelligently, and Dr. Meier-Smith went forward with all his heart, finding entire peace and satisfaction in all his later ministry. Let it be said here that he never allowed himself or others to cast any reflections upon his past ministry, blessed as it had been of God. Nor did he criticise the standing of fellow-laborers from whom he was now separated. It was enough for him to rest assured that for himself service under a branch of the ancient and historic Church was now the only ministry possible.

In October, Dr. Meier-Smith, with his wife, visited Bishop Lee, and on the evening of the Eighteenth Sunday after Trinity, they were confirmed by him in St. Andrew's Church, Wilmington. Very fragrant is the memory of that visit, and the loving reception and wise counsel of that truly Apostolic man, the first Bishop of Delaware. Before the service, the Bishop called attention to the beautiful portion appointed for the Epistle for the day, as expressing exactly what he desired to say to the brother whom he was thus admitting into the Episcopal Church. "I thank my God always on your behalf for the grace of God which is given you by Jesus Christ; that in everything ye are enriched by Him in all utterance and in all knowledge, even as the testimony of Jesus Christ was confirmed in you : so that ye come behind in no gift; waiting for the coming of our Lord Jesus Christ, who shall also confirm you unto the end, that ye may be blameless in the day of our Lord Jesus Christ." — 1 Cor. 1–4.

The Bridgeport home, where an eventful seven years had been passed, was finally left in November, and the family spent most of the winter following at the homestead in New Rochelle, with Dr. Meier-Smith's parents.

Thoughtful men, and Christians generally, were much perplexed at this time by the condition of the negroes of the Southern States in their new and untried position as Freedmen. The Episcopal Church, recognizing its responsibility toward them, organized a Freedman's Aid Commission, under the care of the Board of Missions.   Through the kindness of friends, especially the Rev. Dr. Wharton, Dr. Meier-Smith was appointed to present the plan and work of the Commission to the Episcopal Churches of New England, during the period which must pass before his ordination.   In the months of January and February, 1866, he was engaged in this work.   Rectors of prominent parishes invited him to deliver addresses, in which the proposed work was laid before their congregations.   From these visits an extended acquaintance was formed with clergymen, and some knowledge of Church methods gained.   He also passed the necessary examinations for Orders.

During his visit to Boston in January, he wrote to his wife: " For a feather in my cap, the Bishop called on me yesterday, and asked me to take his place and read prayers at a special service wherein he is to preach on Sunday evening next, at Tremont Temple, for the Young Men's Christian Association.   I regret that my probable absence from the city will prevent my serving him. He said I might use the Prayer Book, or extemporize, or blend prayers together, infusing Prayer-Book language and Collects as I pleased.   He preferred the latter, as most certainly do I.   On Monday, I heard Dr. Nicholson lecture in St. Paul's Church on a chapter in Romans.   The most refractory Old School Presbyterian could not have been dissatisfied with aught said or done."

To his Wife.

BOSTON, January 17, 1866.

Daylight at last appears.   Imprimis, I have survived all my examinations for Priest's Orders, the work being completed this morning.   The examiners were the Bishop, Drs. Huntington and Wharton, and Rev. Mr.

Coolidge. It was a very fair examination, not by any means rigid, yet a fulfilment of the Canon, done with exemplary fidelity. The Bishop is very courteous and keenly humorous. He says he likes me " because I am not a Yankee." How glad I am that I shall never have to be examined again by any bishop or councils !

He writes in his " Record of Services ": " March 6, 1866. I was ordained by Bishop Eastburn to the Diaconate in Emmanuel Church, Boston, Rev. Dr. F. D. Huntington, Rector. My presenter was Rev. Mr. Snow. During the six months' interval, I have made addresses in behalf of the Freedman's Aid Commission. I enter with devout thankfulness upon my work again."

On the evening of the day of Dr. Meier-Smith's ordination, he preached in Emmanuel Church on the " Oneness of the Church," from the last two verses of the eleventh chapter of the Epistle to the Hebrews. On the following Sunday, he preached three times in New York, — for Dr. Tyng of St. George's ; at the Church of the Ascension for Dr. John Cotton Smith ; and at Holy Trinity, for Rev. S. H. Tyng, Jr. On the next day he received the following letter : —

NEW YORK, March 13, 1866.

MY DEAR BROTHER, — I am just starting for Washington, and can only write a few lines, but I am unwilling to leave without saying to you how gratified I am at the impression made by your services on Sunday last ; I hear but one opinion expressed. Most devoutly do I thank God for it. Though I have said but little, I have nevertheless felt the deepest anxiety with regard to your entrance upon our ministry. My prayer has been that God would guide you and give you acceptance with our people. Thus far everything is all that could be desired. At St. George's and the Ascension you will ever be welcomed with the warmest interest.   How grateful we should be for these things !

Tell your wife how much I love her for being present with you at these services.   No doubt her heart went up to God for you.

In one sense it was no more for you to stand up and preach the Gospel as you did last Sunday, than in all the Sundays which have gone before ; but in another and very peculiar sense it was widely different.   You have now entered your new relations, and your work is before you.   To human view the prospect is fair enough, but it is the Lord's work, and His will alone should be the guide.   He will place you where you can best serve Him.   Sometimes He disposes for a time of His servants very differently from what a human wisdom would dictate.   But I cannot say more ; you will have my warmest sympathy and most earnest prayers, and it will give me the greatest pleasure to contribute in any way I can to your usefulness and happiness.

Give my best love to Mrs. Meier-Smith and the children. God bless you all.

Your old affectionate friend and brother,

H. DYER.

He officiated constantly during the next six or seven weeks, principally in New York, Boston, and Troy. Great kindness and many attentions were extended to him by both clergymen and laymen, which were most gratefully appreciated at this crisis.

Six weeks later he received Priest's Orders ; and thus wrote in his "Record" : "On April 20th, I was ordained Priest by Bishop Eastburn, acting for Bishop Potter, in Holy Trinity Church, New York.   Rev. Dr. Dyer presented me, and Drs. Dyer, Tyng, and Gallaudet, and Rev. Messrs. S. H. Tyng, Jr., H. M. Beare, and others, united in the laying on of hands.   Bishop Eastburn gave an address in place of the sermon. It was very kind, courteous, and catholic, making recognition of my past ministry, and speaking most hopefully of the future. In my last record I wrote, 'I know not what is before me.' During the few weeks of my Diaconate, I have received calls from St. Matthew's Church, Jersey City, St. Michael's Church, Trenton, St. John's Church, Troy, and overtures, pressed by Bishops Randall and Eastburn, to take charge of the Church of the Messiah, Boston. These, however, I have declined in favor of a call to the rectorship of Trinity Church, Newark, New Jersey, and I shall begin my labors in this parish on Sunday, May 6th, the fifth after Easter, 1866."

From a " Memorandum of Events of Especial Interest during the year ending April, 1866." "The man to whom of all others we feel the most deeply indebted is our friend of eighteen years, the Rev. H. Dyer, D.D. His counsel freely sought from the first was so free from partisanship, so catholic and devout, that it could hardly be deemed encouragement. But when the long-weighed question was settled, he gave the heartiest of welcomes, and has since been unwearying in efforts to secure a favorable introduction into the Church."

Dr. Dyer, who knew all the steps which led to his friend's transition into the Episcopal Church, has kindly prepared the notes which follow, giving his own impressions at the time, which remained unchanged ; together with a loving tribute to the long and close friendship between himself and Dr. Meier-Smith.

New York, February 9, 1887.

My acquaintance with Dr. Meier-Smith commenced during his early ministry in the Presbyterian Church, and continued to his death. Various circumstances brought us by degrees into very close relations of friendship and Christian fellow-ship. After his removal to Brookline, and settlement in charge of the Congregational Church in that beautiful pre-cinct of Boston, and during his residence of several years there, our associations became very intimate. Having to spend much time in Boston on several occasions, I was often an inmate of his lovely and attractive family. The same was true while for some seven or eight years he had charge of a parish in Bridgeport. Frequently, when visiting that city to take the Sunday service in one of the Episcopal Churches, I was the guest of his family. These intimate associations dur-ing a period of nineteen years or more, gave me an exceptional opportunity of studying and knowing the man, of under-standing the elements, traits, and habits which made up his character, as well as the motives and spirit which shaped his life and conduct in all the relations of life ; and I can bear the strongest testimony to his generous, sympathetic, and noble nature.

He was greatly respected by the whole community where he lived, and deeply loved by all who knew him, and most deeply by those who were nearest to him and knew him best. He was a charming companion for old and young, full of play-ful pleasantries, of unaffected and genuine kindness, yet always preserving the dignity of a true Christian gentleman. Nowhere did the excellencies of Dr. Meier-Smith's nature shine with brighter lustre than in the circle of his own family and among his intimate friends. To know him was to love him. It was these traits which made him so popular, particularly among the young, and so endeared him to his people. He was greatly respected and esteemed in the par-ishes where he was settled. I do not wonder it was so, indeed, I should wonder if this had not been the case.

I have often been asked why with such surroundings and in a career of marked success and promise, he made the great change in his Church relations ? As we had not a great deal of conversation on this subject, I can only say that Dr.

Meier-Smith was a very thoughtful man, not at all given to change, never taking up new things because they were new, or dropping old things because they were old. On the contrary, he was very deliberate in action, never jumping to his conclusions, but reaching them after careful and mature examination. He always had a reason for what he did. The change, therefore, was not the result of any sudden impulse or emotion, nor did it proceed from mere taste or preference, nor from disappointment in the results and promises of his former ministry, nor yet again from unworthy motives of ambition. None of these things moved him. In his former relations he was very prosperous. He had already reached a high position as a preacher and pastor, and as a man of culture and progress. Everything was bright and promising. Few men could have had a more attractive future. To make the change in the face of such an array of circumstances, required the deepest convictions and a very high degree of moral courage. I would say, therefore, that nothing but convictions attended by patient thought, careful study and examination, earnest prayers for divine guidance, and a solemn sense of responsibility, led him to take this important step. To doubt the honesty and purity of his motives would, to my mind, be simply unmanly and unchristian.

After he entered the ministry of our Church and during his rectorship of Trinity Church, Newark, and St. John's Church, Hartford, I saw much of him, and know how much he was respected and beloved in those parishes and communities. After he became a Professor in the Divinity School, Philadelphia, our intimacy continued, but I saw less of him than formerly, not because of any diminution of friendship, but simply from a change of circumstances. My health became very infirm, confining me mostly to my house, so that we could not often meet ; but my affection for him, and interest in him and his work continued to the last. When his sudden and unexpected death was announced, it was a great shock to me, and I felt and said that in the removal of Dr.

Meier-Smith, I had lost a deeply loved brother, and one of the truest and best friends I ever had. I can never cease to remember with love and gratitude the genial, cordial, and whole-souled manner in which I was always received and trusted by him and his family.

Our pleasant and I trust profitable intercourse will be a cherished treasure so long as I remain in this world, and I trust and hope that death has only interrupted it for a season.

I should like to say a few words as to the truly catholic and Christ-like spirit which Dr. Meier-Smith displayed throughout his whole ministry, and the fidelity with which he held and preached the simple Gospel of Christ. While he was a sincere Churchman, he never felt or spoke unkindly of Christians of other names. In leaving the Church in which he was educated and where he exercised his early ministry, he bore with him the regrets and sincere respect and love of all with whom he had been associated; and these feelings he fully reciprocated. We mourn when such a man is taken away, and yet we rejoice and take courage from the good example which he has left us. May we follow him as he followed Christ.

XI.

THE FIRST RECTORSHIP; TRINITY CHURCH, NEWARK.

1866–1868.

TRINITY Parish, one of the largest and most important in New Jersey, was the Mother Church of the city of Newark, and dear to many of the oldest and most influential families of the State. It was not without anxiety that Dr. Meier-Smith accepted its rectorship, which but for the encouragement of friends he would hardly have ventured to do. For one as yet unaccustomed to the methods of the Church, it was a grave responsibility to accept immediately so prominent a position. But the invitation to assume the charge of the parish was hearty and unanimous, and the Vestry and Wardens, fully understanding the case, promised all due forbearance and cordial support in his untried work. He accepted their overtures gratefully, not even caring to visit the parish first, saying to the committee who presented the call, " Gentlemen, you are willing to take me on faith, and I take you in the same spirit." The family moved into the rectory, opposite the venerable church which stands among the fine old trees of the Military Park, and the new life of home and Church began under bright auspices.

The first Sunday is distinctly recalled. The congregations were large, as was the attendance upon the Holy Communion. It was the first time that Dr. Meier-Smith had taken charge of the entire service and of the celebration of the Holy Communion, and he felt the solemnity of the new experience. The people were hearing their chosen Rector for the first time, and many were watching with critical eyes, to detect the novice through the long and complex service. At the close, a friend whose watchfulness was owing to his desire that the new Rector should make the best of impressions, remarked, "Everything was admirably done; there was but one expression in the whole service by which one could detect that Dr. Meier-Smith was not to the manner born. He used the word *house* instead of *church* in giving a notice of services, — something no Episcopalian ever does." "Yes," responded the Rector, "I recognized my blunder the moment the word slipped out, and said to myself, 'my friend Mr. P—— will not allow me to forget that.'"

The first year of the rectorship in Newark was perhaps the happiest in all respects of Dr. Meier-Smith's life. The enthusiasm natural to so radical a change, made after years of perplexing thought, pervaded all his work. He was just forty years of age, and in full physical and intellectual vigor. Newark is so near the metropolis that it was easy for him to renew old associations with relatives and friends, and to fall into the large professional circle of the great city. While the prospective life looked very bright, the thought would sometimes come as a check, "surely such unalloyed happiness cannot last."

Newark proved to be an attractive place of residence from a social point of view. An intelligent and refined circle of families enjoyed the informal and intimate intercourse which results from the traditions of two or three generations of friendship. The new Rector of Trinity was soon made at home, not only in the households connected with his own parish, but in many others.

He had valued friends of years standing among the Presbyterian clergymen, and they, with the Episcopal clergy of the city, offered him a cordial welcome, and with all these fellow-laborers he enjoyed the pleasantest fraternal intercourse during his residence in Newark. Bishop Odenheimer, a man of genial manner and great kindness of heart, was always an affectionate friend, and Dr. Meier-Smith became sincerely attached to him.

Among the clergy of the Diocese, with whom he became especially intimate, were Rev. Dr. Clark, of Elizabeth, Rev. Dr. Abercrombie, of Jersey City, and Rev. Dr. Gray, then of Bergen Point, and afterward for many years Dean of the Divinity School in Cambridge, Massachusetts. All of these much loved friends have entered into rest.

Dr. Meier-Smith's hospitality and enjoyment in the entertainment of guests at his own fireside and table found ample scope for exercise during his residence in Newark, as the rectory of Trinity Church was a natural rallying point, not only for the clergy of the Diocese of New Jersey, but for bishops and clergymen from other parts of the country.

Almost a stranger in the Church, he thought himself much favored in occupying a position which gave him many opportunities for extending acquaintance, and forming friendships which remained unbroken throughout his life.

The increasing congregations of the first year, and the hearty assistance given by the parish to the Rector's efforts to enlarge the influence of Trinity Church, were all that he could have desired.

Dr. Meier-Smith entered the Episcopal Church in a season of much internal agitation. The lines were closely drawn between High and Low Churchmen. The traditions of old Trinity were with the latter party, though "radicals" were not to be found. The Rector identified himself with Low Churchmen, but not with extremists, with whom he had no sympathy. He had not left Congregationalism to assist in bringing unchurchly ideas of either order or doctrine into the old historic Church.

One of the vestrymen who had been influential in calling him watched him anxiously, fearing that from inexperience he might be unsuccessful in a time which tried the tact and wisdom of mature sons of the Church. At the close of the first month's service he wrote to his Rector as follows : —

" . . . Allow me to thank you for all your sermons so far, especially for the very striking discourses of to-day. It was evident to me the first Sunday, that we were most fortunate in selecting you as our Rector, and that all you needed for complete appreciation was to ' get the range ' of the congregation. Such sermons as those of to-day, so practical, so close, so pungent, show that you have not been long in seeing what class of preaching suited us best. I do not know that I ever heard sermons I admired more. Do not be afraid of tiring us. Give us *all* of your sermons."

Church Unity was not then as prominently before the minds of Christians as it is to-day, and Episcopalians held little fraternal intercourse with other churches. The various denominations of Newark, during the autumn of 1866, arranged a course of sermons upon this subject, and Dr. Meier-Smith was invited to preach one of the series as a representative of the Episcopal Church.

He was not a little surprised to find some members of his Vestry objecting strongly to his appearance in the Methodist Church, where the sermons were to be delivered. He, however, accepted the invitation, and preached to a crowded congregation, among whom were many of his parishioners; and the expressions of surprise and gratification with the wisdom and tact of the discourse, and with its broad and catholic spirit, were significant, as showing that the doctrine taught was seldom heard in the Church. A friend who had tried to dissuade him from preaching the sermon, said afterward, "I am not convinced that Dr. Meier-Smith ought to have preached at all on that subject, but if it was to have been done, mortal man could not have done it better." A few days afterward the same gentleman wrote to him : —

"Do you ever lend your manuscript? And if you do, will you lend me your 'Unity' sermon of last Sunday evening? I want to read it over. I congratulate you most sincerely on that effort; it could not have been done better by any one, if so well. I wish all your congregation had heard it, and really think it should be published for the good of everybody. No one could object to its spirit, or do aught but admire the skill, judgment, and eloquence with which you presented boldly moderate Episcopal views. I was exceedingly delighted, and so was every Episcopalian there; while 'those of the contrary part' had no cause of complaint, and indeed made none."

The text of this sermon was the command of our Lord, "Go ye into all the world, and preach the Gospel to every creature," and its main thought was the union of various branches of the Church for aggressive work. This, he said, might be accomplished before the time was ripe for organic unity. A note was here struck which was in accord with the aspirations of many Christian hearts, and from time to time its vibrations have been heard. To-day there are indications that it may prove to be the key-note of a grand marching chorus for the "One Army of the One Lord."

A mission in the south part of the city, previously commenced, but for some time suspended, was reopened in the autumn, and services were held in a chapel which was placed under the care of an assistant minister of Trinity Church.

Its growing work was of much importance in the view of the Rector, who was very active in arousing interest in it, and in raising the means for its support. The first Confirmation under his rectorship took place on the Fourth Sunday in Advent, when he presented thirty-five candidates to the Bishop. The service was naturally one of profound interest to him, and a fitting close to a year of such varied and momentous experiences. With devout thanksgiving he acknowledged the gracious guidance which had led him into his present ecclesiastical relations.

There are very few notes to be found in Dr. Meier-Smith's handwriting respecting his Newark rectorship. The compiler of these reminiscences has to rely largely on her own memory and that of her children. She is most thankful that her husband counted her worthy to be the sharer of his inmost thoughts and purposes and hopes. Slow to speak freely of these to even intimate friends, it seemed always a pleasure and relief to him to share every interest with the one on whose entire sympathy he knew he could always rely. Nothing, from the sermon he was composing to the weightiest matter of general church interest, was withheld from her; and she will be pardoned for believing that she is a faithful witness, as she writes of his views and methods of work. Among other expressions of satisfaction with the new relations was one frequently heard from his lips. " I am astonished that I have so little impression of strangeness. In fact, I feel as if I had come *home!*" His position as Rector of one of the largest parishes in the Diocese impelled him to a prominence he never sought, and which he would gladly have avoided while yet a novice in the Church. In his own estimation his parish offered a sufficient field for all his powers, and he would have been well content, had duty permitted him, to give little attention to outside matters. In his study, work was somewhat changed. Many old sermons were laid aside as unsuitable; others were re-written, and with especial enjoyment preparation was made to follow the course of the Christian Year. No pulpit work could be more congenial to him than that which was called forth by the successive seasons of the Church. Preaching the Gospel as manifested in the Life that is the Light of the World, was a mission which kindled all his enthusiasm.

Early in the year 1867, a mission in East Newark was revived, and in all directions parish work was enlarged. Earnest personal labor for individuals, and sermons with reference to Confirmation marked the Lenten season. The Rector's high ideal of the consecrated life was fervently presented in familiar addresses, and the effect was seen in the increasing congregations at the daily services, and in the number presenting themselves for Confirmation. Dr. Meier-Smith's revered friends, Bishops McIlvaine and Lee during this season were guests at the rectory, and preached to his people. There were sixty communicants added to the church in the first year of Dr. Meier-Smith's rectorship, a second Confirmation taking place at Easter. The Diocesan Convention was the scene of some excitement, parties in the Diocese taking opposite sides on the questions which were agitating the Church. A memorial was presented by Hon. Cortlandt Parker, praying the next General Convention to take steps toward legislation to arrest the Ritualistic movement. This received many signatures, but it also met with very strong opposition. Dr. Meier-Smith was at this time a member of a club composed of prominent Low Churchmen, which met at the office of the Evangelical Knowledge Society, of which Dr. Dyer was secretary. Here were brought forward by men of radical Evangelical views, their objections to the statements of the standards of the Church regarding Orders and Sacraments, and to the " Romanizing germs " in the Prayer Book, as they styled various parts of the Ritual and Service. Dr. Meier-Smith was often appealed to as a new-comer, and sometimes with expressions of wonder that he could have chosen to enter a Church within whose fold some of her own children found so much that was dangerous. Sympathy was expressed for the disappointment he must already feel, and on one occasion he responded to such remarks with the question, " Brethren, where would you go if you left the Church ? " The answer was given by one, " Perhaps into the good old Presbyterian fold, where we would be at least safe from Romanizing views of Orders and Sacraments." " Allow me to read you something," he replied, and stepping to the book-case he took down a volume, and read statements of doctrine respecting baptism, the Lord's Supper, and the ministry. " How does that strike you ? " he asked. " Worse than our own standards," said one. " Rank Popery," said another. " Where did you get that ? " " From the venerable Westminster Confession of Faith on which I was brought up," he replied. " You can hardly expect me to find fault with the doctrines of the Church of my adoption and my mature choice, when assuredly I could never have entered it, had it not been essentially the same on these vital points with the Church of my nurture." Expressing great astonishment, these good brethren then declared that there was nothing left for them to do but to form a new sect, which result some of them not very long afterward were prominent in accomplishing.

The Rev. Charles E. McIlvaine, a son of the Bishop, and a son-in-law of Bishop Lee, was called, during the summer of this year, to the charge of one of the chapels. A warm attachment grew up between the Rector and Mr. McIlvaine. Their relations were always harmonious, and Mr. McIlvaine's work was lovingly appreciated. Of a singularly frank and affectionate nature, he was greatly beloved by all his friends and parishioners, and most sincerely mourned, when yet in his young manhood he was called to a higher service and the rest of Paradise.

In the autumn of 1867, the Evangelical Societies held meetings in Philadelphia. Dr. Meier-Smith was one of the speakers, and while in sympathy with the object of the meetings, he deplored the radical spirit and uncharitable criticism displayed by many present. Approaches toward secession were made by some fiery speakers, and near the close of one of the meetings the venerable Bishops of Ohio and Delaware entered the church, and listened to some of the " Disunion " appeals. One after the other, these veteran leaders in the cause of Evangelical truth arose, and in language of dignified eloquence, sternly rebuked the disturbers of the peace of the Church, amid the profoundest silence on the part of the great congregation. The scene was one never to be forgotten. The stand taken by these honored fathers gave great encouragement to Dr. Meier-Smith to maintain firmly his position, which he believed a thoroughly consistent one, of non-partisanship in connection with pronounced Evangelical convictions.

This year closed with every prospect of increasing influence and usefulness, both in Trinity parish and in the relations of its Rector to the Church at large. A shadow was however falling over the home, as an unexpected cause of anxiety appeared, in the failing health of his son. This seemed to be owing to overwork in preparation for college, and to fatigue and exposure connected with a long daily journey to his school in New York. Parents and physicians expected a rapid improvement from a break in study, and this for a time was the case.

Early in 1868, the cause of solicitude increased, and aroused the gravest fears for the future. And here, as this record of memories has been prepared for those who have known much of the years of anxiety which followed, it seems fitting to speak briefly of the trial which overshadowed so many years of Dr. Meier-Smith's life. The fond hopes for the future of this only son. which the bright promise of his early years had awakened, were from this time gradually resigned, as year after year the sad truth was realized that an invalid life was to be his portion. The responsive temperament of the tender father suffered keenly; and with alternations of hope and fear,—often with a perfect recovery apparently at hand, the hope aroused only to be followed by disappointment,—his life became heavily weighted with care and sorrow.

No memorial of him could be complete which failed to recognize the effect upon his life and work of the experience of these years of anxiety. The strain upon his sympathies, and the unremitting effort to find relief for the suffering invalid, added much to the sense of burden and responsibility which must ever press upon a faithful clergyman. Thank God, he was permitted to see in his later years such progress toward restoration as to afford him much relief from care, and the comfort of hope. To the brave endurance and Christian submission with which an almost life-long trial has been borne by the chief sufferer, a word of loving tribute may be permitted. The lesson of such a life has been felt by all who have come under its influence, and his parents have ever borne grateful witness to the countless ways in which he has been a help and blessing during the long years of his disability.

XII.

THE FIRST RECTORSHIP; TRINITY CHURCH, NEWARK.

1868–1871.

THE conflict between the radical men of opposite parties in the Church increased in bitterness in the early part of the year 1868, and it was difficult to maintain a position of moderate and conservative Churchmanship. The Rector of Trinity was expected by some in his own parish, and by others without, to espouse the cause of the discontented Evangelical Party. The "Protestant Churchman," of New York, a weekly journal, was placed in the hands of an editorial committee of five, of whom Dr. Meier-Smith was one. He understood, when he accepted a place in the management, that the paper was to fairly represent the views of the Evangelical men of the conservative wing, as well as of those who were earnestly advocating changes. But this proved to be a mistake, and he retained his position but a few months, unwilling to be refused the privilege of appearing under his own signature, in defence of the policy of consideration and comprehensiveness in which he believed, and which he thought best expressed the spirit of the Church.

During Lent of this year, Bishops McIlvaine, Lee, and Randall, visited the rectory and preached in Trinity Church. Their influence, and Bishop Randall's eloquent presentation of the needs of his great missionary jurisdiction, were a help to the Rector in sustaining firmly the work of the Church Boards. While he gave his aid and influence to the voluntary societies, he thought that loyal Churchmen should support the work under the charge of the whole Church, and called for the offerings of his parish for the Board of Missions, as well as for the other organizations.

The "Record of Services" for this year indicates the subjects which engrossed the minds of thoughtful Episcopalians at the time: "What is Baptismal Regeneration?" "The Scripturalness of the Liturgy," "The Church System showing Christ," "The Ritualistic Movement." Two sermons and several addresses were given to awaken interest in Foreign Missions, a subject always near his heart, and one the importance of which he thought the Church had failed to keep prominently before her members.

The class of fifty confirmed in Holy Week was one of much promise to the Rector. A large proportion were young people between fifteen and thirty years of age, whose regular attendance at the Confirmation classes, and earnest purpose of Christian life, testified to the faithful instruction of their pastor.

His work seemed to himself so free from sensationalism and so unobtrusive, that it was a matter of surprise to Dr. Meier-Smith to find that he was watched with marked interest by some prominent clergymen and laymen. From some of these friends he received during this year a number of letters which greatly strengthened him in his position and work. His modesty would not permit him to assume any other reasons for these tokens of kindly regard than the prominence of his position in the Diocese of New Jersey, and the fact of his recent entrance into the Church, — considerations of some weight in a time of unusual conflict within the Church.

When the time for the summer vacation came, he went with his family to Lake George. In the enjoyment of the pure air and inspiring surroundings, renewed vigor came to the invalid for whom the past months had been filled with so much anxiety. Upon the return to Newark in September, a complete recovery seemed at hand, in view of which a reluctant consent was given by his parents to their son's desire to resume his studies, but cautiously as this began, it was a fatal mistake, as a few weeks' experiment proved.

In October, 1868, the General Convention met in New York. The sessions were of much interest from the general excitement upon the subject of Ritualism, and from the attitude taken by some of the pronounced agitators. The petition praying for legislative action before alluded to as prepared for the Diocesan Convention of New Jersey, was presented. Though it received some support, many who were relied upon to promote it, declined to do so, and it was referred to a committee and indefinitely postponed.

Those who recall Dr. Meier-Smith's work during the year 1869, speak especially of the influence upon it of the domestic sorrow which grew deeper as the winter advanced. His sympathetic temperament, strained by the solicitude he felt, and the care which fell upon him, entered as never before into the sorrows of others. Never was the faithful pastor so fully able to minister to the various forms of trouble he met in his large parish. Sermons came fresh from a heart learning precious lessons through its own experience. "I know how to speak to sufferers as never before," he exclaimed to his wife. "It seems to me that I must have made a miserable failure of it before; I have had so little idea what real affliction could be."

The Lenten days of 1869 were very anxious ones at the rectory. Early in March a rally of strength followed a serious prostration in the condition of the invalid, but again, during Holy Week, there occurred a sudden failure, the heart being much affected. Good Friday was a day of sad watching and earnest prayer, as the father and mother realized that they might be called upon to resign this only son.

When Dr. Meier-Smith read, during the Morning Service, the passage from the Lesson commencing, "Because thou hast not withheld thy son, thine only son," the emotion and tenderness with which the words were pronounced, touched all present, and many hearts were uplifted in the prayer that the young life might be given back to those to whom it was so dear. Before Easter dawned there was an encouraging change, and marked improvement followed.

The "Record of Services" this year shows earnest presentation of the subjects of personal repentance and faith in Christ. The Rector was cheered by many interviews sought by those who were impressed by his faithful instruction, and a large Confirmation class was the ingathering. After Easter the effect began to appear of three years' arduous work in a new field, added to the burden of the domestic anxiety of the past months. Dr. Meier-Smith suffered much with his head and eyes, and with loss of nervous strength. His Vestry, unsolicited, voted him a six-months' vacation free from all responsibility for the parish, but he declined to accept more than four months. This vacation, commencing after Trinity Sunday, was passed for the most part in the White Mountains and at Lake George.

He returned much benefited by the long rest, and cheered by signs of improvement in the condition of his son.

The parish missions gave much promise at this time, and as party feeling had somewhat lulled since the General Convention, the Church year opened auspiciously with the prospect of enlarging work on all lines. During Advent, lectures were commenced for working people, of whom a large number had some nominal connection with the parish, though few came to church. After Epiphany, 1870, the lectures given were upon historical or scientific subjects, popularly treated with illustrations. Through this work Dr. Meier-Smith made personal acquaintance among a class before unreached, and the fruit was seen in a greatly increased attendance upon the Sunday evening services, when he preached simple and often extempore sermons. The subjects of written sermons, as recorded, indicate the thought and experience born of the many months of solicitude. The " Resurrection of the Body," "The Life after Death," " The Intermediate State," " The Eternal Life begun Here," were among the topics of sermons preached between Easter and Whitsuntide.

He wrote to Dr. Dyer, under date of May 1, 1870, —

. . . To-day I complete four years of my rectorship in this old parish.

They have been blessed years, for which I thank God, and under God, you, most of all men, my dear friend and brother, for the kind introduction which placed me here. In my own home there has been great sorrow, as the Lord knows. But in my parish work there has not been a serious obstacle to encounter. If only I could be the instrument of making my dear people know and love the Saviour better, and do more for him, I should be the happiest parish minister alive. I would n't go back to Congregationalism for a good deal!

Good-night.   Ever affectionately yours,

MATSON MEIER-SMITH.

The next letter was written shortly after the well-remembered case of "Intrusion," to which it makes playful allusion.

Dr. Dyer had officiated at a marriage in Trinity Church, and sent the fee to the Rector.

TRINITY RECTORY, NEWARK, May 28, 1870.

DEAR DR. DYER, — "Damages" can't be paid under the law as I read it. True, the "Courts" decided that trampoosing into other parishes and preaching in conventicles was trespass, — *in re* Stubbs & Boggs *vs.* Tyng, — but this was not done in conventicle. Cathedrals and those Churches which are Cathedrals *ab excellentia*, by all sound law are not Methodist meeting-houses.

It is therefore not clear that I could have presented you even had you preached after climbing in at the Chancel window; the thing being done in Church and therefore presumably with the consent of the Rector, or his connivance at least.

A Rector to insure the protection of Canon law in the premises must show that the Chancel window in that case had wire netting outside (*Hoffman*, p. 22); else he does not take ordinary care of his rights and cannot recover (Bishop *Cardozo*, p. 350).

Now, had you preached in spite of my prohibition, or under circumstances which exhibited undue violence of determination to effect entry on your part, I might accept the "damages" as a sort of settlement, — being very unwilling to enter upon litigation, — lest, like Stubbs, etc., I get my foot in.

But under present circumstances the case is not so clear. You could show that I was absent from my post, and therefore *could* not do the work. You could probably show that I was absent with full knowledge that the parties wished to be married. Therefore, that I *would* not do the work.

On the whole I think it safer that you pocket the damages, — for I won't.

By the way, though I have heretofore acted on your principle and believe it to be a good one, you are the first clergyman who has ever proffered me the "fee." Give my love to Bishop Potter, and tell him I don't mean to give him a chance to reprimand you. I will give your love to my Bishop, and tell him that *Stubbs*-town stops before Newark begins.

Truly yours,

M. M.-S.

P. S. I have since writing learned that my church has been degraded into a meeting-house, the Rev. Dr. ——,[1] of New York, having speechified in it last Monday night! But that was after your officiating therein.

Referring to a probable invitation to a responsible post other than that of a parish clergyman, Dr. Meier-Smith wrote to Dr. Dyer from Lake George, in the summer of this year: ". . . Now, that is the whole of the matter. Understand that I am not and do not seek to be a candidate for that position. If I were called to it or to any other position in the Church on the ground

---

[1] A distinguished Presbyterian clergyman.

of a specific fitness, I should most earnestly and faithfully consider the call . . .

"You say truly that I love the parochial work and the pulpit. My whole heart is in this. My only ambition is to be successful in this, — a wise and faithful pastor and rector, a good and influential preacher of the everlasting Gospel. While God spares my life and strength this alone I covet. When He lays me aside from this, then I gratefully take whatever else He permits me to do."

The six weeks' rest in summer was chiefly spent at Lake George, where there were many of his friends and parishioners. At this time his wife's health was much affected, and some alarming symptoms caused serious fears during the ensuing autumn. He began to be apprehensive that without relief from his home anxieties, he could not bear much longer his heavy public responsibilities. The fear deepened into conviction, and the year 1871 opened overshadowed by the apprehension that he must seek relief from the charge so happily entered upon five years before, and which had been in all parish aspects so successful. He was in doubt whether to ask for a protracted leave of absence, or to resign completely, and he conferred freely on the subject with friends both in and out of his parish.

Mrs. Meier-Smith's health did not improve during the winter, and medical opinion was decided that for both her and their son a radical change was the only hope.

Early in March, 1871, the Rector's resignation was sent to his Vestry. The closing portion of the Letter of Resignation is here given: —

TRINITY RECTORY, March 8, 1871.

. . . Were I to consult only the promptings of my heart, I should frankly and trustfully ask you to grant me a leave of absence for a year, and hope to return to friends and a parish I so dearly love, to give you thereafter my best services and years. But my judgment is against my heart in this case, and I find myself compelled to act upon the painful conviction of duty, and to lay before you my resignation of the rectorship, to take effect after Easter, and if you please the first Sunday after Easter. Let me, dear friends, here record my grateful sense of all your kindness and generous affection. Our intercourse, personal and official, has been unmarred by a single disagreement. And I cannot conceive of a more cordial and agreeable relationship between a Rector and his parish than this which it has been my pleasant lot to sustain during the five years which will expire near the time of my departure. I most devoutly commend you, and all whom you represent, to the blessing of our God and Saviour, and shall ever be in holiest bonds,

Your loving friend,

MATSON MEIER-SMITH.

Before action was taken upon the resignation, his friend Mr. Cortlandt Parker wrote to him:—

"The Vestry are universally and deeply regretful, and will only acquiesce because they believe it is a wise decision for you to stay away a year or more, and they cannot see their way clear to offer so prolonged a leave of absence. Whatever men can do to testify their high personal regard and warm appreciation of your services, will be done."

Although convinced of the wisdom of his decision, the necessity was hard to meet. Very many of his large congregation had become dear personal friends, and the unbroken harmony of the years of his rectorship only made the wrench the more painful.

This, his first charge in the Church of his adoption,

was ever very near his heart, and to the end of his life he felt a deep interest in its welfare.

When the Vestry accepted the resignation, they accompanied their action upon it by the resolutions which follow : —

" *Resolved,* That the Wardens and Vestry of Trinity Church, Newark, and the Parish, part from their Rector, Rev. Dr. Meier-Smith, with the greatest personal esteem and regret. The five years he has spent among us have been years of perfect peace and unanimity. No dissension exists or has existed in the Parish. Its general situation is eminently prosperous. He has preached a pure Gospel. He has done it with ability of the highest rank. As a theologian, sound, clear, and learned ; as a man, genial, kind, and generous ; the impersonation in his daily life and walk of the gentleman and the Christian. He has adopted the plans of the Church with hearty approbation, and carried them out with zeal and enthusiasm. We trust that health may soon return to his beloved family, and that he himself, rested and renovated by absence from habitual toil, may be hereafter even more successful in preaching that Gospel in which alone he seeks to glory.

" *Resolved,* That in view of the expenses to which Dr. Meier-Smith may be subjected, and as a testimony of the regard felt for him by the Vestry and congregation, the sum of one thousand dollars be paid him in addition to his salary up to the time his resignation takes place."

Among notices in the religious and secular journals, one was peculiarly gratifying as expressive of the kindly feeling still cherished for a former associate by some Presbyterian friends.

From the N. Y. Evangelist, April, 1871.

" Some of our readers have very pleasant recollections of the Rev. Dr. Meier-Smith, and probably always read his name of late years with the comfortable reflection that the Episcopal body really owe us Presbyterians a good turn in consideration of the excellent stock of which he comes, and the well-furnished condition in which we, or our Congregational brethren, handed him over into their preserve, when he signified a wish to go. He has been very useful in that Church, always preaching an excellent sermon, even in the Presbyterian sense, and rendering the prayers better than most 'to the manner born.' He has been the esteemed and efficient Rector of Trinity Church, Newark, for five years past, but has recently, for reasons of health, sent in his resignation."

The resignation was to take effect on the first Sunday after Easter, April 16. At the Confirmation which occurred on the Sunday before Easter, thirty candidates were presented. Of the services of the last Sunday his wife wrote to a friend : —

"Our last Communion with this dear church! Matson had appointed an extra celebration especially for all who had been confirmed during his rectorship. The church was very crowded. He preached no sermon, but made a very tender and beautiful address, which he found it hard to get through with. I did not go out in the evening. I could not bear the strain of any more partings."

At the close of the " Record of Services " before entering the Episcopal Church, it may be remembered that he wrote, " Here endeth the First Lesson." The closing words concerning his work in Newark are, " Here endeth the First Lesson of the Evening Prayer." The words seem to imply that while in the very prime of mature manhood, he discerned in the near future the shadows of even-tide. The first heavy sorrow of his life had come to him while in Newark. Nor this alone, for he was realizing keenly the suffering of a great professional disappointment. To relinquish, at the end of five years, his first work in the Church of his mature choice was a severe trial. While his sunny and affectionate temperament made him yet the stay and comfort of those dependent upon him, life and future work had lost already the brilliant colors with which they had been invested five years before. The hour for "Evening Prayer" had struck, and he heard in the distance the tolling of the Vesper bell.

From the "Record of Services": "The impaired health of my wife and son, and my own need of repose, the result of the combined toil and trial for three years past, led me to resign my charge as Rector of Trinity Church, and to plan a visit to Europe with my family. The resignation was offered March 8, 1871, and accepted, to take effect the first Sunday after Easter, April 16.

"During my ministry in Newark, I have preached and lectured five hundred and twenty-six times. The aggregate of preaching has been twice every Sunday for five years.

"I have baptized one hundred children and twenty-six adults.

"I have married fifty-one couples.

"I have buried eighty-seven persons, and presented for Confirmation two hundred and twenty-three persons, more than one fourth of those presented in the parish for forty years past."

Extracts from two letters from Bishop Odenheimer show the affectionate relations existing between the Bishop and Dr. Meier-Smith:—

March 16, 1870.

MY LOVING AND BELOVED FRIEND AND REVEREND BROTHER, — Your good and kind words affect my heart and make me love you more than ever. My chief concern is that your noble boy's health should be still feeble, but I pray God to have him and all of you in His holy keeping, and to comfort your heart and home by the restoration to health of one so dear to you.

BURLINGTON, NEW JERSEY, March 22, 1871.

DEAREST DOCTOR MEIER-SMITH, — Your letter awaited my return home from a visitation, and I hasten to express my very sincere regret that I am to lose your most acceptable and efficient services, even for a short time, in my Diocese. I know that you have good ground for your action, and I can only submit, hoping that it will not be long before you will return to your country and Diocese, refreshed in strength, with your wife and son renewed and invigorated by foreign travel.

I have no personal correspondence abroad, but I give you an official letter, which is as full of personal feeling as if I were writing to all the clergy and laity, individually. I hope the letter may be of some little service.

Send it, with your card, and if any one to whom it is sent cares for the Bishop of New Jersey, he will open his heart to one of the best beloved and most honored Presbyters of the Diocese.

God bless you and your wife and children !

Ever affectionately your Bishop and friend,
W. H. ODENHEIMER.

Many letters of affectionate leave-taking were received by Dr. Meier-Smith. A few sentences from one are given here : —

. . . And now, my dear Doctor, I have only to add the cheap but earnest expression of my highest respect and sincere love for you in the long relation which we have occupied, — regarding you as my pastor, my friend, and my most congenial and cultured associate in the world. It has been my loss that I have enjoyed so little of a companionship that was most grateful and cheering to me.

For all your kindness to me and my children how can I thank you? Especially on their account, for whose sake I have so often thanked you in my heart of hearts, that you have so considerately given them the advantage of your refined home atmosphere.

.   .   .   .

May God bless you for it all, and may He spare us to meet again, when I pray that you may be able to look upon every member of your dear family restored to perfect health. I thank God for every remembrance of you, and so may He have you in His holy keeping.

Your friend,   JAMES S. MACKIE.

Some months after Dr. Meier-Smith's death the same friend wrote as follows: —

". . . I thank you very much for your kind remembrance in sending to us the copy of official tributes to your dear husband.

"Mrs. MacKie and I read it with loving and tender interest, and yet could not feel that, from all the various sources of appreciation and love, the beautiful character of your husband had been justly portrayed,— not from lack of appreciation, but simply because he was 'one among ten thousand and altogether lovely.'

"In all my large intercourse with men, I never met one who had the elements of human sympathy and attractiveness so largely developed as in my dear old Rector. I never met a man whose confidence and esteem I so yearned to possess as his. . . ."

The two letters which follow are tributes to the memory of their former Rector, from other beloved parishioners: —

From Hon. Cortlandt Parker.

NEWARK, October, 1889.

. . . I was very fond of Dr. Meier-Smith. He was a very manly man. He knew how to feel for his fellow-man. He thoroughly loved the right and the truth. He had not a mean hair in his head. He was a real Christian, not in word or pretension, but in works as well as faith, and he was a very able man. He was really great when occasion nerved and excited him. One of the finest speeches I ever heard was an impromptu from him. I built my conception of what he could do by finding then what he did. . . .

I suppose that he was among the soundest and most learned theologians we ever had. He certainly was a deep, strong thinker of purest Evangelical doctrine, utterly free from cant, charitable to all other Christians, and to all shades of true Christian belief. His mental structure was somewhat unexcited. He was never known in his fulness, but when something greatly stirred him. I saw him on two or three of those occasions, and then he was great. I remember one especially, the funeral of Mr. W. R——. No one expected an address; Dr. Meier-Smith did not expect to make one; but as the service ended the spirit moved him, and he poured out one of the most touching and tender sermons that any one ever heard. His delivery then, too, was eloquent in the extreme. Episcopal congregations require the clergymen to do everything; those of other denominations rather wish to do most things themselves. Dr. Meier-Smith, not broken in to the new demand, did not at first make himself fully known to his people generally; but after awhile they found him out: they found how tender were his sensibilities, how ready his hand, how inexhaustible was his pity and his charity. He sometimes did himself injustice by concealment of his inner self.

I remember one incident which affected me deeply. I had engaged to accompany him on the errand of administering the Communion to a young man, once a student of mine, who from being an unbeliever had been brought, largely through Dr. Meier-Smith's influence, to faith in the Death and Atonement of his Lord, and who was dying with consumption. He lived a mile or more away from the rectory. We went; the service was performed ; he gave the poor fellow his blessing ; and then as he entered my wagon he said, " Pray, if you please, drive home a little fast, I left Mrs. Meier-Smith quite ill when I came away."   I reproached him for going, but was met by the quiet remark, " I did not know how long this poor man might have to live."   Fortunately, when he got home things were better than when he left.

But I must not spend time in dwelling upon this sadly pleasing theme.   I will only add that Dr. Meier-Smith was a manly, tender-hearted, Christian gentleman of high intellectual calibre, keeping himself in the back-ground by the avoidance of all pretensions and by a sort of dislike to self-exhibition.   Knowingly, he neglected no duty.   He was especially beloved by the poor to whom he was a faithful pastor and friend.

From Mr. Bloomfield J. Miller.

" I desire to write a few lines as a slight tribute to my dear old Rector and friend, Dr. Meier-Smith, from one who loved and esteemed him for his uniformly kind, gentle, charitable, and Christian-like characteristics.   To know him was to love him.

" He was one who could be relied upon to rejoice with you in prosperity, and sympathize with you in adversity.   His ear was always open to those in trouble, and his material help was always freely extended to those who needed it.

" In the truest sense of the word he was a Christian gentleman, and when the Great Father called him, every one who had had the privilege of his acquaintance felt a deep sense of great and irreparable loss.

" The young and the old alike found in him a friend who would inspire them with hope and courage in the dark and dreary days, and who would extend the kindliest mantle of charity to cover the sins of the past, and a strong right hand to lift them up to higher planes."

From Rev. Montgomery R. Hooper, an assistant minister of Trinity Church, during Dr. Meier-Smith's rectorship, the following appreciative letter was received: —

" . . . The death of your dear husband was a great blow to me. One more of my old and true friends is gone. Though I had not seen Dr. Meier-Smith for nearly twenty years, I felt just as sure of him and just as near to him as if I saw him daily.

" His rare qualities of gentleness and kindness and genial tolerance impressed me deeply when as a young man I worked under him, and now that I have seen more of the world and of men, these qualities seem rarer and more valuable than ever.

" I had an entire confidence in your husband, and would have confided in him as if he were a brother, and my regard and love for him have deepened and strengthened as I have learned more of life."

XIII.

LETTERS FROM EUROPE.

1871.

ON the 22d of April, 1871, Dr. Meier-Smith and his family sailed for Southampton, England, in the steamship " Rhein."

Many of his late parishioners came to bid farewell and to offer their affectionate wishes. An absence of eighteen months was contemplated. The time was a memorable one, the Franco-German War having closed but three months before. The Commune reigned in Paris, and the news of the fall of the Column of the Place Vendôme was flashed across the channel on the day of the arrival at Southampton.

United Germany, flushed with victory, was at a high pitch of enthusiasm, and hardly a more interesting time could have been chosen to visit her historic cities. Continental travel on some familiar lines was, however, impossible, and this party of wanderers accomplished what few Americans have attempted, a somewhat extended trip in Europe without a sight of Paris, a visit to which city is averred to be the highest aspiration of some of their compatriots.

Notes of the ensuing months are given in extracts from Dr. Meier-Smith's letters, which were written in journal form and in careful detail, for the entertainment of his parents. To quote largely from the letters of description would be superfluous in a day of almost universal foreign travel, and only such selections are made as, from the expression of his impressions or from his chosen view-points, appear especially characteristic of the writer.

SOUTHAMPTON, ENGLAND, May 2, 1871.

MY EVER DEAR PARENTS, — Never more dear, or quite so dear as now that the Atlantic rolls between us! Thanks be to God, we are safely here, landing about six o'clock this morning.

England! How strange it is to me to think that I am so far from home and the dear ones there! They say London was never so fearfully full. The French troubles and the International Exposition have drawn thither immense crowds. I have but a moment to add to Mary's letter, and must say good-by, with all its meaning. God bless and keep you, and my dear sister's family, and us, through our journeyings, — and how gladly and gratefully shall we meet again!

Your loving son,

M. M.-S.

SOUTHAMPTON, May 4, 1871.

MY DEAR PARENTS, — Was it your wedding day yesterday? Oh, those happy years you have had, full of blessings, though some of them were sorrows for the day! God grant that the years may be lengthened yet, and your golden wedding may be this side the golden gate! It seems as if I had been quite a while in England, but I remember that I only landed two days ago. Our cousins, Mr. and Mrs. George N. Dana, of Boston, have run down from London to meet us here, and last night our brother and sister, Mr. and Mrs. Arthur W. Parsons, joined us. They have gone to-day to the

Isle of Wight, whither we purpose to follow them. So we have felt quite home-like and jolly. To-day we all dined in our private parlor, and it was a reminder of old times. Emily has sent off a letter to-day telling of our visit to the venerable ruins of Netley Abbey. This was our first ruin, and we think a great deal of it.

"The Cottage," Bonchurch,
Isle of Wight, May 8.

Here we are, a merry family party, at housekeeping on the Isle of Wight! We are possessors for a few weeks, more or less, of a house on the estate of Lady Pringle, sister of the Marquis of Breadalbane. Earl Fitz-William was the last tenant. Who these big-bugs are I do not know, and certainly do not care; but the names are very tremendous, and so I give them. We arrived here last evening, and the morning has revealed the beauty of the place to our delighted eyes. "The Cottage," a large house in Old English style, looks out upon the Channel, and off toward the horizon and France.

Lady Pringle's agent furnishes everything, including silver and servants. Bonchurch is a delightfully secluded spot, though very accessible. It is embowered amid exuberant foliage, enriched with every variety of romantic formation, hill, valley, lofty downs, and deep chines. Every inch of ground is under culture; the fields are framed in hawthorn hedges; the roads, narrow and in perfect order, twist and turn and roll along up hill and down, among cottages and little hamlets, and the loveliest pictures of rural life that mortal eye can desire. Just now I wish I were a poet. Then I might sing, and tell you something of that which we feel, but which is all beyond pen or pencil, unless to him who *nascitur non fit*.

Yesterday was Sunday. How good it was to have a "Sabbath" again! Those two horrible days on shipboard were not Lord's Days. I went with Mary and Emily to the parish church of St. Boniface. It was so home-like, and we had the Holy Communion service. Just as when I was a little boy, ever so wee, I loved to catch my dear mother's hand, and felt safe in the dark, or when taking a walk, so I love now as a man,—and never more did I feel it than I did yesterday,—in that sacrament, to take hold of the hand of the unseen Lord, and feel its throb and warmth, and know the love that sways, and how safe are all interests in Him. In the evening I went to an Independent Chapel, and heard an earl preach,—a layman. Earls do not preach any better than other folk. This one kept saying "in our midst," which barbarism is enough to condemn anybody. This afternoon I visited what must be the smallest church in the world, built in the twelfth century. It was formerly eleven feet broad and twenty-five feet long. It has now been enlarged, and is forty-five feet long. It has its little chancel, pews, a Rector, and a very full congregation.

God bless and keep you all.

LONDON, May 21.

Strange to me it seems to be in this great historic city of the English-speaking people, to look upon the palaces, and edifices of less pretence, and the churches and cathedrals which have been looked upon by kings and common people for so many centuries.

Before closing the Isle of Wight history, I must tell you that we called, with an introduction from Bishop Odenheimer, upon Miss Sewell, the author of "Laneton Parsonage" and several other works for the young. She is a delightful little body, and took us at once into her warm circle. I told her playfully, that *one* thing I did not like in England, — namely, that amid all the beauties surrounding them, the wealthy people appeared to be selfishly exclusive. Around their elegant places they erect stone-walls, from six to ten feet in height, and so not only wall out the view of their own grounds from foot-passengers, but wall off prospects beyond them.

I told her that in America, the wealthy man who adorned his estates did nothing of this kind, but suffered his neighbors and all stragglers by the way to look upon the beautiful creations of his fancy and wealth to their content. And so every man contributed to the general elevation who indulged his own cultivated taste. She laughed, and said it was their national trait to be "John Bull" and exclusive, but she would take me behind the walls, and show me what was concealed, and how the very formation of their island rendered such high walls necessary. And she was as good as her word, for showing that some of the walls were partly terraces, and partly "ha-ha" arrangements, she introduced me to some of the most exquisite pictures and beautiful grounds I ever saw. Among other things, in one garden a little oaken door into what seemed a cavern, opened into a fernery, a little grotto, a hot-house full of various ferns, rich, luxuriant, — making one think of the period when the Carboniferous Age was the way of the world.

The Tower of London.

LONDON, May 23.

[After a description of the usual Tower routine, he says:] By the time we had gone the "round" our guide pointed the way out, and the party which had been led about under his instructions, slowly made their exit from the gates. But my little wife was not at all satisfied. This would not do. There were more things in the Tower of which we had read, and we must see them. The warder said it was impossible to gain access to them except by special order from the governor of the Tower. We must apply to him by letter, and possibly he might issue the order for our admittance. But the governor was just then away from home. I proposed to wait and try again; but Mary asked the ticket master if there were not some way of gaining the point, and he directed us to the "senior yeoman," or "chief warder of the Tower," who was standing at the gate. In very discreet obedience to her commands, I applied to this magnificent looking individual, and told him that we had come thousands of miles to London, and this historic spot, and as Americans, could not abandon our hopes and desires for a glimpse of those things which are rarely shown.

"You shall see them, sir, — I will accompany you myself. The governor is absent, and I can take you everywhere."

So down we went beneath the great White Tower. into the depths, and saw the fearful dungeons, — one in particular, dark as a tomb, wherein Sir Thomas More, and Fischer, the Lord Bishop of Rochester, had been immured, and whence the latter went forth to die. There was another room in another part, where Fischer was also confined, more comfortable, light, and airy, in what is now the governor's house. Our guide put us into one of the dungeons, and bolted us in, so that we had a momentary taste of darkness, powerlessness, and woe.

Thence we ascended, and visited the Bloody Tower, and entered the room wherein the two young Princes were smothered; and near by, the stairway, recently discovered and *unwalled* (to coin a word), down which their dead bodies were thrown.   In this room other murders were committed, — persons of historic note.   In this room Sir Walter Raleigh had quarters for a while more comfortable than the dungeon, and here his son, Carew Raleigh, was born.   From this place we went into the Church, — "St. Peter's," — interesting as the place where lie interred many eminent persons, — as Queens Anne Boleyn and Katherine Howard, Sir Thomas More and Bishop Fischer, Thomas Cromwell, the Earl of Essex, Lady Jane Grey and her husband, and many more.   We stood over some of their graves.   And we went down into the vaults under the Church, among the sleeping places of the illustrious dead.   Then our guide bade us wait in the courtyard a few moments, and presently he conducted us into the governor's house.   To make a retrospective diversion for a moment, — I forgot to speak of what interested and moved me most in examining the Bloody Tower. Near by the chamber of the murdered Princes, we were ushered into a beautiful room, nicely furnished now, the room wherein those Martyr-Reformers, Cranmer, Latimer, and Ridley, held conference touching their course, and their answers which they should make to their Popish persecutors.   That was a holy spot to me.

But to return to the governor's house.   There we entered the room wherein Archbishop Laud — the bigoted, it may be, but sincere High Churchman — was confined, and the window through which he stretched his hands to give his benediction to the Earl of Strafford, who preceded him in the march to execution a year or two. Close to this was the apartment which the venerable Bishop Fischer had occupied, to which I alluded when speaking of the Bloody Tower, and whence he wrote to Sir Thomas Cromwell that he was in need of more comfort for his advanced age, being eighty years old.

We were then ushered into the room wherein Guy Fawkes and his fellow conspirators were tortured and examined concerning their infamous plot, by the Lords and King James. The event is commemorated by a monumental tablet on the wall.

Here, too, is the room through which Lord Nithesdale escaped after his condemnation, arrayed in the garments of his wife, — possibly Jeff. Davis had read the story, — and a shred of the cloak is preserved, as well as a fac-simile pattern of it, which the warder threw on Emily's shoulders.

And we saw the death-warrants, the original papers, elegantly bound, with others of similar purport, in large folio volumes, which consigned to execution many illustrious persons; we marked particularly the names of Lord Russell, Algernon Sidney, and the Duke of Monmouth. We saw too, and handled, the grim axe which was borne, by officers appointed, in front of those who were on trial; its sharp edge turned away from them until they were condemned, but toward them as soon as death sentence was passed, and which was carried in front of them on the way to the block.

These, you will perceive, were things which the majority of travellers do not see. We were greatly favored, and I gladly made a handsome fee-present to the obliging man who gave us this hour and a quarter of attention, instruction, and pleasure.

It was a memorable day's work indeed, so to move among the places where kings and queens, princes and nobles, martyrs of the State, and martyrs of Jesus have moved in ages past, and to look upon the places where they suffered, some of them, and places where others mingled in all the splendor of royal magnificence and display. To feel that I have stood there, — to be able to say, " I was in the room where Cranmer, Latimer, and Ridley conferred and prayed together in those ' days of tribulation,' " — pays for crossing the seas.

To his Sister.

London, June 8.

London, city of such histories, is a great Babel. It is perfectly immense. It has neither beginning, middle, nor end. Miles and miles, straight and crooked, go in what direction you please, and the same dingy and gloomy houses are on either hand, dark gray and smoke-begrimed, or blackish brown and smoky. . . .

Though the signs are English, and the newspapers are printed in English, I am not yet sure what language the people speak. I find many words and sentences which I cannot catch without great effort, and some are beyond me altogether. And the difference between England and America can be felt in many indescribable ways. Take the average middle class which make up the bone and sinew, and in fact the brain of the nation, more or less, and the man of republican institutions is vastly superior to his brother, trained beneath aristocracy and *snobbydom.* I see no middle-class Englishmen who for up-and-down independence and self-conscious manliness are the equals of those in similar grades of life with us. I cannot imagine among Americans, *well-dressed men* dancing attendance on you to open your cab-door, or to look at you get into it, or get out of it, and then touch the hat most menially, and ask for a gift of a penny or a sixpence.

Yet here they do just this, and what wonder all the street loungers in rags, and dozens of little boys, bother you for the same service, — or plague rather, — and similar gifts. The English are a mercenary crowd. From the Earl of Warwick, who charges a shilling for showing his house and grounds, — nominally his house-keeper's perquisite, — down to the boy who brushes your boots, not one John Bull is above taking your extended shilling, or happy unless he gets it. Make all due allowance and subtraction from this sweeping remark, and you will have the fair view of the matter.

LEAMINGTON, June 26.

. . . This morning I took a most delightful walk to Cubbington (odd name), a rural parish, and called upon the clergyman, in company with my brother-in-law, Mr. Parsons. The walk was through fields of grain, and through private property, yet along a regular pathway, laid out and kept in order, with sign-boards, and even lighted and neatly railed in some parts. This pathway is one of the old pathways of England, free from the Roman days, — pathways which no landholder can close, though they go through his premises anywhere and everywhere, whether he will or not. The farmers till the ground on either side, but infringe not a hair's-breadth upon public rights. The passenger may not leave the pathway for the right or the left, it may be, without peril of trespass, but he may roam the kingdom at will, through fields and parks, if only those ancient and sacred ways lead him, safe and undisturbed, be he rich or poor, a gipsy or a foreigner.

11

LEAMINGTON, June 27.

I have taken two more of those delightful English walks. This forenoon, in company with Mary and Emily, I went to Lillington, — my second tramp in that direction. We went into a sweet little church-yard, and read the inscriptions from the grave-stones. There was one quite odd, — a pauper's grave, I suppose, but evidently a pauper whose very friendlessness is his distinction. It ran thus : —

In memory of
William Treen who died 3 Feb., 1810.
Aged 77 years.

" Poorly lived and poorly died,
Poorly buried and no one cried."
" Blessed are the dead which die in the Lord."[1]

This afternoon's ramble was a solitary one. It was along a pathway such as I described yesterday, to " Guy's Cliff," whereof I gave you some account in the previous letter. It was a lovely pathway through fields, among cows and sheep, with the greenest of grass on either side, and the most fragrant perfumes filling the air. The hay-makers were busy, and the mown grass was surpassingly sweet.

"The pathways of the fathers!" I do not wonder that so many good men use this expression, and then follow in ecclesiastical matters all the ideas of their forefathers, as the people of Old England do. For the pathways over their English fields, generations have trodden, and no ways could be more direct, more delightful, or easier for the feet.

I stood again upon a bridge over the Avon, beside an old mill wherein an undershot wheel plashes away, and looked at the elegant mansion of My Lady, the widow

---

[1] This grave is mentioned in Hawthorne's " Our Old Home."

of Lord Percy. And from the public road I gazed again, through the vista of the trees, whose interlacings make a wondrous aisle of Gothic arch, upon another front of the great house; and turning away again to tramp this time over a dusty road and through village streets, I thought of my dear American land and my loved ones and of our free American people and happy homes and open-hearted ways, and my thoughts grew warm, and I leaped forward in them to the time when travel should be over, and I should see those shores again, and once more resume the good work of life.

CHESTER, July 2.

This day I attended service at the Cathedral. It is a venerable old building. Morning service was in the choir. The Lord Bishop, Dr. Jacobson, was preacher. The sermon was very plain and unpretending, but a most delightful one. The music was like all I have heard in English churches, simple, fervent, choral; only, as ringing beneath those lofty arches and through the aisles, very grand and inspiring. At 6.30 P. M. was what is the most popular service among the common people of England; and this, held in the nave, was attended by a very large congregation, the preacher being the Canon Resident, the Rev. Charles Kingsley, a preacher of great force, fervent, pronounced, vigorous, of Saxon words, of sledge-hammer blows, — the most of a speaker I have heard in England; one of whom we should say he had never written or could write a work of fiction, so directly practical is he in thought and expression, were not his writings known and his position established.

EDINBURGH, July 4.

Of all the cities I have seen, this Edinburgh takes the palm. For situation it is unrivalled. Had it the

St. Lawrence flowing by its Castle, as that river sweeps around the rocks upon which the Citadel of Quebec stands, I verily believe nothing could be grander in the world or in all time. After a late breakfast and some private rambles about the streets, we visited the Castle, which stands upon a bold precipitous rock, three hundred and eighty feet above the level of the sea.

. . . Very near the Crown Room was the room of Queen Mary, the bed-chamber, of very small dimensions, in which she gave birth to her son. In the large apartment adjoining was a beautiful portrait of Mary at the age of eighteen, when she was Dauphiness of France, and most surely after seeing this I can credit the family tradition by which my Mary and her mother claim descent from the Royal House.

York Minster.

July 8.

It is simply impossible to communicate the emotions with which I stood in this magnificent temple, and gazed upon the grandeur of its arches, its massive columns, its exquisite beauty of proportions. It is to my mind grander than Westminster. Strength and beauty are in Thy Sanctuary, O Lord of Hosts! We stood at the separation between the choir and the nave, beneath the lofty opening into the tower, just as the great bell of the Minster struck the hour of noon. Never have I heard such sublime reverberations, so sweet, so awful, in their peerless tone. It was like the archangel's trump, and they swelled and rolled through the arches. It was worth crossing the ocean to hear those twelve strokes.

One asks what is the use of these cathedrals? Modern churches are infinitely better for the modern use of

Christian people, doubtless. It is better, too, to multiply now, plainer, smaller, simpler edifices for the extension of the Church of God, and to devote more sums and skill and strength to the diffusion of the Gospel. This I do not doubt. But within these vast piles of everlasting rock what histories have been enacted, what battles for truth been fought and won, what generations of saintly men and women have been trained for Eternal Life! What volumes of prayer have arisen! What displays of God and of Christ have been made! Yes; all these amid many errors too, showing how even in the corrupt ages there has been working the leaven of a vital Christianity, showing that in spite of Satan the gates of hell shall not prevail. I begin to see new meaning in the expression the "One Catholic and Apostolic Church," and in that other, "The Communion of Saints." I grow larger and broader and more catholic of spirit every time I tread those ancient floors.

Cologne, July 18.

As I am writing, — quarter past eight, — the descending sunlight reposes above the turrets of the Cathedral; a little steamer is shooting down the Rhine, which drives along so vigorously northward, bearing Alpine snows to the sea; people are leisurely travelling over the bridge of boats; the band of the hotel is discoursing sweet music in the garden beneath us; people are gathering for their little treats of coffee or salad or punch or beer. Everything again, as last night, is *so* German. And what an air these men have! They salute you so grandly. They step so proudly. The helmeted soldiers and — the band is now playing " America " — the sentinels look so aloft. The style of the conqueror pleases them and becomes them. They are proud of " our Fritz," and proud of

Wilhelm, and proud of the German Empire, now a fact realized. And so, I confess, is *my* German blood.

This morning in the Cathedral, where we went to look at the skulls of the wise men, the young priest who was our guide began to explain in German. I said, "parlez-vous Français," to indicate that we could comprehend French better than German. He at once with an ineffable disdain said, "*Do you speak English ?*" and then proceeded to enlighten us in our native tongue most admirably.

COBLENTZ ON THE RHINE, July 21.

MY EVER DEAR PARENTS, — I am writing this in the Giant's Hotel, why so called I know not, seated in a cosey parlor, from which the outlook is upon the beautiful Rhine, the famous bridge of boats being at our feet, and opposite aloft, Germany's proud fortress, — Ehrenbreitstein, the "broad stone of honor." This Castle is a magnificent stronghold, reposing on a lofty and precipitous hill, defiant of all armies, serene beneath the imperial ensign of the United Germany and the "Kaiser und König," whom the German people almost adore.

To-day I made an excursion to see a physician, Doctor Unschuld, at Neuenahr, a small watering-place on the Ahr, a few miles from Remagen, which is on the Rhine about halfway between Coblentz and Bonn. The whole vicinity thus visited in every direction is most charming. The hills are clad with vines to the very tops. And significantly do the fields utter hygienic oracles, for they blossom with wheat which speaks labor and wholesome food, and with scarlet poppies among the wheat and grain, bidding us repose. You would be greatly amused to hear me endeavoring to speak in French and in German, particularly the latter.

I carry a phrase-book in my bag, and my bag on my neck, and so load up and fire away at random. I manage generally to make myself understood, but find my match the instant any reply is made, which is always utterly and infinitely incomprehensible. My resource then is to look for somebody to speak English or French, and so interpret for me.

STRASBURG, "ALSACE," July 25.

We left this morning by rail at about 10.30 for Strasburg, the city of the great siege a year ago. Approaching Strasburg the signs of the war's work are abundantly apparent. Marks of shot and shell are visible on all sides. Devastation indeed there must have been. Within the city many ruins remain. But the old Cathedral rears its lofty spire serenely, and we are quietly housed in the Hotel de Ville de Paris, where Germans reign and English is spoken.

And here — God bless and love and keep you, while I say, good-night.

July 26.

After breakfast I visited the bankers to procure some "Napoleons," and then sallied out with Mary and Emily to see the famous Cathedral. On the journey we had opportunity as yesterday to observe the remaining effects of the war, houses broken and dismantled right between other houses apparently all unharmed, splendid edifices in ruins, shot and shell ornaments for sale, mementos of the direful days, women and young girls arrayed in deep black. Although it is said orders were given in the beleaguering armies not to injure the Cathedral, still even this edifice bears many marks of rough treatment, though accidental.

BERNE, SWITZERLAND, July 27.

The ride from Bâle to Berne was the route by Herzogenbusche. I had said before I left home that Switzerland I cared not whether I saw or not. Everybody raved about it, but mountains were gloomy to me, and I *would* not like it. So much for *contrairiness*. I give it up. Even this German Switzerland is the most exquisite country for lovely beauty my eyes have ever seen. What the other Suisse will be, I do not venture to conceive.

The road lay along the hills and valleys, rich and verdant, with the most romantic and peaceful varieties of scenery; strange combination you will say, but the two adjectives precisely express it. The lovely little villages and hamlets and châlets were at every bend in the road, all so simple, so picturelike, so inconvenient for the enjoyment of life, I admit; but all the prettier for this. And at last, as we approached Berne, a perfectly superb view of the entire chain of the Bernese Alps burst upon us. Their lofty peaks shot up into the air like spires of icebergs, flashing in a flood of sunlight, as if snow-clad and the snow in rifts and furrows, or like brilliant clouds piled up along the horizon. And in the play of the sunlight they seemed to my eye to dance like the flashing of the Northern Aurora. It was like the gorgeous dream-pictures of the Pilgrim's Progress, the gates of glory and the hills of heaven. It was such a vision as might precede a new apocalypse. Had this burst upon me a quiet traveller, not whirling amid dins by steam, methought I should have waited to see and hear things unutterable. But things unutterable they were which our eyes *did* see, and to the ear of our hearts the Alp voice spoke in that vision. Mary's eyes filled with tears at the strange emotion. It seemed so new,

so like the portals of the World-Infinite in the distance,
golden, silvery, ineffable for grandeur and for glory.
From my parlor window where I write, — mine for a
few hours in the Bernerhof Hotel, — I look upon these
mountains now while the evening mists gather upon
them. I know not the names of those sublime Teachers; but as they stand there robed before our eyes, guard-
ing on the horizon one of the loveliest landscapes that
ever feasted mortal eye, they silently discourse of things
illimitable and things eternal. They speak of faith and
of life. They speak of God, and to my ear they speak
quietly of Him who, mid "mountains and the midnight
air" taught the world to pray to Him who is unseen.
Oh, if only you dears at home could look this evening
with us upon those heights! In the descending sunlight they are sublime.

But to descend from the everlasting hills, all things
around us and near at hand are sweetly beautiful. The
air is vocal with music of birds. The little balconies
and windows and terraces all around are filled with
men, women, and children, enjoying the placid evening,
and looking upon the marvels of glory.

LAUSANNE, August 6.

The wind is whistling without as if it were a winter's
storm, though it is a fine night, and the day has been
exquisitely beautiful. The Sunday is more regarded
here than in Germany. The shops are shut. I do not
know how well people go to church, excepting that at
the English service this morning there was quite a full
attendance. In the courts of the Lord I feel at home;
everywhere else I feel strange. The familiar prayers
and the sweet service of the Holy Communion refresh
me. But in the streets, among crowds, — do you remem-

ber it somewhere in the Acts, that Paul was "in Athens [that great City], *alone*"? I begin to understand this. The Cathedral we visited the other day, cathedrals being supposed to be worthy visitation. We had read that it was erected about the middle of the thirteenth century and consecrated by Gregory X., in the presence of Rudolph of Hapsburg. And we saw that it was a large Gothic edifice of simple construction. But entering it, we found nothing specially worth seeing, excepting the great bareness and general absence of all ornament which marks the antagonism of the Swiss Reformers to even the semblance of papal art. Images of the Virgin and saints in various lofty niches were decapitated and otherwise maimed. Poor Saint Sebastian, full of his arrow-holes, stood in an ignoble retreat behind a pillar in the porch. Altar and screens there were none. Pure spirituality was symbolized in the complete stripping of the sacred edifice. But when I learned that only one service was held there on Sunday, and that at 9 A. M., I feared that the Reformation had gone too far, and that probably undevout rationalism ruled.

GENEVA, August 16.

This afternoon I made a short excursion to Nyon, a village an hour distant, going by train and returning by boat. Upon the dock, while waiting for the boat, I had good opportunity, for some twenty minutes, to observe Prince Napoleon (" Plonplon ") and his wife Clotilde, who accompanied for a " farewell " the brother of the Princess Clotilde, Prince Humbert, the heir to the throne of Italy, son of Victor Emmanuel. M. Napoleon has quite the face of the Buonaparte family, and resembles the first Emperor. He is, however, a tall and large man, of good figure, dressed very genteelly and looking *so* clean! His eye is brilliant, and his manner quite fascinating, and when he said good-by to his royal brother-in-law, he did it with extraordinary grace. Mme. Clotilde is a very plain-looking personage, no handsomer than her father in the face, but of course better looking by far, inasmuch as she is *petite* and not at all gross. The Crown Prince is a slim and quiet young fellow, quite dark, as a true Italian, with a most ordinary style of face, lines and eyes quite after the fashion of his father's, heavy mustache, and a manner entirely unselfconscious, democratic, or republican rather, for simplicity. He was attended by a fat fellow who may have been a general or a prime minister or a valet. He was so fat and oily that I dubbed him "Count Fosco," after Wilkie Collins's character.

M. Humbert, Victor Emmanuel, *Regis Romæ*, worthy even of *Il Re galantuomo*, was trying to travel *incog*. Poor fellow, he could n't do it. I looked at him with thoughts of pity, — pity for the responsibility which he must some day carry on those not broad shoulders; pity for the aches which sometimes must throb away in that poor skull of his when he is king, and has to manage his ministers, keep his eye on the Jesuits, take care of the Pope, lead forward the people, maintain his own throne, govern Italy, and keep the peace with Europe, or fight as it may be.

INTERLAKEN, August 19.

From our balcony in this hotel to-day, we looked out and saw through the partings of mountains, in all her glory and marvellous beauty, the Jungfrau. The clouds rolled away for a little, the sun played upon her form, and she stood robed in spotless white, "a bride prepared for her husband." Not snow *capped*, but snow *clad*, a vast summit of mountain, intensely

white, — a sort of world of snow and ice. And yet
no thought of iciness, for the Jungfrau is warm and
lovely. Seen from Geneva, Mont Blanc, at very early
morning, or just at the sinking of the sun, was a magnificent grandeur. But it was only a mountain. This
Jungfrau is not a mere mountain. She seems to live
and think. One might look up to her and speak to her,
and verily be amazed if she deigned no notice of his
address.

Luzerne, Switzerland, August 24.

. . . . To-day I saw a diorama of views from the
neighboring summits of the Rigi and Pilatus. A sign
was up over a curiosity shop, to the effect that a franc
and a half would give the grand vision. So in I went.

"Will you walk into my parlor, said the spider to the fly ?"

I entered and — pop ! — downstairs comes Monsieur
the Showman, and invites me up into his great place of
observation. I was ushered into a dark room, and the
door was carefully closed. My showman entered with
me. He was the lecturer. I was the entire audience.
The green curtains were mysteriously rolled away, —
before me reposed a panorama of Mt. Pilatus. " Now
you sall zee de sunset ober de mountains, if you please,"
— and shadows fell apace upon the scene, and a dim
sunset haze made quite an effect.

The Rigi view came next. " Now, sare, if you vas
upon the Rigi Culm top zu would valk around to see
de wue [view]. But as zat is not possible for to do ici,
ze diorama will go round." Presto, " ze diorama "
ground its way by slow jerks. The pointings out were
quite laughable. " Vare you see dat lake wis-a-wis,
dat is de lake Zug. Und now dat lake wis-a-wis to zu
is de lake ob four Cantons. Dare, où you see de leetle

vite spots, dat is Luzerne, — und où you see de snow mountains, dat is de Jura chain," etc., interminably.

The picture was, however, remarkably fine, and I was as well satisfied as if I had climbed the heights.

Munich, August 28.

The hotels are crowded, so many persons going to see the Drama of the Crucifixion at Ober Ammergau. I cannot imagine how Christians from America or England can endure such a spectacle. It may be that the rite is a religious one, and the result of a solemn vow a century or two ago, and that the people enter into it as a religious service; but it seems to me horrible to witness any man personating the Saviour in his trial and his woe.

. . . I had the effrontery in the course of my peregrinations to call upon that man so famous as the leader of the Anti-Infallibility School, Doctor Döllinger. I introduced myself as one of thousands in America who entertained for his course a profound admiration, and for himself great sympathy. He received me with the utmost cordiality, and we had quite a chat about the Vatican Council, and the Catholic Church, and fraternity between true Catholics and Protestants. Dr. Döllinger is a spare man, thin and wiry, with long, dark-brown hair, wrinkled face, and keen, dark eyes, a comical and determined and most intellectual expression, homely, piquant, powerful. He is in appearance the hard-working professor, — not at all the well-conditioned priest.

Nuremberg, August 31.

It was very interesting to observe the evidences of the contrast between the Swiss, or Zwinglian and Calvinistic, Reformation and the German, or Lutheran. In

the Swiss Cathedrals and Churches, all images and
ornaments and symbols of the Roman Catholic age had
been removed or mutilated. You may recall that I
mentioned the appearance of the Lausanne Cathedral as
being so destitute of ornament. The one at Geneva was
almost as much so. The visitor entering the Lutheran
Churches here in Nuremberg, would have no idea that
he was not in a Roman Catholic Church, excepting for
the fact that there are plenty of seats for hearers, and
plenty of pulpit convenience.

All altars, pictures, Madonnas, crucifixes, candles,
images of saints, and shrines of saints remain as they
were, only they are not used.

DRESDEN, September 5.

I have seen that great thing of Dresden, — the Sis-
tine Madonna. Many a time as I have looked upon
the engraving which depicts it, and then upon what is
better than any engraving, — the beautiful photograph
from the crayon sketch so familiar to us, — I have wondered if I should ever gaze upon the original. And it
was with peculiar emotion that I stood yesterday in the
little corner-room of the Royal Gallery, and saw it
face to face. There is singular beauty and purity in
the conception of the Virgin herself. It appears to me
that in this, Raphael surpassed all other painters, and
himself. The child is not more wonderful than the
mother.

BERLIN, September 8.

The walk to the Gardens led me through quite a remarkable forest-like park. Just think of thick woods,
acres in extent, thick as those at Conway in the White
Mountains, with ride-ways and drive-ways, right in the
midst of a city. On one side of the street, magnificent

residences, and thick shades on the other ; palatial splendor on the one hand — a five minutes' walk, and the thick dark back-woods of the far-back country.

Even in this brilliant city the German is the German. Along this beautiful and fashionable " Unter den Linden," on piazzas and balconies, men and women sit at little tables, and eat and drink and smoke, and scrutinize the passers-by. Germany loves out of doors.

I have just this day received my dear sister's letter of August 25, telling me how poorly our darling mother is, but having the postscript pencilled that she slept well last night. So I take a crumb of comfort, and hope and pray that the Lord will order that we meet again ere long, and that I may help gladden my dear mother's heart by narrations of travel, and by the ministrations of a loving son.

Van Dyke's pictures of the Saviour impress me very much, particularly one I saw to-day of Jesus being mocked, having the purple robe, and the reed put in his hands ; such weariness and wornness, such distress, more, a painter could not put into a human face. Another picture of Christ dead, mourned over by Mary Magdalen, Saint John, and an angel, was quite suggestive. An admirable Rubens of the Resurrection of Lazarus was also most worthy of mention, Lazarus looking as if he had been dead.

In a large hall leading to what is called the " New Museum," are some fine mural decorations by Kaulbach, — splendid frescos. One represents the Confusion of Babel, with Nimrod as king in the centre, and the descendants of Noah's three sons in groups, scattered, and indeed confounded, in speech.

Another impressed me greatly, representing a legend in a Battle of the Huns, wherein the combatants were so exasperated that the slain rose in the night, and fought in the air. The city of Rome is in the distance; above, borne on a shield, is Attila with a scourge in his hand, and opposite him, Theodoric, King of the Visigoths.

This afternoon I took a carriage, and drove with Mary and Emily out to Charlottenberg.

The Mausoleum, erected for the parents of the Emperor, is a beautiful temple, with its chancel and altar. Scripture legends are on the walls. Two white marble tombs, with effigies representing the meritorious dead in repose, stand in front of the altar. The figure of the queen is beautiful. It was a satisfaction, as I looked at her lovely face, to think how entirely her imperial son had avenged, in the humiliation of the second Napoleon, the insolence offered that mother by the imperious first Napoleon. Over the crucifix, behind the altar, is a beautiful fresco. The Lord our Saviour, by whom kings reign, is seated in the centre on a throne. On either side of Him kneel in adoration the king and queen, casting their crowns at His feet. Under it are in German the words, "I am the Lord and there is none beside Me."

I like the strong *religiosity* which comes out so in the German nature, and asserts itself so strongly, whatever must be said of the religious character of the nation.

BERLIN, September 11.

I write to-day wondering how these lines will find you. I am solicitous in the highest degree, from the tenor of the last advices from home; yet I trust, by the great favor of our God, before this my dear mother is convalescent, and that this will meet you in comfort and peace. As the time draws near in which we expect to be voyagers again, I have a strange shrinking from the embarkation, since I leave behind me unattained what I had for my own self most desired, and much beside that I wished to see and do. Yet I am persuaded that the over-ruling hand of God has moulded my plans and disappointed me. I could not endure to remain in Europe, with my mother in a failing state, and had I not engaged my passage when I did, I should see no way of coming until mid-winter.

BREMEN, September 15.

This is written from our ancestral city, and the home of our relatives, now so few, however.

Bremen presents a pretty appearance, with many new houses in blocks, and many attractive residences detached. The gardens and little parks are well laid out, and the city seemed to give us a home-like welcome.

Arriving in Bremen, I went to see Cousin Emily Pauli. She lives on a street which fronts upon the old ramparts, or "Wall," as they call it, but which are now simple promenade pleasure-grounds, and very attractive. To-morrow I am to drive with her.

I learn that Mr. John Meier, the old burgomeister, is very ill, and therefore I suppose I shall not see him. Emily Pauli says he has been talking about my coming, and expressing great delight and desire to see " Matson," of whom he had heard so much in former years.

BREMEN, September 17.

MY EVER DEAR FATHER AND MOTHER AND ALL OF YOU DEAR ONES AT HOME, — As I write this date, I perceive that it is just one month before our day of sailing. The thought fills me with conflicting emotions. What will be before that month expires? What shall be when the voyage is over, if God in His kind care bring us safely across the sea? I hope and pray that we may meet, —all of us, — with thankful hearts, and that our lives all spared and health renewed, we may rejoice together. But as God wills, who orders all things well. There is somewhere a quaint hymn by Richard Baxter, beginning, " Lord, it belongs not to my care whether I live or die," in which hymn, I think, are the words, " Christ leads us through no darker rooms than He went through before." And somehow I like that hymn, though I cannot now recall another word or vestige of it. When we are able, as we think, to take care of ourselves, — by any foresight to avoid evil or calamity, to engineer our own way, — then we feel as if all things belonged to our care, and we are sometimes sore troubled and perplexed. But when to carry out our plan is impossible, and circumstances are out of our control, then we can throw all care and sorrow upon God, and ask His help, and rest upon it. I learned this at sea, and I am learning it anew almost every day. Tossing on the ocean in a little box of wood and iron, one realizes human impotence.

. . . Yesterday I set out to inspect the ancestral city. First, we went to the venerable Rathhaus, or Senatorial and City Hall of time immemorial, where the Burgomeisters were wont to meet, and the Senators to rule affairs. And in the queer big hall of the assembled Wisdom (for the Bremen Senate, or Government Council, is or was called the " Wittheit " or the " Wisdom "), hung with pictures of whales, and models of ships upon the windows, among the aristocratic names, shields, and armorial bearings, I observed the arms and names of the Meiers emblazoned for the coming generations to reverence. From the Senate house we went to the old Cathedral, " the Dom," of which my grandmother used to speak, and, by the way, we went to church there this morning, and heard a German sermon, of which I understood not a single sentence. In the Dom, which is a fine old church, is a curious apartment called the Blei Keller, an ancient vault for the dead, which, like three or four others in Germany, possesses such quality of air that putrefaction does not take place in it. In this vault were several corpses lying in open coffins, which, it is affirmed, have been there kept for periods from one hundred to four hundred and thirty years. They were not skeletons, but more like mummies, the skin shrivelled and tight over the bony frame-work, though bone color, and not black, as the Egyptian mummies are.

. . . From R——, on the way back to Bremen, we stopped at " Horn," the country-seat of the Burgomeister, Mr. John Meier. Mr. Meier, as my last informed you, is quite ill, and evidently going his way from hence. I found him in his parlor among his family, in good thick dressing-robe, and received an exceedingly warm and touching welcome. He said he had heard so much about the " wonderful grandson of his Uncle Caspar " from my dear grandmother whom he loved so warmly, that he longed to see me in Bremen. He inquired about many things, which proved that his interest in the various members of our family was not a thing for effect, and he was tolerably well posted respecting us. He asked after my father and mother, and their health, and was much moved at the report I was compelled to make. With messages of great affection, he bade me good-by, — for the call was necessarily short, — and expressed many thanks that I had come. He was a dear old man, and reminded me so much of my mother in the contour of head and face that my heart went right out to him. Mrs. Meier took us into a parlor to see the family portraits. . . .

It really has been a great pleasure to see these relatives, and to find them so cordial to a stranger, simply because he is one of the family. And I am very glad that my daughter has had a peep at them too.

LONDON, October 9.

. . . In the afternoon I went to the Royal Chapel in the Whitehall Palace, — a chapel once the banqueting hall of kings, and itself all that remains of the original palace. The attraction was the preacher, Prof. F. D. Maurice, — a famous Broad Churchman of many years, one of the most liberal and cultivated divines of England, a writer of great beauty and wide charity. He is a very fine-looking old gentleman, with an intellectual countenance, much above the average of the English clergy. Maurice has a keen dark eye, a face with many lines of humor in it, yet under the greatest control, a mouth that speaks promptly, and a lip and chin that will neither be vacillating nor obstinate.

.   .   .   .

I cannot say I am tired of the Old World. I cannot say we have gained even all I had hoped to gain. But I can say, mortal man could not do much more or better under the circumstances than we have done. The invalids, I think, have made some progress.

For Emily's sake, more than any other, I am sorry that our travel has been abridged, and that we do not pass the winter in some continental city. But she is so good, so charming, so self-forgetful, so great a blessing and comfort, that I know she will come again some day.

For myself, I can speak when I see you. I was not all right when I left home. The relief from the parish care and sermon-writing has been of very great benefit. The entire change in ways of life, in the mere food and air and exercise, has proved also exceedingly beneficial. Though the solicitudes have been something of a drawback, and have given me two or three more gray hairs and crow's-feet, I am better in mind and nerve, as well as elsewhere, corporeally. Then the mental refreshment for us all. Though we have not been in either France or Italy, we have made thorough acquaintance with English, German, and the French and German-Swiss ideas and ways. We have seen the life of this metropolis, of British villages, and of continental cities. We have been among historic places. We have been picking up facts and philosophizing. We have seen treasures of art. We have found the world bigger than it looked before, and have learned, I think, to prize more than ever our own land with all its defects, our own country with its free institutions, and our better type of religion, — that I mean which is Protestant, Evangelical, earnest, and aggressive. I, for one, as a clergyman, am glad too to be able to hold up my head among others, and to say, " I have been there too, and I know what I say and why I think." I long again for a Sunday in America. Somehow nothing has seemed like our American Christian Lord's Day on this side the water. And I long myself again to be about my loved and chosen work, in some parish; to do good, and to preach the blessed Gospel, and to feel that I am useful, working, blessing others, every day and every week. I sometimes think I would not have resigned my Newark charge if I could have at all foreseen events. But, again, the hand of the Lord was in it. It was necessary to have the entire break-up. . . . Your devoted son,

MATSON MEIER-SMITH.

To Dr. Dyer.

MY EVER DEAR DR. DYER, — Your letter to me, — as well as those to Emily and Mrs. Meier-Smith, — came speedily to England, and thence followed us to Bonn, where it was as cordial and meat and all sorts of genial things. It did us good, for I was blue, among these chaps who can't speak English, and whose guttural Deutsch no well-bred American can be supposed to comprehend. But I make out. By my patent-combination language of Deutsch-French-English and the Symbolik, and that used by the deaf and dumb, I compel all nations to understand me. I wish I could compel myself to understand them in return.

You have been in Coblentz, I believe. We have passed several days in this " Hotel of the Giants," looking upon the Rhine and up to Ehrenbreitstein opposite. By the way, how much this German Fortress looks like Edinburgh Castle. I am having my first taste of a genuine Continental Sunday. In Brussels, last Sunday was not unlike that in any American city. There was less racket and hawking of wares than in London. I saw no shops open. In this city it is just the week day. People are coming and going, buying and selling, precisely like yesterday. Yet they go to church too. I shall have more faith in the " Sabbath Committee's " mission one of these days.

It is a good work that the English Church does, in that she keeps service in these cities. I attended service last Sunday on the Rue Belliard, in Brussels, and found a faithful and fervent young man preaching the Gospel. This morning I have been to the English Chapel in the palace of the Prussian Queen (or Empress), and found it good, though the preacher was more legal than Evangelical, more of John Baptist style, than of the preacher of a finished Atonement. Adjoining the Church of England chapel in the palace, was one for the Lutheran service which her Majesty attends. Talk about candles and crosses and ritualism! The Lutherans were no iconoclasts.

After I wrote you, I heard some better preaching. For one, I heard Canon Charles Kingsley. He was preaching for the times, and against the corrupters of the Reformation Doctrine. From the good old Bishop of Chester I heard also a sweet, good sermon, and a fair talk from the Archbishop of York, — not much of a sermon, however.

I do hope there won't be any terrible *muss* at the Convention General. What can be gained by a going off? I am sorry that the C—— affair is what it is. But I am sure a C—— would not, *mutatis mutandis*, be sustained in the Presbyterian Church to-day, and I doubt if *the* C—— himself could be ordained in the Presbyterian Church, if he held no more, and knew no more on the Baptism question, than he appears to hold and know so conscientiously to-day. Give him years, and more time for thought and experience, and I am sure he would come to the conclusion that the Baptismal Regeneration of the Prayer Book is Scriptural truth, and practically held in every Christian household; in other words, that the germ of the highest and purest Christian life is always, in Old Testament and New, in all ages, that which springs in infancy, which is then implanted by a Covenant God and Saviour, and which, nourished, — amid many vicissitudes alas, indeed, and sometimes it may be blasted, — brings at last the fulness of manhood in Christ. Oh, if only our Evangelical brethren, dear and beloved, would spiritualize what is fossilized in the Church, and use with power, in God's name, what is exhibited like mere crown jewels in a case by too many of our clergy, we should never think of separation. Fidelity like this I am persuaded would gain the day, and make our Church system what it ought to be.

I say most earnestly, use the Prayer Book as it is; press upon the hearts and consciences of our people spiritually, our doctrine of baptism and its obligations, of the Lord's Supper and its meaning and requisitions. Show the wonderful, the inexhaustible, the illimitable love, peace, and resource of our glorious God and Saviour, and demand of men a true, devout, and consecrated churchliness in view of this, — and this will be more to the glory of God and the salvation of men, and for Christian unity, than all the squabbles about canons and liberty any of our brethren get up.

With my dear love to my brethren, this is what I think.

Do write again when you can. My wife and children join me in warmest love.

Ever and ever yours in Christ,
MATSON MEIER-SMITH.

XIV.

WORK RESUMED.

St. Luke's, Philadelphia. — St. George's, New York.

1872.

THE homeward voyage was made in October, and was a tedious one of two weeks' length, with constant storms and adverse winds. The change of plan which shortened the proposed vacation of eighteen months to less than half of that time, was principally owing to the enfeebled condition of Dr. Meier-Smith's mother, who appeared to be rapidly failing, and suffering much from the fear that she might never see her children and grandchildren again. It was a great disappointment to abandon the purpose of a winter in Italy and Southern Germany, but there was much cause for gratitude in the improved health of the invalids, although all the benefit anticipated from the trip was not realized.

While Dr. Meier-Smith was greatly invigorated by the entire change and the relief from professional labor and responsibilities, he did not feel ready to assume a parochial charge immediately, preferring a temporary work for some months to come.

Amid the kindly welcomes from friends, there were many invitations to supply vacancies, and there were engagements for every Sunday, much to his satisfaction; for, as he remarked, " after six months of fasting he was hungry for preaching."

Bishop Coxe urged him to come to Buffalo, desiring him to take the rectorship of St. John's Church in that city, and he visited the parish, and preached there. After his return to New York, he received the call, which he felt compelled to decline, fearing that the climate would be too severe for himself and his family.

In February, 1872, he accepted an engagement to take charge of St. Luke's Church, Philadelphia, until after Easter.

The work in this large and important parish he was willing to assume temporarily, while not ready for settlement, as it gave him an introduction, much valued, to social and church life in Philadelphia.

The winter and spring were overshadowed by an epidemic of small-pox, with which Philadelphia was visited. There was also some prevalence of the same disease in New York; and in March, his mother, although an invalid and confined to her room, was attacked by it, and died after a very short illness. The loss of this beloved mother was a severe bereavement to her devoted son, who, although called to her immediately, did not reach her until all was over. Her sudden death under such unexpected circumstances added painfully to the sorrow of this affliction.

The engagement at St. Luke's Church included the charge of the Lenten services, and the preparation of the Confirmation class. It was distinctly understood that Dr. Meier-Smith was not to be considered a candidate for the vacant rectorship. There were circumstances which, in his own view, made it undesirable for him to take such a position were it offered to him. He preferred a less conspicuous work, and one which would allow him more time for study and writing. These considerations made his work at St. Luke's an independent one. He made many very warm friends in the large congregation, attracted equally by his strong and thoughtful preaching, and the frank and kindly manner which expressed his genuine interest in all to whom he ministered. It is often made the occasion for humorous comment, that the good people of Philadelphia are disposed to receive with especial cordiality all who, by birth or tradition, are associated with the early history of the city. Dr. Meier-Smith's descent from the old Lutheran pastors, Drs. Muhlenberg and Kunze, gave him a ready entrance to some of the best social circles. Before the term of his engagement closed, there were many in the parish who were anxious to retain him permanently; but he gave no encouragement, and accepted an invitation to fill the place of the Rev. Dr. Tyng, Rector of St. George's Church, in New York, during his absence in Europe.

Bishop Howe, the former Rector of St. Luke's, confirmed a class of nearly fifty at the close of Dr. Meier-Smith's work there.

The duty at St. George's commenced in May. Dr. Tyng expected to be absent six months, but returned at the close of the summer. The position as assistant minister of the parish was retained until November, though he officiated in several other places during the time. The summer home was with his father, at New Rochelle.

FROM THE "RECORD OF SERVICES."

November, 1872.

I desire to put on record in these pages the delightful and affectionate nature of my intercourse with Dr. Tyng, during my association with him as his assistant and temporary substitute at St. George's. It has also

been a very profitable relationship. The simple ministry of the ever-living Jesus, the Friend, the High
Priest, the Saviour, and the continual preaching in
great simplicity the blessed Gospel of faith in Him,
as the comfort, the salvation, and the inspiration of the
soul, are blessings which cannot be too highly appreciated.   I have found Dr. Tyng unvaryingly gentle,
generous, courteous, loving, and worthy my high regard
and love. The result of observation and of mature age
is, that I regard preaching as more and more a *practical
business*. It must be made to *do something* with men.

May I have wisdom and grace more than ever
before — and the *gift* — to move men for Christ, and
to do the work of Jesus!

During the summer of this year calls were declined
from St. John's Church, Ithaca, New York, and the
Church of the Ascension, Staten Island.

XV.

RECTORSHIP OF ST. JOHN'S CHURCH, HARTFORD.

1872–1876.

IN October, 1872, Dr. Meier-Smith accepted a call to the rectorship of St. John's Church, Hartford, Connecticut. This parish had for its first Rector the Rev. A. Cleveland Coxe, the present Bishop of Western New York; and among other well-known clergymen who have held the rectorship, was the Rev. Dr. Washburn, so long Rector of Calvary Church, New York.

St. John's had been a large and influential parish, but the policy of multiplication of parishes had prevailed in Hartford, and it had lost much of its strength. Dr. Meier-Smith was strongly urged to attempt the work of restoring the church to its former position. Though he felt very doubtful of success in this direction, Hartford, as a place of residence and as a field of labor, presented many attractions. It is a beautiful city, and, as the seat of Trinity College, is a centre of churchly and literary interest. He looked forward hopefully to opportunities for influence among the students, his solicitude for his own son having awakened a strong interest in all young men, whom he regarded henceforth as having a peculiar claim upon his sympathy.

Such considerations induced him to accept the call, and on the first Sunday in Advent he assumed the rectorship. In consequence of very inclement weather and a heavy snow-storm, the congregations were small, and this entry appears in the "Record": "I pray that the Lord may give me grace to do a good work to the glory of His Name, notwithstanding the somewhat discouraging aspects of the beginning."

The members of St. John's parish received their new Rector with affectionate welcome, and the friendly reception everywhere met counterbalanced the first rather chilling impressions.

Bishop Williams extended a cordial greeting, and was ever the kindest of friends. Dr. Meier-Smith became warmly attached to him while in Hartford. The Bishop's personal attractiveness, force of character, and scholarly attainments, strongly impressed him, as they must all who come under his influence.

The winter of 1872–73 was exceptionally cold and damp, and Dr. Meier-Smith suffered much from heavy colds and weakness of throat. The church was often imperfectly warmed, with the result of smaller congregations than the Rector hoped for, and no little discomfort to himself. He was somewhat disheartened. "Clearly," he said, "it is not my forte to bring up a 'run down' parish!" He was the last man to claim gifts suited to all lines of work, and certainly never over-estimated his ability in this particular direction. The work necessary to rapid success under these circumstances was not altogether congenial to him, and he doubted whether he possessed the elements necessary for it; yet to be otherwise than faithful and laborious in every recognized duty would have been impossible for him, and probably he was more successful in the eyes of others than in his own.

When the services of Lent commenced, the attendance upon them increased so rapidly that the Rector began to look more hopefully upon the future. At the daily service from eighty to one hundred were always found, a large attendance in proportion to the Sunday congregations. The number presented at the first Confirmation gave evidence of faithful work. Among them were those who said that the Rector's appeals and instruction had brought them to a decision, weighed for years and constantly postponed. The Sunday-school had dwindled into almost nothing, but during this rectorship new life was imparted to it by his efforts, aided heartily by faithful teachers. A Guild was formed, which infused enthusiasm into teachers and scholars, and soon quadrupled the number in attendance, as also the offerings of the children for missions. The much coveted honor of admittance into the "Orders of the Silver and the Golden Cross" will never be forgotten by some who were then young parishioners of St. John's. The members of the Sunday-school were made to feel themselves the helpers of the Rector. The school met before the afternoon service, and one object of the Guild was to secure the attendance of all present at the Evening Prayer, which followed. A youthful choir was formed, aiding the quartette as a chorus, and the sermon was short and simple. The older people were gratified by the interest of the children, and the result was a "live Sunday-school" and a full church in place of the hitherto much neglected "Afternoon Service."

The first Confirmation occurred on Good Friday, when seventeen were presented.

Among topics of sermons written during this year, these are noted, — "Christian Liberality in Offerings," "Gifts as a Part of Worship," and "The Call of God for Liberal Response to Church Missions."

It has been said that Dr. Meier-Smith was an ardent

advocate of the work of Foreign Missions. The following article, written for the "Churchman" while in Hartford, gives some of his often-pressed arguments for its promotion : —

"That Mr. Max Müller on the 'Day of Intercession,' in Westminster Abbey, should have offered a suggestion to the effect that Christian missionaries change their tactics, and begin tinkering Buddhism and Mohammedanism into more earnest life, is, to our mind, one of the coolest things on record. We wonder that the hoary stones within those venerable walls did not 'immediately cry out.' The reported sentiment is, unhappily, not a new one. It was very far from being one of those occasional and solitary flashings of perverse genius which are as suddenly extinguished as they suddenly blaze forth. Unbelief has said the same thing a great many times. And it is to be feared that the sentiment is not altogether unfamiliar even at Christian firesides. There is certainly a most appalling apathy concerning the business of missions to heathen lands. Are we wrong in attributing the indifference in part at least to just this style of scepticism which cropped out so forcibly without regard to the proprieties of the occasion ? The Foreign Missionary enterprise is pronounced by not a few a Quixotic scheme. Men who give this as their verdict are Christian men. They bring plausible arguments and stubborn facts to the support of their position. They draw the balance-sheet between the expenditures and the results. They compute the sacrifice of health and wealth, of life and energy, through eighteen Christian centuries. They quote the census of Paganism. Against the Christians found in heathen lands, they offset the pagans dwelling in Christian lands. There are as many Chinese idolaters in the United States to-day, we hear, as there are Christian worshippers in China, and more perhaps than there are converted heathen in China and India together.

"They review the intellectual warfare between Christianity and philosophical Paganism which is going on in the world, and tell us that it is as hotly contested in Britain and Germany and America, as in India itself. In fact, it is made to appear a matter of serious doubt whether Christianity or Paganism is making the more converts. So far as actual idolatry is concerned, — which is the worship of the invisible Deity under material forms subsisting, temporarily or permanently, in sacred places, — it is averred that this is quite as much a feature of nominal Christianity as of Buddhism.

"There may be other explanations of the indifference to Foreign Missionary work, and various other exceptions may be taken to the service, and to its methods, as the Boards of the Church pursue them. But this mode of argument — the appeal to results — is a summary process which the rectors of our parishes have to meet with a frequency which is painful, if not embarrassing.

"The Epiphany appeal of the Foreign Committee of the Board of Missions suggests one form of judicious answer to this practical scepticism. We commend it to our readers, without reproducing it here. In this appeal, testimony of four Indian governors is cited respecting the results of missionary labor in India. Sir Bartle Frere, Governor of Bombay, bears strong witness to the moral, social, and political effects of the missionary work among the intelligent Hindoos and Mohammedans of India. To the temperate language of the appeal, we might add some words. We might remind those who criticise and disparage the results of Foreign Missions, that they themselves are among those *results*, — albeit, possibly, amid slippered ease, — and their positive unbelief on this question not the ripest nor best-rounded fruit thereof.

"Our ancestors were heathen. Britain was Foreign Missionary ground in former days. Nineteen centuries ago — however insignificant the results reached by these sagacious accountants — there was not a square foot of earth outside Palestine which was not soil of heathenism.

"But this is not the argument we prefer in urging the great duty of carrying the Gospel to the heathen. With results of missions, whether past or prospective, we have nothing to do. They are entirely apart from the question of the Church's duty, or the personal obligation of every Christian. The problem of the Foreign Missionary service is not, in our understanding of it, simply to supplant the false religions of the world by the introduction of our average modern Christianity, with its base alloy of worldliness and unbelief. Nor is it even to Christianize heathen nations, in the true sense of the term, through the ordinary agencies and instrumentalities familiar in the Church. Doubtless, we are to labor and pray as if this were the precise consummation to be reached. This is our bounden duty, and the only practical method of any service whatever. Above all things, we are not to fail of duty in this direction, through scepticism about results. Were it revealed that such a consummation, to be gained by present agencies and processes, was the ultimate of the Church's service, it would be a sin to have any misgivings about it, or to look for an iota less than the perfect and literal accomplishment.

"The problem assigned to the Church, we believe,

however, to be an entirely different one from this. It is a problem upon which all the light vouchsafed is that which radiates from the seasons of Advent and Epiphany. We pray, as our Lord taught us to pray, 'Thy Kingdom come.' That kingdom, as we read His holy words, is to be introduced in its glory upon earth, with entire and absolute independence of all human works, and the times and seasons of human adjustment. The object of the missionary work, the object of the Apostolic Commission itself, — for they are one and the same, — is to prepare the way for this. The Gospel is to be preached among all nations, 'for a witness.' From among all nations and tribes an 'elect' people is to be gathered, — to be a waiting Church, waiting for Him who is always 'at hand,' NEAR, and whose EPIPHANY shall be for splendor, as for suddenness, like the lightning from one end of heaven to the other.

"Such work has the Lord Christ given us to do. His word is 'Occupy — until I come.' This His work must be carried on, with or without success, regardless of expense, — whether of gold or of life, — until He Himself, coming in the clouds of heaven with holy angels and the risen saints, summon His militant Church away from the warfare to the 'exceeding great reward.' Do we hesitate concerning Foreign Missions? Are we believers in Christ, or are we Infidels?"

Among his letters of this period was one to a friend who purposed going upon the stage : —

. . . You are making a great venture. Some of your friends feel badly about it. I admit that I wish it were in some other line, on general principles. But I am free to say to you and anybody else, that I have no sympathy with those who consign the stage and its company to a wholesale and unmitigated perdition, without even Christian burial. I recognize in the drama high educational and moral possibilities, as, in the personal character of some who make the stage a profession, the highest and noblest qualities. And it may be ignorance on my part wholly inexcusable, nevertheless I fail to see why one may not assume that profession with true and laudable purpose, as any other, not merely for wealth and fame, but for moral and benevolent ends, and be faithful, by God's help, in carrying out this purpose. I think I know you well enough to say that you have not been unmindful of this consideration. And yet I foresee for you difficulties and obstacles, neither few nor trivial, to the realization of such an ideal. I pray that you may have wisdom and grace to surmount them. In the good long' ago, my dear ——, when we were boys together, we had a Friend and Lord to whom we were wont to bring our affairs, and of whom to seek the wisdom and grace we needed as little fellows, in our boyhood's battles and endeavors. That good Friend and Saviour has not deserted us, neither you nor me. We have been led in different paths, but with all our errors and imperfections — and it is with an unfeigned hand that I write *our*, meaning my own — He is still our unchanged and unchanging Lord and Friend. The Man, but *such* a man! The " Christus Consolator et Adjuvator." Yet more, the God-Man ! As I grow older He is more to me, in my increasing manhood and capacity and need. May I hope you find Him so to you, led around and tried as you have been. And whether on the stage, or elsewhere, I pray that the thought to serve and honor Him may ever be a controlling thought with you, while " to your own Master you stand or

fall," however and whatever others may "judge." I
fervently wish you all success that may be for your
highest good; this I pray and trust you will have. I
want more for you than even our old friendship perhaps warrants me in expressing. But anyhow and
under all circumstances your friend of a lifetime,
heartily and truly,

M. M.-S.

While the period of the Hartford rectorship was a
quiet and uneventful one so far as his own parish was
concerned, it was a time of lively interest and vigorous
discussion in the Church at large. Occurrences in connection with the meetings of the Evangelical Alliance,
in New York, in 1873, were the ostensible causes of renewed agitation by radical men of the Evangelical
school. They had been laboring long to secure conces-
sions from the Church to their own views, and especially
to alterations in the Prayer Book. The course taken
by Bishop Cummins resulted, as some who read these
pages will recall, in bringing out intense feeling among
Churchmen of all shades of opinion, and in directing
the eyes of all Christian people to our Communion.

The extracts which follow are from a characteristic
letter to Dr. Dyer. It was written just after the
" Cummins defection," which resulted in the establish-
ment of the Reformed Episcopal Church : —

. . . I don't feel half as much like " Evangelical
Alliance" as I did a few weeks ago. . . .

. . . The tone of much of the sectarian press is anything but Christian and charitable. They talk sensibly
enough of "Cumminsism," and its baselessness, but they
show exhilaration at the chance of poking their fingers
under our ribs. They know better. They know that

Ritualism for doctrine is not our characteristic. They know that the Church holds Justification by Faith only, — not by feeling as with some of them, — and that we don't talk of "sacrifice," "priest," and "altar" in any sense wherein Presbyterians and Congregationalists forty years ago would not have indorsed the sentiment; nor in any sense which their average, unaltered standards do not now indorse, and yet they assert that we poor Episcopalians mean everything in the Romish sense, or ought to. . . .

Blessed and dear old Saint Stephen of St. George's.[1] How grandly he spoke the truth *pro Christo et Ecclesia!* I wanted to go down and put my arms around his neck, and hug him as a son a father. And what an inspiration was Bishop Alfred Lee's open letter to George David,[2] and with what golden sentences it ended! *Inter nos*, I have sent two editorials to the " Churchman " lately, " Unity, Unity, Unity," and " Intolerance." I was requested to give something which outsiders could comprehend. Criticisms are in order. . . . Did Cummins talk at random when he made the allusion supposed to be to Dr. Muhlenberg? I fancy I hear my venerable cousin smack those expressive lips of his, and in deep guttural say, " Bah ! " The stir-up has done good here. Connecticut men say that it brings us all closer, as it shows stronger love of Church principles on all sides. I have talked with the most conspicuous Baptist, and the most conspicuous Congregational clergymen here, and find that neither have the slightest sympathy with the Cummins proceeding, from its first fence-jumping to its final secession.

---

[1] Dr. Stephen H. Tyng.　　　　[2] Bishop Geo. David Cummins.

One of the published articles alluded to in the foregoing letter is given here, as clearly expressing his sentiments on a subject of so much discussion at the time.

UNITY, UNITY, UNITY!

Now that the various journals, religious and secular, have had their "say" about the Evangelical Alliance, and as well concerning those whose honest convictions were adverse to some of its ideas, we have a fact to state which we wish our brethren of various Christian affiliations would accept in good faith. We desire this as a simple matter of justice and truth. It is a matter we wish to have understood, whether it be appreciated or not.

The fact is this. The Protestant Episcopal Church entertains an unfeigned and most lively interest in all signs of the times which indicate approach to closer union among Christian people, and in everything which may fitly express the unity pertaining to followers of our Blessed Lord. Such, we are well aware, is not the popular impression, but precisely the contrary. Yet we believe the fact to be as we have stated it.

Another thing is true. The fact stated is not, as some may aver, *in spite* of the peculiar principles of the Church, but a fact which grows out from these principles, — the very principles which are vulgarly called "exclusive," and associated, like the phrase "High Church," in many minds with narrowness and bigotry.

We do not propose to argue this point at length just now. But for its bearing upon the fact we have stated, it is sufficient to say, we are broad enough to recognize all the unity which exists, and to thank God for it. We believe that the Son of God organized and equipped a society, — an Ecclesia, a Church, — which organization is Scripturally called the Body of Christ. Christ is the Head of this Body. In this organization He dwells by His Spirit, the Vitalizing Force. He Himself uses the figure of the vine and its branches to illustrate His relation to His people. The life-sap from Him, the True Vine, flows in all the branches, imparting life and vigor to every twig or tendril, and producing in their full rounded beauty the rich and luscious clusters of all Christian fruit. In the completeness of this organic unity are — the Faith, once (and once for all) delivered to the Saints; the Sacraments; and the Apostolic Ministry, called into being, ordered, sent, in due procession by Himself the Head, His accredited agents, — their duties assigned, their instructions ample, their limitations definite.

This organic unity — that of the Church, the Body of Christ — is, moreover, indestructible.

Now, this statement of doctrine is not an *unchurching* form of words. It is not at all necessary for us to say that they who, amid the convulsions of the Reformation period, were separated from the Apostolic order, yet retained the faith as best they might, were sundered by that separation from the Body into which they had been baptized. It requires something more than involuntary error to separate from Christ. No more is it necessary for us to make such affirmation respecting the spiritual progeny of those Continental Protestant disciples, in whom the life which flows from Christ manifests itself by abundant fruits of the Spirit. Nor do we make any such affirmation. Nor does any conclusion to this effect follow from Church principles or premises. That all baptized Christians pertain to the substance of Christ's body, we unhesitatingly admit and proclaim;

and this is perfectly consistent with the statement that the relations of some in this number to the Body in its completeness, are similar to the relations subsisting between a vine and certain branches which are partially detached. Partial detachment is the principal fact of sectarianism. The evils of sectarianism are but morbid growths from this anomalous relation.

Now, the claim of the Protestant Episcopal Church is not to be exclusively the Body of Christ in this land, but to represent in completeness of organization and historical continuity that organic unity which the Lord founded when He founded the visible society, the Church. This claim, we believe, can be made good alike against Rome and the Protestant bodies which are destitute of Apostolic orders.

To preserve the features of this organic unity in their completeness, and with them certain benefits not of the essence of the unity, — for example, such as the sacramental liturgy, — we hold to be our sacred trust. As among Christian denominations, we might say that this was for the Protestant Episcopal Church in the United States a *raison d'être.*

By reason of these principles, accordingly, as we have already said, Churchmen must take a lively interest in whatever seems to move their separated brethren toward the contemplation of organic unity, and the best methods whereby to express their conviction of it. We have no denominational pride to be considered in the matter; but we have the most entire confidence that, the organic unity fairly comprehended, return to the historic Church will be only a question of days. It will be a time for mutual congratulation when the modern latitudinarianism, "Ye are of one spirit, no matter of how many bodies," shall give place, and the solemn pleading of the

Holy Ghost be everywhere heard, urging spiritual unity upon the ground, first, of the "one Body."

An affirmation respecting the temper and tone of our clergy and laity in this matter of kindly interest may count for what it is worth. We believe there are very few who will not subscribe to the spirit of this article. We are confident there is neither priest nor layman within the comprehension of the Church who would fail to recognize, with devout gratitude and Christian love, those lineaments of pious life and holy faith which mark the Family of our blessed Lord, no matter where found or in whom. Our rules of order may be rigid. In the popular apprehension we may be exclusive in our ways. But there must be rigid rule and exclusiveness after a sort, in the faithful custody of any important trust. But we are not for this the less disposed to say, "Grace be with all them who love our Lord Jesus Christ."

And our desire for the unity of all Christians in the completeness of Church organization — for we have repeatedly expressed our lack of faith in any union less than this — is unfeigned and absorbing. The very extreme attitudes which appear in individual illustrations, seeking affiliations with non-Episcopalians on the one side, and with Rome, or, some will say, Oriental Churches, on the other, are but anomalous expressions of this consuming fire of catholic love. It is no mere formality that on bended knees we say daily unto God, " We pray for Thy Holy Church Universal; that it may be so guided and governed by Thy good Spirit, that all who profess and call themselves Christians may be led into the way of truth, and hold the faith in unity of spirit, in the bond of peace, and in righteousness of life."

The extract which follows is from the latter half of the paper on Intolerance : —

"Now, concerning this word intolerance, which is our text, there might as well be an understanding. There is a vulgar impression that it sums up all ecclesiastical villany. It is a very common word, — when men wish to speak opprobriously respecting something they dislike, but are powerless to change. But we hold that as there is such a thing as a 'toleration' which is consummate abomination, so is there an 'intolerance' which is highest virtue. There is an intolerance which is the strongest safeguard of social purity and peace. There is an intolerance without which no man's home or life would be secure for a day. Law involves intolerance. Government involves intolerance. Law and order pass away the instant there is anything less than absolute intolerance of all breaches or infractions of the same whatsoever, — even the least. The Church is in this sense intolerant. What is not forbidden by her law, she endures, even though it be foreign to her spirit or opposite to her tastes. What is forbidden by her law, she tolerates not for a moment, — though her judgment be pronounced slowly, and after, it may be, too protracted deliberation.

"Are other denominations of Christians less intolerant than the Church ? Or are they prompt to assert their denominational principles when occasion may arise ? Should the whole House of Bishops propose some time, with a charity transcending even the amplitude of the Evangelical Alliance, to commune with our Baptist friends in expressions of 'love,' — would they be admitted even to such an affiliative banquet with dry vestments and dry-shod ? Our Presbyterian brethren subscribe to a confession of faith which affirms that 'Neither Baptism nor the Lord's Supper may be dispensed by any but by a minister of the word lawfully ordained.'   Are these brethren so far from intolerance that they would suffer the Quaker Mrs. Smith or Mrs. Smiley to administer a sacrament in their churches, or receive one at the fair hands of either of these irreproachable 'Sisters' from among the 'Friends,' — or, as some would say, 'The Quaker Church'?

"The Church we love, and to which, thank God, we belong, is intolerant, — not of human error, for so was not her divine Master; not of human infirmity or defect, for the time is not yet when there shall be 'neither spot nor wrinkle nor any such thing,' but intolerant of every attempt to pervert or impair the order which Christ has appointed, and the doctrine of Christ as she has received the same.   To the Apostolic Ministry in continuous succession, and in three Orders of Bishops, Presbyters, and Deacons, and to the two Sacraments, in all the Scriptural and primitive, as well as Catholic richness of their significance, she is irrevocably pledged. Touching these, she cannot waver.   She may be maligned and abused for her fidelity to these.   She may be persecuted and accounted the offscouring of all things for these.   But if she remains upon the earth, she will upon this continent welcome the advent of her Lord and Head, holding fast these things 'once delivered.' This is her intolerance."

In the same year he wrote to Dr. Dyer: "Hartford folk are nice people.   So are the clergy.   *My* particular folks are æsthetically highish, but they love the simple Gospel.   So that suits me, and I am having a good time."

Clergymen of marked culture and ability were pastors of non-Episcopal churches in Hartford, and he enjoyed their society none the less that he had once belonged to their own ranks.

With the Faculty of Trinity College, especially with Professors Johnson and Hart, warm friendships, much prized, were formed. With them there was the full accord in theological views, and in Church position, most desirable at this time, as the contest grew in strength and bitterness through the open division in Church ranks. The result of all the excitement was to bring into deeper sympathy and closer union all who loved the Church more than any party in it. Probably no better time could have been chosen to institute the Church Congress, which was founded during Dr. Meier-Smith's residence in Hartford. He was among the number who met informally in New Haven, in the spring of 1874, to confer with reference to such an organization. The outcome of this conference was the first Church Congress, which met in New York in the ensuing October. Among the topics of discussion one was, " The Relation of the Church to other Christian Bodies," and another was, " Mutual Christian Obligations of Capital and Labor."

The keynote which has never been lost seemed to be struck at the outset. The Church Congress has proved that Episcopal clergymen are ready to meet the questions of the day, in spite of the impression of those who have supposed them to be only concerned on matters of Order and Ritual. As a centre of union and of powerful influence on the thought and progress of the Church, Dr. Meier-Smith regarded its annual meetings as of great importance, regretting that he was so seldom able to attend them, through pressure of engagements. With everything which promoted Christian Union and Church Unity, he was in hearty sympathy. Breadth of thought, with its full expression, grew more necessary to him and characteristic of him, as he advanced in years.

In February, 1875, he visited Newark, and preached two sermons, by special invitation, in Trinity Church. Dr. Nicholson, his successor in that rectorship, had recently made public his sympathy with the seceding brethren, and his intention of joining the new organization. The Baptismal Office and the Ordinal were the points upon which he founded his defection.

A letter from a Vestryman of Trinity, conveying the request to preach two sermons in reply to Dr. Nicholson, contains this sentence: —

"I regard you as altogether the best informed and ablest theologian who has been with us in Newark. Judicious exposition of theology seemed, *me judice*, to be your forte. I remember to have been much struck with your sermon on Baptism. Besides, you came from a Calvinistic denomination, and are well posted on their views, and on those of kindred sects."

In June of the same year, he preached the Convention sermon in New Haven.

When Dr. Meier-Smith assumed the rectorship of St. John's, he was not without hope that the parish might regain its former strength and influence. Though this hope was but partially realized, he had no reason to feel that his work was an unfruitful one, as much advance was made on previous years. The standard of religious life was raised by his faithful and earnest preaching; congregations greatly increased, and large Confirmation classes were presented. But he labored under many discouragements, especially in regard to

the financial matters of the parish, which induced him
to consider favorably suggestions made to him, in the
third year of his rectorship, to become a candidate for
the vacant Chair of Homiletics in the Divinity School
of Philadelphia.

Respecting these propositions he wrote to Dr. Dyer:

". . . The notion about the professorship has been,
from various sources, dinging at me for some time.
W—— suggested it to me first last winter, I think.
You know he once had an idea of getting me into Gambier when I was *in transitu.* I know enough of myself
to know that I can teach; and I have found out that I
can influence young men. And if I were really compe-
tent for the place, —and I could, I think, fit myself for
it easily, — I should enjoy the work most thoroughly."

There was a growing consciousness in his mind that
the pastoral work which he loved so dearly, he could
never again hope to carry on with the vigor and enthusiasm of earlier years. His physical strength had been
somewhat impaired for several years, during which
time, his devotion to and sympathy with the invalid
members of his household had caused a great nerve
strain. A work free from the excitements and responsibilities of a rector's life looked inviting to him, especially as it was in the line of study he most loved,
and one which would bring young men under his influence. Yet he would not have given the subject any
serious consideration had he believed that his best loved
work, preaching the Gospel of our blessed Lord, would
have to be abandoned. Nor, indeed, had he contemplated less work, upon which point he expressed himself decidedly in a letter to Dr. Dyer: ". . . Don't let
anybody suppose I seek a 'dignified retirement from active work.' I am not prepared to become a trilobite or

any other fossil yet. Let the Lord order. I wish I were always as willing in everything to say this; for beyond the question of the most usefulness, I care nothing personally about this particular thing. If it had not been said to me a good many times that I was cut out for this sort of business, and that my friends might as well find it out, I would not have alluded to the vacant professorship."

To Dr. Dyer, in September, 1875, he wrote: " . . . This is a case in which more than ordinarily I take pleasure in thinking that all is in the hands of the Lord who knows what is for my good, and for the good of His work. The chief personal solicitude I have in the matter is on my wife's account. If I could shake the idea out of her little pate, of her responsibility for all the woman's work in the parish, I should not care half a peck about the question. On the other hand, I say as frankly that I regard the work of such a teacher as among the highest works, and should enter upon it, if the way were pointed out clearly, with the strongest convictions. I have a letter this morning inclosing one from W—— wherein is this sentence: ' What very exact theologian can speak of the extent of your friend's Broad Church tendencies?' *He* does n't know, neither do I. I will trust you to defend me against charges of heterodoxy. My 'Broad' is not *Colensoïsh*, nor the lack of positive convictions. I say 'Credo' and I mean it. While I can keep good temper with those who are of the other part, I am in spiritual sympathy with the earnest Christian believers and workers who hold the faith as Evangelical Protestant Christians hold it, and with such only; and my 'Broad' lies in two facts,— first, I don't care two pop-corns whether the chap next me spells it *shibboleth* or *sibboleth ;* secondly, while I hold very decided views of Church Orders, I like a good hand-shake, every now and then, with all who love our Lord Jesus Christ, with the entirety of the flock of our Blessed Lord. . . . By the way, how much it is the fact that theological sides taken are as much matters of temperament as anything else. I have seen a despondent, pre-doomed, reprobated Calvinist, of the ultra-marinest blue, converted into a light-hearted, loving fellow, ready to hug the Arminian brother, within fifteen minutes,—the means of conversion being a dish of Saddle-Rocks on the half-shell, and a toby of Bass's Pale East India. . . . Now my matters I leave with the Overseers of the School, and with the Lord, with no anxiety about the result. I want to have my work and years and record, if the Lord will, among the broad and evangelical men in the Church, and not among 'high and dry,'—'High' and 'Low' are words I care not for, if I can see the devout Christian, full of faith and good works, and the sympathetic helper in bringing men, women, and children to the dear Lord."

Late in the autumn of 1875, Dr. Meier-Smith was elected to the Chair of Homiletics and Pastoral Care in the "Divinity School of the Protestant Episcopal Church, in Philadelphia." When his name was brought before the Boards, objection was made by a member of the Board of Overseers, that he had heard that the candidate was not orthodox on the doctrine of future punishment. Bishop Lee wrote to him telling him of the objection, saying, "It is stated that you hold the views commonly known as those of the Restorationists."

The reply was as follows:—

HARTFORD, December 2, 1875.

MY DEAR BISHOP LEE,—. . . I don't know whether I am orthodox or not, in the opinion of the man who started the nonsense, on this point or any other. I did not stop my thinking when I left the Theological Seminary; but I certainly have never taught nor do I hold either a Restorationist or Universalist theology. Nor am I aware that I hold anything inconsistent either with the recognized position of our Church on the question of future punishment, or maintain any different attitude respecting the fearful facts revealed, from that maintained by leading evangelical thinkers among our own clergy, and those of other educated denominations. I accept, heartily and simply, every word of our Blessed Lord and all teaching of Scripture. But I recognize in these holy words, heights and depths of mystery and meaning unmeasured yet, if not unmeasurable. I am, my dear Bishop, with highest regard and loving thanks,

Faithfully yours,
MATSON MEIER-SMITH.

His decision to accept this appointment was communicated to his Vestry, with his resignation of the rectorship. The acceptance of his resignation was accompanied with affectionate expressions of regard, and of regret in parting with the Rector. The Vestry requested him to continue in charge of the parish until after Easter, which he consented to do, with the understanding that early in the year he should commence, in part, his duties in Philadelphia, and must be relieved of much of the pastoral work.

The Christmas Festival of the Sunday-school was made the occasion of many warm tributes to the retiring Rector, who had made for himself a strong place in the affections of the younger portion of his congregation, and their parents and teachers. "No one has ever done so much for our young people," said one and another, as they greeted him tenderly. The charm of his warm and sympathetic nature made itself as strongly felt in these days of his maturer ministry, as in his fresh and buoyant youth. The discipline of almost thirty years of steady labor with its burdens and responsibilities, its rewards and disappointments, had mellowed and softened the enthusiasm which, early in life, had sometimes led to an over-sanguine trust in others. Yet it had not changed his hearty responsiveness and kindly thoughtfulness, or made him less unselfish and unwearied in labors of love for all to whom he could minister, either as friend or pastor. Thus in Hartford, as in all his former pastorates, he left behind him the memory of one whose presence and daily influence were cheering and uplifting and in perfect harmony with the spirit of his public ministrations.

From the Bishop of Connecticut the following note was received in reply to Dr. Meier-Smith's request for a letter dimissory.

My dear Doctor, — I hate to send this! I hate to lose you! For all the comfort you gave me I thank you, and pray God to bless you and yours most abundantly!

Affectionately yours,

J. W.

From letters of sympathy written by members of St. John's parish and other friends in Hartford after the death of Dr. Meier-Smith, the extracts are taken which close this record of his four years' work in that city.

From James A. Smith, Esq.

HARTFORD, April 2, 1887.

. . . I loved your husband for his strength and clearness of mind, and the warm friendship of his soul, which always made me feel stronger and better for meeting him.

The news of his death gave all his old friends in St. John's a great shock, and you may feel sure that many hearts here, with mine, deeply sympathize with you and yours in your great, great loss.

From Edgar T. Welles, Esq.

NEW YORK, April 1, 1887.

It is impossible for me to tell you the shock that the news of your great bereavement gave me.

Your dearly loved husband, loved by all who knew him, was one of the *reliables*, — a friend ever and always to be depended on, — and one whom you would always think of as near with a glow of satisfaction.

And now he has gone forever from us. It is hard, very hard to realize, and harder for us as circumstances have so controlled, that we have not been fortunate enough to be able to see as much of each other recently as we should have done.

And now that I am able to be here more regularly, he is taken away!

It is a great personal loss, but to you, my dear friend, it is irreparable. To you and yours I tender my warmest, deepest sympathy. May God have you in His holy keeping.

From Rev. Dr Pynchon, then President of Trinity College.

". . . I always regarded him as a gentleman of the best type, a sincere and most warm-hearted and hospitable friend, a man of a particularly genial temper, and evidently designed by nature to be one of those whose function it should be to sweeten life.

"If this so appeared to the outside world, to friends, how much more must these qualities have endeared him to his own family ? I feel that you have all met with a peculiarly severe and trying loss."

XVI.

LIFE AND WORK IN PHILADELPHIA.

1876–1887.

IN February, 1876, Dr. Meier-Smith commenced his work in Philadelphia, spending three days in each week there, familiarizing himself with his duties, and arranging for the full course of lectures to commence in the following autumn. Until after the Easter vacation, he remained in charge of the pulpit of St. John's, Hartford. It was not until May that he removed with his family to Philadelphia, where he had purchased a house. The marriage engagement of his daughter occurred a few months before leaving Hartford. This event was a cause of much happiness, strengthening ties of affection between his own family and those of honored and much-loved friends.

The excitement of the great Centennial Exposition had already begun, and Philadelphia for the next six months could hardly be recognized as her own staid and conservative self. Under these circumstances not much could be done at the Divinity School but to make acquaintance with the Faculty and the students, and to survey the new field.

The summer was spent with his family near New London, Connecticut, and in September they took possession of their house. To one of his strong domestic tastes there was much satisfaction in a home presenting a hope of permanence, which was an hitherto unknown experience.   His complete contentment with his surroundings at home, and the opening of his new work, are well remembered.   The life now commenced differed essentially from the past.   The busy days, full to the brim with pastoral duties, pulpit preparation, and parochial supervision, were exchanged for days of quiet, methodical work, with the regular hours of the lecture room and the study.   When asked by a friend how he liked such a complete change, and if he did not miss the more exciting life now over, he replied, " I confess to feeling a little like a fish out of water, or rather like a boat which has steered out of the current; but on the whole I like it, and I rather think it is going to like me.   I believe it is the better work for me now."

If the steady routine and the carefully arranged hours made the life in some respects easier, there was no less call for the full powers of the man.   He was not one to content himself with the exact amount of labor expected, but conscientiously put the best of himself into all that he did, as truly as when a parish clergyman.

His life being now one of so much less variety, and moving on in a beaten track, it seems best no longer to follow it year by year, but to give reminiscences of the ten succeeding years from three points of view, — the Work in the Divinity School, Church Work and Clerical Associations, and the Home Life.

WORK IN THE DIVINITY SCHOOL.

The Philadelphia Divinity School was founded by the late Bishop Alonzo Potter.   It was ever very dear to that venerated prelate, and as he did not propose to make it simply a school for the Diocese of Pennsylvania, it was placed under the care of Boards composed of clergymen and laymen from several dioceses, principally from Pennsylvania, New York, and Massachusetts.

Thus, being neither a Diocesan nor a General Church Seminary, it has been under disadvantage as to the number of students naturally drawn to it. From the same reason, it has presented some unusual attractions to able and thoughtful young men of uo strong party predilections, and numbers among its graduates names widely known and honored in the Church. At the time Dr. Meier-Smith was called to the Chair of Homiletics, the Faculty consisted of the Rev. Drs. Goodwin, Butler, and Hare, and the Rev. Francis Colton.

The three elder professors were men of eminent scholarship in their respective departments, and men of influence in Church councils. Mr. Colton was a brilliant Hebrew scholar and a fine teacher.

Dr. Meier-Smith felt it an honor to be the colleague of such men, and during all the years of his intimate association with them nothing interrupted the warm friendship and the high regard mutually entertained. Of the five composing the Faculty after he entered it, only the venerable Dr. Hare remains. Mr. Colton was early called from a work full of promise. Dr. Goodwin and Dr. Butler, both Dr. Meier-Smith's seniors by many years, survived him for three years, and passed to the rest of Paradise crowned with fulness of days and honorable service in the Church.

The full work of the professorship commenced in the autumn of 1876. Dr. Meier-Smith entered upon it with enthusiasm, and it grew upon his hands. The preparation in his study was work exactly to his mind, and the intellectual labor of the past years proved a good

foundation for it. Never a careless student and ser-
mon-writer, he was not in danger of becoming a superficial teacher of sermon-making. Never undervaluing
the great work of preaching, he was well prepared to
magnify his office, and train young men to the practical
work of the ministry, and especially to its highest duty
and honor, — the preaching of the Gospel. For several
years his lectures were in large part freshly written or
extensively revised, as each year he could see where
to improve his instruction. He was careful not to
fall into a rut, or to grow dull and monotonous. To
keep abreast of the thought and methods of these
days of ever-widening views and rapid progress was
his steady aim.

He left a large number of manuscript volumes, com-
prising his notes of lectures, more or less fully written
out. They embrace courses upon Homiletics, Pastoral
Duties, Parochial Administration, and other subjects
necessary to the full equipment of the pastor and the
preacher, and many lectures on Liturgics. There are
also historical sketches of Foreign Missions, not only
those of our own Church, but of other branches of the
Church Catholic.

They show the same careful study and vigorously expressed thought which mark all his written sermons.
These lectures were seldom read just as written. They
were used chiefly as notes for free and extemporized instruction, often of the most informal nature. No text-
book on Homiletics was quite satisfactory to him, and
he had in mind, in preparing his lectures, a probable
revision and future publication of his main course of
instruction. Upon his methods as a teacher, the Dean
of the Seminary has written with affectionate appreciation and with critical impartiality. His tribute, first

printed in the "Churchman," is appended to this sketch of the work in the Divinity School.

Dr. Meier-Smith's lectures are found written, as were all his sermons, in distinct hand, unmarred by erasures or abbreviations.   Friends of his own profession, looking over his manuscripts, invariably comment upon the neatness and finish of his work.   This painstaking method of work resulted from the fact that nothing in the line of his duty ever seemed to him unimportant. The simplest expository lecture was faithfully studied, and, if written out, took its appropriate expression in his own mind before he commenced to write.   Perhaps this careful and conscientious labor hindered, to some extent, a showing of his real ability outside of his regular work.   It was a familiar and playful response with him, when asked to write for the press, " Oh, I 'm too lazy for such hard work !"   It was rather that he had a dread of the severe labor he knew it would cost him to produce the realization of his high ideal.

The new work commenced hopefully.   The class entering the school in 1876 was one of unusual promise, with a large proportion of able men and good students. There seemed at once to be a mutual attraction between them and the Professor of Homiletics, and the warm friendships commencing then continued, not only through the Seminary course, but with several of the number during the rest of Dr. Meier-Smith's life.   He felt that much could be done for his pupils by personal influence, and he wished to be their pastor and friend. They were frequently guests at his house, and his frank and winning manner, and unvarying courtesy, placed them at ease with him, and encouraged a free confidence.   There have been ample testimonies to the place he held in the hearts of many of his students.

To no one could they go, if in doubt or perplexity, with more certainty of a patient and sympathetic hearing, or more assurance of wise and judicious counsel. Long experience as a pastor, and large intercourse with men, well fitted him to understand the needs of these young men ; and all who knew him, and who read this record, know that to appeal to him for help always meant to receive it. If no more practical aid was possible, they received the certainty that the need or anxiety had been thoroughly appreciated by an elder brother's heart. There were some among the many who came under his instruction whom he never reached. But in every class, the best and strongest men gave him gratifying assurances of their obligation to him, as friend and teacher, as well out of the class-room as within it. It was his practice to seek out the more retiring students, most of whom were strangers in the city, and to do what he could to make them feel at home in his house, inviting them to his table, or for a social evening, and often thus breaking the loneliness of a holiday for those who could not go to their distant homes. To have found his unrestrained cordiality abused, would at any time have caused him more pain than many could feel from such a disappointment. Naturally trusting and guileless, he expected trust in others, and suffered keenly on the few occasions in his life when he found that his confidence had been misplaced.

At the time Dr. Meier-Smith commenced his work at the Divinity School, an old mansion with large grounds, in West Philadelphia, was occupied by the Seminary. There were many inconveniences resulting from the imperfect adaptation of such a building to the needs of a divinity school, and after a few years this property was sold, and the present location secured. The cornerstone of the fine edifice erected upon Woodland Avenue and Fiftieth Street, was laid at the Commencement of the Seminary, in June, 1881.

Professor Colton, who was secretary of the Faculty, died within the first two years of Dr. Meier-Smith's professorship, and he succeeded him in that office. This position he retained until the close of his work. He found that there was need of some supervision of domestic matters connected with the comfort of the students who lived at the School, which seemed, in the absence of a resident Dean, to be no one's duty; and he volunteered his services for such work, believing that he could advance the interests of the Seminary, and remove some grounds of dissatisfaction. Such a post he held by desire of the Faculty and the Bishop, until he was relieved, after the removal to the new building and the appointment of Dr. Bartlett as resident Dean. Through this position he was brought into close relationship to many of the students, and became familiar with the household economies, to a degree somewhat amusing to his family, who knew how little of such care had heretofore fallen upon him. He had the satisfaction of feeling that this service, on which he expended much time and thought, was productive of substantial good, hardly appreciated at the time. The practical knowledge he gained in this experience was of benefit in contributing to the conveniences of the new building, in the arrangements of which he took a warm interest.

In 1885, Rev. Dr. Edward S. Bartlett, Rev. John P. Peters, Ph.D., and Rev. Dr. Joseph F. Garrison were added to the Faculty. New vigor in administration and a higher standard of scholarship gave an impulse to the progress of the Seminary. With these colleagues,

Dr. Meier-Smith was in hearty sympathy, and predicted greatly enlarged usefulness in the work of the school from these additions to the corps of instructors.

During all these years Dr. Meier-Smith wrote to his friend Dr. Dyer with the frankness of close intimacy. To the larger experience and wise counsel of his friend he appealed in any perplexity, and many of his letters are so characteristic that there is much temptation to insert them. But that which constitutes their charm precludes their appearance to any extent. Much relates to very personal matters, and without explanation might be misunderstood. Under date of March 1, 1877, Dr. Meier-Smith writes to Dr. Dyer concerning his work at the Divinity School. " . . . You do my inmost heart good, by the kind way you speak of my success, so far, in the professorship. I was more anxious to succeed, for my friends' sake, yours particularly, than for any purely personal reasons, I am quite sure. I want indeed to be successful for higher reasons. . . . The fellows seem to take to me. They don't act as if I were stiffness personified, and I enjoy the work immensely. I only wish for more students, and for more who have had superior preparation. Many of the boys have enjoyed but limited advantages. I work hard over them, and the work grows upon me with its possibilities and responsibilities. I think we can turn out good material. One of these days, if I can get hold of some good layman, I should like to get some fuuds much needed now for library uses. In fact, between you and me, there are several things that want ' tinkering,' for the most effective working of the School. But I won't write anything to set you thinking. I only want to show you that I am busy thinking outside of ' chair ' limits."

Referring to the discussion going on respecting the "Order of the Holy Cross," and Bishop Lee's letter to the Bishop of New York, he wrote to Dr. Dyer, under date of Jan. 8, 1884 : —

. . . What exciting things are going on ! Such a stir here in Philadelphia over the reported new departure of Bishop Potter ! . . . I have so warm a regard for the Bishop, and such unbounded faith in his glorious intentions to go out to the outcast and perishing, and in his common-sense, and his disdain of both the nonsensical and the effete, that I cannot fault him. But — but — is there any grace in an ill-fitting robe, and a rope around one's " midst " ! The " crackit " however we shall always have with us, and we must bear with their infirmities though we cannot " abide " them. . . . The Divinity School is on the move. Certainly the additions to the Faculty are immensely valuable. Dr. Bartlett is admirable in professorship and Deanship. He is scholarly as teacher and practical as Dean. Dr. Peters does not allow the Hebrew to be a " bugbear," and awakens enthusiasm. Dr. Garrison is a very full man, with unusual presentation faculty, and is popular and successful. Now if the Executive Committee will show that they are as progressive as the Faculty, things will "rush." The *morale* of the School seems to be excellent. The residence of the Dean is a great help. I think now for instruction we have no superior in the Church, and excepting in a single department (!),[1] I fancy that so far as we go, we are equal to any school in the Church. I hope, my dear Doctor, you keep bright as ever. You await the revelation of the Lord from heaven, and what peace and glory must this be in your soul! Ever affectionately, your brother,   M. M.-S.

[1] A modest reference to his own work.

The following extracts, taken from among many letters received from former pupils since his earthly work was ended, bear witness to his influence as friend and teacher : —

From Rev. L. W. Burton.

". . . I can echo all that has been so aptly and affectionately said of Dr. Meier-Smith in the published letters and resolutions.   What position could be a more responsible one than that he filled ?

" I am sure a conscientious realization that he was shaping men for the ministry of Christ, to many scattered congregations, was always combined with a tender regard for the students themselves.   I am certainly still feeling his influence over my work, and every day's deeper experience of life, and understanding of God's Will, are making me appreciate, more and more, how right he was in his views and advice as to our calling."

From Rev. N. H. Burnham.

". . . For the last twelve years he has been a kind and constant friend.   As such I owe him more than I can ever express.   I must add that as my instructor he is equally deserving of my lasting gratitude.   I seldom write a sermon without seeming to feel his genial presence, and to hear his voice uttering words of kindly criticism and instruction.   I cannot realize that my dear friend and wise, kind counsellor is gone forever."

From Rev. J. J. J. Moore.

". . . His unvarying kindness to me during my three years' course in the Seminary will ever live in my most grateful remembrance.   My nervousness and diffidence always received at his hands the utmost consideration, and his hearty, ready sympathy saved me from much anxiety and actual pain.   He was one of the few men who can understand such a temperament, and to whom I would care to go in time of perplexity and trouble.   Men of his genial nature, quick perception, unfailing patience, and sympathetic counsel, are so scarce in this world that I cannot forbear offering this mite of true appreciation, of grateful and lasting regard."

From Rev. George McIlvaine Du Bois.

". . . For my own part I have always believed that I owe more to Dr. Meier-Smith than to any other member of the Faculty.   His method of teaching his department was excellent.   He made timid men bolder, and gave all his pupils self-reliance.   He knocked out the sensitiveness or foolish pride which stands in the way of usefulness, and taught men to be broader, tougher, and more manly.   He took a personal interest in the young men, and tried to aid them and develop them in every way.   I know moreover his laboriousness in preparation, though it was also a fact that he depreciated his own work, though it may have cost him hours of study.   I am sure the Class of '79 are unanimous in their regard for Dr. Meier-Smith, and their appreciation of his work."

From Rev. W. H. Burr.

". . . I can never forget either Dr. Meier-Smith's kindness to me, nor the strength of his goodness, — he was always a man, a true man.   I shall never forget many of his words, and how deeply they impressed me.   They set a thoughtless, pleasure-loving college boy to thinking, and made him seriously ask for the first time, ' What is life?' "

From Rev. E. G. Richardson.

". . . I wish, while expressing my deep sympathy with you and yours, to add a special word of gratitude for valued, helpful influence.   It is difficult for a pupil to tell precisely what he owes to a respected teacher, but I am distinctly conscious of being indebted to Dr. Meier-Smith for a germinant enthusiasm for the work of the ministry, and also for the beginnings of a habit of hopefulness in the midst of its perplexities."

From Rev. F. S. Ballentine.

"... How inadequate are words to express the worth of such a character! I can't but think, however well others may have known him, that I saw some sides of his character while with him at the Divinity School, which led me especially to know what a noble, manly man he was. He prized a manly character above everything. If he found that, he cared not for minor differences. And how he did pity one who lacked breadth, — one who could not see beyond his own little rut. I am glad to remember the kindly interest the Doctor took in me. The memory of him will always be to my life as a sweet-smelling savor."

From Rev. W. M. Harrison.

"... My intercourse with Professor Meier-Smith was most pleasant all through the Seminary course. His lectures I always found interesting and instructive, especially in those matters which related to our practical work as pastors and preachers. There was no one of the Faculty more interested in the personal welfare of the students, as students; and no one more ready to give them the benefit of his wider knowledge and experience, both when they were under his instruction, and when they had left the Seminary. Well do I remember writing to him for advice soon after I had graduated, and his reply so full of sympathy and encouragement, and so helpful to me at that time."

From Rev. R. S. Howell.

"... I cannot express to you the comfort it gave me to draft the testimonials of our reverence and affection for the friend who has gone to the home he loved so well. Every word seemed so merited and so true. I had difficulty in

restraining myself from expressions, which, though the outcome of deep respect and regard, I felt would not have been
sought by the modest, manly spirit we delighted to honor "

From Rev. L. H. Schwab.

". . . I think what must have struck most people as they
came in contact with Dr. Meier-Smith was his great power of
sympathy. It was what attracted many very strongly to him,
and this trait of his character leaves the most abiding impression upon the memory. His kindly smile, the warm and
hearty grasp of the hand, with which he greeted you, these
are things which one does not meet every day in the cold
world, and when you come under the influence of such a
warm nature the impression is lasting. This sympathy of
his certainly gave to many a young man, struggling hard, a
new hope and courage. In his teaching perhaps the chief
characteristic was the entire absence of red-tape and formalism. It was his endeavor to teach the men to think, and thus
to get the best out of them by a natural process of development.   His lectures were often very informal and familiar
talks. His strong sense of humor and lightness of spirit made
his recitations different from those of other professors, as the
lesson which he was trying to teach was enforced and illustrated by some pointed anecdote or happy saying, and yet
underneath it all there was a deep earnestness which every
now and then would come to the surface in some earnest
words of serious warning or spiritual advice ; and many
have carried away the strong impression which such words
of evangelical fervor made upon them, when the students
were exhorted above all things to preach ' Christ Crucified,'
and to preserve the consciousness of the responsibility for
men's souls to which they were called.

"This blending of an innocent joyousness with a deep, intense seriousness was, I think, one of the strong points of
Dr. Meier-Smith's character. As I write, the recollection of
him comes up so distinctly before my mind ! What a

blessing that we may look forward to seeing again those we have loved so much here!"

From Rev. Frederick Burt Avery.

July 11, 1890.

. . . I have tried repeatedly to renew our acquaintance and to tell you how much I loved your noble husband.

Dr. Meier-Smith was a very dear friend to me, from the day I received his cordial letter of welcome to the "Divinity School," on through the course, and to the time of parish work as a priest in the dear Church which he loved and taught me to love. For I was not "born and bred" in our Church, but had come, as he had, from the Presbyterians. This made one of the strands of the strong rope of sympathy which seemed to bind us together. He was personally my friend, as he tried to be to all the students in many a practical way, securing remunerative positions as assistants, visiting us in our rooms, giving us valuable suggestions as to ways and methods of work, study, and recreation. He did not forget that the young men were still boys in their home feelings, and in this, his wife, always so hospitable and cordial, enthusiastically seconded his efforts to make us feel at home in "De Lancey Place," not only when specially invited to "splendid suppers," but whenever we might "drop around."

Some of these pleasant memories of course still linger to recall those happy days, as they touched the "natural man's" sensibilities and affections. Divinity students are very human. But while these social amenities marked dear Dr. Meier-Smith's relations to the students, they were merely incidental to the career of the young men for whom, and with whom, he was laboring, in order to make them "workmen who need not to be ashamed," well furnished and equipped for their life's work. He was a great reader and a hard student, a real lover and judge of good books. From his researches he gave us "treasures new and old," and did not simply confine his lectures to a few "books on homiletics." His Churchmanship was not that of a partisan.   " Broad " in his sympathies, " High " in his ideals of ministerial rectitude, " *Lowly* " minded, feeling the necessity of meekly obeying the Master's precepts, yet ever ambitious to excel in every good word and deed.   While evangelical in his presentment of the " faith once delivered to the saints," he believed thoroughly in institutional religion and the authority vested in the Divine Orders of the Visible Church of Christ.

His criticisms of our sermonic efforts, and our delivery of the same, while at times severe, were always just, discriminating, and kind.   He knew how to " speak the truth in love."   While he taught us to be very loyal to the Church's standards, and was a thorough Rubrician, he interlaced the offices of the Prayer Book with the " Rubric of Common-sense."   In this latter gift he excelled, and frequently, with a forceful incident of his own experience, or by a most practical illustration, presented the profoundest of truths, fastening them as nails in a sure place in our memories, from which they can never be obliterated.

I might add many more reminiscences of our beloved preceptor in Pastoral Theology, and then still fail to do justice to the memory of one who was more than a teacher, — a friend and pastor to those whom he tried to make realize their high calling as under-shepherds of the divine Master.

He made a deep impression upon my own life.

May our Heavenly Father grant me the privilege of the blessed reunion with him and the saints gone before, in the Paradise of the Redeemed and Blessed for evermore!

The Rev. Edward T. Bartlett, D.D., Dean of the Divinity School, contributed the following to the " Churchman," June 18, 1887 : —

" I desire to write a few words in memory of a dear friend and fellow-worker whose services to the Church will not soon be forgotten, but a record of some of them may be still further promotive of good.

"Two months ago the Rev. Matson Meier-Smith, D.D., Professor in the Divinity School in Philadelphia, was suddenly called away from his place and work on earth. The shock was so sudden, and the loss so great, that it scarcely seemed possible to those who had worked side by side with him to bear the one or speak of the other with entire calmness. Now, however, that the mind has become somewhat accustomed to the great change caused by his sudden departure, it may be possible to say a few words that will convey some notion of what his work was in the Divinity School.

"Dr. Meier-Smith was peculiarly gifted with a sincere, quick sympathy with all sorts and conditions of men. Dignified, and commanding respect wherever he went and whomsoever he met, he was remarkably free from that self-assertiveness which so often accompanies personal dignity. He knew how to yield and subordinate himself, how to practise a genuine, easy, graceful Christian humility, without the sacrifice of self-respect or the respect of others. There was no appearance of narrowness, dogmatism, or arrogance in him, though he was a man of positive convictions, which he was accustomed to express freely whenever there was occasion.

"The professorship he held was that of homiletics and pastoral care. His course of instruction was well planned and methodical, but its special characteristics grew out of the fact that he endeavored to make his lectures personal conversations between him and his pupils, — not the less direct and consecutive for being free from formality. The wise, loving, charitable, and manly principles that he had learned to apply in his own pastorate of twenty-eight years were those which, during his eleven years' professorship, he sought to implant in those who were preparing for such work. His influence tended to strengthen in his scholars traits of manliness, true Christian self-reliance, strength, courage, and meekness. He gave principles, not rules, and was extremely careful to show those who heard him that men must for themselves look at things straightforwardly and clearly, and adapt their application of principles to the peculiar and ever-varying circumstances with which they would have to deal. His own work in the pastorate for many years had given him experiences the harvest of which he knew well how to gather and store up. Sympathy, and a desire to understand and be fair to all men, had enabled him to profit by such experiences, and it was evident that he was always thinking kindly and carefully of all that he had passed through, with a view to learning how it might be turned to profit for those whom he instructed. His method thus was inductive. He did not deal with preaching and pastoral work as a theorizer merely. His theory was reached after a careful collation of facts, by a patient, careful, kind-hearted consideration of them. He was not only a clergyman and a priest of the Church ; he knew laymen, he understood them, he showed great ability in working with and not merely over them, and no one could attend his classes without feeling that with great common-sense and wisdom he was exercising such an influence over them as would send them out to be good leaders among the laity.

" His power over his classes was all the greater because of the solid, quiet basis from which it worked. It was a genial quality which drew his men to him personally while yet it left them free from any overwhelming personal influence. Wit and humor played a large part in his remarks and criticisms. He was always ready with a smile, which was good-natured and which never hurt the most sensitive feelings, yet which performed a most effective work. Satire, severe but altogether free from bitterness and perfectly courteous, was at hand when needed. But he was an attentive and appreciative listener, a true critic, looking for the good points rather than the bad. Having found the best there was in a man, he desired to cultivate that to the full. It was evident that he had in mind the difficulties men would have to meet through their own limitations, and was trying to understand each man separately on his own merits, and to assist him to that enlargement of character which is the best of all safeguards against the peculiar difficulties that are encountered in the ministry. To train a young Christian man into being his own best self, and to live in the highest regions of his character, — that was Professor Meier-Smith's great aim in his work in the Divinity School. Strong and liberal in his own views, he never attempted to interfere with earnest convictions in other men, any more than with individuality of character, but only to help them to clearness, sincerity, and truth.

"Self-forgetting, unobtrusive, ready with kind feelings and kind words, ready to help wherever he could, he is greatly missed by his fellow-workers, and his memory will be forever blessed."

XVII.

CHURCH WORK AND CLERICAL ASSOCIATIONS.

BEFORE Dr. Meier-Smith accepted the professor-ship offered to him in Philadelphia, he expressed strongly, to friends, his unwillingness to resign the work of a parish clergyman, unless he could find frequent opportunities to preach. "The work I love best in the world," he said, "is to preach the glorious Gospel of our blessed Lord, and I cannot lay it entirely aside. An educational post too often means that the *preacher* is shelved." He was assured that he would find no lack of occasion to exercise his much-loved calling in so large a city, and the experience of the subsequent years was in this respect all that he could have desired.

From the "Record of Services" it appears that he preached more than five hundred times after his re-moval to Philadelphia, which is an average of once each Sunday throughout the whole time.

He came to Philadelphia without any extensive ac-quaintance with the clergy of the city. The cordiality with which he was welcomed, and the friendships formed in various parishes, and with their rectors, made his work among them a very happy one. For the first two years he was at the service of his friends in various parts of the city and its suburbs, and responded cheer-fully whenever he could give relief to an overworked brother. He assisted in the services and at the Holy Communion, frequently gave aid in the Lenten lecture courses, and was often called upon for addresses and lectures. During the ten years of Dr. Meier-Smith's residence in Philadelphia he became a familiar figure in the chancels and pulpits of Holy Trinity, St. James's, St. Luke's, and other prominent churches. From the large circle of friends made in these parishes, he had many kind proofs of his acceptability as a preacher, and from the acquaintance thus made much delightful social intercourse resulted. When he was so suddenly removed from his labors, a well-known layman paid him this high tribute: " I think there was not, in all Philadelphia, a clergyman so beloved in so many of our parishes as Dr. Meier-Smith." His own modest estimate of himself was such that an expression of this nature would have overwhelmed him.

The absence of past heavy responsibilities was a great relief; yet he gave many a loving and half-regretful thought to the pastoral work now over. " I do love to *know* to whom I am preaching," he often said. And to his sympathetic nature, a blessed work ceased when he found it no longer his place to minister consolation in hours of suffering, or to guide and help the struggling and weary. He missed, also, the regular celebration of the Church's great Feast. " I never celebrate the Holy Communion," he said to his wife, " without devout thanks that I am permitted such an honor; and I do love to administer to my *own* people," adding with a sigh, " that I suppose I am never likely to do again."

The summer vacations of the Divinity School were always passed away from the city, and for several years he preached quite constantly during these vacations.

He was in charge of the Chapel of the Episcopal Theological School, in Cambridge, Massachusetts, during two seasons. One summer he spent in Germantown, and preached for two months at the Church of the Transfiguration, in West Philadelphia, of which his son-in-law was temporarily in charge.

During the first three years of Dr. Meier-Smith's professorship he wrote few sermons, as his time for study was engrossed by his necessary work for the Divinity School. After this, and during his four years' connection with the parish of St. James's, he often wrote two or three sermons in a month, returning with vigor to his old work.

Recalling the main features of Dr. Meier-Smith's preaching, as remembered by many, and verifying the impression by looking over his " Record of Services," the distinctly evangelical character appears which marked all his previous work. The epithet is not used in any party sense, for in these late years he seldom wrote or preached a strictly theological discourse. The blessed Gospel message, in its simplicity and fulness, he loved more and more to deliver. Probably he cared less than formerly for oratorical effect, and he certainly preached more quietly. But in fervor, in pathos, in earnestness, and with increasing solemnity, he " preached Christ." The Life and Words of the Blessed Lord were his favorite themes ; mere ethical topics were seldom chosen. In the last three years there were many sermons preached relating to the Future Life. He read much, and thought deeply upon eschatological subjects; and the sermons inspired by this line of study glowed with an enthusiasm born of his enlarged and hopeful views. On many points he agreed substantially with some of the advanced writers in the Anglican Church, and while he was careful not to speak dogmatically on subjects not of positive revelation, he spoke frankly and openly of his growing convictions, and his belief in the " Larger Hope."

The complete union of the believer with his Lord, — Christ formed in him, — was a favorite theme, with the precious truths flowing therefrom for strengthening and consolation. The present life, as but the commencement of the grander stage of being, and that there is " no death for the one in Christ," were truths he emphasized in all their phases, as those who heard him frequently can testify. Christ, the Second Adam, the Head of a Redeemed Race, was another favorite subject, and, inseparable from this, brotherhood in Christ for all believers, and the hope of the " Universal Brotherhood," the bringing in of the " Fulness of the Gentiles." The notes of an increasing spirituality, and of a tender sympathy with human needs, witnessing to his own deepening inner life, were discerned in all the preaching of these years. A sense of failing physical strength, of which he was doubtless conscious, probably led his thoughts in the directions indicated. The shadow of the future, or shall we rather say, the light of the setting sun, fell upon him, and his spirit was thereby stirred to its inmost depths.

Never had Dr. Meier-Smith enjoyed such opportunities for fraternal intercourse with those of his own profession, as during these Philadelphia years. Bishop Stevens, a man of model life, wise and tender in all his administration, and in bearing a true Christian gentleman, was well beloved by all his clergy. There was much that was sympathetic between him and Dr. Meier-Smith, who was greatly drawn to him. Discussion of matters bearing on the interests of the Divinity School brought him and the Bishop much together, and very affectionate relations existed between them. Among the parish clergy some of his most intimate friends were the Rev. Drs. Miller, Watson, Currie, and

McVickar, with several of the younger rectors, to whom he loved to give assistance as they needed it. He was freely called upon for help, and as freely responded. Scarcely an unemployed Sunday appears in his "Record."

In 1879, from Epiphany nearly to the close of Lent, he officiated regularly at Holy Trinity Memorial Chapel. In February, 1881, his connection commenced with St. James's Church. For nearly four years it was his parish church, and he was the Rector's assistant in the pulpit, taking part in the service if he did not preach. The venerable Dr. Morton, for more than fifty years Rector of this parish, and whom he had frequently served before this regular engagement, was taken ill in February, 1881, while away from Philadelphia, and Dr. Meier-Smith became the preacher in charge until Dr. Morton's recovery, and continued to assist him every Sunday until the summer vacation. He also delivered a course of Lent lectures. In the winter of 1882 he gave a course of Confirmation lectures at St. James's, and conducted a weekly Bible instruction by invitation of a number of ladies.

Between Dr. Morton and himself there grew up a loving friendship which continued to the last. When, in the year 1890, the venerable Rector of St. James's was called to the service of the Upper Temple, he had been sixty years in this his only parochial charge, and three generations of loving parishioners mourned his departure. With the congregation of St. James's the pleasantest social relations existed, and Dr. Meier-Smith found again a renewal of the work always dear to him, when, now and then, he was asked to assist in parochial visitation, and to administer consolation and help to the afflicted or perplexed, to the inquirer or the mourner.

The whole term of his service with this parish was one of unbroken satisfaction. He could have had no position more thoroughly to his mind, and it was a cause of gratitude, that he could in this way supplement the work of his professorship, without any interference with its duties.

Among letters received giving impressions of Dr. Meier-Smith's preaching, there is copied, by permission, one from Miss M. P. McClellan, a lady for whom he cherished a warm regard. She thus relates an incident of her first acquaintance with him : —

" . . . I honored and loved Dr. Meier-Smith, and have mourned his loss as one whom the world needed, and whom the Church could ill afford to spare. I counted it a privilege to know him, and greatly valued his warm friendship. I shall never forget the occasion when I first became acquainted with him. It was on an Easter evening, 1880, I think, at Holy Trinity Memorial Chapel. I had frequently heard Dr. Meier-Smith preach before, with great appreciation of his fine sermons, but that Easter sermon was so grand that I felt impelled to speak to him and thank him for it. I asked a friend to introduce me to him, and he received me with such a kind and cordial greeting, that he won my confidence immediately. After a delightful little conversation in which he spoke of the joy with which he always pondered and wrote about the subject of the resurrection, I turned to pass down the aisle, when I heard him call my name repeatedly, until I turned and went back to where he stood on the chancel steps in his surplice, and well do I remember the earnest, eager expression of his bright face, as he said, 'Miss McClellan, after awhile we shall know all about these things! We shall *know* for ourselves!' His manner and the tone in which he spoke impressed me greatly. I understood how real, and how near, the future life seemed to him. From that time I can recall many and many an occasion when Dr. Meier-Smith's valuable instruction as a teacher, and his cheering words and ready sympathy, helped and strengthened me.   I once received a little note from him which I have prized as showing how pure and true was his love for the Master whom he served.   He wrote, 'I must thank you for the beautiful Christmas card you sent me, and most particularly for your kind words added.   And I want to say that more than any possible plaudits or honors, do I prize just such expressions from members of Christ's flock, telling me that through some poor ministry of mine, the dear Lord has come nearer to them and blessed them.'   When I next met him he repeated what he had written, and the tears in his eyes proved the sincerity of his words."

Dr. Meier-Smith was a member of the " Clericus Club," and highly prized its meetings.   The members were men of wide culture and independent thought, and their discussions were refreshing and stimulating.   He compared it often to his old Boston Club, the " Winthrop," referred to in the sketch of his life in Brookline.

It has been difficult to choose from among the many letters which have been received, testifying to the place Dr. Meier-Smith held in the respect and affection of his clerical brethren.

The extracts which follow are typical of nearly all, every one of which bore its own message of sympathy and consolation.   To the hearts so sorely stricken, such words of appreciation were grateful beyond expression.

With the Rev. Dr. D. S. Miller, Dr. Meier-Smith was very intimate.   The tender words written by Dr. Miller a few days after the shock of his friend's sudden death, are given here.   The last sentence seems prophetic, as within a few months he also entered into rest, after a long life of faithful service in the Church.

". . . I must say a word to you about the loss of our dear friend. I should have done it before, but I have been ill and without energy these few days, and somehow I did n't feel like writing a letter of condolence to the wife, and in formal fashion. For he was so true a man, — so loyal, so kind, so tender, so much above words himself, that only one's heart should speak of him, and mine does. I can hardly name a man in the ministry whose loss I shall feel so much, — as if a light had gone out from our horizon. God be thanked, we know it is well with him, and he has gone to reap his full reward! And we who are all getting among the shadows of the way must soon join him. The Lord comfort you, and give you strength!"

From the Rev. Dr. C. G. Currie.

". . . I honored him not only for his ability, but for his noble qualities as a man. He was a man all through, — incapable of a mean action, or of an uncharitable word concerning any one. He had the qualities that cant pretends to have, but he abhorred the cant."

From the Rev. Dr. W. F. Paddock.

". . . His memory will be fresh and fragrant, his example stimulating and beneficent to his friends, clerical and lay, who have been in any way associated with him. It is a glorious thing to leave behind such a pure and stainless record."

From the Rev. Professor Peters.

". . . I shall venture to copy and send you the following passage from a sermon I preached in New York on Whitsunday: 'On my mantelpiece stands the photograph of a late colleague of my own, and every time I look at it the memory of certain beautiful traits comes up before me, and above all of a peculiar thoughtfulness and consideration of the feelings of every one with whom he came in contact ; and a spirit is present that bids me seek to acquire that same thoughtfulness, that same consideration for the feelings of others, which was in him so lovely. This spirit for their help he has bequeathed to those who knew him.'"

From the Rev. A. H. Vinton.

". . . Every word said of your dear husband is true, and much more could be added of his manliness and truth, his breadth of mind, his charity, his strength of friendship and encouragement of the young minds that were trying to find themselves.

"Rather used to snubbing from my elders in the ministry, I shall never forget the kindness shown, over and over, to me by the Doctor, and the memory of his friendship shall be ever sweet and lasting to me. Something of this I tried to say to you, telling you how deeply and truly I sorrowed with you, when the sudden news came last spring, but I was interrupted. I am very glad even at this late day to be able to tell you what has been so long in my heart, for I have mourned the loss of a noble friend, and, as it seemed, the too early death of a son the Church could, in these days of ill-balanced minds, little afford to lose."

From the Rev. J. W. Ashton.

". . . I have felt myself unequal to the task of expressing myself in relation to the subject which the memorial pamphlet suggests. I say 'task,' but never should I say *that* in relation to anything which concerns, or is associated with, the memory of your dear husband; and yet the expression of my feelings on account of his departure from us amounts to that; because I do not know what words to employ when speaking of his unselfishness and nobleness of character, of his friendliness and sweetness of disposition. He was my friend, and in more ways than one I am under obligation to him, — if one friend can be under obligation to another, — for words and deeds the recollection of which will never fade from my mind. As the season draws on I shall remember again, as I have often done since, how he preached for me at Grace Church on a certain Christmas Day when my dear mother's death and my father's dangerous illness rendered me unfit for the functions of the pulpit. He preached for me several times besides then. I used to tell him that I never could repay him for his assistance. I regret that I never was able to do so. Nevertheless, I shall leave the payment of that debt to the Lord, who I know will repay him tenfold, yes, a hundredfold, for all his kindness and love, — 'And the King shall answer, and say unto them, Verily, I say unto you, inasmuch as ye have done it unto one of the least of these my brethren, ye have done it unto me.' Dr. Meier-Smith was a man whom I knew and was associated with, in one way and another, under peculiar and diverse circumstances, and I have never known him to be anything else than large-hearted and broad-minded.

"My simple tribute to the value of Dr. Meier-Smith as a friend and fellow-minister may not prove to be altogether unacceptable. I deeply sympathize with you and your family in your great sorrow.

"I wish to add that the first intelligence of Dr. Meier-Smith's death reached me through Bishop Coxe, with whom I have enjoyed many pleasant conversations concerning your husband. The Bishop cherishes sweet memories of Dr. Meier-Smith, and it is agreeable to talk with one who knew him so well, and loved him so dearly."

From the Rt. Rev. O. W. Whitaker, D.D., Bishop of Pennsylvania.

". . . I write now to tell you how just and true I feel that all these loving words which have been written of your husband are. They tell only what all who knew him could testify, and there is no exaggeration in them. I feel his death as a personal loss. He had always been so kind to me, that I looked forward with pleasure to the hours I hoped we might spend together."

XVIII.

HOME LIFE.

THE chief object of these pages has been to present a sketch of Dr. Meier-Smith's life as related to the work he was permitted to do for Christ and the Church, and only incidental reference has been hitherto made to the place he filled in his family.

The curtain must be slightly lifted now, for if the sketch is not partially filled in, — if some suggestion of him in his home is not attempted, — it must fail as a life likeness. The hand which has held the pen with such calm impartiality as it could command, trembles now; and the heart which has been bidden to hide that which was nearest to itself beats more rapidly, as memories of the home life of the last years, so full of benediction to his own family, are to be briefly recorded. These later years were marked by more exclusive enjoyment of his home than any that preceded them. When not engaged in his public duties, Dr. Meier-Smith had but few of the interruptions to hours of quiet and domestic peace which had been inseparable from his life as a parish clergyman. To one of his domestic tastes this gave great satisfaction, and a tendency to retirement at his own fireside grew upon him with advancing years. He could rarely be induced to seek recreation for himself without his family. Now and then he yielded to entreaties of friends, and promised to join them in some jaunt or excursion; but ever when the time came he found some plausible reason for staying at home.   So it came to pass that, excepting for a night or two at a time when called away on business, he never went from home, save during the summer vacations, and in company with his wife and children.

Though the years flowed quietly on, they were not without events of deep interest to the family circle. In December, 1876, Dr. Meier-Smith's only sister, Mrs. Robert Jaffray, died, after long years of suffering borne with heroic patience.   Beloved for her beautiful Christian character, her loss was great to her family and friends, and this bereavement was keenly felt by her devoted brother.   They were much alike in sweetness of disposition, in sprightliness and buoyancy, and in true unselfishness.

The marriage of Dr. Meier-Smith's daughter, Emily Stuart, to the Rev. Henry Ogden Du Bois took place on the sixteenth of May, 1878.   The ceremony was performed in St. Luke's Church, her father officiating, assisted by the Rector, Rev. Dr. Currie.   To part with this dear child and only daughter, whose devoted ministrations were made so necessary by the delicate health of her mother and brother, would have been a great trial.   In the kind Providence of God no separation was called for, which was a cause of devout gratitude to the loving father, to whom his son-in-law became as dear as an own son.

The summers of 1877 and 1878 were passed at Cambridge, Massachusetts.   These summers he greatly enjoyed.   The influence of the University pervades the classic old town.   In every direction drives and excursions are of a delightful character, as all know who are familiar with Boston's beautiful suburbs.   Boston itself, with its memories of his early ministerial work, possessed a great attraction for him, and occasionally there was the pleasure of meeting the familiar face of some dear friend of the long past years.

The slow progress toward recovery of his son, so constantly a tender care to the father, was an abiding source of anxiety, and doubtless contributed much to his indisposition to join in any but the quietest of home pleasures. Yet there was enough gain to inspire hope, and he was often able to be a most enjoyable companion to his father. By Dr. Meier-Smith's own desire, his study was his son's sitting-room. The presence of one who bore his heavy cross with almost unvarying sweetness and patience was never disturbing to the father when studying or resting. Once he said to his wife, "Norman does not know how many sermons he has inspired!" For years he was his son's companion in the daily walk for exercise. Many an invitation or proposed plan was cheerfully laid aside to give place to this sacred duty.

The birth of a granddaughter in March, 1879, brought a new joy into the household, and the delight with which her grandfather welcomed her grew with her lovely infant life. "Did I love my own little ones as much, I wonder?" he often asked. Certainly, in the more hurried days of his earlier work, he found less time to enjoy them. His comment upon the name given her was, "How could it be improved! Mary Constance! The name of all among women dearest to the Christian heart, added to the most characteristic of womanly virtues!" He chronicled every budding gift and grace, and was a proud man when the little maiden was old enough to be his companion in a walk or drive. Nothing was too much to do for this little princess, who repaid his affection by her marked preference for him as play-mate and obedient attendant. From her infancy it was his pleasure to carry her up the two long flights of stairs, when the hour for bed came. Whatever he was doing, — reading or sermon-writing, — it was laid aside the moment the little voice was heard at the foot of the staircase, " Grandpapa, I 'm waiting for my pony ! " This was kept up until she was so large a girl that every one remonstrated. But not until his own severe illness, when she was six years old, interrupted it, would the fond grandfather resign this loving service.

A few weeks in the summer of 1879 were spent in the rural seclusion of Crosswicks, New Jersey, and Dr. Meier-Smith preached nearly every Sunday for his friend, the Rev. Dr. Du Bois, then Rector there.

The Rev. William R. MacKay, who chanced to hear him preach once during that summer, wrote after the death of Dr. Meier-Smith of the abiding impression produced upon him by the sermon he heard on that occasion in the following words : —

" . . . The closing words of the memorial pamphlet are like a picture, and just the picture of his real self which he left deeply impressed upon my own mind, as the true self-hood of the man. The one sermon which I heard him preach was a revelation to me of what true preaching is ; it changed my whole idea, and I hope has made me something of a real preacher to my fellowmen.

" I shall always be grateful to him. That sermon is always before my mind as a model, — so simple, so clear, so full of help for man in trouble, and the preacher lost in the message that he had to tell ! ' Grant him Eternal Rest, O Lord, and let Light Perpetual shine upon him ! ' "

The vacation in 1880 was passed in Bridgeport. There were yet old friends and parishioners remaining there, and to meet them, and recall the past, was very pleasant. He had a remarkable memory for names and faces once familiar, and seldom failed to recognize both, with his ever-ready cordiality, although years might have passed since a meeting.

The quaint old town of East Hampton, Long Island, was the summer resting-place of the family in 1882. Nowhere on the Atlantic coast are the changing moods of the ocean more invigorating than on the south shore of Long Island. It was an inspiring, health-giving summer, much needed after a year of especially laborious work.

The next year a cottage was taken at New Rochelle, near the old homestead, the choice of this place being made in consequence of the failing health of Dr. Meier-Smith's father, and also of his father-in-law, who was then residing there. Early in June his wife's father entered into rest, after a long illness. In the city of New York, with which his honored name was identified for more than fifty years, Norman White will not soon be forgotten as a man of marked force and grace of character. Fruitful in all good works and prominent in all religious circles, he is especially remembered in connection with his service in the Management of the American Bible Society, and in that of the Sabbath Committee, of which he was one of the founders. Eight children survived this revered and beloved father.

The long life of Dr. Albert Smith, Dr. Meier-Smith's father, closed in February, 1884, at the venerable age of eighty-five years. Though feeble in health, he retained his mental vigor to the last. He died at his old home at New Rochelle, whither his son made frequent pilgrimages for consolation and solace to his loneliness. Dr. Meier-Smith parted with his father on the day before his death, not knowing that the end was so near, and had scarcely returned to Philadelphia before he heard of his release.

Early in this year Dr. Meier-Smith's family observed signs which indicated that he was in a less vigorous state of health, but his work went on as usual, and it was only the anxious eye of love that detected them. Sometimes after hearing him preach his wife would say to him, "Did you not feel well this morning? I noticed that you were very quiet, and that your voice had less than its usual power." The answer in a cheerful tone was almost invariably, "Is it so? I was not conscious of it at the time, but now it seems to me that I was not quite up to 'concert pitch.'" In his Diary, are found frequently recurring remarks that indicate a lowered physical tone. "I found myself unusually tired after my walk to the Divinity School." "Dr. M —— urged me to go to the Epiphany this morning [regular meeting of the Clerical Brotherhood], but knowing I was not in trim for the debate, I excused myself." Still no one thought him seriously threatened.

An event which called out his ever-ready sympathy occurred in May of this year, when death entered for the first time the large circle of brothers and sisters, so dear to him by his marriage. A brother-in-law much beloved since they were together in England, in 1871, entered into rest after three years of great suffering. Dr. Meier-Smith was much with him during the early part of his illness, doing all that was in his power to help and comfort him and his family.

In the year 1884, a purpose long in mind was carried out, and Old Lyme in Connecticut, the home of his paternal ancestors, was chosen for the summer vacation. It is a quaint and picturesque town, beautifully situated where the Connecticut River loses itself in

Long Island Sound. A very pleasant sojourn was anticipated, during which researches were to be made among the localities sacred to his father's kindred.

There being a number of Episcopalians in the place with no church of their own, Dr. Meier-Smith commenced to hold services in the cottage parlor. But all plans were abandoned when, after a few days, an illness began which lasted the entire summer. A malignant carbuncle appeared on the back of his neck, and rapidly assumed alarming proportions. Many weeks of intense suffering followed, endured with heroic fortitude. Dr. J. H. Packard, his family physician, was sent for, and performed an operation that gave some relief, but which was followed by great prostration, from continued high fever. The surgeon when he left him had serious fears as to the result, and undoubtedly Dr. Meier-Smith was for a month in great danger. Convalescence began in August, but it was not until November that he was able to resume any work. Apparently he owed his life to the skilful and unwearied care of an admirable nurse, whose ministrations he remembered gratefully. As may be supposed, the whole summer was one of sad care and anxiety, overshadowed with the fear that he had come to the home of his ancestors, which he had never visited before, only to die there. But his life was given back to the prayers of those who loved him, and it was a life consecrated afresh to the service of his Lord and Master. As soon as recovery seemed assured, a thanksgiving celebration of the Holy Communion was held in the parlor of the little cottage. At the close of the service he whispered to his wife, "I pray that henceforth my life may show something of the experience through which I have been led. May my life be 'hid in Christ'!" In other conversations he told her that during the days and nights of extreme pain and weakness, when unable to speak, he had received views of the glory of God, of the love of Christ, and of the power of faith to support in the darkest hours, which were well worth all the suffering. "Life and death have put on a new meaning to me." From this time until he rested from his labors, there was a marked change in him, which was noticeable to all who saw much of him. He never regained his physical vigor, and it is probable that a disease was slowly progressing, of which the visitation of the summer was a symptom. It is a wonder to his family now that they were not more alarmed at the increasing signs of enfeeblement. But they were slight and subtle, and he made so light of them himself that it was easy to put the fears at rest, with the hope that the fine constitution which had carried him through so much, would certainly rally in time, and that many years were to be added to the life now more precious than ever to those who had so nearly lost him. The six months which passed before Dr. Meier-Smith preached again, and the half year spent in Europe, make up the one twelve-month which is lacking to complete a record of forty years continual service in the pulpit. It was two years before he ceased to be fettered by the stiffness of neck, and sensitiveness of brain, caused by the terrible carbuncle. That he made as fair a recovery as he did was a surprise to his physicians. Often does his wife recall meeting him unexpectedly in the street, and noting from a distance, with sinking of heart, the slow step and slight stoop which had taken the place of the erect carriage and firm tread of former years. "Is he growing old before the time?" she asked herself. Other signs which will be spoken of hereafter might have told her that he did not expect to see the length of days given to his father and to so many of his ancestors.

In the summer of 1885 the beautiful town of Litchfield among the hills of North-western Connecticut was selected as the place of rest. It is an old historic town, memorable as the birthplace of many whose names are identified with the early history of the nation. The house occupied by Dr. Meier-Smith's family dated from Revolutionary days, and retained some old Colonial marks. The drives abound with charming views of hill and valley, with the mountains of Berkshire in the distance. The elevation is high, and the air invigorating. For the first time in some years Dr. Meier-Smith enjoyed driving himself, and many hours precious to memory were passed with his wife in exploring this lovely country. Litchfield attracts to itself a refined and intelligent circle of summer residents, Yale University being especially well represented. In this congenial society, some friends of the old Boston days were met for the first time in many years.

While he made much gain in strength, the elevation of Litchfield proved very unfavorable to his wife and son. Thus again his solicitude for those dear to him clouded the summer, and he failed to realize all the anticipated benefit.

During this vacation he preached a number of times at St. Michael's Church. The following remark of a lady whom he met in Litchfield gives an intimation of the impression he made upon strangers. She said, "I can never forget that lovely Dr. Meier-Smith. I only saw him a few times, but words of his have helped me ever since. No one ever came into my life for so short a time who did so much for me and left such a lasting impression."

Dr. Meier-Smith was sufficiently acquainted with the premonitory symptoms of the disease which was slowly sapping his strength, to have detected them; and, as the succeeding months are remembered, the conviction grows that he believed his days to be numbered, feared that there was no remedy, and was unwilling to seek a medical verdict upon his case, because of his determination to spare his family, as long as possible, the distress of hearing an unfavorable opinion. At all events he insisted that he needed no medical aid, and was "doing well enough." Indeed he appeared brighter and more vigorous during the following winter, 1885–86, and repeatedly said that study and speaking were again enjoyed.

Throughout Dr. Meier-Smith's life in Philadelphia his days were very systematic in routine. Correspondence occupied an hour after breakfast. Then came his hours at the Seminary, from which he returned about two o'clock. After dinner and the relaxation of an hour with book and cigar, the rest of the afternoon was given to out-door business and exercise, and sometimes to social visits. The evening found him almost invariably in his study, in the enjoyment of the open fire which was a necessity to him. He studied and wrote until eleven o'clock. Work was then laid aside, and certainly to one of the occupants of the study the best hour of the day began. Some book of mutual instruction or amusement was read and discussed, and conversation was so fresh and animated that when the midnight hour struck, the remark was often made, " We have been talking as if we had not been together for years, and as if it might be years before we met again!"

Not often was he tempted out of his study in the evening, but others of the family were welcomed there, and his wife's chair was always ready for her on one side of his writing table, no matter how busily he was plying the pen. In early years there was seldom a sermon in progress for which she had not composed the audience of one for a private rehearsal. Bit by bit, he gave it all to her. While this became impossible as years went on, she was not often seated near him for half an hour while he was writing, without a welcome interruption with the question, " What do you think of this ? " And then after reading a few sentences to her, he would say, " Perhaps I had better go back a few pages," until the result was that she heard the whole manuscript. For several years she was kept much away from church, either from her own weakness, or from her attendance upon her son. Yet all that time, — ah ! with what pleasure does she remember it, — never was a new sermon to be preached without the question being asked a little anxiously, " Shall you be able to go out this morning ? " " Why, do you want me ? " was the reply. The answer being, " Oh, no, not unless it is entirely best for you to go ; but I *should* rather like to have you hear my new sermon ! I think it will please you." Now, as she reads, one after another, these sermons into which he has put so much of himself, connected with each there is the memory of the comment and discussion which so often grew out of the reading, and which she sometimes told him was a revised and improved edition.

Those who read these pages will not think that too much has been said of the ready sympathy, the kindliness of manner, the winning smile, and the perfect naturalness which gave the charm to Dr. Meier-Smith's personal presence. But how may we show what this meant in the home so dear to him! The unselfishness and simplicity of heart of which these graces were the fruits were revealed there continually. He lived only for his work and for those he loved. Not that his bright humor was never clouded, nor that his words were never hasty, for he was naturally impatient and out-spoken; but that the light clouds passed so quickly, and the sunshine of his tender and ever ready helpfulness appeared so soon, that the prevailing impression was of a presence at once cheering, invigorating, and supporting. If he looked on the dark side of passing events, it was but a temporary view. He foresaw the sure coming of the "better hour or day." He was not easily ruffled with small annoyances, nor was he one of the bustling, hurrying folk who are so often also the *worrying* folk. He was deliberate about everything, willing that time should correct mistakes, and quite sure that it would. We have said before that he was a born care-taker, helping naturally and easily in domestic perplexities, and as an ultimate authority in ways and means, always satisfactory. He was methodical and exact in affairs, and safe and prudent in business matters to an extent not always to be found among clergymen. Bills and letters received immediate attention. No one who worked for him, no tradesman or mechanic, ever had to wait for his pay. "Time is money to them," he would say, as he paid their bills promptly. A wise administration of domestic economies taught him the same prudence in expenditures when a parish clergyman, so that he was very successful in financial matters coming under his supervision. Such characteristics every family knows go very far to make up a personality upon which every one in the household must needs depend, and combined with the manner which makes friends everywhere, the rough places are smoothed in many practical ways. Any one, for instance, who had occasion to travel in his company, would be struck with the quiet command of circumstances he assumed. The best of everything came to him easily, as he knew just what he needed, and how to secure it without annoyance to others. In the crowded hotel dining-room, his party were usually well seated and promptly served. No doubt there was a magnetism in the kindly tone and smile with which his orders were given, though something of the old-time dignity which expects to receive its due was not wanting. How much of life's care and fret and turmoil are due to the absence, in many admirable characters, of just those traits which were conspicuous in him whose loving life we are recalling! How impossible it seemed to take up life's burdens when he was called away who had cheerfully lifted so much of their weight!

Those who served in Dr. Meier-Smith's household became truly attached to him, and were glad to remain long in his family. They received from him words of kind greeting, thoughtful consideration for their comfort, and often a playful remark which helped the wheels of the domestic machine to run smoothly. In every shop where he was known, and where his orders were left, he had more than acquaintances, — he had friends. He was quick to commend when well served, and if occasion required criticism, it was so free from sharp fault-finding, that naturally every one took pains to please him. Touching proofs of the affectionate esteem in which he was held by such friends came to the knowledge of his family after his removal. It was told that when in the early morning word was passed from place to place in the vicinity, " The Doctor is dying," no one needed to ask who was meant. " Every one called Dr. Meier-Smith ' the Doctor.' He seemed to belong to us all." The shutters were closed in one of these shops, and no business was done for several hours. Though he resided in the neighborhood of a number of medical men, and several Doctors of Divinity, he was " *the* Doctor " to these friends. Said one and another, " Every one here feels that he has lost a dear friend." A young girl who met him daily on her way to school, and perhaps never exchanged a word with him beyond the morning greeting, would hardly be comforted when she heard the news, so strongly had she been attracted to him. Said a lady living in the same street, but having only a slight acquaintance with him, " The whole day seemed brighter when I met Dr. Meier-Smith and received one of his smiles and greetings." To the very last the words, already quoted, of his early friend Dr. Dexter, were almost as apt as in the days of his youth, " Like a sunbeam he went everywhere ! "

His charities were unostentatious. As freely as possible he responded to all calls, but especially were his sympathies appealed to by those sufferers who were silently struggling with adversities of fortune for which their education had ill fitted them. With gentle tact he discovered their necessities, and in gracious and loving manner he relieved them ; making the recipients of his gifts feel that *he* was the debtor by their acceptance of them. To many such his death was a blow only second to that which fell upon his own family when God called him away.

It has been said that there were other signs than decreasing physical strength which might have raised the question whether his earthly work was to be continued much longer. Friends outside of his own family, who saw him frequently, say that the genial and tender traits of his character shone with increasing brightness during the last two years of his life. Unlike many who as they grow older are easily fretted and oppressed by small cares, he became more quiet and restful. His patience with trying people was now almost unfailing, and a kind excuse for their infirmities was ever ready. In his class-room his students observed that much of the playful satire which had formerly enlivened his instruction was repressed, and that he appeared unwearied in his efforts to give help and encouragement, and when criticism was necessary, to offer it without wounding.

Though the attempt to give a true representation of him who forms the subject of these pages may have been in part successful, his friends will feel that one important element of his individuality has been almost left out. To portray him in connection with his work was the aim proposed, and a natural prominence has been given to the characteristics which were most exercised as teacher, preacher, and pastor. But in his home, among his intimate friends, and when extending the hospitality in which he so much delighted, his natural mirthfulness, and the gay sparkle of his humor, made a strong impression. When he felt perfectly unrestrained, this playfulness was constantly coming to the surface. In younger days his tendency to apply original and terse epithets, and to see things from the laughable side, if there were such a point of view, was almost irresistible. Years and cares had their sobering effect, and chastened the native buoyancy, but enough remained to identify him with the young and merry spirit that did "good like medicine," and is so affectionately remembered by the friends of those long past years.

It would be out of place to insert many anecdotes concerning Dr. Meier-Smith which are fresh in the memory, and which are yet told by his old friends and parishioners.

One writing of him said, "His bright humor made him such an essentially *live* man that I cannot think of him as having passed out of our earthly life."

A clergyman about his own age met him one Christmas morning. Dr. Meier-Smith's "Merry Christmas" rang out when some paces distant, his face expressing his sympathy with the joyous greeting. His friend, being inclined to the dark view of life, solemnly exclaimed: "Have n't you gotten over that sort of thing yet?" "No," was the somewhat indignant reply, "and I hope I never shall while the world is full of the blessings springing from the birth of the Lord Christ!"

In these days of rapid communication, any regular correspondence beyond the most business-like notes, brief and hurried, appears to have become a thing of the past. Few letters are kept, and the material which has heretofore been the most valued part of a memoir is likely to be wanting in the future. Dr. Meier-Smith wrote a great many letters, until within the last twelve years; but most of his correspondents are gone, and the letters have disappeared. Such of his letters as are included in these pages, his friends will recognize as eminently characteristic; others at hand are equally so, and would be of much interest as expressing his views in his own forcible manner, but they are withholden because of their purely personal character, or on account of their frank reference to events of too recent occurrence to be appropriately introduced.

With the Rev. Dr. Dyer correspondence was always maintained; although in the last two or three years it

was much interrupted by the invalid condition of this
dear friend. Dr. Meier-Smith's professional position
during his residence in Philadelphia gave him opportunities, of which he always availed himself, to use his
influence in behalf of friends, especially for his younger
brethren and his pupils. To his responsive heart it was
a second nature to write a letter, or seek a personal interview, whenever there was hope of aiding any struggling or anxious friend. Many such letters, could they
be printed, would testify, as no other words can, to the
elements of character which made him so much beloved
by all who knew him.

Extracts follow from two letters to Dr. Dyer.

" . . . Our dear Dr. Muhlenberg is gone to his rest.
Every line I read about him impresses me more and
more with the saintly beauty of his life. How like his
divine Master! What an example for imitation! I
often think that such a life and work, and to be identified with a 'St. Luke's Hospital' and a 'St. Johnland,'
is the highest of human honor. . . . So the Europe
plan is postponed. I trust for the best. Are you
growing stronger again? I hope so. I cannot express
the deep and affectionate interest I take in your health
and comfort. The good Lord keep you through a happy
and serene evening, by and by melting into the Eternal
Day!"

Referring to Dr. Dyer's "Records of an Active Life,"
he wrote from Southampton, under date of September,
22, 1886.

. . . Your book is a good instruction. It shows how
a man can be most useful, and find distinguished honor
by simply doing the day's work as God gives it to him

to do. The best of ordinary legends for the memorial brass is that " He served God in his generation and then fell on sleep." How blessed and peaceful and light is your eventide! Soon it will brighten into " no night there "! Good-by, dear old friend.

Ever affectionately yours,

M. M.-S.

Dr. Meier-Smith's own family have but few letters remaining from these later years. His brief absences from home allowed only a hurried note or telegram announcing his return. The tender and watchful love which shrunk from any separation, they understood so well as the cause, that they are consoled for the loss of letters that would now be such cherished relics.

A few extracts are given from letters to members of his own family circle on occasions calling for sympathy. They are types of many, and will serve to show why they found so warm a place in the hearts of their recipients, and have been affectionately treasured for years. Such letters were to his friends *more* than characteristic, — they were his very self.

Fancy and humor played about his pen, as in his conversation, and the tenderness of his heart found ready expression when the sorrows or joys of those dear to him called for his notice.

To a Sister-in-law.

Bridgeport, December 16, 1862.

My dear, darling, pet Julia, — Stiff hand as I am at congratulations, I must drop you a line at least, to say how heartily and lovingly I do unite in your new found joy.

But, pens, ink, paper, — they are a perfect nuisance just now.

Give my love to C. C. J. Tell him I like him. Tell him I, for one, welcome him to just the best circle of brotherhood and sisterhood that man ever saw or, — if *this* unworthy dust may slip out for the nonce, — angels ever peeped upon.

It has a pokerish look when one sees two life currents, starting from widely distant hills, come down gushing, dashing, bubbling, foaming, surging with impetuous emotion, suddenly, inevitably, to blend and make one stream.

We shiver a little, and wonder how it is to be with them.

But if God sent the two rills out from their springs on purpose to make a river of them, there is nothing to be feared. They *will make* a *river*, and they will go together to the sea, hand in hand, laughing right cheerily, dancing right merrily, leaping the rocks right joyously, now soberly sweeping with deep and silent motion through the sombre chasms, now serenely through the plains.

I believe in fore-ordaining; I believe in Providence; I believe God looks after His children.

My dear sister, I long to press you to my heart and give you the warmest kiss I ever gave you.

Your brother,

MATSON.

To his wife's youngest sister, whose birthday was the same as his own : —

2015 DE LANCEY PLACE, April 3, 1884.

DEAR SISTER GRACE, — The almanac reminds me that to-morrow, the fourth, is my annual Humiliation Day. It is a day also of rejoicing among angels and admirers of the beautiful, for you graced this planet with your rising beams some twenty odd years ago. It was like my effrontery to have chosen for my nativity the same day, without consulting the siderial "Vennors," and finding out who was to come after me! My best atonement for this unblushing behavior is to beg your acceptance of the inclosed, as a small compensation, and to say that I put a dollar a year for each year of manifest, apparent, and undoubted difference of age. You are in your bloom; I am in my decrepitude. Twenty-five years hence you will be still in your bloom! I shall be in "lean and slippered pantaloon." But despite senility on one side, and youth and beauty on the other, I am ever, your loving old brother,

MATSON.

To his Sister-in-law Helen.

PHILADELPHIA, December 26, 1881.

DARLING SISTER NELL, — I was still puzzling over the conundrum, " Who sent a cup and saucer and plate to whom, from Tiffany's ? " when your sweet note came explaining all.

Thank you, dear sister, for the gift so choice, and for the loving words, more precious still. But let me say that my " coffee times " will not be my only times for thinking of you; for you, dear child, you are in my heart and thoughts often and again, more than you dream, in these your days of so much sadness and brave sorrow-bearing. I suppose that in the great cycles of Providential movement, — cyclones I might call them, — there are rough and terrible things, which like earthquakes and tempests make for good in the end.

God's children can go safely through them, and come off more than conquerors, weather-beaten into heroes, transfigured through the storms into those who wear white with the Lamb, and stand on Mount Zion. Other people get swamped, and somehow reach shore, — through the life-car, or ropes of the surf-men, and it takes them ages to get over the battering and bruising. You, dearest sister mine, have hold of God's hand, the warm flesh and blood hand of the Only Begotten. God grant you, in dear Arthur's convalescence and in your dear children, a new year of brighter days and growing joy!

Your own loving brother,

MATSON.

To the Same (after preaching in New York).

2015 DE LANCEY PLACE, February 28, 1882.

DEAR SISTER NELLIE, — The little postal card received this morning was verily a surprise. I had no idea that so many or any of my loved ones were in the congregation, although I saw in the dim light of the church a face which suggested you so strongly that I warmed toward it; yet it was not distinct enough for recognition. And now I am glad to learn that you were there; for when I was writing that sermon some three weeks ago, I was thinking of you, and wishing I had leisure to put into a letter, just to *you*, some of the precious things as they came to me, and some asides for your own ear and the comfort of your dear, stricken, and sorrowing heart.

' The long outlook toward the extreme reaches, and the faith-vision which sees the God in Jesus near at hand, and hears the voice, " It is I," are the sufficient comfort in days when nothing short of the Infinite can bring any approach to peace or calm. " There is a rest that remaineth," into which we from time to time enter. It is a lofty boon if given to our poor nerves and our

tired spirits to abide in it always. Do any ever reach
this gift? I have another text for you, "There hath
no temptation [that is, trial] taken you, save such as is
common to man," — that is, fitted to our human nature
and our best development, as well as common in the
sense that many share it.

You are not an exceptional sufferer, and God's plan
will work out more than we think for good, — "exceeding abundantly."

I know by sad experience how hard it is to believe
this; but sometimes faith triumphs, and we peer for a
moment through parting clouds into heaven's fathomless
blue.

Give my love to all those whose names you indicated,
and with my good-night kiss, darling sister, believe me,
ever your loving brother,

MATSON.

To the Same.

PHILADELPHIA, February 19, 1884.

DARLING SISTER, — That exquisite chair appeared at
my door this morning. It is a marvel of beauty and a
wealth of love. Your dear eyes and your deft fingers,
your nerves and your warm blood, and your sweet sis-
terliness are all in it. Can I tell you how I thank you,
how I shall prize it, and how, when my eyes are dim
with force-abating age, I shall be gladdened by the
vision of it? Shall I dare *sit* in it? That is the question. I gently deposited myself therein on trial. But
it seemed a sort of sacrilege to treat the beauty so
familiarly.

. . . I did not think that my dear old father was
so near his rest when I left him yesterday. But I
thank God the conflict is finished for him, and in the
new life and the new brightness of Paradise he awaits

with Christ's departed the opening of the Gates Eternal. "Not that we would be unclothed, but clothed upon, — that mortality might be swallowed up of life."   Saint Paul never wrote brighter words from the human side of this thing we call "death" than these.

And now, again, thank you for the chair; and good-night.   And the dear God bless and comfort you always, my pet and darling little sister, wishes and prays your brother,

MATSON.

In the spring of 1886, Dr. Meier-Smith arranged for extensive repairs and enlargement to his house.   When the time came to decide whether the proposed work should be carried on, he was asked, "Do you feel strong enough to look forward to an extended term of work here ? If not, it might be better not to undertake this, as in case you feel compelled to retire from active duty, we may wish to go back to our early associations, or to live in the country." His answer showed that whatever were his fears for himself, he had no thought that he was commencing the last twelvemonth of his life.

"I think I am stronger than I have been at any time since my illness, and do not see why there may not be years of good work yet before me.   At any rate, as we cannot forecast the future, it is better to arrange to do our work as comfortably as possible," — adding after a pause, — "if I break down before my time, I should be glad to know that I had provided such a home for my family as I want them to have."

Before the meeting of the Diocesan Convention, Bishop Stevens announced his wish to have an assistant, in view of his increasingly feeble health and advanced years. Who should be his helper and successor in this large and important diocese? This was a question of great interest and much discussion. Most of Dr. Meier-Smith's friends united upon Dr. Phillips Brooks, and while he shared their admiration for the distinguished man and preacher, he regretted their choice, as he felt sure that Dr. Brooks could not be induced to leave his chosen field, and that time would be lost, and votes thrown away. Thus it proved; and after Dr. Brooks declined, and remained immovable in his decision, the Convention adjourned without an election, to meet again in June. Dr. Meier-Smith was out of town, and was unable to be present. While Rector of Trinity Church, Newark, he had formed a pleasant acquaintance with the Bishop of Nevada, then a parish clergyman in New Jersey, and when he became the choice of a majority of the Convention, Dr. Meier-Smith sent him a warm letter of congratulation and welcome. Bishop Whitaker responded cordially, and their relations, after he came to Philadelphia, were very friendly. When death so soon interrupted them, the Bishop earnestly expressed his sense of personal loss, saying that Dr. Meier-Smith was one of the very few clergymen of Philadelphia whom he had known previously, and that he had "counted upon him as a right-hand man and helper."

In the month of May the circle of Mrs. Meier-Smith's brothers and sisters was broken by the death of her half-brother, — a young man whose unusual gifts and fine character gave promise of a brilliant future. The blow fell with crushing weight upon the widowed mother, now bereaved of her only child, and Dr. Meier-Smith's sympathetic heart was greatly moved.

He often spoke of this bright young life so early

closed on earth, and of his certainty that he had entered upon a greater and nobler work than any he could have done here.

In June he went with his family to spend the summer at Southampton, Long Island. The home in De Lancey Place was left for six months, that the alterations decided upon might be made. Very sweet is the memory of that last summer, which seemed peculiarly free from the anxieties of other vacations. Southampton, the oldest town in the State of New York, combines the attractions of a modern sea-side resort, and a venerable New England village; for it was from Massachusetts and Connecticut that its first settlers came, and many historic marks remain. The ocean view is unbounded, and the breezes unfailing. The rush of fashionable life has hardly invaded it, and society is refined and intelligent. Many clergymen were there, — some old acquaintances among them, — and every one noticed in Dr. Meier-Smith a lightness of spirit and enjoyment of society which indicated a sense of returning health. He took long walks again, and said that he had not enjoyed exercise so much for five years.

The coast of the eastern end of Long Island is marked by low sand hills, or "dunes," upon which there is some vegetation. They form a soft outline of artistic beauty. Upon the dunes at Southampton stands a picturesque little chapel, — "St. Andrew's Dune Church," and here he officiated, preaching every Sunday for two months. He enjoyed this work, and there were many among the friends he formed while in charge of these services who spoke of him afterward gratefully and affectionately, and who will long associate the little chapel with his ministrations.

Late in the autumn the family returned to their enlarged and renovated home. Dr. Meier-Smith spared no pains to carry out in every detail all that could meet the wishes and tastes of those so dear to him, and took a loving satisfaction in the attractive result of the thought and care he had given to the work. "I am thankful," he said, "and my mind is at rest, now that I see you just as comfortable as I have desired you should be." In his new and beautiful study he took great delight. There he and his wife spent much time alone together, their son having decided to remain through the winter at Southampton. As the year drew toward its close, the outlook for the one so soon to open seemed unusually bright. Affairs at the Divinity School were in an encouraging state, and many things combined to promise a happy winter.

Just after Christmas, Dr. and Mrs. Meier-Smith visited their son in Southampton, and were cheered by finding him unusually well and happy. He thought his father looking worn and tired, and noticed that he was very quiet; but he said nothing to his parents of the fears aroused by his appearance.

The last day of the year will never be forgotten by the compiler of these memories. A wild winter storm of snow, sleet, and wind was in full sway, a heavy surf thundered on the beach, and from the windows could be seen the grand line of white breakers. The surroundings added solemnity to the thoughts which are natural to serious minds in the last hours of the dying year. Thanksgivings for the mercies of the months past, and the prayer for a blessing on the new-born year, which were offered as the midnight hour struck, were tender and fervent. An undefined impression was felt that an experience, yet unknown, was in the near future.   Yet it was with hopeful hearts that they returned to their home, grateful for the improvement apparent in their dear invalid.

When Dr. Meier-Smith returned to the Divinity School, he was surprised to be met by congratulations on the benefit his trip had been to him, with the remark that he had been looking far from well before his absence.

XIX.

EVEN-TIDE.

1887.

JANUARY — FEBRUARY — MARCH.

OF the eventful weeks which passed quickly and peacefully from the opening of the year 1887 until the middle of March, there is little to record. Dr. Meier-Smith's diary shows a regular fulfilment of his duties at the Divinity School, and of pulpit engagements for nearly every Sunday. He and his wife were more constantly together than for many years. He seemed to be unwilling to be away from her for even a few hours, desiring her company in his walks, and laying aside his evening study for conversation with her. The peculiar tenderness of his attention she attributed to his knowledge that she suffered much in the separation from their son, who had been for so many years her constant companion.

Early in the year he commenced to write a new course of Homiletical lectures, in which he seemed to take much satisfaction, expressing a hope that they would fill a need in the plan of instruction which had not yet been met.

Among letters which he wrote was one to Dr. Gouverneur M. Smith, under date of January 18, 1887.

MY DEAR COUSIN, — It was a most pleasant sensation, sharpening appetite for breakfast, this morning, to find some lines from you. And among the curious psychological, not to say neurological, things, did you ever note family relationships in chirography? I puzzled a moment over the address of the envelope. Your writing suggests your father's very much. There is a resemblance to my father's in his stronger days, perhaps more than you may notice, in my present writing, although I can see a trace of it with all the admixtures of other elements, careless habits included. Two or three times within a few years, I have had a note from Chief-Justice Waite, who, you know, is one of our third cousins, or thereabouts. The first writing from him fairly startled me, so extremely suggestive was it, and side by side with one of my father's in his old age, it seemed as if the man of sixty and the man of eighty-three had written on a match for a prize. Family voices in various generations have marked similarities. Is it the *rule* likewise with manuscript? What is the explanation? Are these facts for some yet unformed deduction as to enlarged and multiplex *personalities*, or some new doctrine of blood tides and blood unities? I submit the questions to my medical philosopher-kinsman, whose conservative character never allows his imagination to run away with him. . . .

Throughout the months of January and February, there was even more than the usual brightness and cheerfulness apparent in Dr. Meier-Smith's life at home. He was more inclined to mingle in society than for some years past, and to the entertainment of friends and relatives, extending the hearty welcome and warm hospitality always characteristic of him, more lavishly than usual.

Among the latest visitors was his brother-in-law,

Charles Trumbull White, with his wife. With him there was an affectionate and sympathetic intimacy, the more tender on Dr. Meier-Smith's part, because of the failing health of this dear brother. Nearly three years later a lingering decline, borne with a Christian martyr's heroism, closed a life of rarely beautiful unselfishness and devotion to Christ and His work.

One of the latest letters to Dr. Dyer was written on Ash Wednesday :—

. . . In regard to the Divinity School and its outlook. Certainly the Faculty is doing all it can to elevate scholarship and attract students, and there has been a respectable addition to the number. But between the requisitions of the Faculty, and the oppositions, in a polite way, of certain of our brethren of another school of thought in the Church, we lose students. If they connect themselves with certain parishes, they are apt to leave us for New York or Berkeley.

What is the remedy? Some bishops assume the right to control the places of study of their candidates, and I think that if our dear and lenient Bishop would tell his young men that he has something to say on the subject, it would be good for the young fellows themselves. I have noticed many times within forty years, that freshmen in theology are wise beyond their years, and more learned and orthodox than their instructors. It was so in Union Seminary in my day. But I would not seem to criticise my Bishop, for doubtless he weighs each case, with a knowledge no one else has of the special facts. And speaking of Bishop Stevens, how beautiful is his endurance and fidelity! I have learned to love him very warmly, and he grows upon my respectful admiration. I love to go and see him occasionally. He is so sweet and heavenly minded, looking forward "to be with Christ." When I talk with him and with you, I come away fervently desiring that I may know the same glorious hope and peace and quiet triumph, if I be spared to your years. How faithful is our God and Saviour to His servants!

My wife and daughter join me in dear love to you and yours.   Ever most affectionately,

MATSON MEIER-SMITH.

An interview with Bishop Stevens in February is referred to in his diary. The Bishop was very feeble, and could talk but little, but Dr. Meier-Smith spoke with deep feeling of the tenderness of the meeting, and of the sweetness and Christ-likeness of the Bishop. "I think I may never see him again. He seems to me very nearly ready to depart," he remarked to his wife. Nor did they meet here again, but at that time no one could have thought that the venerable Bishop would survive his friend.

On the last Sunday in February, he took charge, in the absence of the Rector, of both services at Holy Trinity Church. The sermon in the morning, though but recently written, was one which was more doctrinal in subject, and less subdued in style, than was usual in the sermons of his later years. The subject as given in the title was, " Sin the Ruin, Repentance the Remedy." It was somewhat startling to his wife, who was unprepared for the subject or its treatment. At the close of the service a number of persons spoke to him of the deep impression produced, remarking that the sermon was one of the "old-fashioned" kind seldom heard now. Walking home with his wife, he said to her, "You are very quiet; I think you did not enjoy my sermon." Her reply was, "I am afraid I was not in tune for it; I wanted something else this morning." He seemed a little troubled, and during the walk reverted to the subject, saying, "I wish you would read over that sermon, and see if there is anything harsh or severe in it. I desire more and more to speak the truth in love." Little did she know that she had listened for the last time to the beloved husband who had been so long her pastor and teacher. How slow would she have been, could she have foreseen the near future, to speak a critical word to him who always honored her by his desire for her approving verdict upon his public work!

The two letters which follow are among the last he wrote. The first one is to a brother-in-law, and is dated Sunday evening, March 6, 1887: —

MY DEAR CHARLES, — My heart is glad as I think of you to-day, and I thank God with you, that you have been helped to see your way clear to the outward stand of the Christian, and to the Table of our Lord.

That the obstacles which have hindered you in the past would sometime be removed, I have not suffered myself to doubt, during these many years of our acquaintance and most agreeable relationship, knowing as I did your high principles, and your deep sympathy with all that is real and true in religion and in life. And at the same time I fully appreciate the many and great difficulties which often do stand in the way of just such a step, with conscientious men who know themselves, and know other men, and are distrustful regarding any step which seems to invite observation.

It is a great point gained when one commits himself openly and forever on the side of God and His Son Jesus Christ, and lets everybody know that his life in this world, and his outlook for the future, whatever the drawbacks or discounts of our imperfections, are to be ruled by, and to depend upon, this determination and belief.

I am sure you will be a happier man, stronger to be, and stronger to bear, and stronger to accept all the lot, now and hereafter, which the Father ordains. And I do most fervently trust that you will find spiritual enrichment and peace and joy and more and more of that "peace of God which *passeth* all understanding," as you participate freely in all means of grace, and especially, from time to time, in the holy and life-strengthening Sacrament.

And I add to my prayer that God relieve your bodily infirmities, that you may find length of days and stronger health and greater comfort, as you advance toward the evening, and the blessed *to-morrow!*

With love to dear Julia, and assurance of loving remembrance from us all here, I am most affectionately,

Your brother,

MATSON MEIER-SMITH.

To the Rev. B. B. Beardsley.

PHILADELPHIA, March 8, 1887.

MY DEAR FRIEND AND BROTHER, — I entirely agree with your views expressed in your note of yesterday. There is only one thing, so far as the point in question is concerned, to be preached and declared to men by any Christian minister, or any who hold the revelation in the Old and New Testaments, and that is, the duty of immediate repentance and settlement with God in this present life; and to hold out any hope or chance of better things in any life to come, or in any future of this life, is to speak without authority, and in violation of the most solemn responsibility. Nor within the range of my acquaintance and reading, do I know of any persons claiming allegiance the slightest to the traditions or doctrines of a Catholic or Orthodox Christianity, who would teach otherwise than this.

Certainly those tinged with the new Orthodoxy of Andover, and the suspected missionary candidates, disclaim any such contrary purpose, and avow their adherence to the rule I have stated. Any " Larger Hope," so called, has respect exclusively to those who have not had the Gospel preached to them at all, and it pertains to none to whom the salvation offer is brought near.

In lands nominally Christian, it is held by some that there are cases of those who have, by painful circumstances, been equally debarred, and whose fault is similar to that of the disbarred heathen, — the fault of Christian negligence. I do not know enough about such cases to affirm anything about them. I hope all things. I can't say how *many* or how *few* I believe of the " all things." Hence my charity is not up to the Pauline. I think the Andover brethren do not teach second probation. They simply conjecture a probation, turning upon the acceptance or rejection of Christ for those who have had nothing of the kind in this life. It is doctrine of equal chances in grace only ; whether true or not, that is another question. Farrar's doctrine is, — so far as it is doctrine, — that moral conditions and laws are permanent. If a man repents in the next life, the unchangeable love of God will receive that man. But the *if* is the great word, and he argues no probability to the effect that such a thing will be. At least such is my recollection of the impression I have received from him.

Annihilation is in the views of those who hold it,

the final and eternal punishment. There is no second probation with them. I find another writer, a Presbyterian, who seems to teach that death is the penalty of sin, and therefore all die. But Christ has redeemed from death, therefore all will arise.

The elect Christians arise to life and glory; the remainder to a new probation under redemption, after which comes the Judgment, with its issues final, and possibly annihilation in the second death.

So speculation runs *ad infinitum.*

. . . Our friend Pettingill has indeed gone. Could he come to us, what would he tell us now?

Very truly yours,
MATSON MEIER-SMITH.

It was in the first week of March that Dr. Meier-Smith wrote his last sermon, It was from the Epistle of Saint James, the first chapter and the twelfth verse.

He preached it on Sunday, the 6th of March, at St. James's Church, and this was the last time that he officiated there.

Will it be said that the sketch which these pages present has been drawn with too partial a pen, and that love has woven a veil of silver tissue about its subject, that hides deficiencies and reflects a light from itself?

Surely no such verdict will be given by those who were admitted into the intimacy of Dr. Meier-Smith's home, or to whom he came near as pastor and friend. But were it so, there could be only gentle criticism for her who was blessed, for eight and thirty years, with the love of one whose whole life was a ministry of unselfish devotion.

To the children who have the right to know something of the inner life of their beloved father, it may be permitted to speak freely here of the last precious days,— days which were as an ever-brightening pathway by which God was leading him into the perfect day.

Often in the still hour, just before retiring, sat hand in hand by the glowing embers the two whose lives had been so long in perfect union, and talked of the life in Christ,— here in its feebleness; there, the other side of the veil, in all its glorious fulness. These sacred communings after all was quiet in the house began in the days of youth and early love, and were never given up. But in these last weeks there was a depth of earnestness and a ripeness of thought which makes the memory of them precious beyond all that had gone before. He who led the thought, allowing imagination free play, spoke unreservedly of the future life and of the state of the blessed dead before the Resurrection. These themes, he said, had been constantly before his mind since he had been himself in the "border land." He had no sympathy with such materialistic views as are represented by books like the "Gates Ajar." "Yet," he said, "I often think that the continuity of our life will seem to us unbroken, when we pass through the 'Portal we call Death;' and that this will be to us a great surprise. . . . I expect," he said, "that my thought and study and work will go on; my love, my service for that love,— all this I shall find the same, only with infinitely enlarged possibilities. If I go first, I know I shall often be near you and our children. If you go first, I shall believe the same of you." Again the talk would be on the hope of the complete annihilation of sin,— the glorious victory over all to be finally achieved through Christ. Then it would turn upon the return of the Lord to His waiting Church. These soul-inspiring communings would close with a prayer which revealed the power in his own soul of the faith he had preached, — a faith which the storms of life had never shaken, and which was founded upon a rock. And there was a note of personal intimacy with, and loving dependence upon the Master to whom he spoke, which caused mingled joy and pain to the listener. "He is growing away from me," she sometimes said to herself. "Is he to leave me?" Reassuring herself with the thought that surely God would not have given him back to her at the time when — two years before — their separation had seemed so near unless they were to pass into the evening of life together, she suffered her fears to rest. But by all this she should have known that the sheaf was ripening for the harvest, and was soon to be gathered in.

The notes that follow are a part of those written by Mrs. Meier-Smith three months later, recording while fresh in her memory the incidents of the next three weeks.

March 6. Matson preached at St. James's Church. He also celebrated the Holy Communion. I was suffering much, and felt unable to go out. Had I known that this was the last opportunity of hearing my beloved husband, and receiving the Holy Communion from his dear hands, what could have kept me away! On his return he came to me, and putting his sermon in my hands said: "There, little wife, read that; I think you will like it better than the one you heard last Sunday."

This day, the sixth of March, was the twenty-first anniversary of his Ordination by Bishop Eastburn.

March 12. We left home to spend a few days with Norman, lunching in New York, and arriving at Southampton in the evening. He was well, and delighted to welcome us. We found our nephew, Stanley White, there, who preached the next day in the Presbyterian Church. His uncle went to hear him, and expressed much gratification at the bright promise he gave for the ministry he was just commencing. Sunday and Monday were mild and spring-like days, and walks to the beach were much enjoyed. Norman thought his father very bright and well, and much improved since his visit in December.

March 15. Very cold, windy, and bleak. The night was so severe that it was hard to keep warm, and I felt anxious lest my husband, who since his long illness had been sensitive to cold, should suffer from such a change. I think now that he may have taken a fatal chill that night. The next day he assured me that he was all right, and he took a long walk, calling on some old family friends sojourning at the time in Southampton.

March 17. This morning early we bade our dear Norman good-by, and went to New York. My dear husband and I had much pleasant conversation during this journey. We talked of our plans for the coming summer, and of some entertainments to be given to the students and others, after Easter.

In New York, we made a number of calls. Matson, thinking that I looked tired, offered to call a carriage. I assured him that it was unnecessary; but looking at him, and observing an expression of weariness in his face, and an unusual pallor, I assented to his proposal. Never was his manner more tender and loving than during this whole day. He was very merry over our little supper in the train, and when we arrived in Philadelphia, about ten o'clock, he said, "It is years since we have had such a lovely journey together!"

March 18. Matson appeared so very tired this morning that I urged him not to go to the Divinity School, reminding him that he had not expected to return until to-day. He thought, however, that he ought to go, as he was in the city. The next day he felt better, and in the afternoon we had a long walk together. My brother Erskine and his wife came to us for a short visit. To be with this dear brother was always an especial enjoyment to my husband.

Sunday, March 20. During Saturday night Matson suffered considerably with pain, which he thought was caused by a slight cold. He had an engagement to preach in the evening at the Church of the Incarnation, and I proposed that he should telegraph to the Rector, Rev. Dr. Newlin, that he was not able to fulfil it. But he said he would rest all the morning, and was sure that he would be quite himself again in the evening.

I was suffering much that morning, and decided to go to my physician for relief. When I was ready he arose from the bed to go with me. He looked so ill that I begged him not to accompany me, and after a little hesitation he said, "Well, if you are sure you can get along without me, perhaps I had better keep still." As I left the room a premonition of trouble came over me. I said to myself, "He feels more ill than he will allow, or he would not let me go without him. It is the first time since our marriage that he has permitted me to go anywhere alone when I was not well."

In the afternoon he said he was much relieved, and quite able to fulfil his engagement. He had a very long ride to take to the Church, and I was anxious about the fatigue and exposure.

As he entered the library upon his return, late in the evening, I was alarmed at his appearance. His face had a gray pallor, and he looked exhausted. I exclaimed, "I am so sorry I let you go. It has been too much for you." He replied, "Not at all; I have felt well, and much enjoyed preaching." We talked a little about the sermon, which was the one he last wrote, and which he had preached at St. James's a fortnight before. The text was, "Blessed is the man that endureth temptation, for when he is tried he shall receive the crown of life." No words could have been more fitting with which to close his public ministry, than the last sentence of this sermon, spoken on the last Lord's Day of his earthly life. "To-day the warfare of the Cross! To-morrow the Crown! Righteousness, peace, and glory for evermore!"

My brother Erskine, my husband, and I sat in the library until midnight, and when we retired he said he thought that his indisposition was over.

On Monday morning, however, he came down late to breakfast, and finding himself still suffering, remained quiet through the day. That evening we sent for our physician. The doctor said he did not consider the trouble serious, and that a few days of quiet would relieve him.

March 22. At three A. M., I was awakened by Matson, who was suffering great pain, which became so intense in an hour that I called Emily and her husband. Finding all our remedies were unavailing, we sent for the physician. Not before eight o'clock was there much relief, and then he was greatly exhausted. There was some fever, and he was very quiet, not disposed to talk, and under the influence of anodyne.

On Wednesday, the 23d, he was much more comfortable, and we were encouraged to think of a speedy recovery. About six o'clock the next morning, Thursday, he was attacked with another violent paroxysm, which lasted some hours. The doctor thought it neuralgic, and could not account for the great prostration which followed. I wrote in much anxiety, yet guardedly, to Norman and to my brothers. I was certainly apprehensive, but not of a fatal result; rather of a long illness, perhaps typhoid fever.

He said but little, dozed when not in pain, and only complained greatly of thirst.

Friday, March 25. Matson rested well, and seemed much more comfortable. His little granddaughter came in to see him, and he said to her, " Is not next Monday your birthday ?" adding, " I am so sorry I cannot go out to get you a present. Ask Mamma to get something very nice for you from Grandpapa."

Dr. Packard brought in another physician in consultation, and we received an encouraging report after their examination. No intimation was given to us that our beloved one was in an alarming condition, nor do I feel sure that he thought himself dangerously ill. He certainly said nothing to me that implied such an impression ; indeed he was much of the time sleeping under the influence of morphine. The only thing I recall which assured me that he was thinking more deeply than he was able to express, was a question as to the day of the month. When I told him that it was the 25th, he said, " The Feast of the Annunciation ! The day I love." The almost feminine tenderness of his spirit had always invested this day with a charm for him. He delighted to celebrate the Holy Communion on this festival, while he was a rector, and while living in Philadelphia always received it, when possible.

When the physician saw him at noon, he said to Emily, " You may know that I think your father really better, as I shall not come in again until evening." Early in the evening another paroxysm of suffering commenced, and we sent in haste for the doctor. During the two hours that passed before he came, our efforts to relieve the distress were fruitless. Though greatly exhausted, he surprised us by exclaiming with a strong voice, " Send for the doctor, and tell him he must either take away this pain, or *see me die.*" After he was relieved and sleeping, we had a full consultation with our physician, who said that in his opinion the pain was principally nervous, that there was no inflammation, and that he could only account for his exhaustion, and the severity of his suffering, by the evident weakness of his nervous system ever since his dangerous illness in 1884. At my earnest request, the doctor consented to spend the night with us, saying, " I do so, not because I think Dr. Meier-Smith needs me, but that I may be a comfort to you." He insisted, as a condition, that I should go out of the room, leaving Matson entirely to the nurse, as he himself was within call. It was not until about two A. M. that I went to my room, leaving my dear husband sleeping quietly. At four o'clock I went in, and found him awake. I kissed him, and he said, " I am getting on nicely." He asked me to get something for him, which I did, and as he held my hand I said, " I want to stay with you, dear." He answered decidedly, " No, darling; you are worn out, and I insist upon your going back to bed," which I did.

Saturday, March 26. Two hours later, I was awakened by the sound of suppressed voices in my husband's room. I found the doctor and the nurse endeavoring to administer stimulants to him. He was very pale, with his eyes closed. In answer to my inquiry, the doctor said, "It is a sinking turn." I think it was the physician's manner, more than his words, which made me know instantly that my beloved one was to leave me. I called Emily and her husband, telling them to come at once if they would see their father again. From that moment all hope left me, yet I remained perfectly calm. I suppose all that human skill could do was done. Another physician was sent for, and hypodermics were given to stimulate the heart, but all was in vain, for heart failure had occurred. When Emily came in, she kissed her father and asked him how he felt. He whispered, "More comfortable." From this time there was no further sign of suffering.

As I remember the succeeding hours I am amazed at my self-possession and my ability to give every necessary order. Surely it was a strength not my own which so upheld me that I did not utter a moan, or shed a tear. The very gates of Paradise seemed opening before me, as I watched my beloved husband, in perfect repose, going down into the river without a groan or a shudder. They said he was unconscious during the hours that followed. I do not think so; I believe that he was half with us, and half away, unable to speak, but calmly willing to have it so, and gently resting in the arms of his Saviour. When I whispered words of support from the Psalms or the Gospels, he pressed my hand. I know he heard me. Dean Bartlett was with us, and read the Commendatory Prayer. Twice as I sat with my arm supporting the beloved head, he kissed me in response to my request. I said to him, "My darling, you know how gladly I would go with you if I could, but I must wait for our children's sake! If you know what I say, kiss me." He pressed my hand and kissed me, though now very feebly. I said "Can you give me any word for our dear Norman?" I saw his lips move, and putting my ear down to them, I heard distinctly "Love!" It was fitting that the word which so expressed his whole life, should be his last on earth!

During these waiting hours all was peace and calmness with him and with us. His eyes opened sometimes with a far-away gaze, and a few moments before the last an expression of wonderful brightness passed over his face, as though he had a sight of ineffable glory. Then he slowly closed his eyes, as he was gently borne over the river.

When it seemed that he could remain with us but a few moments longer, I asked our dear friend Dr. Mills, who though not the attending physician, had hastened to us in response to our summons, to tell us when the end was at hand. He replied that there could be but a few more pulsations of the heart. I said to Dean Bartlett, "Will you give the blessing I want?" He divined my meaning, and with tender voice and uplifted hand, pronounced the benediction in the office for the Visitation of the Sick, which my beloved husband had used so often for the departing spirit. "Unto God's gracious mercy and protection we commit thee! The Lord make His face to shine upon thee, and be gracious unto thee! The Lord lift up His countenance upon thee, and give thee peace both now and evermore!" As kneeling around the bed we responded, Amen, Dr. Mills said "It is over!" The spirit had passed to its rest while the blessing of peace alone broke the silence! The hour was half past eleven.

Around the bed were Emily and her husband, my brothers-in-law, Dr. Lee and Mr. Starin, Dean Bartlett,

Dr. Mills, and our faithful Agnes. It seemed almost that our mortal eyes could see the divine Arms which upheld him and supported us. What else could have enabled us to go through these hours as we did, conscious of no wish to withhold our departing one, but only of an overpowering sense of the divine Presence, and that we were standing so near the veil which now separated us from him that we could almost discern the glory of the Paradise into which he had entered.

Telegrams came to us during the morning from Norman, which much comforted me, assuring us that he was hastening homeward. He did not arrive until late in the evening, and I was able to meet him with entire composure.

In the days that followed we were greatly comforted by the testimonials, constantly received, of love and esteem for him who had so suddenly been taken from his home and work on earth. Relatives and friends, his brethren of the clergy, members of the Divinity School, and many others, offered all the consolation that it is possible to receive from human aid and sympathy. The Vestry of St. James's offered the Church for the last services, expressing the desire that they should take place there. We knew that his preference would have been for the most quiet and unostentatious arrangements, but felt that it was due to his many friends in that parish to yield to their wishes, and that he should be carried to his last resting-place from the Chancel where he had so often ministered.

The funeral services took place on Tuesday, the 29th, at three o'clock in the afternoon. There was a quiet assembling at the house, principally of friends from New York.

My beloved husband was scarcely changed by his

short illness, and was beautiful in the serene majesty of Death. Robed in surplice and stole, he held in his hands the little Prayer Book which I gave him at the time of his Ordination. On the casket lay Palms and Easter lilies. As I kissed him for the last time, I could hear his voice with its joyous ring in the text which more than any other I associate with him: "Our Saviour Jesus Christ hath abolished Death!"

The services in St. James's Church were conducted by the Rev. Dr. Bartlett, the Dean of the Divinity School. Bishop Whitaker presided, the Faculty of the Divinity School and other clergymen being in the Chancel. His students of the Seminary bore the casket, followed by the Vestry of St. James's Church.

The simple and beautiful service of our Church was said. The music, as he would have desired, was grand and triumphant, closing with the noble hymn, —

> "For all the Saints who from their labors rest,
> Who Thee by faith before the world confessed ;
> Thy Name, O Jesus, be forever blessed,
> Alleluia !"

Many of the clergy of the diocese, and a large number of friends from the various parishes of Philadelphia were present, testifying to the general regard and affection cherished for him in the city where for eleven years he had exercised a faithful ministry.

On the following day all that was mortal of my beloved husband was laid at rest in Woodlawn Cemetery, New York. A granite monument in the form of a coped tomb has been placed there, on the top of which lies a polished cross. On one end of the stone is engraved the text, "Our Saviour Jesus Christ hath abolished death ;" and on the other end are the Greek words, "*ΕΙΣ ΤΟΝ ΣΤΕΦΑΝΟΝ.*" On the side is carved in raised letters,—

MATSON MEIER-SMITH, S. T. D.

April 4th, 1826.   March 26th, 1887.

Collect for All Saints' Day.

O Almighty God, who hast knit together thine elect in one communion and fellowship, in the mystical body of thy Son Christ our Lord; grant us grace so to follow thy blessed Saints in all virtuous and godly living, that we may come to those unspeakable joys which thou hast prepared for those who unfeignedly love thee; through Jesus Christ our Lord. *Amen.*

LETTERS FROM FRIENDS

AND OTHER TRIBUTES.

19

Letters from Friends.

FROM among the letters of sympathy received by Dr. Meier-Smith's family, a few from personal friends have been selected from which to make extracts.

The limits of this volume forbid the introduction of many others which bear equally strong witness to the affection of the writers for the friend who had been so suddenly removed from them.

32 St. Mark's Place, New York, March 27.

My very dear Mrs. Meier-Smith, — How can I express in words the grief and sorrow which fill my heart at this moment!

The sad tidings of dear Dr. Meier-Smith's sudden removal by death have so surprised and overwhelmed me, that I can do no more at present than to say that you and all the sorrowing ones have my profoundest sympathy and earnest prayers that our God and Saviour may be to each and all the support and comfort you so much need. I will not speak of my own deep sense of personal loss. You know what have been our relations for so many years, but of these I must not speak now. My thoughts are of you and yours. I wish I could say or do something to comfort you. But I am utterly powerless. I can only turn to my dear Lord and ask Him to be very near to you. He will minister as none other can. To Him you may pour out your whole heart and feel assured He will hear every sigh, and count and treasure up every tear. I wish I could write more, for my heart is full, but I am too feeble and too much overpowered by my emotions to do more than say these few words. God help and bless you all, so prays

Your loving old friend,

H. Dyer.

From Edward A. Strong, Esq.

Boston, March 29, 1887.

. . . You will know that I can in some measure understand, because I knew Matsou, the extremity of the grief to you and your children because of his departure, and by love and sympathy enter with you into the shadows. But I may say out of the fulness of my heart that the world is poorer to me since Matson Meier-Smith has left it. I loved him truly, much as I could have loved a brother. You and he are the earliest friends associated in my mind with my wife. He joined our hands in the indissoluble clasp of a true marriage. He has done me a great deal of good in the years gone by, by his Christian cheerfulness, and indeed helping me not a little, as I fain believe, to escape the misery of a morbid element in my religious life. Contact with him was always a tonic of hope and good cheer to me. . . .

I do not forget your dear children. God bless them! Ah, what a husband, what a father, what a friend!

From the Rev. Prof. Martin Kellogg.

Berkeley, California, November 17, 1887.

. . . But how much there is which cannot possibly be put into type! All written description and written eulogy fails to bring out, to near friends, the warm and vital personality of the departed. It is well that the survivors can " read between the lines," and put in for themselves all that filled up and rounded out the life and presence which have ceased on earth. No memorial book is needed for you. His whole life is ineffaceably engraven on your heart.

From Edmund Clarence Stedman, Esq.

NEW YORK, November 6, 1887.

. . . He was, in truth, an ideal exemplar of Christian manhood, — strong, faithful, intellectual, loyal, devoted. Your life has been richly "worth living;" were you not his wife for almost forty years?

From the Rev. Prof. Edward A. Hincks.

ANDOVER, MASS., November 1, 1887.

. . . I am glad to be numbered among those who cherish his memory. I recollect most vividly and with affection his manly face, pleasant voice (one of the most tunable I have ever heard), his kind, helpful words. He was a true friend, born to cheer and help others.

From the Rev. L. C. Baker.

PHILADELPHIA, March 27, 1887.

. . . Dr. Meier-Smith's sudden death has come upon us like a great shock, and filled us with a common sorrow. His Church, the Divinity School, the city, and his neighbors, will all greatly miss him.

I had not known Dr. Meier-Smith long enough to know him intimately, and yet a short acquaintance was enough to reveal to me his kindly, genial nature, his large-hearted Christian spirit, his broadly human sympathies, his neighborly kindness, his gentleness and courtesy. I had counted it as a pleasure in store for me that I should know him better.

From the Rev. Dr. T. H. Hawks.

SPRINGFIELD, MASS., January 7, 1888.

. . . I am very glad to be permitted to join with a great company of friends in assuring you that in your sore bereavement you have the deepest sympathy of all who knew him. . . .

You rejoice, as we all do, in the noble service he was permitted to render in the pulpit and the professor's chair, and the testimony of many witnesses that he did a great and good work cannot fail to comfort you.

From the Rev. W. W. Andrews.

WETHERSFIELD, CONN., November 8, 1887.

. . . I thank you for the Memorial of your dear and honored husband, which you have had the kindness to send me. It is most valuable for the testimonies to his character and worth from those who knew him best in the later years of his life, and who could speak with the warmth of personal affection.

But a like testimony could have been borne by very many who knew him in earlier life, and when laboring in another Communion, and whose love for him, and admiration of the beauty of his life, was not less, perhaps, than that of those with whom he was most closely associated at the last.

It was my happiness to know him, both before and after this religious or (more fittingly) ecclesiastical change, and he was beloved by me at every stage of his life. I was struck with the heartiness with which he welcomed me to his house, when he could no longer invite me to his pulpit ; and I honored at once the fidelity with which he stood by the laws and ways of the Church, and the Catholic spirit which overleaped all barriers of sect and party. It is a great joy to think that such a gift of God to His Church, and through the Church to all His creatures, is an abiding gift, never to be withdrawn. He rests now for a little while, but the time of true and blessed activity is still to come ; and then all that was most characteristic of him, all his noblest powers and qualities, will come forth transfigured and glorified. In that day we shall forget all the sorrow of his present hiding away in the resting-place of the blessed saints who sleep ; for he and we shall then have found our true sphere both for work and for Communion.

From the Rev. Prof. Peters.

NEW YORK, March 27, 1887.

. . . You do not know how good he has been to me, how kind and unselfish. It seems to me as though he never met me without showing me some kindness, some little word of appreciation, some offer of the most friendly and affectionate and helpful sort. I have gone to him so often when I was fretted and worried and despondent, and he was always ready to listen and help me, as though he himself had no troubles and nothing to do but bear mine. It seemed to come so natural to him that I do not think he knew the great value of the services he rendered me. The Father will tell him and reward him, and may that Father comfort and help you now !

From the Rev. Francis Lobdell, D.D.

BUFFALO, November 9, 1887.

. . . Please accept my thanks for the pamphlet which you so kindly sent me. I have read it with great interest. The testimony of those who have known your husband so intimately for the last eleven years is none too emphatic. I have known him more than twice eleven years. We ended our ministry among the Congregationalists in the same city, and about the same time. For more than a year we had talked freely together on the subject, and I shall never forget the earnestness with which he advised me not to hesitate to apply for Orders in the Church, saying that if he were as young as I he would not delay a minute, but he was afraid he was too old to make the change ! And yet three months later he was a candidate for Holy Orders !

And I think he was never so happy as after the change was made. He has done a splendid work in the Church, a work which will follow him.

From the Bishop of Western New York.

BUFFALO, March 27, 1887.

MY DEAREST COUSIN, — A Sunday newspaper has just been sent in to me, by a friend, in which I read — oh, astounding news! — that my beloved friend, Dr. Meier-Smith, has gone before me, young as he was compared with me. Can it be so? Oh, most sudden and most painful! I loved him, and he lately wrote me one of the best letters I have had from anybody for a long time. Daily have I designed to write and thank him for it. It did not require an answer, for it was an answer to one of mine; but it deserved one, and I was grateful for it.

Must it be so? God's holy will be done, and may you be able to sustain this fearful blow. Divine Love often calls for heroic faith, as when Abraham puts forth his hand to slay his son. Let us, with like faith, say only, "It is His will. Amen."

I am going to Church, and will bear you on my heart in prayer.

Little did I imagine that it would ever be my lot to write you on such a subject. But God sustain you, my precious cousin, you and yours!

Affectionately,

A. CLEVELAND COXE.

Tributes.

THE RECORDED MINUTE OF THE TRUSTEES AND OVERSEERS OF THE DIVINITY SCHOOL.

AT the joint meeting of the Trustees and Overseers of the Divinity School of the Protestant Episcopal Church in Philadelphia, held June 8, 1887, the following minute was placed on record : —

On the 26th day of March last, the Rev. Dr. Matson Meier-Smith, Professor of Homiletics and Pastoral Care in our Divinity School, was removed in the providence of God from the cares and duties of the present world to the felicity promised to God's people.

His death came suddenly upon the members of his classes, his fellows of the Faculty, and upon his many friends. Only a few days before they had seen him in his accustomed place ; and scarcely a hint of his illness had reached them, when the sad report came that he was dead, and they should see his face no more. He was a man to be remembered by all with whom he came in contact. Genial, earnest, generous almost to a fault, full of kindly purposes, considerate even of those with whom he differed, his death left a void not only in the immediate circle of the Seminary and the Church, but in the large round of the world about him. But in all his kindly and frank ways he was faithful to his Church and his creed, and to the service of God and man, to which he had devoted his life.

Professor Meier-Smith was born in New York, in 1826. His earlier days were passed in the house of his father, a prominent physician and a member of the Presbyterian Church ; hence he was trained in the religious views of that body of Christians. He came, on his mother's side, of the race of the Muhlenbergs, and was a descendant of one of the most celebrated ministers of that name in the Lutheran Church in America. After his graduation at Columbia College, his mind fixing itself upon the sacred ministry, he was educated in the Union Theological Seminary, and ordained in 1849. His career as a minister was attended with great success and favor, and in 1863 he received from Columbia College the degree of S.T.D. But his thoughts soon after were turned toward our own Church ; and after the usual hesitations and delays, he was finally ordained to the Diaconate in this Church, by Bishop Eastburn, of Massachusetts, in March, 1866.

In this new field he held several important charges, and wherever he ministered he left behind him a precious memory which lingers still. He loved his great work of preaching the Gospel, and was seldom happier than when enabled to engage in it ; so that in the years in which he was at work in the Divinity School he was in the pulpit nearly every Sunday. To this position of the Chair of Homiletics and Pastoral Care he was chosen in 1876, holding it for over eleven years. The record of these years is fresh in the minds of all the members of this Committee, who know with what zeal and fidelity he fulfilled his trust, and more need not be said here. He did a good work ; he earned a good name ; he has won a good reward from Him who knows us as we are. These things cannot be forgotten by those who knew him. While, therefore, we resign him to his place in our memories, as the Church has already consigned him to the bosom of his God, may we all be able to say, " Let our last end be like his."

COMMUNICATION FROM THE FACULTY OF THE DIVINITY SCHOOL.

MY DEAR MRS. MEIER-SMITH, — I am directed by the Faculty of the Divinity School to convey to you the assurance of our deep sympathy with you and your stricken family, and also to communicate the following notice, which was ordered to be entered upon our minutes : —

We wish to place on record our grief at the loss of our dear colleague, the Rev. Matson Meier-Smith, D.D., who passed hence Saturday, March 26, in the sixty-first year of his age. For eleven years he had occupied the Chair of Homiletics and Pastoral Care. He was likewise Secretary of the Faculty, — a position which, without hope of reward, he filled year after year with unvarying patience and a faithfulness beyond praise.

He was dear to us for his unfailing kindliness, courtesy, and consideration of the rights, thoughts, and feelings of those with whom he was associated. Whatever kind or friendly thing could be said of or to any one, he knew how to say. His many affectionate services were rendered so unobtrusively that few realized till afterward the value of that which he had done for them.

His own heavy burdens he bore with unselfish cheerfulness, always ready to help bear the burden of another.

So sudden is his removal that our sense of loss and bereavement can scarcely be measured even by ourselves.

Yours sincerely,

April 2, 1887.   JOHN P. PETERS, *Secretary.*

COMMUNICATION FROM THE STUDENTS' ASSOCIATION OF THE DIVINITY SCHOOL.

TO MRS. MATSON MEIER-SMITH :

At a meeting of the Students' Association of the Divinity School, a committee was appointed to express to you the sympathy of the students in your present sorrow.

Our acquaintance with Dr. Meier-Smith and our intercourse with him in life at the School have been such that we feel as individuals that it is a personal friend who has been taken from us.

Now that his work among us is ended, and we can no longer profit by his present instruction, we can only trust and believe that his work shall live, and that the seed sown in the past shall bear fruit in us; that, being dead, he shall yet speak.

It is scarcely necessary for us to speak of our sorrow, or of the lightening of it that comes from our hope for the dead in Christ. Knowing that both he and you shared also in that blessed hope, we ask for all those to whom his death has brought grief, the peace that comes from Christ our common Master.

Very sincerely,

L. W. BATTEN,
LAURENCE B. RIDGELY,
WILLIAM DU HAMEL,
Committee.

March 28, 1887.

RESOLUTIONS OF THE ALUMNI OF THE DIVINITY SCHOOL.

WHEREAS, At a meeting of the Alumni Association of the Divinity School of the Protestant Episcopal Church in the city of Philadelphia, held on June 8, 1887, a committee was appointed to draft resolutions touching the recent demise of the Rev. Matson Meier-Smith, D.D., Professor of Homiletics and Pastoral Care, and Secretary of the Faculty, therefore be it

Resolved, That the death of the Rev. Dr. Meier-Smith has deprived the Divinity School of a faithful, zealous friend, the Faculty of a distinguished and able member, and the students of a peculiarly sympathetic guide and counsellor.

Resolved, That during a pastorate covering a period of twenty-eight years, the manly principles he taught by his life and work were such as to ennoble all with whom he came in contact.

Resolved, That the sad and afflicting dispensation of Providence which has removed him from our midst has deprived many of a dear personal friend, the community of a good and faithful citizen, and the Church of a wise, able, and effective laborer.

Resolved, That we sincerely sympathize with his family in their deep affliction for the loss of one who in domestic life was the affectionate husband, kind father, and generous protector.

Resolved, That a copy of the above resolutions be conveyed to the family of the deceased as expressive of the deep respect and sympathy of the Association.

Signed,

R. L. HOWELL,
MARTIN AIGNER,
L. W. BATTEN,
A. D. HEFFERN,
F. M. TAITT,
Committee.

COMMUNICATION FROM THE CLERICAL BROTHERHOOD.

An Association representing the Clergy of the Diocese of Pennsylvania.

MRS. MATSON MEIER-SMITH:

DEAR MADAM, — The brethren in the ministry of your late beloved husband, assembled in their Brotherhood-Meeting this morning, appointed the undersigned to convey to you the expression of their deep sympathy with yourself and your household in the sad bereavement which has just overtaken you.

In behalf of the Brotherhood they would also express to you the high esteem and tender regard in which he was held by them, and their sense of the loss which they and the Church in this Diocese have sustained by his departure, so sudden and unlooked-for by them. They recall with a melancholy satisfaction his ever warm and genial manner, his prompt obligingness in service for others, his devotion to duty, and his deep interest in all that concerned the cause of Christ and His Church.

That he has been called away from us so soon, we, for ourselves, deplore ; that he has been called to a higher life and ministry, we have a good hope ; and for that hope we give thanks to Him who " by His death overcame death, and by His rising to life again brought life and immortality to light."

Praying for the abundance of God's grace to be granted you and yours in this the hour of your deep trial, we remain,

Your friends and brethren in Christ,

BENJAMIN WATSON,
ISAAC GIBSON.
H. L. DUHRING.

March 28, 1887.

From the Address delivered at the Diocesan Convention, May 3, 1887, by the Bishop of Pennsylvania, the late Rt. Rev. William Bacon Stevens, D.D. : —

"We were all greatly startled a few weeks ago when we heard of the unexpected death of Rev. Dr. Matson Meier-Smith, who departed this life on the morning of the 26th of March, in the sixty-first year of his age.

" A graduate of Columbia College and of the Union Theological Seminary, New York, he began his ministry in the Presbyterian Church. After eighteen years of service, as pastor of Congregational churches, he found himself greatly drawn toward our Church, and in 1866 was ordained Deacon, by Bishop Eastburn, of Massachusetts.

" As a clergyman of our Church he became Rector of Trinity, Newark, New Jersey, and St. John's, Hartford, Conn.

" In 1876, he was elected Professor of 'Homiletics and Pastoral Theology,' in the Philadelphia Divinity School, and held that chair at the time of his decease.

"Dr. Meier-Smith was a man of much loveliness of personal character, genial, sympathetic, tender, yet always manly and upright. His scholarly abilities were large and well cultivated. His pastoral work was ever regarded as very acceptable to all classes in his several congregations; his sermons were carefully prepared, and were often of marked power; his home life was beautifully tender and sunshiny, and his Christian bearing as a man, as a clergyman, and as a professor very distinctive and true. He might almost be said to have died in the harness, for the Sunday before his death he preached in the Church of the Incarnation; and that very night he was taken ill, and before the next Lord's Day dawned he was called to be 'forever with the Lord.' It seems almost something more than a coincidence, and more like one of those unconscious prophetic utterances, spoken under impulses which we cannot describe, and pointing to a future still behind the veil, that the last words of his last sermon in the last week he lived should be these:—

"'To-day the warfare of the Cross! To-morrow the Crown! Righteousness, peace, and joy for evermore.'"

"Death is another life. We bow our heads
At going out, we think, and enter straight
Another golden chamber of the King's,
Larger than this we leave, and lovelier,
And then in shadowy glimpses, disconnect,
The story, flower-like, closes thus its leaves,
The will of God is all in all."

SERMONS.

20

SERMONS.

THESE sermons, selected from the large number left in completed form by Dr. Meier-Smith, have not been chosen because they surpass many of the others either in breadth of thought, originality of treatment, or excellency of style.

His careful choice of topics, his habitual clearness of expression, and his conscientious care in preparation insured great uniformity in the attractiveness and force of his pulpit utterances. The selection was determined rather by the fact that while these sermons well represent Dr. Meier-Smith's manner of dealing with themes widely different, and thus are a fair illustration of his ordinary preaching, they are also all of comparatively recent date, one of them indeed being the last either written or preached by him.

It is hoped that as they are read by those who in memory will recall the earnest spirit and tender unction as well as the persuasive eloquence and forceful utterance of the preacher, these sermons may be endued again with something of the interest and power that attended the living voice.

E. N. W.

UNITY AMID DIVERSITY.

There are diversities of operations, but it is the same God which worketh all in all. — 1 CORINTHIANS, xii. 6.

THERE is an important sense in which every individual of mankind stands purely and entirely *alone*, whatever be in other respects the points of contact with others, or the relationships of race. In this sense each one lives unto God, having a dependence and a responsibility unshared by any other being. In the common intercourse of life the fact is recognized. There is conscious personality, or selfhood. There are rights pertaining to me, and rights pertaining to the other one who is not I. There is a circle about my own individuality which no alien foot may cross, and there is a circle around my neighbor within which I cannot intrude.

Yet, strangely, when Christian people deal with facts of the spiritual life, within the domain of what may be called personal and individual religious experience, taking the term in its common acceptation, this momentous elemental fact is oftener forgotten than remembered. A vast perplexity and much uneasiness, not to say unhappiness and consequent cramping of energies and usefulness, is engendered by a readiness to make other persons' lives and spiritual records tests and touchstones of our own. And not a little Christian charity is sacrificed when, in a similar forgetfulness, we make our own knowledge or moral success or private conscience the measure and rule whereby we judge others about us. Many a one has lived the years of life subject to bondage, and never able to rejoice in the liberty of Christ, afraid even to come unto the Holy Table and receive the sacramental Body and Blood, simply because the conscious spiritual life failed to correspond with that which was typical in the local community, or with the portrayal in the journal of some favorite saint. And many another has grieved, amid unuttered sorrows, over the apparently hopeless case of souls dear after the flesh, who never seemed to be religious in the right way, —that is, the set way of the books or the sect,—and yet doubtless were among those who feared God and sought to keep His commandments.

Now, that the great fact of personal individuality is not destroyed in the Kingdom of God, or neutralized by religion, and that a common-sense recognition of this fact is right in matters of the faith, is a truth clearly acknowledged by Saint Paul in many places, and especially in this chapter and this text. In the Body of Christ, the vast Church of His redeemed and baptized flock, there are many members of various use and honor, and various gifts of spiritual endowment. And in the grand arms of Divine charity all are to be comprehended. For amid diversities of gifts and operations there is the same Spirit, the same Lord, the same God working all in all.

For our present purpose, and in the line of thought I have indicated, let us then first apply the principles enunciated by the Apostle to the facts of *diversity in the beginnings* of the conscious religious life of the Christian believer.

We may select or call up at random from the Christian company — under any names, I had almost said — a few individuals familiar to our acquaintance, say out from the present congregation, and question them respecting facts in their spiritual history. We may ask one and another: When did you begin the Christian life? Under what circumstances did you first recognize yourself as a disciple of Christ and a believer in Him? Or, if the person was born outside and far away from the Church of Christ: By what steps and through what pathways were you guided to her portals and the hopes of her children? And we shall find that the paths by which they were led, and the circumstances wherein the consciousness of faith and holy purpose was reached, and the personal acts of faith and devotion which marked the occasion, are as different as their names or nationalities or complexions; as markedly individual as their natural personal traits.

With one there is no remembrance of any particular time or circumstance suggestive of what in a common parlance is called "Conversion." Made in infancy a member of Christ, and nurtured in the Church of God, there has never been a day wherein there was a thought alien to the Christian position. It was always the habit to serve God, always the intent and purpose, and never has this one doubted the Divine grace or the Divine provision. Of the convulsed experiences whereof some may tell, this one knows nothing at all.

Another will tell of a life given to selfishness, pleasure, worldliness,—a life in which God was forgotten,—and of some *awakening* to the sin and peril and shame of such a life in a world where God is known and wherein the Son of God once lived and died for man's redemption. Awakened — and a good word is that, for men need to be *awakened* amid their sins and fatal repose, *awakened* out of their sleep to see the facts which environ them, and the judgment ahead of them, — awakened was this one to unwonted thought; awakened to inquire who he was, whence he came, whither he is going; awakened to see himself a sinner, defiled greatly peradventure, — a sinner against law and goodness and grace, verily a defiant sinner, defiant because so willingly blind and so heartily godless; awakened to see himself, although of good repute among men and a very Pharisee as touching the law, a sinner in God's sight. And this awakened one will narrate how he sought God's face, saying, "Father I have sinned," and began thenceforth to live beholding the things unseen and eternal.

One will tell of struggles with temptations, with self-will and pride, long and fierce, before, in the spirit of the little child, submission was made of intellect and heart and life to God, or the proud man bowed to receive the holy gift in the Christian Baptism. One will tell of dark days of despondency, and of light coming slowly, with hope and peace, as the Gospel of Christ gradually dawned upon the spirit. To one, there was attraction in the pure life and words of Jesus, and the heart sought His yoke. To another, the cross riveted the thoughts, and the risen Lord lifted the soul; and from all darkness and sin, or from all self-seeking or worldly splendor, he turned, enamored of that Prince of Life, and sworn in irrevocable fealty to His service for life, for death, in this world, and in all worlds beyond.

The like and yet other tales will be told over a wide range of the Christian profession, illustrating the same great truth of diversity of operation. In all branches of the universal Church, and amid all Christendom, on the one hand churchly nurture rears in churchly ways, within the courts of God, the Samuels, the John Baptists, the Timothys, faithful soldiers of God and His Christ, strangers to marked *conversion* experiences, but who from the womb have been sanctified, and from childhood have known the Scriptures. On the other hand, within the Church — rescued from ignorance and sin and trampled grace, from the bondage of wrong instructions and burdened consciences, from heathenism — there have always been the publicans crying, "God be merciful to me a sinner;" the prodigals sick of the husks, saying, " I will arise and go to my Father;" the Sauls inquiring suddenly on Damascus roads, " Lord what wilt thou have me to do;" the Augustines, profligate children of praying mothers, paralyzed with terror at Scripture utterances, the sword of the Spirit coming into the soul, and with mighty spasm of the frame putting off the old man and putting on the new; the Luthers affrighted at dire strokes of Providence and struggling onward in bewilderment until Christ's Light is revealed; those whom some special interpositions of mercy bring to God's presence in penitence, like the soldier whose Bible stopped the bullet on its way to his heart; or those again who are moved by sudden tides of memory and tender thought, like one who, far from friends and kindred, was seated beneath the olive trees in Gethsemane, and in loneliness began to meditate on Him who once bowed in agony there for men, and then and there said from overflowing heart, " O Jesus, henceforth to Thee and Thy service I do give my poor self, joyfully, wholly!"

Such are " diversities of operations " in the leadings of the Holy Ghost in earlier stages of the conscious Christian life.

For our second point, I ask you to observe that the

diversity is equally marked in the maturer developments of the same life.

The style of manifestation of the spiritual life and character is to a great extent a resultant of education, temperament, the prevalent surrounding thought, climate, — possibly in more degrees than we may suppose, — and very largely of the ecclesiastical circumstances or relationships of the individual. Providence and grace work together, and are not at cross purposes.

It is a familiar fact that different theological systems or schools of thought and discipline produce piety in correspondingly different types: the strongly Calvinistic, and its most opposite, for example; the high and reverential order of traditional Anglicanism on the one hand, and the ways of dissent and independency on the other, for another example; while schools of devout mysticism bring forth their own delicate fruitage, whether amid the retirement of the monastery, or beneath the sunlight and amid the freedom of the Reformation.

The stern Calvinist Puritan battles for his life among Divine Decrees, Predestination, and Free-will Mysteries, reposing sometimes with a superhuman equanimity in his assured belief, however irreconcilable by human logic his positions of faith; or again, in very depths of woe lest his own calling and election be not sure, he having peradventure lost the signs thereof. A Christian he, dwelling in mountain fastnesses, strong in the arm, bold in heart, nimble of foot as the Alpine hunter, revelling amid torrents, serene beside the avalanche, peaceful and at home where clouds gather blackest and tempests howl fiercest, he recks little of the world below, its ways or its fate. His thoughts are of Him who inhabiteth eternity, and it is for him to crucify all human affections and desires, and to submit to the Infinite orderings. The stern and the terrible, the wrathful, the severe, the man-humbling aspects of God, are his delight.

There is again another child of God whose ripened vision beholds chiefly the other side of the Divine character, the loving beauty of the Father's face. He looks not so much at the Infinite and Absolute and Unsearchable, the God who overthrows the hosts of Pharaoh in the Red Sea, and whose presence is amid clouds on Sinai with thunderings and trumpet sound and earthquakes, as at God manifest in human flesh in the sweet face of Jesus. To this man there are no clouds round about the Throne which are not resplendent with the rainbow which the seer of Patmos saw, nor any frowning summits of Divine counsel or orderings which are not beautiful, tipped with the glory of God's smile. This man has sympathy with man, broad as the Gospel he receives. He dwells in the sunshine, amid lovely valleys, verdurous with perpetual summer, yet ready with the other and with all valiant souls to endure, to labor, to serve as a soldier in any fight of faith and love, to suffer, and to wait as a man of God, obedient to God's will, unto God's glory.

There, again, is the honest face of one of an every-day piety, loving God and loving man. His brain is unwearied by discussions of theological parties; his soul is distracted by no spiritual paradoxes. He is addicted neither to raptures nor depressions. He cannot speak the dialect of camp-meetings, or of more staid prayer-meetings. He does not trouble himself about Church politics, provided only there are no lights on the altar nor innovations in ritual where he worships, and no Canons concerning Orders and no Rubrics are broken by Low Churchmen. He believes according to the creed,

and by God's help he endeavors to live in the communion of the Catholic Church, in all honesty and sobriety
among men, doing good as he has opportunity, visiting
the fatherless and widows in their affliction, and keeping
himself unspotted from the world.

And, once more, we meet the Christian of highly nervous temperament and marked intellectuality, trained
to earnest and discriminating thought, given to self-in-
trospection and analysis of motive, and analysis of all
things whether of man or God, — a man whose spiritual
life is strongly moulded upon the cast-iron lines of the
sect to which he belongs, radical, positive, sure he is
right, intolerant of those who differ, yet true to his convictions and to his God; narrow and intolerant, just
because he cannot help being so, being unable to make
himself over again. This man may be a Presbyterian,
or he may be a Churchman, or he may be a Roman
Catholic by profession. He is stiffly ascetic perhaps in
his nature. His theology may be that of Schoolmen.
He may be given to fastings and prayers. He may
submit himself to penance after the mediæval renais-
sance style, confessing to his Anglican priest in the
vestry-room or the study, and receiving absolution and
direction for penance under cover of relief to his burdened conscience, almost mourning that there is no im-
palement or martyr fire to be risked thereby; or he may
devoutly conform to all the discipline of the old Papal
hierarchy, and carry even superstition and bigotry into
zeal for God's honor till they be almost virtues.

But in all such men, of various kinds and trainings,
coming from all points of the theological compass and
from extremes of spiritual latitude and longitude, we
recognize the fear of God, the love of God, supreme regard for conscience, and obedience to Christ their Lord

as they hear and understand Him, working out these cardinal elements of character, all in their different manifestations. Then, besides types like these produced by education and surroundings, do we not see endless *sub-varieties*, so to speak, in Christian life, results of temperament and constitutional idiosyncracy perhaps? Religion, like water, some one has well said, has flavor of the soil over which it flows, and whose elements, taken up in solution, impregnate it. There are sparkling disciples who see all things with joyous eyes, and whose utterances always delight us. Nothing ever comes amiss to them. There is exhilaration where some others of us would find smart and pain. There are dull disciples, the stream of whose spiritual life and influence runs slowly at dead level, yet it bears weights upon its sluggish tide and carries the good brethren quietly toward the haven. There are melancholic disciples, and sanguine, hearty men and women. There are rude and sturdy souls good for pioneer service, like Samson and Gideon. There are those who, David-like, sweep the harp-strings from deepest, tenderest penitential plaints up to the jubilant notes of seraphic triumph.

There are those whose lifetime is a mixture of conflict and bondage, fightings within and fightings without, with passions and propensities and temptations, with doubts and unbeliefs and fears of death, so that there would be absolute despair but for a poor flickering faith that there is somewhere a God and a Saviour.

There are others, happy souls, to whom from first to last life is a bright service of God, its good things *His* gifts, its trials *His* appointments, the comforts amid them *His* tender caressings; and who ever say, "I know Whom I have believed."

But — and we are now fully prepared for my last point — amid these diversities of religious life and manifestation, there is the great principle of unity; namely, —

It is the same God who worketh all in all.

For the principle of regenerate life is obedience to God, — loving obedience, obedience that believes, obedience coming from faith; and this, being a divinely implanted principle, imparts unity to the variety of Christian life manifested, and creates the true Christian brotherhood, and the family resemblance. Christian people believe God, and obey God. This belief and obedience comes from His Spirit. God renews, moulds, and sanctifies them all.

This is Saint Paul's teaching and the teaching of our Lord, and it is accepted truth in Christian creeds.

Putting which truth together with the facts which so far I have been permitted to recall to you, we may gather up two lessons, the first being, —

The right and duty of preserving the independence of personality in religious life.

For since obedience of the heart and life to God is the main thing in religion, and the way of the life eternal; and since God has made men and endowed them so variously, bringing about rich variety of fruit and flower in the garden of His grace, — it is utterly incongruous to suppose that we can improve upon the divine arrangement, either by toning down the aspect of variety or by bringing about a monotonous hue and absolute sameness. He would be adjudged a lunatic of the first water who made experiments of this sort in the material world, — in his garden, for instance; or as an educator, paying no regard to aptitudes and tastes of a thousand pupils while superintending their development. To be fretted and despondent of God's mercy, and fearfully afraid because, when reading narrations of pious folk who have gotten into print, or poring over books of devout counsel and procrustean beds for self-examination, we cannot, for our very lives, subscribe to every feeling put on record, nor to every sentiment, nor make satisfactory reply to the probings of thought and motive — in other words, because we cannot be at once the good man or woman we are studying — is neither reasonable nor at all expedient. As well might one be discontented because he cannot fashion his countenance anew after an admired model, or add a cubit to the stature, or change body with some other.

Be yourself, and be honest. Be true to yourself. God has a place for you — just precisely *you* — on the earth and in His kingdom of grace. You, with your personal characteristics, are not a mistake upon this planet nor in His Church, any more than any mountain or tree or river or lake is a mistake because it has its own form, outline, course, or scenic effect, different from all others. So serve Him who has made you and redeemed you, and trust Him, in the true and manly independence of His creature and His child.

And our other lesson grows so out of this one that it needs but to be named, it being but the common duty of Christian charity, into wonderful expansion upon which virtue Saint Paul bursts forth immediately after the argument whence our text is taken.

It is the One God working in all Christ's Body, though diversity of operation correspond with diversities of members.

Then judge not, either your fellow-Christians or your fellow-men, or other companies of Christians, denominations or sects, or branches of the Catholic Church other than the one to which you are allotted; judge no man by any narrow thoughts or tests of your own private stock, or the current tests of your circle or sect. Amid diversities of operations are some peradventure neither you nor I can understand; and possibly you and I may be an enigma to some other survey.

Neither let us despair of any, but thank we God for the inworkings of His grace vaster than our ken; for the very vastness of the temple He is building up; for many and various stones that the Master Builder knows how to place; for the glory that shall be made clear when the top stone crowns the pile sublime, — and the Church, made up of our human kind and purged from all imperfection, shall stand, without spot or wrinkle or any such thing, a Church of Glory.

CARE CAST UPON GOD.

Casting all your care upon Him, for He careth for you.
1 PETER v. 7.

HAVING once read or heard words like these can we ever forget them? And who having once taken in their meaning could be persuaded to give up the Christian idea of God and to accept any other "first-cause" doctrine in place of it?

This wonderful universe in which we live! Far beyond us, and encompassing us on every side as in vast and yet vaster concentric spheres, are the revolutions and cycles revealed by our mathematical science supplementing the splendors of the heavens. There is the sublime perfection of motion. The immense and unnumbered stars and systems pursue their way; they never fail nor swerve. We can make accurate computations concerning them. We can stake all earthly interests upon these computations.

Then upon our own earth, how straightforward the march of all things in their order and succession!

Summer and winter, seed-time and harvest, cold and heat, sunshine and black clouds, day and night, keep up their alternations. We keep track of them. Storms drive through our atmosphere, their force invisible, — but on their own paths, some of which we have found out. Particles of all kind of material substance, expired, exhaled, in comminuted or vapory forms, going off from our bodies, from lungs and pores, going off from our gardens and our waste-heaps, going off in the smoke from our chimneys, are — as chemistry teaches and explains — re-gathered, re-distributed, kept in perpetual use and in perpetual transmigration: so that the balance of organic nature is preserved, and no atom is ever lost or extinguished.

The labor of the hand or of the brain is productive *so* surely and *so* inevitably. Then there seem to be just as fixed regularities and certainties in what we call the realm of morals. We speak of rewards to virtue. We say, "Murder will out," and we recognize appropriate penal results for moral wrongs. And when we survey the social life of man, or the State life, we observe the same thing. There is a course of empire. The law of the rise and thrift of a nation is as clear as the law of a tree's growth. The law of decay and ruin is as clear as the process of death in a plant or in a man. What is this all? What is the secret of it? Some men speak of *law* as if this were the full explanation. We hear great wisdom in which words like "force," "development," "protoplasm" come in quite roundly. We have great names of philosophers and scientists sounded in our ears, and are puzzled by their various "hypotheses," — which only mean suppositions or theories.

There are men who do not like to retain *God* in their knowledge; and who travel a long distance to keep that name out of their mouths.

Everything that science and skill can accomplish — the navigation of the seas, the prediction of astronomical changes, the process of invention and discovery — is traced to some law or force, but the explanation goes no further.

Now, we who are Christians love to put the word "God" into our solution of all these marvels. And that word "God" means a good and wise and loving and almighty Father, a Father of omnipresent power and efficiency, and, what is more, of an omnipresent heart full of tenderness and comfort.

Look at Saint Peter's expression in the text. God "careth for you."

Before the little child was born in your house, how many things were done to give it a comfortable welcome to the world, which would have been such a cold place but for the provision. And how you anticipate all the wants and needs of the living, breathing babe! You sleep verily waking, lest any harm come through too sound a sleep or through any neglect. That is care taken for the child.

Go into the chamber of a sick person. There is a a darkened window. There on the table beside the bed stand flowers, put there by thoughtful love. There are the prescribed medicines. There is a plate with bits of cracked ice, and there is a fever-allaying drink; while seated at the bedside is a faithful watcher whom not a breath escapes, nor a delirious word, nor a turn of the hand, nor a motion of the eye. That is *caring* for the sufferer. So is the thoughtfulness which has sent a book for the solace of some sad hour. So is the loving look upon the sick bestowed by a friend coming in.

We take passage and go aboard the ocean steamer. We are keenly alive to the perils of the sea — at least some of us — when we step upon the deck. But everything, even amid the confusion, wears the air of order and discipline. Presently after parting with friends we make our inspection. The arrangements for safety and for a degree of comfort are all we could expect. The officers and men are at their various posts. The bells strike the hours. By and by we hear the rush of the gang of men heaving the log. There in that little room is a chart, and the captain makes his notes upon it after the "observation" is taken, so that he can tell just where we are upon the trackless sea. We look about at night as well as in the daytime; there is increasing watchfulness. The men are always at the wheel. The officers are always on the bridge. Down in the engine room, and amid the fires, always we find men awake, earnest, intent upon duty. And in due time after a certain number of revolutions of the screw and a careful following a prescribed route marked out in New York or in Liverpool, we find ourselves safely landed "where we would be." There has been *care*, to bring us to this happy termination.

The toil of the plowman and the sower and the reaper; the busy industry in the workshop, behind the counter, in the office; the economical management of a household which keeps expenses within income and saves a little for laying up, if only a dollar in a year, —is what we mean when we say that care is taken. Care plans and provides. Care sees that there is no waste, or as little as possible. Care looks after the ten thousand little and, by themselves, insignificant things, which are really so vital in their connections, and so essential to our preservation and happiness.

Fruits and flowers spring from care. Public parks and private gardens thrive by care. Nothing would flourish without it. Hinges would grow rusty, the shingles fall from the roof and the clapboards from the sides of the house, if nobody took any care. Even churches would tumble into ruins, beginning with some leak which lets in the rain, were there no good wardens or faithful people to look after repairs.

Now, Saint Peter says, " He careth for you." Who would strike out, I say again, the Christian idea of God, and travel his pathway on earth with the substitution which some propose for this? "God careth for you." God is full of care, — loving care; care for individual needs; care for the grass and the lilies and the hairs of the head and the sparrows and the cattle, and for you and me. Essayists, lecturers, and schoolmasters may say what they please, but would your heart give up this God? This God to whom you can say " Our Father," and whom you can ask for " daily bread " if you need?

We may be told that the peace and happiness which come from such a faith in God and about God are after all only charms resulting from a delusion. Perhaps. But it is a sweet intoxication to be able to take such an outlook upon the world, — yea, over the flood of waters upon which we are embarked. If it be only an idea, yet it is an idea of wonderful power to sustain and strengthen, that so great a heart beats in love, and so prescient a vision orders in love, and so ready a hand all unseen brings about in love while it upholds and protects. If all the truth lies even in the interior soul, yet may we say with Addison : —

> "How are thy servants blest, O Lord !
> How sure is their defence !
> Eternal wisdom is their guide ;
> Their help, Omnipotence."

Upon Him cast all your care, says Saint Peter.

There is an energetic action about that word " cast." It means something of violence. If we believe in God, we are to put certain things into His hands, or upon Him; to throw them off our perplexed and wearied minds and upon His great broad, unwearying, infinite thought, wisdom, love, and power.

And, what is important for us to remember, the advice is not the tame and quiet exhortation coaxing us to trust as much as we can in God's hands, and worry ourselves at the same time, nor even that we try more and more to trust God, but it is the word of command and of action.

You stand upon God's earth. Plant your foot firmly on that earth. Brace yourself, if needs be. Then lift up and cast, thrust the whole of your care, all your trouble and your life into God's lap and leave it there.

I say your life, for " all the care " is equivalent to life. When we cease from care, we shall cease to be. That means that we cast ourselves first into God's hands. We have to commit others to those hands. We have had to leave our best beloved ones with Him, and all their interests. We know these are safe. So may we and must we entrust ourselves to Him. You are a mystery to yourself, and see only trouble and perplexity ahead of you. You compare yourself to a passenger on a ship at sea, amid fogs, — taking your risk, — helpless, and calm because helpless. Your calmness is stupidity or desperation. Try what Saint Peter commands and commends. Cast your care, yourself, upon God. Grasp the hand that would help you to this uplifting, even the hand of Christ, and throwing yourself and all things upon His love, trusting that, be at peace, go your ways in peace, do your work in peace. If you succeed in your plans, it is well. If you do not succeed in them, it is well also. Your care is cast upon God. In that venture of faith you have left questions of success and failure, after our common ways of thinking, in God's hands. You have cast yourself upon Him. If He breaks your plans and sweeps away your projects, He still bears you upon His almighty wing; and you are in the arms, and the hand, of His care and love.

Let me close with these trustful lines of Whittier:

"I know not what the future hath
    Of marvel or surprise,
Assured alone that life and death
    His mercy underlies.

.   .   .   .

"And so beside the silent sea
    I wait the muffled oar;
No harm from Him can come to me
    On ocean or on shore.

"I know not where His islands lift
    Their fronded palms in air;
I only know I cannot drift
    Beyond His love and care."

THE NEW HEAVEN AND THE NEW EARTH.

And I saw a new heaven and a new earth. . . . And He that sat upon the throne said, Behold, I make all things new. — REVELATION xxi. 1, 5.

IN these words our thoughts are first carried to the sublime vision itself from the record of which they are taken. The vision of the Judgment, wherein the dead, small and great, stand before God, and the sea and death and Hades give up the dead which have been in them, that they may be judged out of the books, according to their works, has passed, and the resplendent vision of the New Jerusalem appears. The City of God descends from God out of heaven, prepared as a bride adorned for her husband. The tabernacle of God is with men, and God doth wipe away the tears from all eyes, and there is no more death, neither sorrow nor crying, neither shall there be any more pain. The former things are passed away. And then the voice of the One sitting upon the throne is heard, "Behold, I make all things new !"

If we study the whole picture, and note carefully the language, we see that there is not a process of new creation going on, a creation of material, nor even a putting chaotic matter into order and beauty, but that it is rather the renovation and reconstruction of the old material. Both in the material things and the spiritual things of the Apocalyptic imagery this seems to be the case. The heavens and the earth are new ; yet heavens and earth for substance. The City of God is new; yet it is the New Jerusalem. And they who sing before the throne sing a new song, or as it were a new song; one in some senses old and familiar, to which their lips were attuned through many processes of sanctifying discipline, yet ever new and fresh in its grander meanings and its celestial harmonies.

The key-note of the revelation here made is *renovation*. The Apocalypse — whatever the true or rather the indiscoverable theory for its interpretation, whether it be a prophetic vision of the earlier struggles of the Church, closing with the great era of the imperial persecution and the final destruction of Jerusalem, or a revelation of the course of conflict, or the general features thereof, through which the Church of God is to be led to its final glory — certainly seems to throw a light upon the whole course and trend of Providence and history. And these words, "I make all things new," may be taken as a summary of the hopeful suggestions of the book respecting the course of history and of human experience, amid all vicissitudes and upheavals, revolutions and catastrophes. There is something great and good being evolved as age follows age, as destruction and revivification seem to alternate. There is One who says, "Behold, I make all things new!" And the end is this whereunto the vision of Saint John reaches, — the consummation of blessedness in the universe of God, and in the full revelation of God in the glorification of His Son Jesus Christ, and perfect redemption, the restitution of all things, the gathering together of all things in Him.

Saint John's keen vision and Saint Paul's inspired utterances point to the same grand end, — the new creation and the manifestation of the Son of God, — toward which all the weary ways of human life, and all the groanings of the old creation are tending, and in which shall be at once their justification and their recompense.

The recognition of this ultimate purpose of God and of the process wherein it is described, the grand renovation of all things through the ages, discovers to us a principle of unity whereby the solution of some of our gravest problems in theology, and the philosophy of events, may be greatly aided.

I will endeavor to indicate in one or two illustrations how we may gather the assistance and comfort thus afforded.

1. Let us begin with our own problem: ourselves, man; and the question, what is man's worth and man's destiny? What significance has the making all things new for him? Is man, are we, among the things made new? A foremost truth of Scripture is at once brought to mind when we attempt this problem; namely, the regeneration of man himself. And it is a note-worthy fact that Saint John, the writer of the Apocalypse, in his later work, the fourth Gospel, gives supreme prominence to this point. The Gospel opens with the Word becoming flesh, and with power being given to men to become sons of God, "not of blood, nor of the will of the flesh, nor of the will of man, but of God;" and the great truth receives emphasis again in the narrative of the interview between Nicodemus and the Lord. Reading various scriptures, and putting together what is said in the Gospels, and by Saint John and Saint Paul in their Epistles, we gather that although the process of renovation began indeed close upon the Fall, with the first promise of grace, and the provisions of religion, the disclosure of the first and fundamental step is not made

until Christ, the Messiah, the Son of God, appears in
our human nature. Christ appears in the "fulness of
time," — that is, when the world and humanity and
God's purposes are ready for the appearing.

In this incarnation, we are taught, is the revelation
of the long withholden mystery, — that is, "The mystery
of godliness," "God," or "He who was manifested in the
flesh." Christ is represented as the New Man. He is
figured to us under the title of the second Man, the
second Adam. The idea presented is that of race head-
ship. The first Adam stands in our theological systems,
gathered from scriptural expression, head of the race
which sprang from his loins by natural descent. In
him they, his children, fell. In him they all die. The
solidarity of the race in Adam is strongly figured, nay,
more than figured; and race ruin is the logical consequence, and the consequence *de facto*.

The re-creation, or the regeneration of the race,
comes by its transference to a new head. That new
head is the second Adam, the Christ. He is the first
born of the new creation. The manhood He assumed
and wore, and joined to His divine nature, is the manhood born of the Virgin, and springs from divine over-
shadowing. Scripture is consistent. There is wonderful
harmony and exactitude in its revelations of supernatural and divine facts and doings. This God-Man is
head of a new race gathered out of the old race, — a re-
constructed and regenerated race. The manhood which
is joined unto and finds its head in the second Adam,
the Lord from heaven, is delivered from power of
death and made heir of the resurrection. As all in
Adam die, so all in Christ live. The regenerate manhood, and that is the aggregate of the regenerate men;
those who by faith and covenant are gathered into

Christ and belong to the race of the second Adam, — these are conformed, by His Spirit dwelling in them, to His spiritual character and similitude in their personal character, and will be conformed to Him, spiritually and bodily, in the unspeakable beauty and purity of His glorious Person.   It is a wonderful picture of hope which faith discerns when she studies the portrayal: "Christ, the hope of glory."   What is our hope in this vision of the New Man who stands central in creation, and whose renovation is a part of that work which He who maketh all things new is doing?

The first man Adam was lord of Paradise.   Even the *fallen* Adam is a wonderful being, a splendid race for endowment and power.   His deeds of might and deeds of good, looked at in our earthly way, are well worthy a child of the skies.   His deeds of evil, his crimes, are a stupendous revelation of the power resident within him.   And yet again, how close are his limitations! "Thus far and no farther," is the law upon him.   There are bounds which he cannot pass.   He is subject to conditions, to toil, to suffering, to deterioration, decay, and death.   He cannot escape therefrom.   No elixir of life is within his compass.   He cannot stave off consequences of sin.   No one of them can by any means redeem his brother.   He is godlike, yet not a god.   He can accomplish many things.   He can weigh the stars and map out their motions.   He can master potent forces of Nature.   But he cannot create a ray of light or a blade of grass, nor breathe life into any nostrils, whether to vivify a statue or to revive a dead fish.   The very earth brings forth thorns and thistles to him.   He can eat bread only in the sweat of his brow.   At the most, he can but temporarily avert or briefly hide from any impending evil or calamity. And great as he is, death masters him. Death has reigned over him. A whole creation indeed is handicapped by its relation to him, and groans in sympathy with his estate.

What hope is there for this creature which is not against hope? What chance for him, except there be some unrevealed law or power within him at last to burst his bonds and transcend all his known limits? Perhaps — Let us not, however, cast aspersion upon any human outlook.

But the New Man, — type as well as head of the new race, head of a race in which the finite and the infinite meet and blend, — how He doth interpret for us what it is to be sons of God! The New Man is master of all the earth. He is master of human woes and of human circumstances, and master of death. There seems to be no word "impossible" with Him. The matter world and the spirit world are subject to Him. The seas subside at His bidding; He can walk upon their crested waves as upon a smooth floor; the fig-tree withers to point His spiritual teaching; bread multiplies in His hand to feed the thousands when He must needs feed them; disease flies at His word,— fever, palsy, leprosy, blindness, lameness; devils are cast out by Him; the mad-men clothe themselves, and are of right mind when He speaks to them; death and Hades surrender their victims at His command. What a wonderful sight was that when the New Man touched the bier at the gates of Nain and the young man rose from his death sleep; or yet more, when, calm and assured, he went out to Bethany and to the grave of Lazarus, and bade the four-days dead come forth, and he came forth, bound hand and foot as the corpses were bound for entombment ! Mark it ! He who summoned Lazarus from the grave was the Son of Man. Then again, the New Man Himself is superior to death. He dies indeed, not because He must die, but He lays down His life for a purpose. And then He asserts Himself, the dead and buried New Man alive again and alive forevermore. He is now man; master of old laws and of new laws; master of new forces, and interpreter of laws until His revelation all unknown.

Scripture, we have said, is consistent. The whole story of the New Man, the Son of God and Son of Man, is a story which befits such a Being, and is essential to the conception of such a Being.

What more have we for light upon our human problem ? The New Man revelation culminates in the Ascension. From the summit of Olivet He has passed into the heavens. It is made known that He will appear again, and that He will be the Supreme Power upon earth,— the reigning king, all things subject to Him. The visions of the Apocalypse portray the glory of His reign. Do we inquire what this means for man; for the race whereof He is head and Prince ? Saint John, whose eye discerned the future in those visions, says, " When He shall appear, we shall be like Him, for we shall see Him even as He is." " Ye also shall sit upon thrones," said this Son of Man Himself, to His elect representatives of His chosen race and body, when He spoke of the full regeneration, the palingenesis of the future. The new race is a brotherhood; the Son of Man is the elder brother. The brotherhood, the race redeemed, the faithful of Christ,—they, by the vision of the Apocalypse, shall dwell in the city; they shall there serve God and see His face, and His name shall be upon their foreheads.

Such is the outlook for man through Christ. By faith in Him men become members of His body, being baptized into Him. He is the head of the new race, the head of the body. To the renovated manhood is given power to be sons of God, — a dignity which surpasses our present scope of definition or thought. God is making all things new, and, central amid the all things, a new people, a new creation of man to serve and praise Him.

2. The renovation work again, it appears, is not confined to the race of man. It is carried on in man's surroundings and conditions, so that the re-established Man shall find abundant re-endowment, and all circumstances fitting to the glory of the regenerated race. As the earth has been carried through successive renovations in ages past, to the end that man should find his place and work in it, and as the shapings of events in history, — all revolutions and upheavals and successions of empire, and all advance in dominant thoughts and age ideas, — have been manifestly directed for human advancement and growth, so the Apocalypse gives us the fuller knowledge that the like process goes on definitely toward the beatific consummation discerned in the vision. The motion of the universe is toward the new heaven and the new earth. There is a shaping power. That power is His who sits upon the throne. His throne is that whence emanates decrees and all laws and all changes and all supreme judgment. From that throne comes the explanatory voice, the voice interpreting Providence and history, " I am making all things new." The processes of Nature and of history may be very intricate, but here is the clew to the most labyrinthian problems they present. There is supreme purpose. There is a throne and power in it. There is

uniform and resistless exercise of purposeful power, — the renovations, — until the time of the perfect restitution of all things, when under the new heavens and upon the new earth there shall stand the city whereof it is written, "the glory of God did lighten it and the Lamb is the Light thereof."

In the recognition of this purpose of a consummation in the first revelation of God in His Son, and the perfect estate through the redemption that is in Christ Jesus, is, as has been already said in part, the key to the solution of history. The consummation is full enough and grand enough to be the issue and result, and thus the explanation of all that has gone before it, — the growth and construction of the earth, the sufferings and conflicts, the revolutions and renewals of nations and individual men. The processes of this world are seen to terminate in that which is immortal, spiritual, and eternal. May we not rest in this great fact ? Or shall we turn to the alternative, — the most relentless pessimism or agnostic fatalism ?

To the eye of Christian faith, then, the whole march of Providence and history is a transformation work. A new heavens and new earth are being evolved before the keen eye of our spiritual discernment In our daily world the ideas which the New Man by His Incarnation put into the world are the transforming and renovating forces. These forces have made the present age what it is, in contrast with remote past ages. It is the potency of the New Man in human life which makes our city, our home, and our life in the world, better, purer, safer than the life of old Pompeii or Pagan Rome or Corinth or the older Babylon. The wars and overturnings of empires, amid seas of fire and blood, which have brought the nineteenth century to us are

but successive steps in the "making all things new."
Behold, He who says from the throne that He is doing
it, is verily the world's Saviour in the most worldly and
material sense, as well as in the higher and spiritual significance! He has made earth habitable for us. What
would this world be to-day for you or me were all the
Gesta Christi eliminated from the scene of our surroundings and possessions, and had we nothing left
which has come from Christ and His Gospel? When
the prophecy is fulfilled, the new heavens and the new
earth will be an abode fitted for the race which is to
dwell and reign thereon.

The separation from sin and woe shall be complete
and permanent. Death and Hades shall have been
cast into the lake of fire. And there shall be ex-
cluded forever all that is evil and pollution, and
whatsoever loveth and maketh a lie.

Oh, brethren, fellow-members of the race of Adam,
what august mysteries and capacities of our being remain before us to be tested! Amid what limitless
possibilities of life that is eternal shall we be versed
some day! Out of the old God is creating the new.
Are we being made over again into the likeness of His
Son? The spiritual renewal and transformation of the
individual man is the first step in the process of hope
and life for that man. The new birth by God's grace,
and the sanctification into the likeness of Christ, are
not mere dogmas of the Church or of theology. The
whole hope of man by the Scripture is made to rest
upon this renewal. The voices of Nature and of history echo to the words of the divine Lord, "Ye must
be born again!"

He that maketh all things new must make us all
anew, that we may inherit with the new-born race, and

the First Born — the God-Man — the highest blessedness of being.

God grant that so we be made His children by adoption and grace, and daily be renewed by His Holy Spirit that we may, in the latter day, rise to the Life Immortal!

22

THE HOLY COMMUNION.

He gave it to His Disciples. — MATT. XXVI. 26.

THERE is a familiar poetic, if not entirely philosophical, deduction from a known law of sound, to the effect that the atmosphere of earth, or the yet vaster medium of surrounding ether, retains in form and living motion every sound and note that has ever been projected from human lips or from any other source. So that — fearful thought, in some aspects of it — words never die. They, once spoken, may strike ears for which they were never meant. They may ever live and move, though we cannot trace their flight, winged benedictions, or winged evils, of measureless influences for good or for ill.

Another familiar and impressive fancy, based upon the laws of light and its velocity, startling when first conceived, yet altogether within the bounds of reason, is that when we look at certain heavenly bodies through the telescope, so great is the magnitude of distance, we see not the rays which to-day are flashing from them, but those which leaped forth from the mighty fires thousands, nay, tens of thousands of years ago. And so could an observer upon some planet much less distant than some of those be endowed with vision keen enough for analysis of objects, he might to-day discern, as a present scene, almost any of the noted events of the past, — the day of the crucifixion, for example, or, farther back, the floods of Noah's time, or yet again the freshness and glory of the virgin earth when morning stars sang together and sons of God shouted for joy, the new verdure and the primeval glow of the sunlit paradise ere it had ceased to be a home for the human kind.

In a sense, then, words are ever living and fresh, through ages, from the lips that spoke them, and things done are ever being done so that time and space almost pass out of reckoning, and all things and all words dwell eternally in the perpetual and eternal *Now*. May we not bring these conceptions to our aid and think of the words of our divine Lord and Saviour as fresh words to-day, just falling from His lips, and behold as a present and perpetually present scene the upper chamber of the Passover in Jerusalem, and the ordering of the Feast wherein He purposed to feed and refresh His people in all the years thereafter ?

It is to the Christian faith a living picture, — more than a picture, an undying group, a transaction never vanishing from the view. The Table of the Lord and His disciples is ever spread. The Master is seated at it still. The words giving His body and His blood are verily issuing from His lips and fresh upon the air. The bread broken and the consecrated chalice are being in this very movement still given into the hands of His disciples. Let the centuries melt from our thoughts, and be as though they were not. The successive generations of communicants are but successive ranks of the congregation going up to that sacred Table where He presides, Master of Assemblies, receiving from Him and orderly retiring that others may follow them.

So to-day, in our turn on earth, we advance to His altar. Priests and people, we alike receive from His own most blessed hand. Other generations shall follow us. It is one unbroken Eucharistic Feast wherein we do eat the same spiritual bread and drink the same spiritual cup until all His sacramental host are nurtured and gathered into Paradise, or the hour doth come for His glory. In this grand Eucharist, which is every day and every hour somewhere upon the earth celebrated by faithful souls, there is perpetual presence of the Lord with His believing Church, — not a corporeal presence in the bread and wine, nor a transubstantiated presence, nor aught merely metaphysical or theoretical, but a presence warm and living as He gives still to His disciples.

1. *He* gave it to them.

Let our first thought, after this conception of His presence, spring from our emphasis upon the first word, " He."

The lofty estimate which the Church of Christ places upon the sacraments is the result of the esteem wherein the Master Himself is held. Instituted by Him personally, and not mediately through apostles as were some other institutions, faith in His divinity places them above all other ordinances whatsoever. One of these pertains to the production of spiritual life. The other pertains to its preservation. We call them, in their grand pre-eminence, " Sacraments," and by this title distinguish them from all other ordinances however primitive, binding, or beautiful.

Then farther, believing that which the Master taught concerning the inflowing of spiritual life from Him into His members, even as sap flows from the vine-trunk into the branches, and regarding these Sacraments as channels through which specific streams of this life flow down, albeit not all the streams, — receiving them as conduits from Him, the Church regards them not as mere tokens or signs of grace which is given independently of them as much as within them. So she differs, and always has differed, in all her confessions, and in all her personal faith, from those who regard them as mere medals or badges; from those to whom they are simple formalities; from those to whom they are transactions in which man gives to God rather than receives from God; from those who esteem them valuable only as certain thoughts are always suggested by them; and most of all. from those who, whether papist or rationalist, modify them at pleasure or set them among the worn-out things which were supposed to be helpful in the primitive days of the Christian Faith. Because He ordained them Himself, — because from His lips issued the commandment to baptize, and again to bless and break and eat the sacramental bread, — these two Christian rites stand forever pre-eminent above all possible ordinances or rites which, however appropriate, faith or love might ever erect. They cannot be set aside. They may not be neglected. They must not be tampered with. They must remain as He gave them, and be preserved and perpetuated according to His words.

2. Let us emphasize the second word, " He *gave*."

A sacrament is something wherein the Lord *gives*, not a something in which He receives. Yet, in the fickle perverseness of human thought, there is a prevalent notion, let us hope it is not widespread in the Church, that man must *give*. And connected with this idea is a fear of sacraments and a great neglect of them, on the part of those who know not what to give when they come before God, or who are conscious (as who must not be) that they can bring no fitness to Him wherein they may be baptized, nor any proper degree of penitential emotion when they must offer up a "feeling" suitable to the intellectual process of recalling the circumstances of the Saviour's death, or the theological doctrines which they are taught to arrange in clusters around the cross of a Redeemer. Nay, brethren, we may indeed give ourselves up anew to God's service in the devotional acts accompanying every sacramental service, and we ought to do this sincerely and earnestly; but, except in that sense, we have nothing to give, we are simply recipients. *He gives*, the gracious giver. He gives the grace in baptism. We offer not perfection of renewed hearts to Him for His acceptance in that service. We cast no new honors at His feet when we, in the loftiness of manhood, come to His font for the washing of regeneration. We are not bidden wait with coming to those waters until we have achieved victory over sin, or until we can exhibit a heroic repentance, or something that shall entitle us to His regard. We come, as we bring the new-born babe, empty of all pretension, and empty of all goodness, and empty of all spiritual power. We come desirous of blessing from Him, and in receptive mood because desirous. We come seeking, and to take, as He will give it, that grace which seals acceptance with Him, and which is the first instalment of spiritual mercies unnumbered, of spiritual life, of imparted strength and spiritual victory. And, in like manner, in the Holy Communion Christ gives and we receive. This is the attitude of a true faith in Him. "Nothing in my hand I bring" may be sung before that Holy Table as nowhere else.

So let no one who would have Christ's blessing stay away from the Eucharistic Feast by reason of the sense of want, of emptiness, of unworthy heart and feeling and service. For here is the empty filled and the feeble is holpen.

3. But what is given in this sacrament? Let us emphasize again, He gave *it*. He took bread and blessed it and brake it, and gave *it*. And He took the cup and gave thanks, and gave *it*. And as He gave the bread, He said, "This is my body." And as He gave the cup, He said, "This is my blood of the New Testament which is shed for many for the remission of sins."

His natural body was before their eyes, and with His own hand of flesh He gave that bread. His natural blood coursed through those veins, and yet He said, "This is my body, and this is my blood." Nor did He say, This bread when you eat it represents merely this body of mine; nor did He say, It shall suggest this body of mine. The holy words of the Institution affirm, "This is my body and blood." And yet the fleshly body and blood were clearly not that bread and wine, clearly not that body and blood which the disciples then and there ate and drank.

But previous to this most holy occasion our blessed Lord had taught His disciples that there was to be special communication of spiritual life from Himself to His people, through a process which He was pleased to call, "eating the flesh of the Son of Man and drinking His blood." At the time, they who heard did not understand Him. In these wondrous words of the Holy Table, however, the mysterious language was not divested of mystery, but sufficiently interpreted. He gave them the bread and bade them eat, saying, "This is my body," and the consecrated wine, saying, "This is my blood." In this sacramental act they were to receive that spiritual nourishment which our Saviour expressed in the terms, eating His flesh and drinking

His blood, — that which He meant when He said, "My flesh is meat indeed, and my blood is drink indeed;" "He that eateth Me even he shall live by Me."

He gave it then to His disciples, and He is giving this in all the ages to them, individually, as they come, in successive generations in their day upon earth, and kneel around His Holy Table, — the altar whereof they have the right to eat. The great sacramental grace, or blessing, the gift, the enrichment, the endowment, the help, the strength, the vitality of most precious value, — whatever it be in its nature or analysis we know not; that supreme blessing which He is pleased to call, "bread from heaven," "His own flesh," "His own body and blood," and the richness of which, and the sustenance of which, the armies of the saints have tested and witnessed, — this, obtainable nowhere but in this sacrament, spiritually received, this blessing, supreme and ineffable, He gave to His disciples, and gives to them to-day.

It is a gift, permit me to say again, which we cannot analyze or dissect. Nor can we in our own consciousness separate it or its immediate effects from those expressions which are the natural emotions of the devout heart; but by its results we may recognize its value. Somehow there is most intimate connection between this sacrament and all ghostly strength; between it and elevated Christian peace, stability, and comfort; between it and the growth of individual spiritual life; between its faithful observance and the continuance, the growth, the spirituality and power of the whole company of all faithful people. Corruptions of this sacrament are historically associated with corruptions in the Church and diminution of spiritual power through them. Detractions from this sacrament are associated with deteriorations in faith and order, and in diminution of spiritual power on another side. The reverent maintenance thereof in its integrity pertains to them in the Catholic Communion who most strongly hold the apostolic faith and practice, and is their highest means of growth and of grace, even as it stands central and most exalted in their worship.

As you come to the Holy Table this morning, disciples of the divine Master, remember that it is He who gives to you the sacramental food, and the blessing of spiritual strength pertaining to it. Let all others fade from the vision, and receive as from that Master alone. Give thanks to Him that as His warm right hand might be grasped by those who lived when He was in the flesh upon earth, or the "hem of His garment," so through this sacrament, coming down through the ages, there is contact with Him for believing souls, and "virtue" goeth out from Him for the healing of their infirmities. Closing the palm upon that bread, you take hold of what is as the hand of Jesus, what He gives as a sensible proof of His presence, like the loving hand extended in the dark to caress and comfort and assure the timid child in its cradle. The voice of this sacrament is, "Lo, I am with you!" It whispers that the shadows shall flee away and the morning shall break. Receive. Believe. Feed on Him present, in your heart, "by faith with thanksgiving." Do your sins trouble you? In His voice, telling of His own sacrifice, can you doubt His forgiveness? Do clouds and darkness fill your day so that you are in perpetual sorrow and tribulation? That voice of Jesus says, "My body and my blood are given for you." Shall not all things be well at the last? Are not all things well now, with this great fact before your eyes, and

He who gave Himself, — your King, the Almighty Ruler?

He gave it. He gives this sacramental food to His disciples. And do you not receive it? Then, why? You refuse, beloved, what Christ offers you. You refuse the sign, and do not respond to it. You refuse in this the thing signified, the grace of the eternal life which He gives in the sign, — that food which except you eat it and drink it, you have no life in you.

Beloved! beloved! it is no small thing to refuse the Holy Communion of the body and the blood of the Son of God, the gift of the infinite love, the means of the infinite grace, offered most freely to every sinner who would repent him of his sins and humbly receive it.

THE MANY MANSIONS.

In my Father's house are many mansions: if it were not so I would have told you. I go to prepare a place for you. — JOHN xiv. 2.

"IF it were not so I would have told you." What blessed words are these! The hope of future life and conception of that life is cheering to the chastened mind, so that the outlook is not cold and dark, but home-like, so that the world to come invites the spirit rather than affrights or repels it. The conviction is born, inborn with the spiritual regeneration, that what God's children need and thirst for they shall some day find, and shall thirst no more; that every immortal spirit shall have enough and to spare of joy in being and of service; that conceptions may be framed which, although to be hereafter corrected in detail, shall nevertheless not be disappointed in the fulness and sweetness of the reality. This hope and this conviction find justification in these words of our divine and adorable Master. Were they essentially wrong or without foundation, He says, "I would have told you." We may look away from this our earth into the vast expanse of the starry heavens, and we may be confident; many abodes remain, and we have grander intervals than those of time and sense, and vaster resource than all earthly habitation and wealth, although it is not given us here to make inventory of the things beyond. Let us take the words of the text first in one of the two familiar interpretations of them, and —

1. Understand our Lord as referring to the grand universe as the Father's house, and the home everywhere, and that there are in this vast edifice many apartments, resting places, abodes, where children and guests may dwell in serene peace. This earth is one of the abodes or chambers. In the vast palace there are countless other chambers. So the Lord comforts His disciples in anticipation of the separation presently to be realized. I am going away from you, and the daily intercourse of eye and ear and hand and mouth will be suspended; but I only pass into another apartment of the house. I shall be but the other side of the veil which so heavily drapes the hall wherein we are together tarrying, and I shall come again to carry you with me to the place more sumptuous within.

From the Christian standpoint it is a good thing to live. Whether immortality and an unending conscious existence be man's inalienable right, and his law of being, or whether it be that this endowment is bestowed only in the regeneration, as man is renewed into the life and hope of the second Adam, the Lord from heaven, may be left to the well-learned controversialists for solution; but to the disciples of Christ the promise is sure, and his personal immortality and hope of glory is matter of revelation. This present estate may be whatever he chooses to consider it. So bare the walls, and so meagre the furniture of his individual lot, and so painful the allotments for his discipline, that he may call it a prison cell with scarce more than a rift in the cold granite for light and air, or a school of hard tutelage and bitter experience. But presently the door will open, and there will be a going forth into something better, into another abode, — an abode bright to our vision, for God's word writes hope upon its front in hues of the rainbow.

Yet let us not call this lifetime a prison, though it be a school of discipline. In the light of Christ, let it rather be the vestibule wherein we await the unfolding of portals with expectancy. Beyond is the Paradise, the grand hall where the redeemed of all ages are assembling, not having yet received the promise in its fulness; where, with the consciousness of that presence of their Lord which is supreme felicity itself, they still await the vision beatific, "the redemption of the body," and "the abundant entrance to the everlasting kingdom."

Wondrous comfort this to stricken souls and to those whose hearts and hopes are bound up in some of these! That life which seems so fearful a wreck, sorrow and suffering having blasted it; that life wherein the poor tenant of a feeble frame has lingered, in the day time saying, "Would God it were evening!" and through the night watches, "Would God it were morning!" that life a burden and a paradox, leading the sufferer and the sharer of the woe to wonder sometimes whether there be a hearer of prayer or a throne of mercy at all, — behold! it is not a wreck, but a waiting time. The morning cometh. Earth is not the only dwelling place, nor is it home; there is life to come. And to those who dwell in bondage through the fear of death, how strengthening and how emancipating the words of the Master, could they but take them in! Our "Saviour Jesus Christ hath abolished death," and hath brought life and immortality to light. Death is but transition. "I go and come again." There are apartments more than one. To the member of Christ, there is no extinguishment of being. To his consciousness there is no interruption, nor is there break in his existence. Indeed, there may be no disturbance of his highest plans and purposes; for his plan and purpose is to fulfil God's will and to honor his divine Redeemer. This is all there is in death to the man of faith or the child of God. It is but the passage through an open door, — a door which Christ hath opened and which no man may shut. Life is here; more and better life is there. Service is here, a blessed service, though the service be only — and that the hardest one — to stand and wait. Better service, yet more blessed, greater and more telling, is beyond. The transition made, that other room gained, the vestibule left behind and the soul standing amid the innumerable company within the hall of Paradise, — what ineffable experiences of joy and gladness must they know who enter there! Pain and toil are over. Weakness and weariness are of the past. The clouds which rested so heavily upon the mind are rolled away. Doubt is gone; fear is gone. When you speak to the weary and heavy laden, beloved, point them to this comfortable hope. Strengthen the hearts of the sorrowing ones with the vision of the New Testament prophecy. When you revolve the puzzling problem of human destiny, and surveying the generations after generations who toil in turn upon the surface of the globe, loaded with poverty, ignorance, and sin, dull and stolid in their lives and their ways, you inquire wherefore do they live, or doubt whether it be for more than gross and material ends, — as to dig and delve and labor for the elect few of higher position and happier lot. Among your many thoughts concerning them, rejoice that there are many mansions in the great house of the Father, and that there is another side of the veil for these as well as for their betters in circumstance and lot. Speak to them words of brotherly hope, words of patience, and words of trust. Speak to them the words of Jesus, more full of hope for them than they ask or even think. The word for them is, "Onward!" Let them hear from your lips the everlasting Gospel, and, believing it, toil in the honest sweat of labor, suffer in calm obedience, and enter into rest. When you stand by the bedside of the dying Christian, speak brave words in his ear. Congratulate him as well-nigh conqueror. When you weep for those gone before, remember the Communion of the Saints, and that between this vestibule and that Paradise of clear delights and brighter hopes there is but a step, but a hand's-breadth, but a breath.

2. Let us take the words of our text in the other understanding of them.

The Lord speaks of preparing a place, a special place, for His people. Whatever be the drift or the destiny of the nations who pass away, or what some have called the "uncovenanted mercies" of the supremely good and gracious God, there is positive revelation of future blessedness and glory for the faithful people of God and Christ. Christian hope is not undefined hope. The Easter sepulchre is assurance to the Christian believer. It is the one positive and material fact upon which in this earthly life he can rest. It is the seal supernatural to those words, "I go to prepare a place for you."

Then we have the Scriptural pictures of the "city which hath foundations, whose builder and maker is God." We behold upon the canvas streets of gold and jewelled gates and the nations of the saved, — a city whereof the Lord God Almighty and the Lamb are the the Light. And here we have mansions in plurality, abodes many, as it were, in the very place our Lord prepares for us.

Whence we gather, leaving the imagination to work out its pleasure, that there will be community of interest and delight, and individual blessedness; so that while in that city of glory the redeemed people dwell together, yet in that city shall be all needful separateness and variety, crowning human expectation, glorifying human development in its manifold directions, and rewarding noble aspirations of whatever kind. There are many mansions, abiding places, homes and life and work and service and blessing for all and for each one, — for all varieties of task and pursuit, for all the aptitudes of the people gathered there. There is, I think, a felicity in our English word " mansion," with its suggestion familiar to our minds, as a true rendering of the spirit of the original word, although not precisely the most literal significance. For the entire spirit of our Lord's hope-inspiring words is opposed to any idea of narrowness or restrictedness. The gifts of God are generous. In yonder City, the New Jerusalem, they shall dwell in mansions of large liberty, not in cramped tents of warfare, nor in huts, as if unwelcome citizens. There is a glorious liberty of the children of God, an enlargement and a freedom giving unlimited scope to capacity and energy. And adding to this conception the separateness implied in the plurality, we may picture to ourselves in that city a citizenship composed of all elect souls from earth, of gifts in infinite variety, together delighting in God's presence, and blending their voices together in the eternal psalm. Plain and unlearned men will find place there, ripening, after the toil and soil of earthly life, in knowledge and power of thought. Scholars, philosophers, scientists, will there pursue their lofty aims, in God's light beholding light more and more. Genius shall find place there, and peradventure the inspirations which on earth reveal themselves in highest art shall be amid that glory yet more potent, moving to new and loftier constructions of harmony and beauty. As well the singers as the players on instruments shall be there. It must be so, else doth the Hand that created destroy some of His most precious handiwork, and the Bestower bring to nought the gifts He hath most richly imparted.

"Many mansions!" And do we err if in this spirit interpreting our Master's words we discern a suggestion of home life, and a blessedness the full equivalent of domestic love and companionship, amid the delights of that city? Though, in most true sense, in the resurrection they marry not nor are given in marriage, does it follow from this that relationships are broken up forever, and that there is in the future glory one sweeping divorce of all that God in the past hath joined together? Are there not words which speak of brothers and sisters an hundred-fold, and houses and lands? And have these words no significance to our human hearts? Nay, with such an utterance as this, "If it were not so I would have told you," surely we need surrender neither hopes nor conceptions of the *home* when we contemplate the life that is to be. Peradventure, we may not prove our faith to be true to the satisfaction of the dry logician whose soul eschews sentiment, and in whose veins runs only cold blood. Yet the words of Christ inspire us with an assured trust. Before our eyes the process of the ingathering is going on. All ages are culled for the harvest. The shock of corn, fully ripe, is carried in by the reaper. The rich green grass waving in the breeze is mown down and borne away. The sweet lilies are plucked from the garden, and tiniest buds are carefully lifted and borne in to the banquet to the master of the assemblies.

Dare we say that with the close of the earthly career there is absolute incompleteness, and that in any case the predestined earthly mission is blasted? To our Christian vision does not the infant of a few days or months, or the young man dying in the blush of his opening manhood, as truly finish the appointed earthly course as the aged Saint Paul? Has not each one had a place, his own place of influence and power, even if unconscious of it, during the days allotted to him? Has not the very babe for whom you mourn to-day had its mission and its power, with its sweet smiles and joyous dances, with its tears and pains and infant innocence, to you and to a circle of loving ones around, lifting you and purifying you, as it had been a presence from heaven lent to you for a time? What a world would this be were there not all the varieties of age in it, as well as of temperament and beauty and endowment! What a world, were there no venerable men and women in it, to be loved and honored, their hairs white with years and their shoulders bent with infirmity, ripened souls, in spirit still strong, elastic, and buoyant, looking forward to the perpetual life! And what should earth be without the boldness and dash and hot blood of youth, or without the gayety and romping of childhood!

And is there no outlook upon the life to come whence we can discern nothing more than a dead level of age and absolute uniformity of feature and tone? Eliminate from your conception of age its infirmity, its querulousness, all the elements which belong purely to bodily exhaustion, and preserve the factors of Christian faith and Christian graces, mature experience, ripened affections, chastened love, all things that are venerable in its spirit and temper, its achieved beauty and honor. From middle age and from youth prune away the grosser features and the immaturities and the unbalanced propensities, and from childhood all mere defect and lack of development, so that we discern the childhood and the youth and the manhood of Jesus. Transfer your best conception of a social state to the bowers of Paradise, and again to the city of the eternal homes. Let the transition through what we call the grave and gate of death be but a crystallization of our various earthly perfections and relationships, so that the distinct ages of human life as known upon earth shall be preserved in their distinct perfections and free from every flaw in the City of God. We may then hail those adorned with wisdom and honor and righteousness, the scarred veterans from lengthened conflict, their hoary heads white as snow, yet not symbols of decay, any more than the very head and hairs of Him whom the holy Saint John saw in his apocalyptic vision, but regal crowns upon regal brows. We may hail our brethren and sisters of equal strength and knowledge with our own ; we may greet with loving hearts other loving hearts, stainless, mature, and mellow in that beauty which comes through conflict and tribulation ; we may hear voices crying, Hosanna ! with all the sweetness and the power of the perpetual youth. Doth not star differ from star in that firmament of glory ?

"If it were not so, I would have told you." And will any man forbid us ? Forbid us, in the face of these words ! Forbid us, in the face of that immortal scene upon the Transfiguration Mount when a picture of the kingdom was given, and Peter and James and John looked upon and knew Moses and Elias ! Nay, let us thank our Master for the comforting words. And we, bearing upon our shoulders burdens of bereavement through life's weary way; we, wounded, bleeding daily from unstanched wounds, travelling along severed from those with whom we were bound up in organic life, as of one blood and flesh and bone and soul and spirit, — by God's own hand, let us look forward; for we must,— yea, God willing, we must grasp again those precious hands, embrace again those glorified loved ones, gather together again in circles of love amid the pleasures which are at God's right hand.

Mansions, and many mansions! Ah, children of God, you will find homes in that metropolis of God's elect. Fathers and mothers and husbands and wives and sons and daughters, — all true heart-loves comprehended within the circle and company of Christ's redeemed flock, whatever the earthly names of them, whatever the purification and perfectings of them, surely they will be known there. God grant to you and me that the circles be unbroken!

For, alas! there is another side to the thought, and there is such a thing as a human perverseness in sin which verily frustrates much of the goodness of God, and thrusts aside and away, ruthlessly, wilfully, madly, all the kindness of His provision, all God would give us or do for us. And well may every one raise the question, have I a mansion in that city, and do I hasten to the beatific vision of the immortal life and to its permanent endearments, joys, and service?

If life beyond be but expansion of this life, — the unseen holy but the grand habitation beyond the veil which separates the vestibule from it, so that the children of God pass from one into the other as the Master hath showed us, — then what we are to-day is a foreshadowing of what we shall be to-morrow, after that resurrection dawning.

What is the trend of the present life? This is the question answer to which may cheer us or alarm us according to the terms of the verdict.

Are we — of simple race indeed, but redeemed by God's own Son who hath abolished death and brought life and immortality to light — more and more obediently walking in God's ways to the everlasting kingdom; or are we more and more ripening in sin and unbelief, more and more without Christ and without God in the world?

VICTORY THROUGH TEMPTATION.[1]

Blessed is the man that endureth temptation. — JAMES i. 12.

TEMPTATION means trial. It is the process by which the goodness or fitness or purity of the subject is tested. The incidental results of the process in the case of moral beings are commonly the development and growth of the good or the evil, according as the trial is rightly or wrongly used.

The blessing is pronounced upon the one who *endures*. This is the emphatic word. Whether the trial be by adversity and severe tribulation, even long continued, as was the case in early ages of Christianity under persecution, or as in the story of Job, the patient man ; or by prosperity and splendid promise addressed to pride, ambition, or lust, such as many have had from the time when righteous Lot pitched his tent toward Sodom, down to the present age of gilded ease and pomp, — the enduring one finds not only divine approbation voiced in his own approving conscience, but also growth in the energy of goodness. Manliness, fortitude, heroism, faith, godliness, are products of the fire. That same fire consumes and melts the dross. The fittest survives the ordeal. Man has had the two typal experiences. And the typal law is verified in number-

---

[1] Preached Sunday morning, March 6, 1887 (the twenty-first anniversary of his Ordination), at St. James's Church, Philadelphia, and repeated Sunday evening, March 20, at the Church of the Incarnation. This sermon was the last one written and the last one preached.

less lives. After the manner of the first Adam, men yield and fall and are cast out from their remnants of Paradise, to feel their discomfiture and the shame of their nakedness and frailty, and to suffer afresh the pangs of conscience, and to hide away from the voice of God in the cool of the day, as did Adam in the garden. And again, after the manner of the second Adam, the Lord from heaven, and inspired by His example, men have been obedient and loyal, have endured temptation, whether allurement to sin or the trial of grievous sufferings, and have come out from the fires conquerors, and more than conquerors, — being conformed unto the likeness of their divine Master and Head.

Now, it is this victory through tribulation or trial which is the blessing of which Saint James writes. And this morning we will ask two questions concerning it; namely, —

1. How is such blessing to be assured to us in our manifold temptations? and —

2. How may we recover ourselves in any case of failure?

To answer the first of these questions, we have but to glance at our familiar laws of habit in the formation of character for our starting point. And then, recognizing that our conflict is one of gravest importance as related to the immortal life, and that among the elements against us are our own moral weaknesses and a potent spiritual enemy, we are to remember the divine strength promised to those who seek it, giving grace and power to prevail, even to the weak and fallen.

The habit law is strong. Every time we do an accustomed thing the more likely we are to do it again, and to do it perpetually under the recurring favorable circumstances, and to do it more easily and indeed more unconsciously. Men educate their fingers to the most delicate and intricate work. Habit outruns volition, and the deft workman accomplishes his task scarcely knowing himself how, or even that he *is* doing it. We go through many good and wholesome works almost mechanically, and without effort, by this law. A thousand unconscious benedictions radiate from the face and the hands of the hospital nurse or the physician, — electric emanations from the well-stored battery of habitual benevolence. Many sinners take no notice of their commonest sins. Profane men are often astonished to learn that they use profane language freely, indeed all the time. They neither notice their own profanities nor those of others. The man of prayer prays almost as unconsciously. His spirit's voice rises to God along the streets and amid his busiest hours, as naturally and spontaneously as the chest heaves for breathing.

So under special trial or repeated temptation, the habit of obedience to God's will and to the law of conscience grows. Men and women learn to suffer and to trust and to say, " Thy will be done, O Father! " as easily as they sleep and wake and greet those who meet them with loving smiles. And they learn to say, " nay," to the tempter, and to bid Satan get away from them, whatever be the form or the *no form* which Satan assumes, — whether to the enticer in meretricious array, or in habiliments of the philosopher, or to the unbidden thought of evil, or to the suddenly uprising spirit of selfish desire.

In the conflict between ourselves and temptation, everything depends upon the way wherein we meet the trial, and our action in each successive assault or experience. We may surrender to the enemy. Surrender is likely to be the result of the next encounter, and again of the next. No one becomes a violent person, a scold or termagant, a destroyer of life or property, at a single step. There is growth into malefactorship from the simplicity and purity of childhood. The story of the forger, or the absconding robber of a trust company, is no novel story. The man who hides in refuge to-day in Canada, or beyond the seas, began his career of fraud in some very insignificant way, and awaked to know himself a criminal, only after many a compromise with conscience, and many a sleeping potion administered to put conscience into lethargy. The sinner whose sins lie in the grosser and more sensual vices fell into the trough of that filthy sea, but he was swimming in its smoother waters first for pastime, assured that he would not be carried beyond his depth or the lines of safe sport.

An ethical fallacy may be framed very easily, and it requires no great ingenuity of logic to do it. Men plead that they are delivered to do their sins, and from the natural infirmity or the strength of lawless desire construct their syllogisms to neutralize the force of moral law. They throw the blame upon their Maker, and rush into abominations. It is simply amazing how finely the hairs may be split and what exquisite distinctions may be made, even by minds not the keenest, when it becomes convenient or delightsome to the eyes to apologize for a sin which has been wrought, and so, of consequence, to prepare the way for its repetition or a greater sin at renewed convenience. This is one way of acting under temptation.

Alas, brethren, how common a way it is among us in this evil world! How many men and women there are to-day (and perhaps there are some in this congregation) in high worldly position and social standing, who know that they dare not face God's judgment, and would not venture to face a keen human inquisition, who dare not even examine themselves or scrutinize their own lives, yet who live in a sublime contentment amid sin, indulging in sin and in gross sin, undisturbed by conscience, saying their prayers day and night, and not even putting away their sins when coming to the Lord's own Table. They love their sins. The pleasures of sin are keen. The stolen waters are a delight. Such is the result and the mastery of habit and of yielding to the tempter under the gilded and fascinating spell. All this we may do, and being tempted we fall.

Or we may *resist temptation.* And to resist it is to endure and remain faithful, and to gain reward of grace and strength and virtue. Scripture counsels on this subject are gathered up in that word, "resist;" Saint Peter uses it, — "resist" the devil and he will flee from you! The moral and spiritual muscle grows by resisting. The athlete with knotted muscles, lifting the load of Atlas, or shouldering the lion while with swift steps he crosses the arena, was once a puny stripling. Self-discipline and resistance of evil solicitation — renewed determination to bear what burden comes, and to honor God in it — grows into grander obedience and supreme moral elevation. The Joseph who was prince of Egypt in that almost fabulous age of civilization and grandeur was the Joseph who to the consummate artifice of the Egyptian temptress said, "How can I do this wickedness and sin against God!" The Moses who stands peerless among the men of the ancient world, and whose ethics and jurisprudence are the foundations of all law since his day, was the Moses who refused to be son of Pharaoh's daughter, and chose the afflictions of Jehovah's people rather than the treasures of Egypt, though he was himself learned in all the wisdom of the realm, and potent in their priesthood.

How shall we overcome and find the blessedness of them who endure? Look upon these men of the past. And look again upon Him who suffered being tempted, and the story of whose first great conflict with the tempter comes so freshly to us in the Lent season. The temptation came to our Lord, brethren, in some respects, as it comes to every man, — namely, along the lines of His appointed career. And it was addressed to His nature in ways so that it is well written, " He was tempted like as we are," and was, what we are not therein, without sin. He teaches us how to be tempted and *not sin*.

I say it came to Jesus as to other men, along the lines of His life, and in manner adapted to Him, He being what He was. The tempter, — for surely if we had not Scripture for it, we should naturally look for a manager of temptation methods, so wonderfully are they fitted as individual traps, — the tempter never makes misfits in the allurements or arguments he brings. It is not his way to offer pearls to swine; for he knows that swine prefer other things to pearls. Nor does he bring ill-odorous refuse to the nostrils of refinement and æsthetic culture. There is no more subtle perfumer than the devil, and it is well for us that we be not ignorant of his devices. Satan tried the supreme Man as he tried the first Adam, with appeal to his appetite. The first Adam was full to satiety, yet he ate the fruit. The second Adam was an hungered after His forty days of fasting, and why might He not convert those stones into bread and eat for His refreshment? Yea, why not? To the first Adam the offer was made of wondrous new knowledge and potency through the gateway of the forbidden.

To the Son of God in the wilderness, Satan made no appeal addressing itself to latent selfishness or desire of personal enlargement in any degree whatever. It was for His work's sake, for humanity's sake, for redemption's sake, for the kingdom's sake, that He might the more surely and speedily plant His throne upon the earth, and accomplish His great service for Israel and for man, that the tempter pretended to advise Him. And it required more than an ordinary penetration at that day to say why the Son of God might not assuage the pangs of hunger by His miracle-working power, or why He might not have made easy conquest of the nation and the world by the adoption of the policy Satan proposed amid the strange phantasmagoria wherewith he assailed the Lord. But the divine Man and Example resisted. He entered into no arguments. He put the word of God against the word of evil policy. He said to Satan, "Get thee hence!" and then the devil left Him. And this same adhesion to the divine word, and obedience to divine will, and conformity to the divine plan and end wherewith He had undertaken His earthly work, distinguished the career of our Master to the end. More than once was He an hungered. More than once must His heart have sunk, and His patience been taxed, as He saw the unbelief and the hostility it engendered; all the time knowing what power was in Him, and how legions of angels were waiting ever, in silent and unseen array, to do His bidding. Yet even through Gethsemane He endured, and said, " Not my will, but Thine be done;" and even on the cross, though the cup of the soldier He would not drink for relief, yet the cup which the Father had mixed for Him, that cup He drank to its very dregs, triumphant Prince of endurance and of suffering, vanquishing the enemy even in that entire life of mortal trial. He resisted not. He swerved not. He obeyed even unto death. So He overcame, and so He bids His people overcome, that they may share His throne. Blessed is the man that endureth temptation, trial. When he is tried,— when the trial is finished and he is approved,— he shall receive the crown of life.

But suppose we fail in our trials, what shall we do, and how may we recover ourselves?

Right upon the trial wherein we have been found wanting, brethren, there comes another trial, thank God, and by His grace,— and this trial, instantaneously presented, simply asks the question whether we will stay prostrate in our fall, and go from bad to worse, or whether we will rise up again and act like true men, despite our failure, and serve God better for the loss and pain we have had.

A Judas may go and hang himself. It were better for that man if he had not been born, who says, I have fallen, and I will now go to other sin, and add sin to sin. It is madness to revenge oneself on God and man in such way.

David, arrested by the prophet Nathan, poured forth his contrition in the immortal Miserere, and was a new man,— that man after God's own heart, faithful thenceforth. Saint Peter fell; but he who was craven before the maiden and the servants and the officers became the boldest and the most courageous of men, in his apostolic zeal unto his own martyrdom; so mighty the repentance, the recoil, and the rehabilitation when the Lord whom he denied looked upon him, and gave him the new chance, whether to abide in Him or to forsake Him.

Fallen once, vanquished once, — ay twice, ay thrice, ay seven times, or seventy times seven, — take strong stand, and, with your eyes opened to your weakness and your sin, break with it, and gird on your sword anew. There are two things to be done now. One is to cease thinking that you are strong enough yourself to cope with your own weakness or your temptation. Wisdom begins in modesty nowhere more surely than in moral conflict. God's help is our reliance more than self-reliance. At any rate, self-reliance without God-reliance never gains the upper hand, although it is useful under God-reliance for many an achievement beside. Seek, then, divine help, and say, "God helping me!"

Then put body and soul into the fight; and let your body be servant and not master in the fight. Shut the eye and turn away the head by forcible volition from the thing that solicits the evil which is in you. Look not at the unchaste image. Thrust into the fire the polluting page. If there slumbers within you the thirst for that which robs you of all discretion and of manhood, dash to the ground the cup which the fairest offers you. Defy social custom, and, like some brave men, turn over your glass upon the table, and suffer not wine to come near your lip. Fly away from the man or the woman or the open vault that tempts you. There is virile and brave courage in that cowardice which is afraid of wrong-doing and is not afraid to run away from it. If yours be lifelong temptation to self-indulgence and waste, to simple ease and pampering, rush, by God's help, into work for good. Make the body work, and keep it in subjection. Better be master in ascetic life, than the sporting butterfly or the lazy serpent on this earth amid eternities. He who taught man to pray, "Lead us not into temptation," has taught us how to make temptation a stimulus to good, and that in the surmounting of it is man's glory.

Then finally remember for our comfort, brethren, that *temptation* is not itself *sin.* Else Saint James had not written, " Count it all joy when ye fall into divers temptations." The Lord was tempted, but He sinned not. The distinction is real. The question of sin or innocence turns upon the response we make. The hammer strikes the wheels under the railway car, and the ring tells whether the wheels are sound or broken. The fault lies not in the hammer, nor in him who wields it. Those strange and evil suggestions floating into our ears sometimes, or mysteriously arising from our disordered flesh and nerve centres, are not sins. That they have so much power with us, and so catch us unawares, may show of what frail substance we are; but there is no sin until we accept and harbor them. The pains of the sufferer, and the groanings and the prayer that some relief may come, are not sins; but to curse God is to die. To submit and say, " If it be possible let this cup pass from me, nevertheless Thy will be done," that is to transform them all into gifts of God's love, and to triumph as Jesus did. To live smoothly and without conflict, as in some favored retreat, or in a convent cell, may be, but is not always, serene calm. But it is greater and nobler to battle amid the world, and to fight one's predestined way under darts of Satan and beneath the hail of his batteries, even to be a scarred and war-worn veteran, hero of thousands of fights, a valiant soldier of God and of Christ! Endure! Yield not! To-day the warfare of the Cross! To-morrow the Crown! Righteousness, peace, and glory for evermore!

THE END.

www.ingramcontent.com/pod-product-compliance
Lightning Source LLC
Chambersburg PA
CBHW021708110726

47902CB00005B/1097